SHARON LEE & STEVE MILLER

DUAINFEY

Baen Books by Sharon Lee & Steve Miller

Duainfey
Longeye (forthcoming)

DUAINFEY

SHARON LEE & STEVE MILLER

DUAINFEY

This is a work of fiction. All the characters and events portrayed in this book are fictional, and any resemblance to real people or incidents is purely coincidental.

A Baen Books Original

Baen Publishing Enterprises
P.O. Box 1403
Riverdale, NY 10471
www.baen.com

ISBN 10: 1-4165-5552-8
ISBN 13: 978-1-4165-5552-0

Cover art by Tom Kidd

First printing, September 2008

Distributed by Simon & Schuster
1230 Avenue of the Americas
New York, NY 10020

Library of Congress Cataloging-in-Publication Data

Lee, Sharon, 1952–
  Duainfey / Sharon Lee and Steve Miller.
      p. cm.
  "A Baen Books original"—T.p. verso.
  ISBN-13: 978-1-4165-5552-0
  ISBN-10: 1-4165-5552-8
  1. Young women—Fiction. 2. Rogues and vagabonds—Fiction. I. Miller, Steve, 1950 July 31– II. Title.

  PS3562.E3629D83 2008
  813'.54—dc22
                                                          2008015225

10 9 8 7 6 5 4 3 2 1

Pages by Joy Freeman (www.pagesbyjoy.com)
Printed in the United States of America

DUAINFEY

Prologue

IT WAS DUTY THAT BROUGHT HER BACK, THOUGH SHE'D WISHED with all her heart to stay. She had her pride, after all; and the Queen had chosen *her*, Navarone Rishlauf, when she might have sent any other of the Wood Wise. Called her by *name*, had the Queen, and spoken kindly of her skill.

She'd spoken of other things, too. Of small shifts in the aether, tiny changes of phase; hints, no more than a breeze whispering against the ear of the Queen's Guard.

Whispers that wise and canny Guard took note of, and dispatched an apprentice to follow, far across the land, to the *keleigh* itself. There, the apprentice had stopped, whether from wisdom or fear, though the breeze he followed blew on, through—

Beyond.

The *keleigh* was dangerous enough. The Barrens—well, and who knew what might have taken root in the wasteland on the far side of the *keleigh*?

Certainly, the apprentice was wise to turn back. No question that the Guard was wise, and asked Queen Diathen to send a seeker more suited to the terrain, and accustomed to facing risk.

Navarone's charge, from the Queen's own lips, had been clear: Follow the whispering breeze where it led, through the *keleigh* if necessary, and into the very Barrens. Scout out the source and learn what she might—safely.

"You stand high among the Wood Wise, Navarone Rishlauf, which wins you the right to this task. You go not as champion, but as the eyes and ears of your Queen. Go, learn, return. That is your mission."

Navarone bowed. "I understand, ma'am."

"That is well." The Queen raised her hand and slid one of her own rings onto Navarone's brown finger.

"To show you the way home, should there be need. Go now. I look for your return no later than Naming Day."

Go she did, following the elusive breeze to the *keleigh,* through—and beyond.

It was Navarone's pride that she had quickly located the source of the whispering disturbance, and had studied them closely and well.

It was her shame that she had not turned toward home until the Queen's ring compelled her to do so, and that she had gone on leaden feet and with a heart that grew more desolate with every league.

She thought of casting the token away, of breaking the Queen's geas and returning to the land beyond the *keleigh.* It was pride, she told herself, and her honor, that kept the ring on her finger and her face turned into the sweet wind from home.

At the near border of the *keleigh,* she had abruptly stopped, as though that which tied her to—the Barrens, as the Fey had been accustomed to call the lands beyond the *keleigh*—as if that bond would break, and, breaking, shatter her.

Standing there, shivering, she had indeed slipped the Queen's ring from her finger and stood holding it in her fist, her body craning back the way she had come, while her rational mind pled honor, and obedience, and duty.

She had taken a bolt—she understood that, if she did not quite understand how, or when. Her appetite languished, and when she forced herself to eat—as duty demanded—the food tasted of ash and gravel. Reason told her that her only hope of healing lay in continuing onward to home. But her heart—ah, how her heart ached to return . . .

In the end, it was the trees that had ransomed her, whispering encouragement as she walked, trembling, beneath leaf and branch. At first, she had paused often, palms and cheek pressed against bark, drawing strength, and resolution. The more distance she put between herself and the land that was barren no longer, the firmer her step became, until she once again moved through the forests as a Wood Wise ought.

It frightened her, how close she had come to abandoning duty, and honor, and sense, and she pushed on, stopping for nothing, running now—away from the *keleigh,* and that which lay beyond, toward Xandurana, and her Queen, and the faithful discharge of duty.

Almost, she had tarried too long; her hesitations and yearnings had cost her time; time even one of the Queen's Wood Wise was hard-pressed to regain. Still, she arrived, as commanded, on the eve of the Queen's Naming Day. When the glass turned, it would begin to count the first hour of the morrow, but the last sands of night had not run out, quite, yet.

A flash of the ring gained her entrance to the Queen's residence, and a page, his aura an undistinguished blur of sleepy greys and browns, was summoned to guide her to the private parlor while one of the guard ran to alert his captain. They should have allowed her first to bathe, in deference to the Queen's honor, but the glass, after all, was quite near to turning, and the ring blazed hot and urgent on her finger.

The page rushed off, mumbling after wine and pastries, and Navarone stood in the center of the room, her legs braced wide and her boots planted solid against the living wood floor, awaiting her Queen's pleasure.

She might have settled on any of several carven benches and taken ease from her journey; there were no precious fabrics here to be affronted by the honest dirt of travel. In truth, she could not bear to sit. It was all she could do, honor notwithstanding, to be still and seemly; not to pace across the room to the windows that opened out to the east, where the glow off the *keleigh* would be a toothy violet blade sheathed in the sweet belly of the night.

Navarone took a breath, centered herself, clasped her hands behind her back, and recalled discipline. Her boots shifted against the floor; she stilled them; took another breath—and at long last discerned the approach of her Queen. She faced the door squarely and dropped to one knee, head bent, hands open, fingers pointed harmlessly at the floor.

"Rise." The Queen's voice was cool; her aura a ripple of silver-washed greens.

Navarone rose, slipping the ring from her finger and offering it on a calloused palm, her eyes averted. The moment stretched, and yet the Queen neither reclaimed her ring, nor spoke.

Cautiously, Navarone raised her eyes, and met a fierce amethyst gaze.

"We had despaired of your safe return," the Queen said.

Navarone glanced down at the ring blazing against her brown skin. "There was much to study," she whispered. "Much to learn."

"Ah." Pale fingers intersected her line of vision, plucked the blazing circle up and lifted it away.

"Come," the Queen said, slipping an implacable hand beneath her elbow. "Sit. You will tell me all that you have learned. The boy will be here with wine directly."

The Queen had not risen to rule because she was weak, or continued because she was a fool. Surely, a mere Wood Wise, exhausted, wounded, and troubled in her heart, was in no wise fit to disobey her command, no matter how gently spoken.

Dutifully, Navarone sat in the wooden chair she was led to, her back to the windows, and a thin table inlaid with bright enamel before her. Across the table, the Queen sat in a similar chair—dressed yet for court, Navarone saw suddenly, with only the crown set aside in deference to the hour.

To the left, the door opened, and here indeed came the boy with the promised wine, and pastries, too, though the scent of them made Navarone's stomach turn. He set the tray on the table and poured into hammered silver goblets, presenting the first to their Queen with a deep bow; and the second to her, with a bow only slightly less deep.

"Leave us," the Queen said to him. "I will call if I have need."

"Ma'am." He bowed again, not quite as steady as he might, and went soundlessly across the floor. The door closed with a small *snick*; it was all Navarone could do, not to leap up and wrench it open, run down the hall and across the courtyard—no.

She took a breath and waited for her Queen to taste the wine, then did the same, carefully.

As she had feared, the taste was dull and bitter. She lowered the goblet and held it between her two hands, leaning forward slightly in the warm wooden chair.

"Now," said Diathen the Queen. "Tell me."

"A new people is come to the land beyond the *keleigh*," Navarone said, trying with all her power to keep the yearning from her voice, to give her Queen the dispassionate and careful report she required.

The Queen frowned, and sipped her wine. "A *new* people," she repeated, with quiet emphasis. "Fey?"

"Not Fey," Navarone answered, with certainty. "Something—other than—Fey, my Queen, though formed similarly." She looked down into her glass, and saw her own reflection in the glossy surface of the wine. Had her face always been so stern, so thin?

"From whence do they come?" the Queen asked, the soft question a startling intrusion into her thoughts.

Navarone swallowed; forced herself to look up and meet that calm and canny gaze.

"It was of course a few days before I was able to understand their tongue," she murmured. "After their speech had become intelligible, I listened especially for whatever they might say of their homeland. It seemed that they would have themselves out of New London, my Queen, but I know not where that might be. One would sometimes look to the east as they spoke the name, so perhaps we might seek there."

"Or perhaps we might not," the Queen returned calmly. "What else?"

What else, indeed. Navarone sighed and found she wanted another sip of wine, ill as it was, to slake the dryness of her throat.

"They have built a large dwelling of deadwood and metal, two days' walk from the outside edge of the *keleigh*," she said, and held up her hand. "The land there is barren no longer, but lush with vegetation and vibrant with benevolent forces."

"Ah," the Queen said softly, and tipped her head, her eyes shrewd. "But these—*new* people. What more of them?"

Navarone inclined her head. "At first, there were perhaps two dozen of them, half to tend to the construction of the house and half to ready the fields and to plant. Once the house was under roof, there came another half dozen of a different bearing and style. These, I learned, were the great family whose dwelling it was; the others being only workers attached to them by a system of allegiance I do not yet understand."

Behind her eyes, she saw a flash of jewel-tones, shimmering and seductive. Her mouth dried and she sipped wine without tasting it.

"This—family," the Queen said, sharply, drawing her back into the present. "They mean to hold house a mere two days' walk from the *keleigh*? Do the emanations not confuse their abilities?"

Almost, Navarone laughed.

"Ma'am, they do not appear to be aware of any force beyond the goodness of the land itself, which is considerable." She moved a hand, in a meaningless, wandering gesture.

"Their . . . abilities . . . are not as ours," she said, in an attempt to clarify that which was surely unnatural. "According to my observations, they neither perceive the *keleigh* nor draw upon the power of the land." She cleared her throat. "This metal that they use—it is dangerous—corrosive." She pulled back her sleeve to show the scar, still livid against her brown wrist. "A moment's contact burns, and yet they handle it carelessly, and take no harm."

Silence. She dared to look at her Queen, and saw the amethyst eyes close—and open.

"What else?"

Navarone drew a breath, sighed it out, and met her Queen's gaze.

"Though they do not use the power of the land, the land rejoices in them," she said, steadily. "Their auras are . . . very beautiful. Potent." She sipped wine. "Intoxicating."

"Are they a danger to the Vaitura, to us, or to ours?"

Ah, the question. The very question, indeed.

Navarone placed the goblet very carefully on the table between them.

"It is possible that they are—without knowledge or intent—dangerous to the Fey. I—" She faltered.

"You," the Queen said, "are ill. Was this done to you?"

"Ma'am, it was not. I hunger for the taste—the texture—of their auras. It may be a peculiarity of myself alone. Certainly, now that I am returned, the effects must fade. In the meanwhile, I suggest that further study is needed."

"Do you?" The Queen's face was stern, the silvered greens of her aura flowed and flared in pale imitation of those others. . . . "Shall I risk another of my Wood Wise against this malaise?"

Navarone leaned forward, her hands open. "They spoke of other settlements, my Queen, sent out from this New London. The land beyond the *keleigh* is wide, and as I have seen it is largely recovered from the wars. If these new people are—numerous, it may be in our best interest to establish relations. That, we cannot know until we send another to spy them out, and perhaps an ambassador."

Silence.

The Queen swept to her feet, and Navarone hastily scrambled to hers.

"We will speak again. Take you to the healers now, and submit yourself to their care until I send for you."

Navarone bowed; the mint-scented breeze of her Queen's passage kissed her cheek. There was a rustle, the sound of the door opening, and the pale aura faded from her senses.

She straightened, ears buzzing, and put out a hand to catch the back of the chair she had been sitting in. Abruptly, she could see them, those glorious, alien auras. Almost, she could feel them, *taste* them. Her *kest* rose without her willing it, hot and heady, as if she might indeed meld—

The door opened. She started, knocking against the inlaid table; the memories of magic shattered as her eyes flew open.

The captain of the night guard regarded her from hooded yellow eyes, and moved a hand, indicating that she was to precede him into the hall.

"The Queen sends me as your escort to the healers," he said, voice devoid of nuance; his aura scarcely a blue shadow against the aether.

"Of course," said Navarone, and sighed, and stepped dutifully forward.

Chapter One

OUTSIDE, THE DAY WAS BLUE AND SERENE. THE SOFTEST OF EARLY summer breezes stroked quiet music along the leaves of the trees in the wild garden, and bore the spicy scent of fresh-bloomed spinictus through the open window and into the ladies' parlor.

The breeze rippled the day-curtains, and the candles burning in their holder on the desk occupied by the elder of the three ladies flickered.

Rebecca, seated at the card table with her portion of the list and a box of cards, laid her pen down, leaned back in the chair and let the breeze stroke her face while she stretched cramped fingers. She had planned on being out in the gardens this noon, but her mother had instead requested her assistance in addressing invitations for Caroline's dance.

It was not of course correctly her sister's dance, but their mother's. Caroline had merely pouted and pleaded and cried until Mother had agreed to the scheme, with the provision that her daughters would do their share of work. Since Rebecca had not teased for a dance—and indeed did not care for dances—it seemed hard to find herself included in all the tedium of readying for the event. Especially when there was a springtime garden to tend.

You will need to know how to manage these things when you are mistress of your own establishment, Mother had said meaningfully, and Rebecca had known better than to argue the point.

Somewhat refreshed, she glanced at the next name on the list, pulled a card to her, picked up the pen and dipped it.

The breeze rustled through the curtains again, a little more strongly—and she smiled as the scent of the flowers reached her.

A sharp exclamation came from the third occupant of the parlor, seated before the gold and white escritoire. The pretty piece of furniture complimented the lady's own white-and-gold coloring, but the legs were loose and the surface too small, so Rebecca thought, for comfortable writing. Nonetheless, it was a charming piece and Caroline made a charming picture seated before it, with her dark day skirt swirled artfully, and her little slipper peeping beneath the hem.

"What is it, my love?" Mother murmured, without looking up from her work.

"The wind made me smudge Mr. and Mrs. Eraborne's card!" Caroline said aggrievedly.

"Write another, then," said Mother patiently. "And be more careful."

Caroline pulled another card to her, dropping the spoilt one to the pile on the carpet.

"Can't we close the window?" she asked. "The wind makes it difficult to write."

"The desk is rickety and moves under your pen," Rebecca said, as she finished Lady Quince's card, and put her pen down. "It is that which makes writing difficult—" she raised her head and met her sister's wide blue eyes "—not the breeze."

Caroline's eyes narrowed, which foretold unpleasant things when the two of them were alone. The Beauty, alas, possessed a thin skin and a spiteful temper.

"It might also help," Rebecca continued, turning her gaze away, and sanding the card, "if you faced the desk straight on and not as if you were riding sidesaddle."

"Your sister gives you good advice," Mother said, glancing at her youngest daughter. "Address the desk squarely and you will make fewer errors. You may make fewer still if you will write at the card table with Rebecca. The escritoire is not as solid a surface as one might prefer."

Sighing prettily, Caroline turned in her chair and faced the escritoire, her skirts ruched and untidy, and dipped her pen.

Rebecca drew the next card to her, picked up her pen, ticked off Lady Quince's name and glanced at the next on the list—

Sir Jennet Hale.

She did not sigh. There was no reason to do so, after all. Sir Jennet was the man to whom her father had promised her hand, and astonishing it was that he had found anyone to take her. That he had located a gentleman of lineage, who was neither a newlander nor a merchant must be to his credit.

As for Sir Jennet himself—Rebecca held nothing against the gentleman, having met him precisely once, at her betrothal dinner. He was a quiet-spoken man of about her father's age, somewhat portly and a bit red in the face, who had recently come heir to his elder brother's estate. His brother's lady having tragically predeceased him, Sir Jennet required a wife to hold his household. That Rebecca was the daughter of an Earl could only increase his consequence.

For herself, she found it slightly fantastical that by summer's end she would have left her parents' home, the land she had grown up on, an elder brother of whom she was sincerely fond, and a younger sister of whom she was, perhaps, not quite so fond, to become mistress of an estate in the Corlands, and the wife of a second son.

There was surely nothing to sigh about in any of that. In truth, she was fortunate to be established in an unexceptional marriage, which her father and her sister took great care to impress upon her.

So thinking, and sighing not at all, Rebecca wrote out Sir Jennet's card in her best hand. She then paused for a moment, pen poised, considering if it would be polite or unbecomingly forward to add a note indicating that she would be happy to see him at the dance. In the end it was the realization that she would be neither dismayed nor gladdened by his presence that stayed her pen.

Sir Jennet was to become a fact of her existence, like rain, or sun, or Caroline's pouting. He had thought enough of her future comfort, during their single conversation, to tell her that his estate included several gardens and a conservatory.

"They'll need a dab o' work, mind," he'd told her, as he poured himself a third glass of wine. "M'brother didn't care to keep 'em up. I hear you're a keen one for the plants and flowers, though, and I'm sure you'll know just what to do to bring 'em 'round."

Her fingers itched to set the neglected conservatory right, and she dared hope that one or another of the other abandoned plots he had offhandedly mentioned might be allowed to become a wild garden. She would not wish to lose her lore.

The door to the ladies' parlor opened precipitously, admitting the young viscount, still in his riding clothes, his fair hair rumbled and his cheeks rosy with exercise.

"Good afternoon!" he said cheerily to the room at large. Laying his hat, gloves and whip on the flower shelf, he strode to the card table.

"Hallo, Becca, old love! I'd made certain you were in the wild garden this day."

She smiled up into her brother's brilliant grin.

"Hello, Dickon," she said in her matter-of-fact way. "Mother had need of me here."

"Oh, aye," he said, picking Sir Jennet's card up and running his eye down the lines.

"Not very loverlike," he remarked lightly, and Rebecca felt herself flush.

"I thought to add something," she said, softly. "But, truly, Dickon, I hardly knew what. Ought I have written that I looked forward to his attending?"

"Only if you meant it," her brother said, putting the card with the rest. His gaze moved to her face, his own serious.

"Father should be flogged," he murmured, too softly for Caroline or Mother to hear. "You deserve better than an old roué with gambling debts and a rotting estate to put right."

This was not the first time Dickon had made his displeasure with her upcoming nuptials known. It warmed her that he cared so much for her comfort, while at the same time making her a trifle impatient. Surely he knew that no one else would have her.

She looked down, and drew the next card to her.

"Father is pleased to have found anyone to take me," she said patiently. "And now Caroline will be free to marry well." She raised her head and met his eyes once more. "Truly, Dickon, I am content."

"You are *always* content of late," he answered, his voice louder this time.

"Indeed," Mother said from her desk. "Rebecca is an example to us all, and she will make Sir Jennet a fine wife. Good afternoon, Dickon."

Rebecca saw her brother's eyes close, his shoulders rising and falling with a silent sigh, then he had turned away from her, and was striding across to the room.

"Good afternoon, Mother," he said dutifully and bent down to kiss her cheek. "Father sent me to tell you that his business with Mr. Snelling is proceeding well and that they will dine together. Pray do not wait the evening meal for him."

There was a pause, long enough that Rebecca raised her head to glance down-room. Her mother's shoulders seemed to droop—then straightened as she looked up at her tall son.

"Thank you, Dickon. Will you be with us?"

"Yes, of course, darling," he said warmly. "My business this afternoon is Gately and the accounts books, and my reward for tending it shall be an intimate meal with my lovely mother and beautiful sisters."

Their mother smiled, obviously pleased, though what she said was, "Piffle. You, sir, are a sad scamp."

Dickon bowed solemnly, and Rebecca bit her lip so as not to laugh. Their mother looked to her youngest, bent industriously over the escritoire.

"Caroline, pray tell Cook that we will be four at dinner. In the small dining room."

"Can't Rebecca go?" her sister asked, petulantly. "I'm writing."

"But I asked *you*, my love," Mother answered, in the tone that meant she would not be brooked.

Sighing loudly, Caroline dropped her pen, spattering ink over her portion of the list, rose, and flounced toward the door.

"Doesn't a brother get a welcome, Lady Caro?" Dickon called, placing his hand over his heart.

Caroline barely spared him a glance.

"Good afternoon, Dickon," she said coolly. "You are quite ridiculous." She was gone in a swirl of skirts.

Dinner in the small dining room was more boisterous than those taken in the formal room, with their father presiding. Mother was in good spirits, which she usually was when they dined alone, once she had finished enumerating the number of times during the month that Father had dined away. Caroline seemed somewhat cast down, though why she should be so was more than Rebecca could fathom. While the beauty of the family was certainly Father's favorite, Rebecca had long suspected that Caro did not find his company enjoyable. And as for herself—unfilial it might be, but she would be quite happy if Father dined away every evening.

Lady Quince, so Mother had heard from Mrs. Settle only this morning, had recently redecorated her receiving parlor. She was therefore questioning Dickon closely on its new style, until he threw up his hands, laughing.

"Mercy, then, Mother! You know I was only there for ten minutes to do the pretty before Ferdy and I rode out! I hardly had time to memorize the number and color of the pillows on his mother's chaise!"

"If I had asked you about a horse you had spent ten minutes with . . ." Mother returned, with a smile.

"Nay, then! Though I risk my reputation as a keen observer of horse flesh by so doing, I must confess that I was this very afternoon in the company of what Ferdy assures me is a pretty filly, indeed, and I can scarcely recall anything of her!"

"No!" Rebecca laughed, putting down her fork and reaching for her wine glass. "Were you ill, Dickon, or bespelled?"

She expected a laugh in return, and perhaps a bogus swoon, but Dickon turned serious eyes to her.

"Odd you should say it," he murmured, picking up his own glass. He looked at their mother over the rim.

"I wonder, Mother, have you met the Quince's house guest?"

Mother tipped her head. "House—ah! Mrs. Settle had said something—a foreigner, I apprehend?"

"I believe his lands are at some distance, though I would hesitate to style him a foreigner." Dickon sipped wine, set the glass down, and addressed his plate once more.

"You, sir, are unhandsome!" Mother cried after he had eaten two or three forkfuls and had said nothing further.

Dickon looked up with an innocent face. "Oh, you are interested? Mind, I did not take note of the fabric of his coat, though I'll allow it to be well cut, if you will—and it suited him. The whole day suited him, it seemed. Very odd fellow. 'Course, I believe Fey often are, according to our lights, at least."

Caroline stirred, and leaned a little forward, interest sharpening her face.

"Fey?" she asked, voice breathy. "You spoke to a Fey?"

Dickon sent her a glance. "Interested, are you? As it happens,

I did. Altimere of the Elder Fey, as he styles himself. Quince met him at the Boundary nine seasons ago; bought the grandsire of that filly I can't recall off him at the time. No man alive could ride the beast, but he was magnificent, and Quince bred him to his finest mare. *That* produced Thunderbolt, the filly's sire, half-Fey and half-mad. The filly, Ferdy tells me, is spirited but not murderous, and Quince counts her his success."

"But a Fey lord," Caroline persisted, her eyes wide and focused on Dickon's face. "Why is he here?"

"Quince invited him to visit, the next time he was on the roam, and Altimere took him at his word. Now he's on the lookout for land, says Ferdy."

"Land . . ." Rebecca murmured. "To farm?"

Dickon shook his head. "Horses," he said succinctly. "Apparently the outcome of Quince's breeding program got this Altimere to thinking about what profit he might realize from half- and quarter-Fey horses. If he breeds here—and produces horses whose sole object is not to murder their riders—then he has a fair shot at the city market." He shrugged.

"If he settles, I suppose he'll become quite commonplace. But as the first Fey in the county—"

"Not quite the first," Mother said surprisingly. "We had a Fey lady and her suite with us the winter Rebecca was born. They put up at the Hound and Horn, as I recall it, and made sure to visit all the houses in the neighborhood. She came to us for tea, she and her—well, I suppose I can only call him her bodyguard. He stood the whole time behind her chair, straight and silent as a blade."

"Really?" Dickon frowned slightly. "I don't remember that."

"You were with your aunt and uncle, my dear. Ask your father—I'm certain he'll recall. He and the lady spoke together privately for some while. She was looking for news of kin, and wished to inspect the—"

"But what does he look like?" Caroline interrupted impatiently. "Lord Altimere."

"Well." Dickon pushed his plate away and leaned back in his chair. He fingered his wine glass and looked up at the pale ceiling.

"He's a tall man," he said slowly, "tops me by a hand or two. Slender for his height—you know how Fey are."

"How should we?" Rebecca asked, interested despite herself.

"*We* don't go to the Boundary to trade, and I was an infant when Mother's Fey lady came to call."

Dickon met her eyes. "True enough. Say then that he's tall and slender, sharp-faced, but with a good, strong nose."

"His hair?" Caroline asked, when he paused. "Is it yellow, like mine?"

"Yellow, oh, aye," Dickon returned slowly; "you might call it yellow—but not like yours, Lady Caro. And his eyes—you see I anticipate your next question!—you might say that his eyes are a pale brown. His coat—attend me now, Mother—was tawny, and his breeches rust colored, his boots polished so high I could see Ferdy reflected in them."

"What did he say?" Caroline demanded. "Was his voice sweet on the ear?"

"Really, Caroline," Mother said. "Such inquisitiveness!"

Her sister lifted her chin. "Why should I not know what this Fey lord is like?" she asked defiantly. "How if I meet him in the village?"

"Caroline!" Their mother was clearly shocked, but Dickon only raised an eyebrow.

"Looking to attach the Fey, Lady Caro?" he drawled, and Rebecca looked at him sharply. "I'd be careful with that one, were I the Earl's second daughter."

"Oh, pooh!" Caroline returned scornfully. "I'm not such a goose as Rebecca. And why shouldn't I look to a Fey lord? *I* may marry where I will."

It was hardly one of Caroline's sharpest barbs, but it cut, nonetheless. Rebecca closed her eyes, and her left hand clenched into a weak fist on her lap.

"Caroline, such self-consequence is hardly becoming," Mother said sharply. "Your father has made an unexceptional marriage for your sister, and you may hope that he does as well for you."

"I may hope that he does immensely better for me!" Caroline answered roundly. "I am not ruined and crippled into the bargain. It's a wonder Father found *anyone* to take Rebecca. Even an old man in need of funds might be expected to have some sensibilit—"

"That will do!" Dickon bellowed, making the china dance on the table. "You are distempered!"

Rebecca's eyes flew open in shock. Her brother's nature was

impetuous, but to shout at one of his sisters over the dinner board? Mother would surely have his—

"I believe your brother is correct," Mother said coolly. "Your nerves are in disorder. Pray retire to your room and compose yourself. I will be up presently to hear how you mean to make amends to your sister."

Caroline lifted her chin. "I needn't make amends for speaking the truth," she said, but the effect was spoilt by the quaver in her voice.

"Perhaps not," Mother returned implacably. "But the way in which the truth was spoken—for that, you owe much. You are excused, Caroline."

It appeared for a moment that the Beauty would argue the point. Her usually pale cheeks were stained red, her eyes flashing fire. But that fiery stare faltered and fell before Mother's cool, dismissive glance. She bundled her napkin onto the table and rose with a mumbled, "Excuse me," which went unacknowledged by both her parent and her brother.

Rebecca, the goose—the *cripple*—Rebecca waited until her sister was decently out the door before she placed her own napkin on the table and pushed her chair back.

"If I may be excused," she murmured, keeping her eyes modestly on her plate. "I would like to walk in the garden before the moon goes down."

"Now, Becca—" Dickon began, and—

"Of course," Mother said, somehow managing to override him without raising her voice. "You missed your walk this afternoon, I know. Take your shawl—and remember to come bid me goodnight before you retire."

"Yes . . ." she murmured and got hastily to her feet, deliberately not meeting her brother's eyes. "Good evening, Dickon."

"'Evening, love," he said softly. "Bold heart wins all, Becca."

It was an old joke, and she smiled for it as she moved down the room, keeping her steps sedate with a sheer effort of will.

As she reached the hallway, she heard her brother's voice.

"Tell me more of your Fey, now, Mother. What was her name, and why should she be searching for kin in our tenants' book?"

The wild garden was ebony and silver in the moonlight. An urchin breeze capered playfully through the leaves, shaking a riot of scent into the silvered air. Rebecca paused by the spinictus bush, its flaming blossoms dyed black by the night, and breathed in the spicy aroma.

Over the rustling of the breeze in the leaves came the high-pitched *peepeepeep!* of the new froglings down in the pod. Rebecca looked up into the indigo sky with its sheen of stars, and awkwardly pulled her shawl tighter. The breeze carried an edge of chill this evening and her withered arm was sensitive to the cold. It hung, useless and aching, down her left side. She could move it somewhat, with concentration and paying a tithe in pain, but the fingers had no fine control, and the limb itself was without strength.

Ruined and crippled into the bargain—Caroline's pettish outburst roiled in her memory, blighting her pleasure in the night.

Sighing, she walked on, her feet sure on the shadow-filled path.

If she had harbored any tender sentiment regarding Sir Jennet's offer, Dickon's candid assessment would have long since retired it. In fact, she had known for some time that the only man who would take her was one more in need of her portion than affronted by her history or her—affliction.

By that measure, Caroline's jibes should not have wounded her—indeed, she *had* only spoken the truth. But it was Caroline's genius to always lay tongue to the most hurtful means of expressing the truth, as it was Dickon's to find the most gentle.

And neither spitefulness nor kindness changed the fact that she had allowed Kelmit Tarrington to take her up into his phaeton, against her aunt's explicit wishes. Once up, she noticed what had not been apparent from the ground—that he was somewhat the worse for his wine.

So much the worse, indeed, that his horses escaped his control while he was trying to kiss her, and it was she who snatched the ribbons from his lax fingers and brought the pair under control—too late. The phaeton went down in spite of her efforts, and Kelmit's neck was broken.

She—she was fortunate to have escaped with her life, so they said to her face.

Behind her back, they whispered that she and Kelmit had planned a secret elopement, which was, Rebecca owned, ducking beneath a tendril of wintheria vine, what anyone who had more sense than a girl of seventeen might well assume. The truth was simply that she, unbeautiful and indifferently courted, had been flattered that the man described by her cousin Irene as "the catch of three seasons" had offered her a mark of distinction.

She followed the moon-bleached path 'round to the medicinal garden, and there she sank onto the bench beneath the old elitch tree, one-handedly pulling her shawl closer. The herbs swayed in the small breeze, silver-grey in the moonlight, and the scents of the night bloomers mingled into a minty sweet breath.

Rebecca drank in the scents, raised her face to the moonlit sky and closed her eyes. By summer's end, she would be married and on her way to her husband's Corlands estate. She would need to take a careful inventory of the plants growing here, and prepare cuttings and seed packets for their journey. The Corlands climate, so she learned from the almanacs and geographies in her father's library, was cooler and drier than she and her plants were accustomed to. That would scarcely be a problem for the hardier of the plants, but there were several she considered indispensable which were more fragile. She would need to take herself into the village and sit with Sonet. Perhaps the herbalist had kin or contacts in the Corlands. Certainly, she would have good advice, and it was possible, Rebecca thought all at once, that the frailer plants could be grown in the conservatory, alongside whatever warmland fruits and flowers might survive there.

She laughed, quietly, into the night.

On her fourth birthday, she had horrified her father and her uncle, who had asked what occupation she should choose for herself, by answering that she would race horses. On her sixth, she had dismayed her mother and her aunt by declaring that she wished to be a physician.

On her eighth birthday, Sonet had come to work in the kitchen at Barimuir, and had been only too happy to instruct the Earl's daughter from her considerable herb lore.

It was an odd calling for a gentlewoman in these enlightened times, though when Father would have protested that he would not have his daughter grubbing in the dirt like a newlander, Mother had pointed out that her own grandmother had been notable for her herbal cures.

After that, Rebecca was allowed to study, and to plant, to harvest and to make up various tinctures and lotions. As long as she went about these things quietly and drew no attention to herself, her father averted his eyes.

The breeze ran more quickly, and Rebecca shivered where she sat on the stone bench. She should go inside, she thought, and opened her eyes. The moon was sinking rapidly toward the horizon.

She stood, pain igniting her arm. Biting her lip, she remained motionless until the flare had died down to the usual dull ember. Tonight, after she had said her good-night to Mother, she would rub the arm with easewerth, which would warm the muscles. Since there was no treatment known either to the lord physicians in the city or to the lowly herb woman of the village which would restore the arm's strength and suppleness, it was the best she might do.

And that, she thought, turning back toward the house along the darkening path, would have to be enough.

Chapter Two

"WHY MUST *I* WEAR WHITE?" CAROLINE DEMANDED, FOR WHAT Rebecca conservatively estimated was the twenty-seventh time since Irene's package had arrived from the city.

"Because you have not yet been presented to the Governors nor made your curtsy to the King," Mother said, just as she had twenty-six times before. "And because your cousin Irene has been so kind as to send the cloth."

Beautiful cloth it was, too, Rebecca thought, smoothing Irene's letter out to read again. Caroline might choose to sneer at mere "white," but the bolt Irene had sent was sombasilk with flowers figured, white-on-white, which would be breathtaking made up into a girl's simple gown.

Not, Becca thought, that Caroline was likely to see it that way.

To her, Irene had sent a bolt of mahdobei, soft and slightly nubby; the color of wheat. It was far too rich a gift, and Becca had considered sending it back, and asking Mrs. Hintchston to make up the sprigged blue she had been saving—but Irene knew her too well.

You will not, her letter read, *return this bolt to me, Rebecca Beauvelley. I want you to picture me saying that* **most sternly.** *No, more sternly than that! For if you do return it, I shall be quite cross, as will Edward when I importune him to ride cross-country with neither sleep nor food to hand-carry it back to you and stand by while it's being made up. I would do these things myself, but I*

21

*am in what Edward's mother insists on styling as "a family way," as if Edward and I weren't a perfectly good family. In any case, Becca, you must have the bolt made up for this **ridiculous** dance of Caro's—have I said yet in this letter how very indulged and spoilt that child is? Ah! Now I have. So, **dearest** Becca! Please do me the very great honor of having the wheat made up into something positively stunning—and tell Hintchston that **I** said stunning, so she will be in no doubt as to what is required! Thank you. Now I may be comforted in my isolation by the knowledge that you will be ravishing!*

There! No more scolding, I promise! Let us move on to gossip!

I wonder if you have heard that Charlie Mason—that would be the elder brother of Gerald, who you had eating out of your hand the last time you came to visit—and what a long time that has been!

Well! Charlie Mason has been taken up by the Purity League for it comes to light that he has built a steam-powered carriage! I, for one, was astonished. I had no idea the lad was so mechanical. In any case, the League has taken the carriage away—and poor Charlie, too, of course. It's a great trial and scandal for the family. There's talk of a Board of Governors' Enquiry and possibly even a deportation, which I will allow to be quite dreadful, if it happens, which it may not, but one never does know with the Governors, does one?

Also, the drollest thing, darling. You know that Edward can't keep a name in his head for more than three minutes. Indeed, it is so very bad that every morning at the breakfast table I make sure to introduce myself to him: Good morning, Mr. Wellburton, how do you do? I am Mrs. Wellburton, your wife of eleven months fortnight. But there, I've lost my thought—oh! Edward, chuckleheaded creature that he is, is quite adamant that he has encountered a Mrs. Hale in town only recently. Well, I daresay there are an hundred Mrs. Hales in the world, and so I asked Edward, Did this lady hold house in the Corlands? and, Who is her husband? And of course the dear idiot knew nothing of any of that, only having been struck, as he had it, by the similarity in name to your affianced husband. He promises to find out something of use, should he encounter the lady again.

*Now, let me see . . . I have scolded, given good gossip, **and** provided you with a mystery! I believe that is sufficient for one letter.*

Your part is to have that dress made—I am not scolding, only reminding!—and to write soon, dearest, and give me all your news, and tell me truly how you go on.

Do give my love to your mother and to Dickon, and say whatever is civil and conciliatory to Caro and your father.

All my love,

Irene

"Let Rebecca wear white, then!" Caroline said angrily. "And I'll have the wheat."

"Indeed you will not," Becca said, putting the last page of the letter face down on her knee. She looked at Caroline, standing pink-cheeked and rebellious in the center of the room. "Irene has ordered me to have the wheat made up, and you know that I dare not set myself against her."

"But it would become *me* so well!" Caroline wailed.

"Caroline, you will put an end to these unseemly lamentations at once!" Mother said sharply. "Sit down this minute and write to your cousin Irene, thanking her for her thoughtful gift."

Caroline stared. "But, Mother—"

The door to the ladies' parlor opened to admit Janies.

"Mrs. Hintchston," he said, stepping aside to allow the dressmaker, bearing the bag in which she kept the tools of her trade, entry.

"Good morning, madam," she said, with a curtsy for Mother. "Miss Beauvelley," another curtsy, followed by a nod, "Miss."

"Oh, Hintchston, you're here at last!" Caroline cried, before Mother could return the dressmaker's greeting. "I will be measured first—"

"Good morning, Mrs. Hintchston," Mother said, as if Caroline's voice were so much birdsong drifting through the open window. "I hope all is well with your daughter?"

"She's on the mend, madam, and kind you are to ask. I hope to have her back in the shop with me next week. In the meantime, she's fretting for something to do—you know how she is, madam; never happy unless she has work in hand! I've brought her 'round some hemming, which she can do while resting on the sofa. And she did ask me to be certain to thank Miss Beauvelley for the tea. Credits it with her being able to come so quickly back to health."

"I am delighted to hear that the tea was efficacious," Mother said with a solemn smile.

"Yes, madam, as I am. Now, if I may—there are gowns to be made?"

"So there are, so there are." Mother moved a hand, inviting Mrs. Hintchston to inspect the bolts laid out on the table. "Mrs. Wellburton has sent some fabric from the city, as you see."

"As I do see!" Mrs. Hintchston moved over to the table and examined both bolts, then looked up, her hand lingering on the mahdobei. "Miss Irene has the best taste in three counties," she said positively, and tipped her head to one side, looking even more like the robin she resembled. "There's to be nothing new for you, madam?"

"Mrs. Janies and I will be reworking the gold-and-purple," Mother said, and Mrs. Hintchston nodded. Mrs. Janies was, after all, her sister, raised in the dressmaker's household and destined for the trade until Janies came to take his post at Beauvelley House, and it was love, so Becca had heard the tale told, at first glimpse. Mrs. Janies had never looked back, and if she pined for her place in the family business, or for her own small shop, she did an uncommonly good job of hiding it. And she was still a wizard with needle and thread.

"So, a dress for Miss Beauvelley and a dress for Miss Caroline," Mrs. Hintchston said, and set her bag down on the table, extracting tape measure and chalk. Caro stepped forward.

"Rebecca will be measured first, please, Mrs. Hintchston."

Caroline actually gaped. "Mother—"

"You were writing a letter to your cousin, I thought," Mother interrupted. "Pray go up to my room and do so. Prudence will give you ink and paper. I will send for you when it is time."

Caroline looked mutinous, but she went, closing the door ... firmly ... behind her.

Becca sighed, then bit her lip, her eyes flying to her mother—who only nodded, wearily, or so it seemed.

She rose and smiled at Mrs. Hintchston. "I was to tell you particularly," she said, "that Mrs. Wellburton wishes me to have a *stunning* dress."

"That would be the wheat, of course," said the dressmaker, nodding. "If Mrs. Wellburton says stunning, then there's nothing for it, as you know, Miss Becca."

"Yes, Irene rules us all with an iron hand," Becca returned. "But, honestly, ma'am, we all of us know that I am not in the least stunning, and frankly I doubt my ability to pull off anything like. If Irene were here—"

"Which she cannot be," Mother interrupted; "a circumstance that she feels keenly, as she writes me. Therefore, my dear, you must needs go on just as if she *were* here to put some starch in your spine, as I believe she phrased it." She sighed. "Edward has been teaching her cant."

"More likely Irene has been teaching Edward cant," Becca said absently. It was true that Irene had always been the spirited one; the one who had thought up adventures and gotten them into scrapes. It had been Irene who had pointed Kelmit Tarrington out to her cousin Rebecca, miserable and ignored in town during her first Season. It had been Irene, too, who had nursed Becca during those terrible days after the accident, and who had wept and begged forgiveness, as if it had all somehow been *her* fault.

Not even Irene, however, could overcome the antipathy of Edward's mother for including a ruined, wanton girl in her beloved son's wedding party. Becca sighed. She and Irene had promised each other when they were girls that they would stand each for the other, at their weddings. Odd, how one was taught to honor promises above all things, for a man—or woman!—who broke their word was, as her father had it, "a damned scoundrel." Life and circumstances, however, took little note of promises—or of honor, either—as far as Rebecca had observed.

"Will your betrothed be attending the dance, Miss Becca?" Mrs. Hintchston asked, pulling Becca's thoughts back to the present.

"I don't believe he has responded as yet," Becca said calmly.

"Yes," Mother said, almost at the same moment, and gave Becca an apologetic smile. "He had written to your father on a business topic and mentioned at the end of the letter that he was very much looking forward to the dance. He has even made arrangements to stay at the the Hound and Horn, though of course there's more than enough room—but there! A custom of the Corlands, I daresay. I had meant to tell you this morning, love, but with one thing and another . . ."

"I quite understand," said Becca, around an unpleasantly hollow feeling somewhere between her stomach and her heart. It had not occurred to her until this very instant that she would rather *not* meet Sir Jennet—which was simply absurd. She was to be married to the man, and would be spending considerable time in his company. If she could scarcely bear to think of spending a few moments with him at a dance . . .

"If you'll allow me, Miss Becca," Mrs. Hintchston murmured, busy with her tape, "I believe I know exactly how to satisfy Mrs. Wellburton and please Sir Jennet."

Please Sir Jennet? Becca thought, and took a deep, deliberate breath. Certainly, it was the business of a wife to please her husband—and she would need to become accustomed to that, too.

"Miss Becca?"

"Certainly, Mrs. Hintchston," she heard herself say, as if from a distance. "I put myself entirely into your hands."

She'd fled into the herb garden when Mrs. Hintchston was done with her, but the rebirth of the growing things neither soothed nor exalted her. Her heart pounding, and her head light and peculiar, she sat down on the bench under the old elitch tree and tried to order her tumbling thoughts, oblivious to both the alluring scent of a rising garden and the beguiling sight of new leaves dancing in the breeze.

When the match with Sir Jennet had at first been proposed to her, she had accepted it without dismay. The marriage would indeed, as her father forcefully pointed out, solve a great many things. Mostly, it solved the problem of what to do with a ruined daughter that one was yet too squeamish to consign to a Wanderer's Village. With her married and away, Caroline would be able to have her Season in town, and a chance to make a brilliant match. Which, Becca thought, shivering in the shade of the elitch, she very likely would. Yes, she was ill-tempered, vain, and a little stupid, but she was also a Beauty, and the world forgave a Beauty much.

The world did not forgive foolish, headstrong girls who failed to consider what was owed to their families. Her father had been quite clear on this point, and he had related to her in excruciating detail his long and laborious search for someone—*anyone*—who would be willing to take "damaged goods."

She had ought, her father had said, rejoice in her good fortune. And while she had never, really, rejoiced in Sir Jennet's suit, she had felt it was—

No. Her mind had accepted the problem as defined and the solution as provided, but she had *felt* nothing.

Now—now her entire spirit rebelled, and the thought of marrying Sir Jennet, leaving her family and her country, depending upon the kindness of strangers in what every knowledgeable resource assured her was an inhospitable and difficult land . . .

"I cannot," Becca whispered, and the new leaves above her rustled in the breeze, seeming to repeat her words.

Surely, she thought wildly, *if I speak to Mother, she will speak to Father, and the wedding may be canceled before it is too late! Surely—*

But she knew better. The banns had been read; the date of the ceremony had been published. The whole village knew. Indeed, the *world* knew! Could she sink further? Could she jilt the man? Would Father cast her out?

And would that, she wondered, be worse?

Becca shivered, suddenly aware that the breeze had come up, and that her arm was aching. She should, she thought, go inside, where it was warm; before the damaged arm grew chilled and stiffened.

But it was some few minutes before she was able to take her own advice, rise, and walk, slowly, up the garden to the house.

Chapter Three

MIST STILL CURTAINED THE TREETOPS WHEN BECCA OPENED THE gate and stepped into Sonet's garden.

Properly, of course, she should have gone to the front door like a civilized woman, and announced herself to whichever of "Gran's" foundlings opened to her. But the doorkeeper would only have sent her 'round back to the garden, anyway, Becca thought, pushing the gate silently shut behind her. It had been a year since Sonet had left the employ of the Earl of Barimuir, and Becca had visited her many times, though she had been inside the cottage precisely once.

Unlike the garden, which was laid out in neat squares intersected by scrupulously raked paths, and the shed, where every tool hung in its place, the house was a mad jumble, every surface occupied by something—sewing in progress, ledger books, candles, trays, cats. Becca must have looked her astonishment, for her teacher had laughed and waved a big hand 'round at the general confusion.

"We've got too many busy people under-roof, that's the truth! And most of 'em subscribe to the belief that it's no use putting something away when they're only going to want it again in a year or two."

Well. Becca stood with her hands folded under her cloak, listening to the soft, usual morning sounds of a spring garden—insect hum close at hand, and the stroke of the importunate breeze against new leaf and stem. High up the trees, a velyre sang a piercing couplet; further off, a raven shouted rude counterpoint. Somewhat nearer to hand, she heard another sort of song, half-mumbled and breathy.

Smiling, Becca moved in the direction of that soft undersinging, holding her cloak close and treading lightly on the raked path. The path intersected another; Becca bore right, the song becoming more distinct, but by no means loud, born on the back of the teasing breeze.

Sonet was surely very near, Becca thought, but where—

There.

Seated on a rock beneath a bitirrn tree was a large lump of a woman, wrapped in a cloak the color of garden shadows. The hood was thrown back, revealing hair the color of the retreating mist, twisted into a tight knot.

Becca stopped in the center of the path, unwilling to disturb the singer, or to put a period to the song. Officially, the Earl of Barimuir deplored and discouraged land-song, calling it backward superstition that had no place in an enlightened age.

Realistically, there was nothing he could do but pretend not to hear when the sowers sang the seeds into the ground in spring, and the reapers sang the harvest out in fall. Everyone did it—everyone who had a stake and a feel for growing things, that was. Land-song was wordless, often no more than a deep hum from the center of the chest, at once soothing and energizing. Very often, as Becca knew from experience, the singer was not himself aware of the song.

She took a deep breath, inhaling the heady green vapors of the garden, as the song-laden breeze capered around her, toying with Lucy's carefully done chignon, and tugging on the hem of her cloak.

She closed her eyes, letting the sensations of the garden fill her senses, while the song and the breeze danced—

And then the song was done.

The leaves sighed, and Becca did, in satisfaction, before opening her eyes and smiling at the green-shadowed figure perched on the dim rock.

"Well, look what the mist brought in!" Sonet called. She slid down the side of the rock, her cloak snagging on a low-slung bitirrn branch, spoiling her balance as her feet touched the ground.

"Storm and lightning!" she yelled, one hand flung out, feet slithering on the new grass. Becca leapt across the pathway and threw herself into Sonet's substantial chest, pinning her upright against the stone. The bitirrn branch, released from its tangle in the herb woman's cloak, whipped back.

"Ah!" cried Becca, hand going to her cheek.

"Spiteful stick!" Sonet snapped, and pushed herself upright, one arm around Becca's shoulder. "Well, it's nothing more than its nature, after all. We can't blame it for that." She took Becca's chin between thumb and forefinger and turned her face. "Let's see, then—tsk. We need to get some fremoni on that before the welt rises." She grinned, gap-toothed, and Becca couldn't help but smile back, despite the sting in her face. "Next time, let me fall, eh?"

"I don't think so," Becca said, following the old woman down the path toward the drying shed. "You could have struck your head on the rock, and *that* would have been serious."

"Serious for the rock, maybe," Sonet said, dryly, and pulled open the shed door, motioning Becca in before her.

Just over the threshold, Becca paused to twist the pin at her throat and shrug out of the cloak with a practiced motion. She caught it, one-handed, as it fell off her shoulders, and hung it on the hook before moving across the room to her usual place. By the time she was comfortably seated on the stool next to the worktable, Sonet had a pot in her hand and a look in her eye.

Sighing, Becca dutifully turned her cheek.

The salve went on cool, immediately leaching the fire from the sting.

"With luck, your lady mother will never know you had a mishap." The relief apparent in the herb woman's voice was comical, and Becca laughed.

"Or she would surely come down here with the largest carving knife in Cook's supply and gut you," she said.

"I don't put it past her, I don't, though she's a fair lady. More likely that she'd take down my poor bitirrn, which I'd rather she wouldn't, because it does have its uses, ill-natured and spiteful as it may otherwise be."

Bitirrn bark was a powerful painkiller, Becca knew, and a few drops of bitirrn berry cordial brought sleep to the most restless patient. Unfortunately, the trees were often sickly, even in the wild, so most herbalists used the less powerful, but hardier aleth to relieve pain, and poppy-laced wine to bring the fretful to slumber.

"Well then, I'll just have to say that I walked into a fence post," Becca said, "and spare both the herbalist and the plant."

"She's not likely to believe that," Sonet said, turning to put the pot away in its place. "Mint tea?"

"Please," said Becca, and smiled.

Sonet turned to the brazier and the flask bubbling there. She measured tea into the chipped teapot, poured boiling water from the flask and set it back on the brazier.

"Well, then, what brings you out in the misty morning time?"

Becca laughed. "You make it sound as if I'm here at cock crow! I assure you that the hour is *quite* respectable!"

"Well, of course it is, which is why you've come with your sister, or your maid, or with his lordship's blessing?"

"Sonet, *you* know Caro doesn't walk out until the mist has dried and her skirts are not at risk—and that I have no maid! As for Father's blessing—he never comes down before midday, by which time I would surely find you awash in those in need of your skill and no time to spare for a novice's questions!" Becca tipped her head, studying the side of her friend's face as she poured tea into mismatched cups.

"If it will ease you," she said, more seriously. "Mother knows I've come."

Sonet's jaw relaxed, and she showed a full smile when she turned to give Becca her cup. "That's well, then," she said. "As long as someone knows you were walking out alone, and where you were bound for."

Becca bent her head over the cup, breathing in; the scent of mint so strong her eyes teared.

"Are there brigands in the neighborhood?" she asked lightly, knowing that theirs was the safest country in the Midlands.

"Not that I've heard," Sonet said, hitching herself onto her work stool. "The problem with brigands being that no one does hear until we hear, if you understand me. It's not like they'll send 'round their card and make themselves known to the neighborhood."

Becca did her best to look stern. "I can certainly understand their unwillingness to embrace civilized behavior, if all the world begins against them." She bent her head and breathed in more steam, feeling the mint clear her head and bring her senses to tingle.

"Well," Sonet said after a moment. "And what *does* bring you out at this highly civilized hour, with your mother's blessing on you?"

Becca looked up. "It occurred to me last evening that I will be needing to transport my garden to—north. And that I need to know which of my plants require extra protection across the winter, and which might not grow at all." She paused. Sonet said nothing.

"Also, I wondered if you would know who the herbalist for the Corlands might be, so I might write and—" She stopped, silenced by the expression on Sonet's face.

"Is there no herbalist at the Corlands?" she asked slowly.

"No," Sonet replied, equally slow. "She was . . . cast out . . . some twenty years ago by the lord of the place."

Becca sat up. "But—why?"

"Well, now. He believed that the way to make room for the modern way of doing things was to cast aside all of the old ways."

"But—healing . . ." Becca began. Sonet shook her head.

"For all he was a landowner, he mistrusted the land and the gifts of the land. He believed that healing should be done by devices created by man, to serve man." Sonet cast her a sharp look. "You know yourself that this is not an unpopular belief."

Becca shivered and her withered arm ached, as if in remembered agony. Indeed she knew for her very self. When she had been freshly . . . damaged. The Earl, her father, unable to accept that she could not be repaired, had carried her to the metropolis, there to place her into the hands of one Sir Farraday, who had strapped her to a table, wrapped her ruined arm in wire, and subjected her to course after course of "electric therapy."

She had screamed and wept, begging him to stop, but he would not. He had been sincerely moved by her distress, and it was with tears in his eyes that he urged her to courage, swearing that the electrically induced spasms were, indeed, strengthening the atrophied muscles; that when the therapy was done, she would stand up whole and beautiful.

He had lied.

She had arisen from the therapy ill and raving, her arm burned and useless; utterly unresponsive. Sir Farraday had wept, and begged her pardon, promising to contact her when he had discovered the error in his calculations, so that she might return to him, and be healed.

Vastly disappointed, and placing the blame for the cure's failure squarely upon her, Father had taken her back home and left her to Mother, and to Sonet.

It had been Sonet who had devised the painful exercises that, bit by bit, won her back some small amount of movement and dexterity. It had been Sonet who made sure that she did those exercises, pain notwithstanding, and who rejoiced with her over every inch of gain.

Here and now, sitting safe in Sonet's workplace, Becca sipped mint tea, and pushed the past out of her mind.

"Perhaps this lord should try one of those devices himself," she said, her voice tart despite the soothing effects of the tea.

"He did," Sonet said softly. "Eventually. When he was ill and dying. It might be that the devices gave him a few more minutes, or a few less. I could have done nothing better. Or worse." She looked down at her cup, raised it and sipped.

"Well," she said. "All that by way of saying there isn't an herbalist at Corlands, not that I know about. It could be that someone's moved into the village, now the old lord's been followed by his brother, who—" She bit off the end of her sentence and pressed her lips together.

Becca shook her head. "Whatever you have to say about Sir Jennet, it cannot possibly be any unkinder than Dickon's transports."

"We'll just leave it that the younger brother has his own faults, then," Sonet said. "As we all do." She drank off her tea and set the cup aside.

"There's some of your usual plants that won't survive the winters up north," she said, bringing the subject abruptly onto Becca's topic. "Fremoni won't. Feverease won't. Nor aleth."

Becca stared. "But—"

Sonet held up a hand.

"Trust the land," she said, more sternly than she was wont. "There are other plants, native to the cold, that will give you what's needful. You'll need to learn those—I have a book, somewhere . . ." She looked around absently, as if expecting to find the book floating in midair, or suspended from the drying rods that ran the length of the shed.

"Ah!" Sonet rose and crossed the room, casually reaching up to the shelf over the sorting table. She groped for a moment, then grinned. "*There* you are!" she grunted, as if to a playful child, and turned with a flat parcel in her hand.

"Feh! Quite a few seasons of dust on *that*! Good thing I had the sense to wrap it in oilskin before I set it away." She pulled a trimming blade from its place and cut the cord holding the packet together while Becca slid to her feet and crossed to stand beside her.

The book that emerged from its layers of protection was well-thumbed, its cover stained and edge-worn; a field herbalist's diary.

"Made that myself when I was no older than Harin," Sonet said, naming her current apprentice, a plump and quiet girl from up-country. "Though with more sense."

"Really?" Becca eyed her teacher fondly. "Now, I find Harin very sensible, indeed, which forces me to ask, Sonet—"

"Eh?" The herb woman gave her a mock glare. "Out with it, Miss!"

"I only wonder what happened," Becca concluded, making her eyes as round and as guileless as she might.

"There's proper respect for an elder in lore," Sonet observed, shaking her head. "Well, I will own it a relief to have a serious 'prentice with me now. Makes quite a change from the last—light-minded to a fault, that girl!"

"Tempery, too," Becca agreed placidly, "and of a nature to take risks."

"Nothing so bad with risk taking," Sonet murmured, opening the cover to reveal a drawing of a leaf surrounded by dense notes. The paper was rough, the ink so vibrant a green that the letters seemed to leap from the page.

"My cold country book." The herb lady's voice was so soft it seemed she must be speaking to herself. She looked up and gave Becca a nod. "This'll be what you want."

"I—" Becca bit her lip. "Sonet?"

"Now what, Miss?"

"No—" She put her hand on the other's arm. "I just—the old Corlands lord. *You* were the herbalist he cast out off of his lands?"

"Younger and hotter of head," the other said mildly. "You knew I was from the north."

"I did," Becca said, "it—I just never realized . . ." She shook herself. "Well. When may I come by to copy out—"

"No sense in wasting your time copying!" Sonet interrupted.

"*I'm* not going back to the Corlands—not at my age! You'll take this very book with you, and glad I'll be to know it's finally seeing some use."

"*Take* it? Sonet, I can't take—"

"You can and you will," Sonet interrupted, thrusting the item into Becca's hand. "It's your master gift."

Becca gaped. "I'm no master," she protested.

The old woman cocked an eyebrow and gave her a gap-toothed grin. "Well, then, Miss Beauvelley, I'm forced to ask—"

"Don't!" Becca laughed, and cradled the book against her breast, defeated. "Very well—and thank you, Sonet. For— For everything."

"Pish and tosh. Now come back over and let me give you another cup."

"Thank you," Becca said again, blinking back a sudden start of tears. "That would be very pleasant."

"I plan," Becca said, reestablished on her stool, with her weak hand curled 'round a newly warmed cup. "I plan to have a busy summer, and take extra medicines, salves, tinctures and cordials with me. With luck, they will be sufficient for Sir Jennet's household and the village until I can plant . . ." She frowned slightly.

"Sir Jennet said that there is a conservatory, though in need of work. I wonder if I might not cultivate some of our usual plants."

Sonet looked thoughtful. "A conservatory . . . I'm not sure what sort of virtue would remain in the plants, removed from the land in such a way."

Becca laughed. "Of course there's land in the conservatory!"

"There is *dirt* in the conservatory," the herb woman snapped. "Have I wasted all my teaching?"

Deliberately, Becca sipped tea. Sonet's tone had struck a spark from her own temper. There was a time when the spark would have become a conflagration, but Becca had learned how to manage her temper, since the accident. She knew that this was not patience, but no one else seemed to.

Not even Sonet.

"Eh, well; I'm a snarly old woman—pay it no mind." Sonet cocked an eyebrow. "My advice is, if you're going to be repairing the conservatory, you'll do best to have yourself an orangery, and plant in chard, beans, tomatoes. The house will welcome fresh fruits and vegetables in winter."

"You're right, of course," Becca murmured, and finished her tea.

"Nay, now. I can tell when you're agreeing only to sweeten me up!" Sonet shook her head with a wry smile. "Take the counsel of your plants and do as seems best to you. I'm proud to say that you were my student, and you'll make those in the Corlands a grand and giving lady, which is something they've sore lacked."

Becca felt her stomach clench, and took a deep, calming breath. "I will do my best in the Corlands," she said softly, and took another breath before slipping off the stool.

"I did promise Mother I'd try to be back before Father came down," she said, apologetically.

Sonet waved the apology away with a large rough hand as she came to her feet and moved over to the door. She pulled Becca's cloak from the hook and draped it 'round her shoulders.

"Thank you," Becca said again, twisting the brooch closed before stretching high on her toes to kiss the weathered, fragrant cheek.

"Take good care, Sonet."

"And you as well, child. And you, as well."

Chapter Four

BECCA WALKED QUICKLY ALONG THE TRACK, SHOULDERS HUNCHED as if against a chill breeze. It was a pleasant, tree-lined way, normally one of her favorite walks, but Becca had no thought for trees, or for the gilderlarks trilling from the side of the path; she barely noted the moist scent of new leaf, or the faint sweetness of the springtime's first honeycups.

No, Becca was thinking of the Corlands, and what she might . . . really . . . hope to find there.

She *had* read the almanacs; she knew that in the Corlands winter came early and stayed late; that high summer, which often lingered lazily into what was rightly fall here in the Midlands, might in the Corlands be a matter of a week or two.

She had known all that, had expected that she would need to discover new plants to replace those that pined for the sun after an absence of a day or two, and those others that were too fragile to transport. Yet to hear Sonet's calm assertion that the oldest friends in her medicine box—feverease! fremoni! aleth!—could not withstand the climate to which she was bound—that gave pause.

Pause, indeed.

She had no illusions regarding her own frailty; she knew herself to be strong beyond what was strictly ladylike. But a land so inhospitable that weedy aleth, which set down roots in gravel and flourished, sun or shade, could not survive it—what toll might such a land take upon her?

Biting her lip, she walked even more quickly, as if she might outpace these disturbing thoughts. Plainly, she needed to question Sir Jennet more closely regarding his land and the conditions she could expect to discover there. Perhaps, indeed, she should write to him—though that would be shockingly forward. Becca sighed. She would ask Mother, she promised herself, and if writing was found to be out of the question, then she would surely have ample time to talk with him at Caro's dance, in just eleven days' time. No, she corrected herself, that must be ten now, unless Caro's crowing at the calendar yestereve was mistaken.

So deep was she inside these dismaying thoughts that she did not for some time hear the approach of the horse. It was the bells at last pierced her abstraction—bells with a tone so high and sweet that they must set anyone's teeth on edge. Accompanying the bells were the sound of hoof beats at canter, and a deal of what might be irritable blowing.

Becca took a step off the side of the path as chestnut filly, white star a-blaze upon her noble brow, came 'round the curve in the path, shaking her head so that her mane slapped the side of her neck, reins hanging loose; saddle, disturbingly, empty.

"Here now," Becca said softly, raising a hand. "Stop a moment, lady."

The horse checked slightly, sending a testy, interested glance in Becca's direction.

"Stand!" Becca said firmly, and at that the horse blew hard, as if to say, "Well, finally!" slowed, and then stood, as she had been bid.

The too-sweet jangle of bells ceased, and Becca gave a sigh of her own.

"Well, now," she said conversationally. "Where have you left your rider?"

The filly stamped one emphatic forefoot, waking an irritation of bells.

"I understand," Becca murmured. "Plainly he is an idiot. I sympathize with your predicament and applaud your forthright action. Alas, we cannot leave him to lie in a ditch."

The horse blew a light interrogatory.

"Well," said Becca, moving forward in a smooth, soothing glide, her eyes decently lowered. "There are those who would judge you harshly for your action, and never ask if it was justified. It is wholly unjust, but we must deal with the world as we find it, and accommodate ourselves to those things which we cannot change." She had reached the filly's side, and carefully raised her hand to stroke the silken neck.

"Now, what we may very well be able to do is convince your rider to have done with those idiotish bells, which I think would please you a very great deal, would it not?"

A slight shake of the head.

"I thought it might," Becca murmured, stroking. "However, for this plan to work, we must find your rider, fool though he is, and show proper consideration for his health. In this way, he will come to understand that you had merely laid out a lesson for him, and bear no lasting enmity."

The filly flicked her ears, apparently in some skepticism of this sentiment.

"Come now," Becca murmured, leaning into the warm shoulder. "Own that he might do very well, eventually, if you have the schooling of him."

There was a pause, as the filly considered this, then a sigh of agreement.

"I knew you would be sensible," Becca murmured. "Attend me, now. I am going to take your reins and the two of us will follow your track back to the place where you left your rider." She paused, then reached up and gathered the reins, pulling them gently over the filly's head.

"I am sorry," she said, as she got them turned around and heading back the way the horse had come, "about the bells. If we walk softly, perhaps they won't be *too* bad . . ."

They walked slowly, indeed, Becca murmuring commonplaces about the weather and the trees, interspersed with praise for her companion's good sense and forbearance. The bells were, unfortunately, nearly as irritating at a whisper as they were in full throat, and Becca made a mental note to read the filly's rider a very stern lecture, indeed. What person of sense needed to advertise himself in such a wise? If—

There was a movement at the edge of Becca's eye. She turned her head, and the filly stopped, blowing lightly against her shoulder.

"Praise harvest!" Devon Jestecost was somewhat the worse for wear, Becca thought critically. His coat was dusty, and torn, his hat was gone and there was a crusty scrape across one rather pale, downy cheek.

"Good morning, Devon," she said politely, and as if there was nothing the least bit unusual in finding him *en déshabillé* at the side of the road, one leg before him and the other bent at a painful and not entirely natural angle. "Did you lose something?"

"Say rather the wretched beast lost me!" he retorted. "Damn, but I'm glad to see you, Becca! Help me up, will you! I've got to get her back before she's missed!"

Becca stood where she was, the filly's nose against her shoulder. "Get her back?" she repeated.

"Well, you don't think she's *my* horse, do you? She's Leonard's."

Becca stared. "What in land's bounty can Leonard want with a horse—" *Like this*, she had been about to say.

Devon laughed raggedly. "Since he has the seat of a pig and the grace of a wood carving?"

It was hardly a respectful way to speak of one's elder brother, though it was. Becca acknowledged, regrettably accurate. Alas, Leonard prided himself on his horsemanship, by which he meant his ability to drive horses. His ambitions lay in the direction of the Four Horse Club, though Becca had heard no less a whip than Robert Trawleigh proclaim him "a trivial whipster."

"Best I can make out is Leonard wants to kill himself in style," Devon said—and gasped, his pale face going paler. "Bring the horse over here, Becca, there's a dear. I'll mount off that rock."

"Will you?" Becca said interestedly. "Perhaps you'd like to stand first."

"Well, I would," Devon muttered, "but my leg—"

"Your leg," Becca interrupted him, like he was seven instead of a supposed young gentleman, "is causing you a great deal of pain, is it not? Come, Devon, you and I both know that what you want is a doctor."

"You're out there," he told her sharply. "The *last* thing I want is a doctor." He sighed, then, and closed his eyes, leaning back in the weeds. "Oh, scythe take it, Leonard will have heard the whole thing from Quince by now."

Becca shook her head. "You told Lord Quince's stable boy that your brother had sent you for the filly?" That would hardly have surprised the boy; Leonard's ineptness in the saddle was legend across the Midlands. What could, Becca thought again, Leonard be thinking? She glanced at the filly standing so still and ladylike beside her. *Not* a cart-horse, this one.

"Well, of course I did," Devon said peevishly. "He wouldn't have let me take her, else. Saddled her right up for me without—"

"With bells on the blanket?" she interrupted him. "Or was that your idea?"

"Scythe, no! What d'you take me for? It's Leonard's tack; he had it sent 'round last night."

"Leonard's lost his mind," Becca pronounced, after due consideration.

"Now, haven't I been saying so for—damn! that hurts."

Becca moved, bringing the horse to the rock Devon had pointed out.

"It's no good," he said. "You're right; I can't even stand, much less ride."

"Yes, but *I* can ride," Becca said. "And had better. First for the doctor. What's her name?"

"Eh? Oh, the filly. Rosamunde. And bells are out some benighted poem Celia Marks has got her head full of lately."

Becca paused with her foot on the rock, the reins gathered in her good hand, and paused, dazzled by a sudden realization. She turned to look at Devon, his face salt white and sweat standing on his upper lip.

"Leonard bought the horse to impress Celia," she said. Of course, he had. Leonard's *other* ambition in life was to secure the hand of the reigning local Beauty.

"She'll be no end impressed when he breaks his fool neck," the gentleman's fond brother returned.

"I suppose. Well." It was, she reflected, a good thing that she had put on a split skirt for the walk to Sonet's. Rosamunde was outfitted with a gentleman's light saddle, which meant she would have to ride astride.

"Becca, is this one of your better ideas?" Devon asked faintly.

"Probably not," she replied. "Do you have a better one?" Silence. "Neither do I. Stay still and try to rest; I shouldn't be long." She turned and put her hand on the filly's elegant neck.

"Rosamunde," she whispered into a delicate ear; "I only have one good arm, and I haven't ridden astride since I was ten. Be kind to me, please."

The ear flicked; Rosamunde turned her head and snorted gently into Becca's hair.

"I can't in conscience ask for more than that," she murmured, and threw herself into the saddle.

It was sorry scramble, but she got herself decently upright, reins in hand. The stirrups were too long for her, and her skirt was bunched uncomfortably, but it would suffice, especially if her mount cooperated.

She leaned forward to whisper into an ear. "To town, beautiful lady." She pressed her right leg against the firm ribs, and Rosamunde turned, heading down the track toward the village at a smooth and seemly walk.

Voices were heard over the bells; and the sound of several horses, approaching. Becca pressed her leg against Rosamunde's side. The chestnut stepped to the edge of the path, and stood quite docile and calm, the voices loud in the sudden absence of tinkling.

Becca recognized the deepest voice as belonging to Lord Quince, and the next loudest to Leonard Jestecost. The third, threading between the others, was light and unfamiliar, and for a moment Becca wondered if the last rider was a woman—Daphne Quince, perhaps, who was a notable horsewoman, and took as much interest in her father's stables as he did himself.

". . . tired of his distempers being dismissed as boyish high spirits!" Leonard was saying hotly as he and Lord Quince came 'round the bend in the path, the elder man a little in the lead and Leonard mounted on stolid, patient Ebonsole, the Quince's teaching horse.

Rosamunde nickered, and stamped, twice. Ebby turned his head—and ambled to a stop, Leonard staring from his back.

Lord Quince pulled up beside him, eyes squinted in laughter, and doffed his hat.

"Good morning, Miss Beauvelley," he said gallantly. "Fine morning for a ride."

"Good morning, Lord Quince," she replied evenly. "It is a fine morning, indeed."

The third rider had joined them, reining his high-necked dark stallion in to the right and and slightly behind Leonard and Ebby. Becca received an impression of height, and of an unlocated glitter, which might, after all, have simply been the sun striking off a ring.

"What the *scythe*," Leonard gritted, "are you doing on my horse? Dismount at once!"

"Here, now, that's no way to talk to Miss Beauvelley," Quince protested. "There's no harm—"

"No harm? *No harm,* you say? To have my horse stolen, and to be made a fool—"

"Peace, peace, young Jestecost," the third rider spoke, his voice as cool and rich as cream. "The horse appears to have taken no hurt, nor has the charming rider. All is, one would consider, well, except perhaps for the vexing question of the young brother who was thought the author of the mischief." He shifted slightly in the saddle and his horse moved forward, showing Becca a tall man, indeed, with golden hair that shone in the sunlight, eyes the color of old ale—

. . . *sharp faced,* Dickon murmured from memory, *but with a good, strong nose . . .*

Those tawny eyes met hers and Becca felt as if her head were full of honey, sweet, golden, and sticky.

"I hope he broke his neck!" Leonard said hotly, and Becca turned to him, feeling the stickiness melt away in a flash of anger.

"In fact, he's only broken his leg," she said keeping her voice calm, and her posture relaxed, so as not to communicate her emotion to her mount. "Rosamunde and I are going for the doctor."

"It appears," the Fey said, turning to Lord Quince, "that my expertise is not needed, after all."

"No, Miss Beauvelley's a wonder with the horses," his lordship said jovially. "If we'd known the filly was going to fall in with her, I'd not have been half so worried."

"It is best to plan for every eventuality," the other said gravely. "For who, indeed, could have anticipated Miss Beauvelley?" He turned again to Becca, though he did not meet her eyes, and swept off his hat, bowing from the saddle with an elegance that made her throat ache. "I am Altimere," he said, "of the Elder Fey."

She inclined her head and glanced down at Rosamunde's mane. "I am Rebecca Beauvelley, sir."

"It is my delight to make your acquaintance, Miss Beauvelley. And my further delight to see you so comfortable in the saddle.

I knew that horse's grandsire well, and he was not one to suffer fools."

"Oh, this one's the spit of him!" Lord Quince said jovially. "Wants a rider her equal or better!"

"Not to mention a rider sensible enough not to burden her with bells!" Becca said, with a meaningful glance at Leonard. He narrowed his eyes, which made him look every bit as disagreeable as it had when they were children together.

"I'll equip my horse as I see fit," he snapped.

Becca shrugged. "You may indeed, and no doubt you'll land in the weeds, like Devon."

Leonard's mouth pulled into a straight line, and his nostrils flared. As a child, those had been indications that he was about to say something regrettable.

That hadn't changed, either.

"I hardly think that a horse that can be handled by a cripple is any danger to me."

Rosamunde stamped and snorted. Becca took a breath and deliberately relaxed, leaning over to stroke the proud neck. "Never mind, lady," she murmured. "He's in a temper and we shan't regard him."

"Excellent advice for all concerned!" Lord Quince said loudly. "Now, then, we have an injured rider ahead. Miss Beauvelley, if you'll be kind enough to lead us to young Devon, Altimere and Leonard will do the needful while I escort you home." He turned in the saddle to give Leonard a quelling look.

"When your brother's situated and you have the leisure, Jestecost, come by and see me. I'll house the filly 'til you do."

Leonard looked as if he thought he might say something—and then as if he thought he'd said quite enough. "Very well, sir," he said stiffly. "I'll call upon you when we have Devon settled."

"Excellent." Lord Quince gave Becca a friendly nod. "After you, Miss Beauvelley."

Chapter Five

"LADY QUINCE ACCEPTS!" CAROLINE SAID EXCITEDLY. AS IF, BECCA thought sourly, there had been any question that mother's oldest and firmest friend in the neighborhood could have conceivably refused to attend the dance.

Becca was not at the moment in charity with the dance, or with Caroline. She had spent far too many hours of a sunny, clement morning closeted first with Mother, making lists of those tasks to be accomplished before the dance; and then in the linen closet with Mrs. Janies, the housekeeper. It was now well into the afternoon, and threatening rain—nothing more, surely, than a late spring shower! But enough for her parent to suggest, in that gentle voice that brooked no dissent, that Becca would do better to be indoors and at her needlework.

Her mother distrusted rain for good reason, Becca reminded herself, as she bent over the embroidery frame. She carried the pain of Evelyn's death, even now, after so many years, and Becca strongly believed that she blamed herself. Though truly, she thought, as she plied the needle with its tail of sunflower yellow, who could have believed that Evelyn, boisterous, bold, and strapping as he was, could have contracted a chill from a half hour's walk in the rain, much less perished of it?

"Celia Marks accepts!" Caroline cried gladly.

"Mark her down on your list, my love," Mother said, without raising her head from her own handwork. "And remember to

47

make a tick on the corner of the note, to remind yourself that you've counted her."

Caroline bent over her list, happy not only in her many accept- ances, but in the lack of breeze from the window, closed against the incipient inclement weather. In fact, it was rather close in the ladies' parlor, but Becca knew better than to ask for air.

"Leonard Jestecost accepts!" Caroline said happily. Becca sighed.

They had gone on in this manner for very nearly an hour before the door opened and Mr. Janies stepped in, bearing a card tray, which he presented to Mother. She picked up a creamy rectangle, and another, slightly larger, and grey, as if it were an impossibly thin slice of silver, rather than being formed from paper.

"Callers?" Caroline slipped out of her chair and bent over their mother's shoulder. "Oh," she said disdainfully. "It's only Ferdy. And—" She gasped, fingers flying to her lips.

"The King?" Becca asked, though she had a feeling she knew who that strange, silvery card belonged to.

"Don't be ridiculous," Caro snapped. "It's from—"

"Lady Quince's house guest," Mother said, seeming to come to herself from a distance. "Lord Altimere." She took a breath, and put the cards back on the tray. "It's very proper of Ferdy to accompany his lordship," she said with a forced calmness that made Becca look at her sharply.

Mother, however, was contemplating the card tray. As Becca watched, she took a deep breath, and picked her needlework up off her lap.

"Caroline, pray sit down and resume your work," she said.

"But, Mother, we must—"

"Janies," she continued, as if Caroline had not spoken. "Please show the gentlemen in."

Ferdinand Quince was a slim man of middle height, at ease on horseback and in the field, and very much *ill* at ease in ladies' parlor or rout. He was Dickon's best friend and Rebecca had known him all her life. While she privately thought he was a little foolish, his heart was good, and she liked him very much.

"Afternoon, ma'am." Ferdy shifted his hat to the hand that held his crop and bowed to the room in general. "I've brought Altimere. Should've done so before this, of course, but—"

"But I have been abominably busy about my affairs," his compan- ion interrupted, his accent reforming the everyday words into some rare, strange music. "Forgive me, madam, I pray you." He bowed gently, like a sapling bending in the breeze, Becca thought.

"Surely," Mother said, inclining her head, "there is nothing to forgive. It is well known that gentlemen must see their business fairly done before they have either time or heart for social calls." She moved her hand, gracefully drawing the Fey's attention to the other two occupants of the room. "May I make you known to my daughters, sir? Rebecca . . ."

Becca slid out from behind the embroidery frame and made her sparse curtsy.

"Miss Beauvelley, I am pleased to meet you again," he said, and swayed one of his boneless bows.

"And I, you, sir. I hope you did not find yesterday's activity too strenuous?"

"Not in the least," he assured her, a cool smile on his thin lips. "After all, I had not fallen from my horse, or broken my leg. That, I submit, would have been most strenuous, not to say tedious. Merely to accompany my good friend Quince and the so-excellent Jestecost on a pleasant morning ride—that must only be pleasure."

"Of course," Becca murmured, well-pleased with him. She met his gaze. The amber eyes were warm, and she again had the disconcerting feeling that her head was filling with honey, drowning all her thoughts in sweetness.

"And," Mother said, her quiet voice drawing the Fey's eyes, "Caroline, my youngest daughter."

Caroline came regally to her feet and curtsied as if to the King. Altimere inclined his head, as if, Becca thought, he *was* the King, receiving no more than his due from one of lesser station.

"Miss Caroline, I greet you."

"Lord Altimere," Caroline responded, breathlessly. "I am *very* glad to make your acquaintance." Which was, Becca thought, picking up her needle again, only a breath shy of scandalous. Luckily, Ferdy was not one likely to carry the story away.

The Fey gentleman raised an elegant, ringless hand. "Please. I am Altimere. There is no 'lord.'" He smiled slightly. "I know—how strange, eh? But in my . . . country . . . the conventions of politeness are . . . different. Indeed, you may consider that Altimere is both my name and my title."

Caroline blinked, and bobbed another, lesser curtsy.

"I see," she said, her tone clearly contradicting her words. She should then have reseated herself, and returned to her task. A show of industry, Becca quoted to herself, never failed to please.

However, Caroline had not yet finished her flirtation with impropriety.

"I wonder, sir," she said glancing down at the scatter of cards and list and pen on the work table, "if you like dances?"

The Fey considered her gravely, tawny eyebrows slightly elevated.

"I have attended numerous dances, Miss Caroline."

"Ah," she breathed, resolutely not looking at Mother. "I wonder, then, if you would care to come to my—to *our* dance on full moon's eve. I will, of course, be pleased to send you a proper invitation, now that we have been introduced."

Altimere tipped his head, his glance intersecting Becca's. "Will you be present, Miss Beauvelley, at this dance?"

"Certainly," she said composedly. "Everyone will be there. Even Ferdy." She gave her old friend a sympathetic smile. "Won't you, Ferdy?"

He bowed. "If you want me, then of course I'll be there," he said with a gallantry that was a little spoilt by the quaver in his voice.

"Well, then," Altimere said, turning to smile at Mother. "If her ladyship agrees that I may be issued a . . . proper . . . invitation, then I will be very pleased to be in company with Ferdy and— everyone." He slid an amber glance at Becca from beneath long, lush lashes; a smile at the corner of his mouth, as if they shared a delightful secret. Becca felt her face heat, and concentrated on her embroidery.

"Of course, you must come," Mother said calmly. "We'll send 'round an invitation."

"You are very kind to a stranger in your land," he said, with another of his odd bows.

"Well, then," Ferdy said, suddenly animated. "That's fine, then! All very neighborly. Which reminds me—" He turned to Becca. "Father said I was to tell you he decided not to sell that filly, after all."

Becca stopped with her needle halfway into the fabric and stared up at him.

"But Leonard Jestecost bought her," she protested, thinking

that Leonard *needed* that horse, or thought he did, to pursue his suit with Celia Marks, and that he would never have willingly given it—

"Father bought her back," Ferdy said, interrupting these ruminations. "Said she wasn't ready yet. Too much heart, not enough head."

That was, in Becca's opinion, more apt a description of Leonard than of Rosamunde, however, it would never do to say so. She bent her attention again to the embroidery and kept her tongue behind her teeth.

"It has been uncommonly fine weather for spring," Mother said, bringing the conversation back onto more convenable footing. Caroline had not been pleased to have heard of Becca's rescue of their neighbor the day before, and that topic must be put aside. "Very often we have wet skies until summer dries us out."

The gentlemen agreed that the weather had been fine, indeed, with Ferdy offering the opinion that they might look for an early haying. They continued in that vein, like characters in a play, Becca thought, since no one else seemed inclined to take up their conversational duty.

She reached for the needle threaded in blue silk, looking 'round the room as she did so. Ferdy was leaning forward, hat and whip in hand, earnestly dissecting the weather with Mother while Caroline sat rapt, making no pretense of industry, her gaze upon Altimere's profile.

Becca bit her lip. It was not her place to correct Caroline's manners—and certainly not in front of guests. From the overly composed note in Mother's voice, however, Becca surmised that her younger sister would shortly be in receipt of some strenuous lessons in comportment, not to mention a stern lecture on the behavior appropriate to a maiden who had not yet had her Season—and might yet be denied the pleasure of attending the upcoming dance.

Perhaps, Becca thought, *I'll be able to escape to the garden after the gentlemen leave us and before the lecture begins.* She glanced aside, but the sky beyond the closed window was even more threatening than previously. Assuredly, they would have rain, and she would be caught in Mother's net, with Caroline. Sighing, she brought her eyes back to the room, and once again encountered Altimere's glance.

He smiled at her, and Becca felt her chest constrict, while her cheeks warmed. She did not, however, look down, which would have been proper. Instead, she boldly met the Fey's eye.

His smile widened. He inclined his head and turned back to give his attention to Mother. Becca forced her gaze down, to the embroidery frame and the pretty picture forming out of silk: a garden in early summer, with roses tumbling shamelessly over a decorative gate and a riot of lesser flowers in the background. That it did not in reality depict a summer garden—fosenglove and teyepia came to bloom weeks apart!—she understood to be a matter of complete indifference to most persons, who would only see the bright colors and the cheerful design and be glad.

"Well," said Ferdy, coming to his feet with ill-concealed relief. "We'll be going, ma'am, before we overstay our welcome."

"Indeed." Altimere rose and swayed a bow. "I thank you for your time and your courtesy, your ladyship. I hope to call again."

Chapter Six

"HARIN GARDENER IS IN THE BACK TO SEE YOU, MISS BECCA," Mrs. Janies said.

Becca looked up from the tablecloth she was mending. She had been glad—wickedly glad—that her infirmity kept her from the silver polishing Mother had declared it necessary to perform—glad for approximately three minutes, which was all the time it had taken for Mother to say, with a firm smile, ". . . while Becca mends the linens we set aside from our inventory."

"Please tell Harin I'll be right with her," Becca said, putting the needle down with relief. "And ask Cook to give her some tea."

"I believe that's already been taken care of." Mrs. Janies sniffed, and Becca bent her head to hide a smile. Mrs. Janies felt that Cook was entirely too free with the Earl's larder.

"Good," Becca said, and nodded. "I'll be there directly," she repeated. Mrs. Janies sighed and inclined her head.

"Very good, miss."

Of course, Harin would have come on an errand from Sonet, Becca thought, trying to disentangle herself from the tablecloth. The heavy linen folds had taken over her lap, and trying to shift them one-handed was proving unexpectedly difficult. No matter where she took hold, the cloth slithered and shifted, eluding capture and becoming even more unruly. Biting her lip, Becca slowly brought her damaged arm up, and laid it across her lap, using it as a stop while she gathered up the slippery fabric.

Unfortunately the arm had weight but little strength, and the cloth went skittering across the work table, before heeding the siren call of gravity, taking needles, thread, and scissors with it in a tangled cascade to the floor.

"Oh..." Becca gasped, perilously—and idiotically—close to tears. She took a deep breath, closed her eyes, and took three more deep breaths. Slightly calmer, she opened her eyes and stood, careful that her feet weren't tangled in the damn cloth.

Deliberately, she walked to the door, opened it and stepped into the hall. She closed the door behind her. *Softly.*

She would, she told herself calmly, see Harin. When that was done, she would bring one of the housemaids back with her to help straighten up the mess.

That was a reasonable plan of action, but it didn't change the fact that she *hated* having to ask for help, for not being able to do simple tasks without creating a mess, for needing someone to cut her meat, for— She took another calming breath and deliberately brought her headlong stride down to something more seemly.

Yes, she thought carefully, her injury did make it difficult to do even very simple things. And the truth was that she would happily trade a year of polishing silver for the ability to actually do so. However, this anger—she was done with anger. She had made a pact with Irene, that she would not be angry, and that she would not be cowed, that she would not be the helpless invalid. There were very many things that she could accomplish perfectly well, and those things she was resolved to do. There were other things that might be managed, with difficulty, and those things she resolved to try to do. Those things that she simply could not perform one-handed, for those things she had resolved to accept assistance with good grace.

It was the last that was the most difficult, but she had managed, at first, with effort—sometimes a very great deal of effort—and then progressively less until it became habitual, simply the way things were.

It had been a very long time, indeed, since her body's infirmity had drawn tears.

"You're all over sixes and sevens, aren't you, my lady?" she muttered. Well. She had schooled herself into what passed for patience and sweet calmness once, she could do it again. And again, if necessary. Sir Jennet surely expected a conformable wife, and she had no wish to disturb his peace—or hers!—by acting him a series of tragedies. All the rumble and ruction attending Caro's dance had knocked her off-center, that was all. A renewed application of discipline would set everything right.

With this bracing thought in mind, Becca entered the kitchen.

Harin was seated on a stool at the work table, a cup of tea and a plate of biscuits to hand, talking with Cook while the latter rolled out dough. Cook allowed no one else to make pastry; she had once told Becca that pie-making was better than prayer for settling the mind.

"Good afternoon, Miss Beauvelley." Harin slid from the stool and bent her head respectfully. Wherever Harin had come from—and Sonet could not be persuaded to say—she had been taught a severe respect for the Landed. She persisted in all the forms even when they were kneeling side-by-side, weeding out a garden patch, and nothing Becca could say brought her to a lesser degree of formality. She'd finally given up, after an appeal to Sonet elicited the response that it was good for an apprentice to show respect to a master.

"Good afternoon, Harin." Becca inclined her head fractionally, ignoring Cook's wink. "I see Cook is taking good care of you."

"And Cook'll take good care of you, too, if you'll let her," that individual said irrepressively. "Just sit you down over there, Miss Becca, and I'll get you a cup of tea to go with one or two of those biscuits. You're getting thinner by the meal. I'm going to start believing that you don't like my cooking!"

Becca blinked, but Cook had already turned toward the teapot. Across the table, Harin stood with head bowed still, which she would do until the Landed told her to do something else. Sighing to herself, Becca went 'round to the other stool and hitched herself up.

"Please sit," she said to Harin, "and tell me how Sonet goes on."

The girl got back on her stool with alacrity, head up, but still not meeting Becca's eyes.

"The mistress is well. There's a sudden fever afoot—three came to us yesterday, and the mistress says that's only the start. Once it gets loose, it will run through every house in the village."

"It will *certainly* do that," Becca said with feeling. "Has Sonet any idea yet of the cause? We've had such a fine spring that it seems unlikely— Thank you, Cook," she added as a teacup arrived at her elbow.

"The mistress thinks it's the something come down on the spring winds. The winter was too warm, she says. Folk always sicken easy after a gentle winter."

"Yes, I've heard that theory," Becca said, sipping her tea and adding to herself, *many times.*

"That being so, the mistress wants us to have a good stock ready to dispense, and she wonders if you might have some feverease to spare her."

"Of course, I do!" Becca said. "Come with me, and—"

"*After,*" Cook said firmly, "you've drunk your tea and eaten one of those biscuits. Or two. There's more where those came from, if you finish the plate."

Becca laughed, and slid a glance to Harin. "You see Cook rules me utterly."

"Mrs. Clowder's biscuits are always delicious," Harin said seriously, using Cook's name. She hesitated before picking up her cup and looked at Becca directly over the rim. "It's true that you've lost weight, Miss Rebecca. It's very apparent to one like me, who hasn't seen you in a number of weeks." She sipped her tea, and Becca did the same, astonished as she was.

"The mistress," Harin said eventually, "says that the healer is often the most at risk, because she is trained to look for signs of ill-health in others, and so forgets to look—within."

Conscious of Cook's eye on her, Becca took a biscuit and bit into it. It was a little dry, and not, Becca thought privately, up to Cook's best, but perfectly edible. She had another bite, and then a sip of tea.

"If there is ever anything I can do for you, Miss Rebecca," Harin said so softly Becca had to strain to hear her, "I would be honored by your trust."

Where, Becca thought, had this girl come from?

As if she'd spoken aloud, Harin smiled.

"I hail from Lunitch."

"At the Boundary," Becca murmured. "You must have seen Fey, then?"

"Now and again," Harin said slowly. "You'll be thinking of the gentleman making his stay with Lord Quince?"

"He has . . . rather odd manners, and I wonder if that's usual."

Harin chewed her lip. "The Fey were here before us, so my granny told it. They stayed hidden for a time, watching us and learning our ways, but even so when they first came 'mong us there were misunderstandings and bloodshed. The Border Lord thought the Fey could be taken and used, and he captured himself a pair or three—this is years upon years ago, now, Miss."

Becca nodded, astounded to hear such a spate of words coming from quiet Harin. "But," she asked, "used for what?"

"Well, now. The Fey have their ways—magic some call it. My granny, she just said that the land loved them better than it does us—which only makes sense when you think on it, since they was here well before us, and the land has known them longer."

"So, the Border Lord wanted the Fey to teach him their . . . magic?"

Harin shrugged. "Mayhap. Or he might have wanted to break them to his service. Whatever his intention, and for all the care he'd taken to bind them in nothing other than iron—for it's known that the Fey have an—an allergy—to iron, and prolonged exposure weakens them. For all the lord's care, though, his pair escaped—one through dying, and one through the window, or mayhap through the wall. All they ever found was the dead one, and the coils of chain on the floor."

Becca took a breath. "I'd think that the Fey Board of Governors would have sent an—an envoy—to the Border Lord."

"Aye, but that's not their way."

"What did they do, then?" Becca asked, barely noticing as she reached for another biscuit.

"Do?" Harin raised her cup and sipped, leisurely. "They didn't *do* anything, Miss Rebecca. To this very day, Fey come 'cross the Border, as the fancy takes 'em. They bring horses to trade, like Lord Quince's guest done. Maybe pottery, or silver work, or carving. They'll come three, four years in a row, then not be seen for seven or more. My granny said the Fey woman she'd bought her best pottery jug from told her that time ran different on the far side of the Border, but my granny didn't know how that could be, Miss Rebecca, and neither do I." She tipped her head, and gave a sly, storyteller's smile. "That jug, though, that she had off the Fey potter? No milk stored in it ever went off, now matter how many days, or how warm the weather. She'd leave it out, on full moon nights, in case any thirsty travelers passed by. She said, though she whispered to me it was the Fey folk she left it out for, to show that the one who lived there meant them no harm.

And for everything of that, Miss Rebecca, my granny told us never to trust a Fey, for they're not human folk, and their ways aren't anywhere near the same as ours."

Becca took a breath. "That is . . . quite a story," she said finally. "I think you've missed your calling."

"Oh, the mistress tells stories enough. She says it's a good thing for a healer to have a store of nonsense and fable to babble, to put those who're fretful at ease."

"She may be right," Becca said. "I see I'll need to apply to you for lessons."

Harin shook her head. "Everyone finds their own stories, Miss. You know that."

"Do I? I'd never thought of it." Becca finished her tea and put the cup down, casting an eye at Cook, who was busily pinching the tops onto her pies. "If I've eaten enough to satisfy Cook, we can get that feverease."

"Oh, aye, I'm satisfied," that worthy said, without raising her head from her task. "Until dinner time."

"Feverease on that shelf," Becca said, pointing. "Leave me a cord for my folk here, but take however much you need of the rest. Is there anything else? Aleth? Poppy?"

"No, Miss, just the feverease. The mistress lent half of our store to Tamli back in the fall when half her village went ill in the fall with the swamp-sweats. The season's too early for her to replenish us—and now we have this."

"So we do," Becca said, rubbing her withered arm absently. "Well, let us hope that this fever does not blossom into an epidemic."

"Oh, aye, we're all hoping that," Harin said seriously, "and planning, o'course, for the worst. Which is how the mistress gets her reputation, so she tells me, for being wise."

Becca laughed. "Sonet gets her reputation for being wise from . . . being wise," she said. "Planning for the worst is hardly frivolous."

"True enough." Harin nodded at the cords of dried plants she had laid out on Becca's work table. "These'll do us, Miss, unless it truly is an epidemic."

"Praise harvest, it won't come to that," Becca murmured, as the 'prentice put her bag on the table and pulled out a cloth sack, the top tied firmly with a workmanlike length of cord.

"Mistress sends you this, Miss, in trade."

"Trade? There's no need for that! Sonet can repay the house when her stores allow it, just as—"

"Said you might have more use of it where you're bound than she's likely to have, hereabouts," Harin continued, as if Becca hadn't spoken. "Had it from a cunning man, she said, in lot with some other exotics. Duainfey, is what the Corland-folk call it. Mistress says to look for it in your northland book, got sketches and the complete list. Use just a leaf-tip for clear seeing. If someone's all in pain and needs release, it's two leaves for an old person and three for a young."

Becca bit her lip. Administering release was not something she looked forward to. During the big sickness she had of course worked at Sonet's side, and stood ready to do everything that was needful. However, Sonet had been clear on the point of protocol: only the healer in charge could offer and administer release.

"Mistress says," Harin continued, putting the sack on the worktable and stowing the cords of feverease into her bag, "it's a rare one, even in the Corlands. These here're rootlings, all dry and ready to plant."

She could not, Becca decided reluctantly, refuse the trade. A medicinal plant rare even in its native land? She would not be the herbalist Sonet had trained her to be, if she did not receive the gift—and learn from it.

"Please tell Sonet that I am very happy to accept the duainfey in trade," she said in a composed voice that fooled Harin not at all, if the sideways glance beneath short, sooty lashes was any indication.

"That's what she'd want, Miss, which you know and I do—having each of us stood her 'prentice." She slung the bag over her shoulder and gave Becca a grave smile.

"I hope to learn as deeply as you have, if you'll hear me say so, Miss Becca. Between you and the mistress, I've lofty examples to guide me."

Almost, Becca laughed. But Harin looked so grave and serious that she swallowed her merriment and instead gave the girl a careful smile.

"You will outstrip us both," she said, the merely pleasant words heavy with a conviction she had scarcely intended. *Are you*, she asked herself crankily, *a future-seer?*

Harin was bowing, even deeper than her usual, but not before Becca had seen the blush staining her brown cheeks.

"Thank you, Miss Beauvelley," she said breathlessly. "Thank you."

Chapter Seven

BECCA LAY STARING UP AT THE DARK CEILING. THE BREEZE murmured gently through the curtains, bringing her scents from the midnight garden below her window, the froglings paean to their pond, and the occasional giggle of a night hawk.

Ordinarily, such homey sounds soothed her into slumber. Tonight, they irritated. Moreover, her left arm ached; she was too warm—and too cool when she pushed the coverlet aside. Her pillow was lumpy, her nightgown chafed, and she was not, in any case, sleepy.

Though she was, she owned, *infinitely* tired of Caro's dance; a sorry circumstance, indeed, as the event was yet three days ahead of her.

Sighing, Becca gave up on sleep entirely, cast the covers aside, wriggled into her robe, stirred the fire, lit a candle, and curled into the battered chaise, Sonet's herbal on her lap.

It was a thin book; much thinner than Sonet's ledger, from which Becca had copied the pages to begin her own book, as an apprentice. The green ink was so strong it seemed that the entries, written in Sonet's clear and careful script, and the careful renderings of leaf, root and berry seemed to float slightly above the page.

Bending above the vibrant page, Becca read of the wonders of the herb alamister, which grew in the ice moors, and was efficacious as a sleeping draught; and of bentolane which, when made into a tea and drunk every day, prevented pregnancy; of cadmyon, used in elixir to soothe coughing. Of the dourtree, the bruised fresh leaves repelling biting insects, while the dried leaves disgusted mice and rats; steeping the bark produced a tea that gave relief from pain, and wine could be made from its berries. It grew along river beds, where it set shallow roots, and resisted cultivation.

Certainly, an altogether useful plant, Becca thought, around a tight feeling in her chest. She closed her eyes and took a deep breath to calm herself, as her riding instructor had taught her to do, so that her unruly emotions did not confuse her mount.

Her chest somewhat easier, she opened her eyes and turned the next page.

Duainfey, read the bold notation. *The leaves, dried and steeped into tea, purifies the blood. The dried and crushed blossoms may be added to watered wine, or made into a sachet for the taming of unruly thoughts. The fresh leaves, taken by mouth, give surcease from pain.*

The page blurred. Becca blinked to clear her vision, and a single tear fell among the green letters, like a rain drop into a welcoming garden. Lower lip caught between her teeth, she blotted the spot with her sleeve, as even more tears fell.

Gasping, she closed the book, and set it aside, closed her eyes and tried to breathe evenly and deeply.

I will not cry, she told herself, the mantra that she had devised for herself in the long months after her accident. *I will not cry. I will do my part without complaint.*

She was panting, her chest so constricted she felt she must surely strangle, and still the tears flowed, faster, wracking sobs now, as if she mourned a death.

"No," she moaned. "I cannot go there—"

And yet, if she did not— *How* could she not? Refuse, after all, to marry the man who would make all as it ought to be: Herself a respectable wife, Caroline free to marry, her father rid of the sight of her and the daily reminder of his failure to rule a mere daughter? Would she run away entirely, and—and live as a wild woman in the hunting park?

Becca hiccuped, caught between a sob and a giggle.

No, she thought, using the sleeve of her robe to mop her face. No, Sir Jennet had been accepted, and so must the Corlands. She would ... She would simply need to think practically. Was the climate she was bound for cold? Then she must see to it that her trousseau contained warm clothing, and plenty of it. Blankets and quilts—Mother's aid must be enlisted, to suggest such items as bride's gifts. She would need to—

Why, she would need to talk to the man, when she saw him at the dance, and—and be frank regarding her concerns. Perhaps—no, *surely*—he would be able to advise her, even, perhaps, assist her. It was, she told herself carefully, the old, useless pride that led to these frights and starts. Had she not resolved to ask for help when it was needed, and to do so with good grace? And if she could not ask for help from her affianced husband ...

And, yet ... ice moors, and a land so inhospitable that even *aleth* would not grow— It was enough to take the heart from anyone.

She swallowed and put her hand on Sonet's book, recalling that there was another source of aid. Sonet was from the Corlands. Surely, she would have advice beyond herb lore, if Becca would simply ask her. It would take asking, of course, just as it had when she had been Sonet's 'prentice. But, she reminded herself sternly, Rebecca Beauvelley was not too proud to ask for help.

Granted, the next few days were overburdened with preparation for Caro's dance, but—after, she would certainly call upon Sonet. In fact ...

She frowned at the notion stirring in her mind, the worn cover of the northland herbal gritty against her palm. Perhaps there *was* another way. She would, of course, still need to leave her family and her land. But she need not go so far as the Corlands, and she need not be married.

Indeed, if she jilted Sir Jennet, she would have ruined her chances of ever marrying.

She closed her eyes against a new rising of tears. Like any properly brought up young woman, she had supposed that someday she would of course wed, bear children and preside over her husband's household. Until the accident, she had never doubted that future, nor her desire for it.

The accident had—changed everything.

"You, Miss Beauvelley," she whispered, "have far too many thoughts in your head. Some worldly advice might not go amiss before you continue further down this path."

The nearest source of worldly advice, however, was—hopefully unlike his sister!—asleep in his bed. But she assured herself; the matter would wait as long as tomorrow morning.

And as if taking that simple decision had released all of her worries, Becca yawned, suddenly very tired, indeed. She uncoiled clumsily from the chaise and went over to the bed, not bothering to remove her robe before she lay down.

Chapter Eight

"GOOD MORNING, DICKON."

The viscount looked up from his papers with a blink and a laugh. "Now, here's a surprise! Don't you know better than to beard a gentleman in his study, Lady Rebecca?"

"I do, actually," said Becca, easing the door shut behind her. "But I particularly wanted your advice."

Dickon cocked a blond eyebrow. "You could have asked it at breakfast, you know. I'm sure it would have been much more entertaining than Caro's transports and agonies over this damned—beg your pardon, Becca—dance of hers."

Becca smiled and moved into the room. "Yes, but you see, it's a . . . private matter, which I did not care to air before Caroline. I fear that I am not," she murmured as she sat in the chair next to her brother, pulling her shawl more snugly around her shoulders, "a very filial sister."

"Well, take comfort from the fact that Caro isn't, either," Dickon said, then, more gently, "Is the arm bothering you, love?"

"It's the damp," Becca said apologetically, throwing an exasperated look at the streaming windows. The rain had come in with the dawn, and the day looked fair to be soggy and dim. Not, Becca thought sourly, that it concerned her. Mother expected her help indoors today with a myriad of dance-related details.

Dickon followed her glance and frowned, leaning back in his chair. "As fine as it's been, we're due a tithe of rain," he commented.

"But I'll wager that you haven't risked an affront to propriety just to talk about the weather."

"In fact, I haven't," Becca murmured. She looked down, saw her hand fisted on her lap and tucked it under the trailing edge of her shawl before looking back to Dickon.

"I . . . have been having—doubts about my . . . marriage. Almost I might call them 'second thoughts,' except I believe that I never once thought about it until now! I only heard what Father said—that I'd disgraced myself and put an undue burden on my family—and on Caro, who was blameless, but must remain unwed unless something was done to mend my error. Then he produced Sir Jennet and—oh! It was just as he said, Dickon, that *here* was the solution. It was rational, and symmetrical, and my mind accepted it."

"But your heart," Dickon murmured, "did not."

"Well . . . no," Becca said slowly. "But surely that hardly signifies. No secret was made of the fact that Sir Jennet needed a wife with a portion and that Father needed to see damaged goods hidden away." Dickon lifted an eyebrow. "You can't think that Sir Jennet cares for me!"

"Be at ease. I don't think that Sir Jennet cares a fig for you, Becca. But whether or not hearts are engaged, a man should have *some* care for his affianced wife, and make some push to become . . . friends, let us say. It would not have been improper of him to ask Father's permission to open a correspondence—and certainly it would have been given! A simple thing, and yet he bestirred himself not at all." Dickon sighed, and looked at her from beneath his golden lashes.

"Before we go further, my love, you must allow to me say how glad I am to see a fire in your eye, and a lift to your chin. You are quite the old Becca, full of passion and purpose. *Infinitely* preferable to the dutiful, dull automaton Mother professes to admire so greatly." He turned his palms up, smiling ruefully.

"Which is to say that, if you are having second—or first!— thoughts about this business now, it only confirms in me an admiration for your very good sense."

"If I had good sense," Becca pointed out somewhat acerbically, "then this problem of myself would require no solving."

"No, that's going a fence too far, my love. The problem of ourselves, in my experience, which you must admit to be vaster than your own—the problem of ourselves is in continual need of solution." He raised his hand, grinning. "No, don't eat me, Becca-beast!" he cried, calling up a name out of the nursery. "I only mean to say that, if not this problem, then another." The grin faded. "Though I will own that this problem is knottier than some. Do you wish my advice on whether or not you should go through with the wedding?"

"No! Or, rather," Becca stammered, "yes. I—Last night, I could not sleep, and so got up to read. Melancholy overtook me, as it has been wont to do these last few days, and I thought—oh, ridiculous things! At first, I thought that I could not marry Sir Jennet, and then I decided very rationally to engage his support, and then the next moment I was certain that I must run off to live as a wild woman in the park—" She frowned at her brother, sitting comfortably slouched in his chair, his expression no more than attentive.

"You hardly seem alarmed—or surprised."

"Nor am I. To be sure, the contemplation of marriage must make cowards of us all. But I am fascinated! Pray continue. What other mad thoughts came to you?"

"As for mad, no more, though I did have one other notion, which may or may not be rational. Therefore, I would like your advice about whether I ought, *really* to marry Sir Jennet, so that I might make a . . . sensible decision about my future." She smiled slightly. "If you please, Dickon."

"Well." He looked up at the ceiling for a time, his face unwontedly serious—and serious still when he looked back to her.

"One of the things my wide experience has taught me, Becca-love, is that it is never enough to decide simply what one will *not* do. One must also decide what one will do *instead*. We must, I fear, take it as a given that the local Parker will not allow a wild woman to stay long in his park. You, however, speak of another 'notion' which you cannily do not dignify as 'mad' immediately. In which case, I must ask you—and myself—what will you do instead, if you do not marry Sir Jennet?"

Becca shook her head. "I—cannot stay here," she said slowly. "That is decided. And I cannot go to Irene—oh, *she* might take me in, but Edward has more sense! My disfigurement, I think, precludes me from taking up employment as a governess, or," she smiled slightly, "a seamstress. The Wanderer's Village is—"

"Entirely out of the question," Dickon said harshly. He blinked, abashed, and waved a hand. "Your pardon, Becca. Pray continue."

She nodded and took a breath. "So. I have thought to ask Sonet to ask among the herbwise, to see if there might be a village or a settlement . . . at some distance . . . in need of an herbalist."

Her brother frowned. "A woman living alone, with only one good arm . . ."

"I might soon take an apprentice," Becca said briskly, having had this welcome thought while Lucy was doing up her hair.

Dickon turned his head to consider the rain-swept day. "It is a better scheme than running wild in the woods," he said at last, turning again to face her. "But, I must ask— Do you think that you can renounce all the comforts you have been raised to, and live as Sonet does?"

Becca made a show of frowning. "I am not precisely certain, but I do not believe it is required to forever have fifty foundlings and stray kittens about."

Dickon laughed—"A score!"

"Indeed. And, really, Dickon, you must have heard Sir Jennet speak of the condition of his estate. I scarcely think I would be less comfortable in my own cot, tending the health of the village." She paused. "Especially if it were . . . somewhat warmer. The Corlands—"

"The Corlands," Dickon said, completing her sentence for her, "is frigid even in high summer, and your injury will never cease to ache."

"It may," Becca murmured, "accommodate itself. After a time. But—I think it unlikely."

"So do I." He frowned in thought, staring down at his papers, but not as if he saw them. "Well. Perhaps you might speak to Sonet and see what she advises. I wish . . ." he murmured, and fell silent.

"What do you wish, Brother?" she asked after a long moment had passed and he had not said anything else.

"I wish," Dickon said again, lifting his head to meet her eyes, "that there were someone whose heart *was* engaged, and from whom you might look for aid. Someone whose regard you might return fully and—" He stopped, as if catching himself in an indiscretion, color mantling his fair cheeks.

"Your pardon, Becca. It never occurred to me until now, but— perhaps the gentleman who was . . . whose ride you accepted—?"

"Kelmit?" Dickon looked so sorrowful that Becca smothered her laugh. "I did not love Kelmit, Dickon. I accepted his offer of a ride because it was a mark of distinction and I had been so miserable—'Brown Becca' was hardly a success, even with her portion. All of the young men were hanging out for golden-haired enchantresses."

"Sharp scythe!" Dickon closed his eyes; opened them. "Becca, my dear. I'm so very sorry."

"Without cause," she said briskly. "You have never been unkind to me—once we were out of the nursery."

Dickon laughed. "Wretch! And here I have given you my most valuable advice!"

"Indeed you have," she said earnestly. "And I am most grateful, Dickon, truly!" She rose and held her hand down to him; he took it between his large, warm palms. "I did not ask you to solve the conundrum, after all! Only to listen, and to advise, which you have done handsomely! I have much to think about!"

"If you say so," Dickon said doubtfully. His hands pressed hers more firmly. "Becca," he said earnestly.

She looked down in to his fair, good-natured face, now shad-owed by care. "Yes, Brother?"

"If you do decide to—unmake this marriage, I will stand with you. If I had my own establishment, you would be welcome there. Indeed . . ." His face grew thoughtful.

"Indeed," Becca teased him. "It is time and past that you were wed, sir!"

The smile with which he greeted this sally was somewhat abstracted. His fingers pressed hers warmly and released her.

"Bold heart wins all, Becca," he said, softly, and it was tears she saw sparkling in his blue eyes.

Chapter Nine

THE WHEAT-COLORED DRESS WAS EVERYTHING THAT IRENE WOULD have wanted, Becca decided, after surveying her reflection critically in the mirror. It was cut low over the bosom with the right sleeve nothing more than a pouf of fabric, which was the style. The left sleeve was long, flowing wide from her shoulder to be captured in a tight cuff at her wrist, which, of course, was *not* the style, but a scheme to hide her disfigurement, so that it would not offend the gentle sensibilities of her mother's guests.

Whether it would please Sir Jennet . . . was something that she would soon know. Her thoughts had calmed over the last few days, and she was now—not eager to see him, no. But willing to meet him sensibly and try, as Dickon had it, to become friends.

She turned back to her study of the mirror. Her hair was down in long ringlets, threaded with a beaded ribbon exactly matching the color of her dress.

It looked well, she thought. Of course, brown hair was not the fashion in beauty, and dark eyes were worthy of notice only if well-opened and round. Her eyes were subtly down-tilted at the outside corners, and her eyebrows slanted slightly upward, giving her thin face an unsettling foreign cast which not even lush silky lashes could redeem.

Becca sighed and looked 'round at her empty room. Lucy had darted in while Caroline was choosing her jewelry to do up her buttons, and Prudence had come in after tending to Mother to comb out and dress her hair. All that remained was for someone to come and help her with her jewelry.

She had chosen the amber set that had come to her from her grandmother, and, one-handed, had hung the drops in her ears. The bracelet was something more of a challenge, but she managed to tease the clasp shut with the strengthless fingers of her left hand. Someone would be by directly to deal with the choker—she frowned as the clock in the downstairs hall chimed the quarter hour—or perhaps not. It was getting late and Mother would want her in line to receive the guests.

Standing, she shook out her skirts, the fabric cool and pleasant against her fingers, and sighed at the necklace, alone and lonely on the tray. Ah, well, no one would be looking at *her* . . .

The door to her room opened hurriedly, admitting a red-faced Lucy.

"I'm sorry, Miss Becca," she said, coming forward briskly. "Miss Caroline was having a poor time of it, and—"

Rebecca put out her hand, touched the maid's shoulder. Lucy bit her lip and looked away.

"Caroline's slapped you again," she said, touching the hot imprint of her sister's fingers on their abigail's plump cheek.

"She does get a bit tempery," Lucy said, pulling away from Rebecca's touch. "Now, let's get you fit out—ah! The amber. Very good, miss."

"Lucy—"

The girl turned, the amber necklace held between her hands, and gave Rebecca a straight look from tired grey eyes.

"It's nothing, miss," she said steadily. "I'd be a fool to complain."

Which was, Rebecca thought, very likely true. If the abigail complained, Caroline would have Father turn her off. Except—she closed her eyes to consider a sudden new thought as Lucy slipped the necklace about her throat.

What if, after all, she married as her father willed? Surely a wife might engage her own maid? And if she had—if she had folk to care for, *familiar* folk from home . . . would that not warm even the Corlands?

"I wonder," she said slowly, as she felt the amber drop nestle, cool and smooth, into the hollow of her throat. "I wonder if you would care to come with me, when I am wed to Sir Jennet."

Lucy gasped, and Rebecca opened her eyes, her gaze seeking the other woman's face in the mirror. It was pale now, the mark of Caroline's fingers standing out in stark relief.

"I'm—I'm flattered, miss," Lucy said carefully. "But—all the way up to the Corlands! I'm Midlands, born and raised."

And to go to a strange country, with a mistress both crippled and odd, bound to a lord who was an unknown quantity . . . thought Rebecca, with a silent sigh. Caroline's temper tantrums were at least known and familiar. *Almost,* Rebecca thought wryly, *I would choose them over leaving, myself.*

Except that choice was not hers to make. Becca made herself smile at the abigail's reflection.

"I understand," she said, and saw the color creep back into Lucy's face. "It was only a thought."

"Of course, miss," Lucy said, smoothing Rebecca's ringlets with a slightly distracted hand. "Why, Sir Jennet, he'll likely get you an abigail of your own, who's been trained in town—"

Actually, Rebecca could only think of one or two things less likely, as she stood there, but there was no reason to say so to Lucy.

Instead, she smiled again and lifted her hand to touch the amber drop at her throat, just as the hall clock tolled the hour.

"Best you take yourself down to the hall now, Miss Becca." Lucy hesitated, then smiled, showing a gap between her two front teeth.

"You look beautiful, miss. That color suits you."

"Thank you," Rebecca said, turning toward the door. "It *is* a lovely dress."

"You look stunning, Becca," her brother murmured, during the first lull in arrivals.

Mother and Caroline stood at the entry to the hall, greeting their guests by name, shaking hands and declaring themselves pleased to see each arrival. Dickon and Becca, positioned halfway down the hall, served as a secondary greeting station. Father, who had started off gamely in the first line, soon left in company with Squire Trawleigh. If Mother felt his lack, her face did not show it. Beside her, Caroline glowed like a star in the white-on-white dress, her blond hair loose on her shoulders, as befit a maiden.

"The dress is lovely," Rebecca whispered in reply to Dickon.

"I'm grateful to Irene for sending the cloth, and Mrs. Hintchston outdid herself."

"It's not the *dress* I'm speaking of," Dickon said, voice rising above a whisper. "It's—"

"Hush!" she murmured quickly as a portly gentleman in a wine colored coat whom she belatedly recognized as her affianced husband entered the hall and made his bow over Mother's hand. "The next wave is upon us."

Indeed, it was so. Scarcely had Sir Jennet passed on to Caroline than Lord and Lady Quince appeared, followed by Ferdy; behind them Celia Marks on the arm of Leonard Jestecost—

"Courage, then," Dickon answered, mercifully back into undertones. "Where d'you suppose Ferdy *got* that coat?"

"Perhaps he lost at cards?" Becca hazarded, and turned to give her hand and a smile to Sir Jennet, pretending not to hear her brother's barely strangled laugh.

"Sir Jennet," she said, as the gentleman bent to kiss her hand. "I am so very glad you have come."

He straightened a little stiffly, but kept her hand in his. "Rebecca," he said. "If I may be so bold as to use your name?" His face was somewhat redder than on the previous occasion of their meeting, and his pale blue eyes seemed a bit moist. His pressed her fingers tightly. Rather too tightly, if truth be told.

"Certainly, sir," she said carefully.

"Rebecca, then. And you must call me Jennet. I very much look forward to sitting with you this evening and observing the festivities."

She kept her face smooth, reminding herself that she did not dance—not anymore—and that Sir Jennet merely meant to be kind. Which was surely, she told herself firmly, a *good* sign.

"That will be quite pleasant," she said, and produced another smile before passing him on to Dickon and turning to greet Lady Quince.

"Good evening, ma'am," she said with genuine affection. "How glad I am that you are here!"

Lady Quince gave one of her comfortable chuckles. "Oh, you'll not need my company at the side tonight, Miss Rebecca! Indeed, you will not!"

With this cryptic utterance, and a roguish wag of her head, she passed on to Dickon, leaving Becca to greet her helpmeet.

"Good evening, sir. How good of you to come!"

"Worth my life *and* my comfort to stay away," he said, with a sidewise grin at his lady that was so fond it that took any possible sting from the words. He caught Becca's hand between both of his big, rough palms and smiled down at her.

"You've heard I've decided not to sell that mare at present?"

"Yes, Ferdy had told us." She looked up at him, wondering at the pause, but before she could lay tongue to something to say, he pressed her hands and let them go.

"You and your mother will be calling on my lady day after tomorrow," he said. "It will be my pleasure to speak with you then, if you'll have a moment for an old man."

"Of course, sir!" Becca assured him, hiding her confusion behind an honestly affectionate smile. "I am at your service!"

He smiled again, seemed about to say something else, then simply made her a small bow before moving on to Dickon.

"Evening, Becca." Ferdy's handshake was firm.

"Good evening, Ferdy. I'm glad you came."

He reddened slightly. "Well, you said you wanted me, which is reason enough," he said, which from Ferdy was gallantry of a high order.

"I will have to think of some other things that you can do for me," she said, trying to tease him and prolong his stop. She was not looking forward to meeting Leonard Jestecost, *or* Celia Marks.

As it happened, she need not have worried. Leonard satisfied himself with a cool, distant bow, and Celia with a sniff, treating Dickon with the same medicine, which was, Becca thought, hardly fair. Not that Leonard had ever considered fairness, and if Celia Marks had ever thought of anything but herself and how to gain advantage, Becca had yet to see evidence of it.

She sighed quietly, shook her head slightly and looked to the first line, wondering who they might have next.

A tall gentleman in chocolate velvet, his thick, buttery hair tied back from his boldly etched face, bent in an attitude of courteous attention toward Caroline, who had her hand most shockingly on his sleeve, her face turned up to his like a flower, while Mother's entire attention was engaged with Mr. and Mrs. Eraborne.

Oh, dear, thought Becca, and sent a glance to Dickon, but her brother was watching something through the open doors of the ballroom. She could scarcely leave her place in line and drag Altimere out from under her sister's hand before anyone else noticed her behavior, and yet—

As if he had heard her thought, Altimere turned his head, his amber eyes meeting hers. One elegant eyebrow arched, and Becca instantly felt that they were sharing a delightful secret, though his face was grave and bland. He inclined his head to her, then brought his attention once again to Caroline. It seemed to Becca that he spoke briefly, a word—two at most.

Caroline blinked, her smile fading as her hand dropped from its improper nestle along his sleeve. She turned, and moved a step to the right, smile brightening again as she greeted Mrs. Eraborne.

Released, Altimere moved forward, walking with a wholly unconscious grace, as if, Becca thought, he were some wild, velvet-furred predator—a great cat or a lone wolf—that had wandered into their hall by chance . . .

He was at her side now, bowing his fluid, boneless bow.

She lifted her hand languidly and he received it as if it were a priceless treasure, bending over it while his eyes—amber, as if the jewels she wore had taken fire and life—were locked with hers.

"Miss Beauvelley," he murmured, and his voice lifted the hairs on her nape and started a shiver of pure pleasure in her stomach. "Allow me to say that you are most extraordinary. We must dance, and you must tell me everything about yourself."

She shook her head, smiling ruefully, belatedly remembering to slip her fingers free of his. "Of me," she said, hearing the words as if she were standing just to the left of herself, "there is nothing to tell, sir. Also, I am sorry to disappoint you, but I do not dance."

He smiled, very slowly, and there came another shiver of pleasure as he leaned close to murmur, for her ear alone, "I am persuaded that you *do* dance, Miss Beauvelley, and I beg that you will be kind to me, a stranger in your land." He straightened, though his warm amber gaze never left her face. "And to say that there is *nothing* you wish to tell—I think you are toying with me."

"I—"

"Hold!" He lifted his hand, the lace falling around his long fingers like sea foam. From the ballroom came the sound of music, barely heard above the din of conversation.

"The music begins!" said Altimere, and extended his hand, imperiously. "Come, let us show the room what dancing is!"

She took a breath, gathering herself to decline—and paused as Dickon turned to them.

"Altimere—good to see you," he said, giving the tall Fey an easy nod. "Becca, I haven't seen you dance in an age. It would do me a world of good to see you on the floor."

Shocked, her eyes flew to meet his. He smiled, and nodded. She felt her mouth tug into an answering smile.

Still smiling, she looked up at Altimere, and put her hand in his.

"Miss Beauvelley," he murmured, as they turned toward the ballroom. "You do me great honor."

Chapter Ten

TO DANCE WITH ALTIMERE WAS TO BE AWARE OF EVERY SENSATION—
the nap of velvet against one's palm, the flow of silk down her
ruined arm, the firm grip of long fingers. To dance with Altimere
was to be delighted by the interplay of muscle and flesh, taking
fierce pleasure in every movement.

"You dance with passion and with grace," he said into her
ear, his voice warm and intimate. "Everyone who sees you must
delight in your beauty, and yet you would have denied them.
Have they angered you?"

Becca laughed, and tipped her face up to his. "No one wishes
to see a cripple dance, sir. Doubtless, when we are done, we will
find that *they* are angry with *me*."

"Can this be so?" he murmured. "How strange is this land!"

She laughed again. "Do you not, in your own country, put
aside the imperfect in preference to those things which are . . . not
ruined?"

He paused as they described an abandoned and quite delightful
loop across the crowded floor.

"To be present when one invokes her *kest*," Altimere said
slowly, "that is a gift. I do not understand, perhaps, this word
'cripple.'"

Becca looked up into his face. "But what is *kest*?"

Altimere smiled slightly. "I lapse twice in the space of a sentence. *Kest* . . . perhaps in your tongue it would be *power*."

"Power?" She shook her head. "Perhaps another word—" she began, but the music ended just then, and they perforce came to a halt among the rest of the dancers.

Her partner bowed. "Shall we, again?" he asked.

She should, she knew, make her curtsy, seek out her affianced husband and content herself with sitting out the remainder of the evening in his company. She had, she reminded herself, begun this evening with the very salutary project of becoming friends with the man.

Her body, though—she was aquiver, as if every thread of her being were—electrified, exhilarated, without the agony that had come from Sir Farraday's equipment.

As she struggled with herself, the music began again. Altimere extended his long, white hand, his eyes smiling down on her—and she could not refuse him.

She smiled and curtsied and held out her hand to his.

"Yes," she said, putting her hand in his. "Let us, again."

Sir Jennet was awaiting them at the edge of the floor when they finally left it, having danced every dance in the set. Her right hand was resting on Altimere's arm, and she was alive to every step, every breath of air and flutter of scent. Her nerves thrummed as if the players had plucked their music directly from her heart, and she was not in the least bit tired. Indeed, she could not recall a time when she had felt so energized, so alert, so—

"Rebecca." Jennet held his arm out with an air of command, his red face stern.

Altimere checked, head to one side as he considered the stout gentleman.

"Miss Beauvelley," he murmured. "Who is this person?"

"My fiance," she said softly. She inclined her head. "Sir Jennet, allow me to make you known to Altimere of the Elder Fey. Altimere, Sir Jennet Hale."

Sir Jennet's face, already alarmingly red, grew redder still.

"I see, as does the rest of the room, that the two of you are on terms," he said icily. He produced a brief, frigid bow—"Sir"—and again extended his arm meaningfully. "Madam."

"I did promise that I would sit with him," she told Altimere's questioning gaze.

He hesitated, then inclined his head. "Of course, Miss Beauvelley," he murmured. He raised her hand from where it rested on his sleeve, bent, and kissed it lingeringly.

"Good evening, sir!" Jennet snapped.

Altimere smiled slightly and bowed, a brief and achingly supple imitation of Jennet's angry gesture.

"Good evening, Sir Jennet Hale," he said gravely, and passed effortlessly through the curious knot of onlookers.

Becca moved a step forward, meaning to put her hand on Jennet's arm. That she was in for a scold seemed certain—nor would it be undeserved. *You are quite as outrageous as Caroline,* she told herself—

Pain knifed up her weak arm, taking her breath. She stared at Jennet. He smiled with a certain grim satisfaction, his fingers tightening around her wrist, until she lost his face in a spangle of tears. Then and only then did he lead her off the floor, pulling her along as if she were grubby five-year-old.

Becca blinked her sight clear—and it was well that she did so, for Jennet was striding headlong toward the chairs arranged in neat clusters at the edge of the floor, making not the least effort to be certain that she followed easily. Happily, she did not stumble, and managed not to tread on anyone's foot, though she came very near to making an exception for Celia Marks, who smiled sweetly at her as she passed, and whispered, "Bad little broken Becca."

"Here, madam, is your chair." Jennet pulled her forward with such vigor that she staggered, her arm screaming agony. She did not, however, *fall,* if that had been his intent, and within the pain, Becca's temper flared.

"Thank you, sir," she said icily, meeting his eye boldly. She inclined her head and sat, adjusting her skirts with her good hand, and taking her time about it.

"Now that you are seated," Jennet said in an angry undertone, "I expect you to *remain* seated, and to refrain from embarrassing me again." He took a hard breath. "Your father assured me that the . . . incident . . . in your past had broken your willful—"

"Sir Jennet." Becca heard her own voice with an astonishment no greater than his, assuming that his sudden lapse into silence was from shock rather than fury. Still, silence it was, and before he could make a recover, she continued.

"If your wish is for an end to notice, then perhaps you may wish to hold your scolding until we are private."

Really, she thought critically, if his face became any ruddier, he would have an apoplexy.

That fate was averted, however narrowly was not to be known. Jennet bowed, stiffly. "Your servant, madam," he stated.

With nothing else, he turned and walked away.

Becca, following him with her eyes, saw him on course for the refreshment alcove. Perhaps he would bring her something cool to drink, she thought, and tried to imagine him regretting his anger.

Unfortunately, the set of his shoulders as he strode onward discouraged such pleasant imaginings. Becca closed her eyes and tried to compose herself. The pain in her arm had subsided to a dull ache, though she would not be surprised, she thought, should she show bruises on the morrow.

On reflection, it surprised her to find Sir Jennet quite so high-tempered, but she supposed a second son, only lately come into his elder brother's honor, might have some retroactive pride. And certainly any man, she told herself sternly, might be some-what . . . annoyed to find that his affianced wife preferred dancing with an exotic stranger than sitting quietly with himself.

Indeed, she continued, warming to her own scold. It had been very wrong in her to dance with Altimere once, much less the entire set! Good sun, no wonder Jennet was angry.

Still, she thought, settling more comfortably in her chair; it *had* been delightful to dance again. She sighed, more blissful than regretful, and closed her eyes.

"Well, then, my dear, where is your escort?"

Becca opened her eyes and smiled at Lady Quince.

"Why, he's given me up to my proper escort, of course." She shook her head at the older woman in mock sternness. "We are both of us irredeemable scamps, ma'am."

"Are we not?" the lady said comfortably, settling her skirts. "Are we not, indeed." She leaned over to whisper in Becca's ear. "He is a handsome one, eh? The pair of you made quite a pretty spectacle on the floor. I haven't seen you dance for an age, Becca! I'd forgotten how graceful you are."

"Yes, but, ma'am, Sir Jennet is . . . rather angry . . . with me."

"Posh!" She disposed of Sir Jennet and his anger with a flick of her fingers. "He'll come about. Men like to possess things that other men want, though he's bound to be a little tempery until that aspect of the matter makes itself felt. Now . . ." She leaned closer. "Quince has asked you to come by and see me on the day after tomorrow, has he not?"

"Indeed, he has, but—"

"He means to make you a gift of that filly of his," Lady Quince interrupted, and raised her hand as Becca began to speak. "Peace! The man's mind is made up, and I will testify, my dear, that once Quince's mind is made up, it's the work of *days* to change it. In this case, however, he has made a decision with which I am entirely in accord."

"Ma'am, you know that I will be going to the Corlands in—"

"Indeed, I do," Lady Quince interrupted amiably.

Becca eyed her. "You are not about to take 'no' for an answer are you, ma'am?"

The lady smiled and fluttered her fan. "You've known me all your life, missy; what do you think?"

"Well, then . . ." Becca looked out across the room, but failed to find Sir Jennet among the gentlemen standing nearby, though she did see Ferdy Quince, speaking with—or rather, listening to—Robert Trawleigh. She really was very thirsty. Perhaps—

"Ah! Ferdy!" Lady Quince brought her son to her with a wave of her hand.

"Mother?" he asked.

"Miss Beauvelley is thirsty, my son. Pray procure her some punch."

"Certainly." Ferdy seemed relieved to be of service—or perhaps only relieved to be out of Robin's orbit. He smiled at Becca. "Unless you'd prefer tea, or—"

"Punch will be delightful," Becca interrupted. "Thank you so much, Ferdy."

"Indeed, you have been well brought-up by someone," his mother observed calmly.

Ferdy bowed. "Would you like any refreshment, ma'am?"

"Thank you, I've been well provided for. Now off with you before Miss Beauvelley expires of thirst."

Ferdy bowed once more and moved away toward the refreshment table.

"That coat is an abomination," Lady Quince said comfortably. "Well, well. He'll be going to my brother in the city when the harvest is done. A bit of town bronze will go a long way,

I'm thinking. Not that he isn't a good lad, mind you. Steady. Dependable."

As if she hadn't known Ferdy all her life, Becca thought, and knew how much of his mother's heart was in his pocket.

"Indeed, ma'am," she murmured, "I'm very fond of Ferdy. He's always been kind to me, and I will miss him very much . . ." she had been about to say, *when he goes to town,* but it struck her abruptly that it was she who would leaving first . . .

"I daresay he'll miss you, too," Lady Quince said. "In fact, I am certain of it." She folded her fan with a snap.

"Here comes the gallant young man with your punch," she said. "And I see Anastasia Snelling waving to me." She gave a broad wink, looking in that moment almost exactly like her husband. "Must harvest the gossip, eh? It was delightful to chat with you, my dear. Do come and call on me, like a good child." She rose ponderously, and shook out her skirts.

"Ma'am—" But Lady Quince had turned away, sailing placidly across the pitching seas of the dance floor, and here was Ferdy, just as she'd said, bearing her punch.

She composed herself to give him a smile and accepted the cup gladly.

"Thank you," she said. He nodded and sat next to her.

"Sir Jennet's in the card room," he said in his abrupt, unpolished way. "Your father and Snelling have a piquet table set up."

Anger flickered. Becca pushed it down and smothered it. Having hurt her, now Sir Jennet wished to punish her, did he?

"Why did he bring you over here to sit, if he didn't wish to—to be with you?" Ferdy asked, sounding much younger than she, though, in fact, he had been born a month earlier than Dickon.

Becca sipped her punch gratefully. "The fault was mine," she said evenly. "Sir Jennet had made it a point to say that he would sit with me during the dance, and then what must I do but accept a dance with—well! an entire set!—with Altimere—which you must own, Ferdy, was very bad of me."

"I think it was very bad of *him,*" Ferdy said, with a show of passion startling in one of his usually placid manner, "to suppose that you would wish to sit out every dance. It was—it was *fine* to see you dancing again, Becca." He hesitated, then pulled himself up very straight. "Becca—" he began—

"Ah, there you are, Ferdy!" Mrs. Settle swept up, a very young lady under her wing.

Ferdy sighed quietly and stood, while Becca tried to puzzle out who—why, yes! The young cousin who was visiting the Markses. The child scarcely looked old enough to be out of the schoolroom—serious doe eyes, pale cheeks, and a distinct quiver of the hand resting on Mrs. Settle's arm. Becca gave her a smile, and received a tremulous return.

"Miss Justina Stanton, allow me to make you known to Mr. Ferdinand Quince, who is in need of a partner for this next set."

"Miss Stanton." Ferdy bowed, and offered his arm.

The child hesitated, looking from him to Becca.

"Please, sir, you needn't put yourself out for me. You and the lady were talking.

I—"

"Nonsense," Becca said, rallying. "We are old friends and will prose on for hours unless someone brings us to a sense of propriety. Miss Stanton, you really must seize the moment! Ferdy is an excellent dancer." This unlikely assertion happened to be nothing less than the truth; Ferdy brought the grace of a natural athlete to the dance floor, and Dickon had insisted that he learn the steps properly. The result was an adept and kindly partner.

Miss Stanton looked somewhat less terrified, though she addressed Ferdy once more. "If you would rather stay . . ." she began.

"Certainly not," Ferdy said stoutly.

"Oh, you must dance with him, now!" Mrs. Settle said. "He will be quite cast down, you know, if you refuse."

Miss Stanton blinked, doubtless wondering, Becca thought, how she had gone from misguided courtesy to *refusing* poor Mr. Quince.

"I—" She struggled briefly, then gave it up with a shy smile. "Thank you," she said, placing her hand timidly on Ferdy's arm.

He smiled down at her and guided her gently onto the floor.

"Well!" Mrs. Settle said, looking about her with an air of purposeful busyness. Apparently she spotted someone else in need of a partner and bustled off, leaving Becca alone.

It was odd, being alone in the very middle of what she was certain Caro would classify tomorrow as a "mad crush." Becca had seen—indeed, been an unwilling part of—several mad crushes, and could testify as to the difference. No matter. They had a achieved a good amount of company, and Caro would be right to claim it a triumph.

The band struck up again. A servant came by and Becca surrendered her empty cup, then forcibly relaxed into her seat to watch the dancing.

Little Miss Stanton was charmingly naïve in her movements, displaying a natural grace as her shyness melted. Celia Marks danced like a wooden doll—or so Becca had always thought. However, hers was obviously the minority opinion, for Becca had never attended a dance where Celia had not stood up for every set.

Dickon was partnered with Amanda Dornet, which was very good of him, and her plain, good-natured face was positively glowing with pleasure. Caro went by on the arm of Leonard Jestecost, neither one looking best pleased—Leonard wishing to be with Celia, of course, and Caroline doubtless wishing to be on Altimere's arm.

... who was not, Becca noticed, among the dancers.

She found herself more than a little sorry for that. It would have been interesting to—how had he phrased it—behold the gift of his power. Very likely he was in the card room with the other gentlemen whose duty to their hostess had been done.

An odd duty, she owned, reliving that moment when he had come to her in the receiving line, insisting that she dance with him and—what had he said? Tell him everything?

Well, she had danced, and though she regretted angering Sir Jennet, still she could not be unhappy that she had. As to the telling of everything—but that had only been a pretty absurdity. Perhaps it was what everyone in his country said—

"So, the angry little man has established his dominion and left you alone?" As if her thought had conjured him, Altimere was before her, smiling, and holding two cups.

"Sir Jennet is playing at cards," she said, and was absurdly glad to hear her voice sound so calm.

"Sir Jennet is a fool," Altimere said matter-of-factly. "He does not know how to value you." He extended a cup. "I bring wine."

"Thank you." She took the cup with a smile.

"It is well." With a swirl of coattails, he sat in the chair next to her. Raising his cup, he touched it to hers, lightly.

"To fulfillment."

"Fulfillment," she said, tipping her head. "An odd toast, sir."

"How so? Do you not wish to be fulfilled? In your art? In your life? In your *kest*?"

"I am not certain that I know what you mean by fulfillment," she murmured, and he laughed softly.

"It may be that the words I use—approximations, you understand—are not as correct as I would wish them. Perfect communication may be achieved, perhaps, only if you partake of my language." He sipped his wine. "But that is a matter for later, perhaps. Certainly, it will wait until you have told me everything. But first—" He touched her cup with a light forefinger. "Drink. The wine is good."

Smiling, she sipped, to find that the wine was indeed good—then looked up at him with a shake of her head.

"I'm no storyteller, sir. If you would like to know something, I'm afraid you will have to ask me."

He raised his eyebrows. "I am to choose what is to be revealed, and the order of revelation, as well? You cede me much power, Miss Beauvelley."

Her lips parted.

He raised a hand. "If it is the custom of this land, so be it. I will ask, after consideration." He sipped his wine, amber eyes quizzing her over the rim of the cup, then sat for a time, head to one side, like one of Dickon's more intelligent hounds.

"I begin to understand the pleasure of this tradition, so different from my own," he said at last, and slowly. "How shall I lead? With a bold question, which tempts your disfavor—or shall I flatter you and win your trust?"

Becca laughed. "If it were me," she said, "I would ask what I most wanted to know."

"A hint!" Altimere smiled his cool, thin smile. "Very well, then, Miss Beauvelley—my first question . . ." He paused, perhaps for effect, raised his cup as if to sip, but instead murmured, so softly she scarcely heard—

"Why have you chosen to join your *kest* with that of the angry Sir Jennet?"

Very nearly she laughed again, but she spied Celia Marks staring at her from the dance floor, and sipped her wine instead.

"Firstly," she said to Altimere, "I have no . . . power. I am a ruined woman, and crippled—broken—into the bargain." She raised her shrouded left arm slightly. "No one would *wish* to marry me, except for their own gain. Thus, we have Sir Jennet." She smiled suddenly, feeling a degree of—lightness, as if speaking the unvarnished truth to this stranger had in some way . . . freed her.

Altimere moved his hand in a gesture reminiscent of Lady's Quince's dismissal of her spouse. "Yes, yes," he said, sounding slightly impatient. "It must be clear to the meanest intelligence that Sir Jennet profits greatly from this proposed alliance. But you—what profits come to *you*?"

The country beyond the Boundary must be strange beyond all imagining, Rebecca thought.

"I profit by making an unexceptional marriage," she told Altimere.

"Unexceptional," he repeated, and touched the tip of his tongue to his lips, as if he tasted the word for sweetness. He sipped wine, and Becca did, watching his face the while, wondering what alien thoughts passed through his elegant golden head.

"No," he said eventually. "It will not do. Miss Beauvelley, you force me to an uncomfortable conclusion."

She raised her eyebrows. "Indeed? And what would that be, sir?"

"I conclude that you are, for reasons you choose to conceal, allowing yourself to be seen as a helpless pawn in this game of alliance. That is your right and your privilege as a woman of power. And yet . . . I wonder if your *kest* has misled you. Surely, it cannot have escaped your attention that this man means to do you harm. To place yourself wholly in his hands—it is a bold act. But is it a wise one?" He leaned back in his chair, smiling once more.

"I could become fond of this form of tale-telling. Mayhap I will introduce the mode, when I return."

"It were wisdom," Rebecca answered slowly, "because it appears to be the only choice available." She took a hard breath. "Now, if you please, sir, I would ask a question of you."

"But how diverting! I accept, of course."

"You say that Sir Jennet means to do me harm. I wonder how you know this."

He tipped his head, his expression arrested. "Is it possible—but I am forgetting how young you must be!" He paused, and looked earnestly into Rebecca's eyes. "I know this, Miss Beauvelley, because I have seen it. It is . . . a small power . . . that I have."

"Saw it?" Rebecca considered him doubtfully. "Could I . . . see it, as well?"

For a moment, Altimere said nothing, and she began to fear

that she had offended propriety. Just as she was about to apologize, he inclined his head.

"I am honored that you think my small power worthy of witness. Here." He reached out and touched her wine cup. "Look into the cup, at the surface of the wine . . ."

Obediently, she bent her head, regarding the glassy liquid with interest.

For a long moment, nothing happened, save once again the sensation of her head filling up with honey, warm and sweet . . . and suddenly, before her, precisely as if she were looking through a window, there was Sir Jennet!

He wore a heavy coat, as if he had just come in from the outside, and he walked down long, dark halls that made Becca shiver as she watched, they seemed so chill and inhospitable. At the end of a particularly long, dim hall, he came to a door, which he pushed open without ceremony.

The chamber beyond was lit by a single lantern, the ceiling lost in gloom, the black plank floor black unrelieved by any covering. There was no fire; the hearth looked as if it had been cold for centuries. A woman huddled over an embroidery frame next to the lantern. She wore a tattered and none-too-clean robe that seemed inadequate for what surely must be frigid air, and her dark hair lay in a tangled, greasy mass along her shoulders. She looked up as Sir Jennet approached and Becca sucked in a breath as she recognized her own face.

Her own face, but—desperately thin, with shadows under her eyes and the bloom of fever along staring cheeks.

"Well, madam?" Sir Jennet said, his voice stern and angry. "How do you go on?"

"Badly," the woman—she!—answered in a faint, shaking voice. "It is cold; I am ill. I ask again for coal, for warm clothing, for a maid."

"And where will I get the money for such frivols?" he asked. "The repairs are costly and necessary. One day this hall will reflect to my honor, as a wife who cannot even dress herself surely does not!"

Of a sudden, the scene vanished, as if someone had drawn a curtain across the window. Becca blinked, and blinked again, at the confusion of a bright, loud ballroom. She was shivering, though the room was quite warm.

"How . . ." she whispered, staring into the depths of the cup again. "How was this done?"

"As I said," Altimere murmured. "It is a small power that I possess."

She looked up into grave and unreadable amber eyes. "Have I just seen the future?"

Altimere frowned, his winging golden brows pulled together slightly.

"The future hangs upon choices made," he said slowly. "What you have just beheld is the outcome of one choice. Other choices may lead to other outcomes."

Becca bit her lip, looked into the cup, and back to his face.

"Show me another choice," she commanded.

He inclined his head. "Look, then."

She bent her head. Once again, the window formed, and she looked out into a wild garden, glorious with strange, exotic blossoms and herself in a dress of shining silver, her hair gleaming in an intricate knot, a diamond collar glittering 'round her throat. She moved slowly among the flowers, and the trees reached down to her, stroking her sleeve, and her shoulders—

The curtain closed. Becca took a breath—another—before she looked up into Altimere's strange eyes.

"I can assist you in the choice from which that future declines," he murmured.

She looked out over the ballroom, her vision darkened by the memory of that cold prison room in the north, her thoughts spinning in the aftermath of viewing so delightful a garden.

"Ah," Altimere murmured. "The so-pleasant Mrs. Snelling approaches with a lady upon her arm. I apprehend that I am about to be asked to do my duty to the house." He rose and smiled down at her. "I am at your service, Miss Beauvelley," he said softly. "I believe you might find an alliance with me to be . . . of benefit."

With that, he rose to greet Mrs. Snelling and the lady. Rebecca raised her glass and drank what was left of the wine, her thoughts in turmoil.

Chapter Eleven

SHE WOULD NOT, BECCA TOLD HERSELF FIRMLY, MARRY SIR JENNET. It was not the first time this afternoon that she had assured herself of this, and she had a sinking feeling that it was not nearly the last.

Despite her strength of purpose undergoing periodic wiltings, she was steadfast in her decision. Even should she discount Altimere's parlor trick with the wine cup—and a wise woman did discount magic—even then, she could not discount the bracelet of bruises around her left wrist or the angry man who had all but dragged her from the dance floor, to fling her into a chair, and— No. She would not marry him.

She had, however, wronged him; which she had freely admitted to Mother last night—or, rather, early this morning—as the two of them sat tete-a-tete in the elder lady's dressing room.

"Your indiscretion angered Sir Jennet very much," her mother said, inspecting the bruises circling Becca's wrist. "That may be a reminder to you, my love, to behave with the good sense and circumspection you have labored so long to achieve." She shook her head. "You must apologize to Sir Jennet. Yes—I know he hurt you. That was ill-done of him. But the first fault was *yours,* Becca. He would have had no cause to be angry if you had behaved as you know you had ought."

Becca had hesitated, the vision in the wine cup still strong in her mind. Almost, she spoke—but her mother had leaned forward at that moment and clasped her hand.

"Promise me, Becca!" she said earnestly, tears standing in her blue eyes.

And so Becca had promised.

Her father, on the other hand, had not bothered with promises, but had descended immediately to orders, leavened with sarcasm.

"A fine way to treat your affianced husband. By all means, show that world that you are still the wild, abandoned piece of baggage that should have broken her neck in that accident and saved us all pain and grief!" He had shouted.

"Now, miss," he'd continued after a pause to see if Becca would cry. "Sir Jennet has asked to speak with you alone this morning. I have given my permission. You will await him in the ladies' parlor and you *will* be meek and mild. You *will* apologize and make whatever amends Sir Jennet deems appropriate." He paused, staring at her hard.

"*Whatever* amends he deems appropriate, Rebecca, am I plain?"

"Yes, Father," she said quietly. "You are quite plain."

"Excellent. I suggest you go now and wait for him to come to you."

She curtsied, turned—

"Rebecca."

She turned back. "Father?"

"If Sir Jennet calls off the marriage, I will remand you to the Wanderer's Village," he said coldly. "I cannot have you disrupting my household any longer."

Becca took a deep breath, made another curtsy—and left.

It had been several hours since that interview. Becca sat behind her embroidery frame, alone in the ladies' parlor. Cook had twice come in to give her tea, and to leave a plate of biscuits. The tea was strong, and it was the reason she was slightly . . . less dull than she might be, with a dance, and an hour's sleep in her immediate past.

"I will not," she whispered to her embroidery, "marry Sir Jennet."

The threat of banishment to a Wanderer's Village—that was frightening. Still, she might yet escape to Sonet, and Dickon had said he would—

The door opened, loudly. Becca started, and rose as Sir Jennet strode into the room.

She bumped the embroidery frame as she did so. It wobbled

crazily; she snatched at it with her good hand, missed—and the whole went crashing down, silks and needles dashing across the floor in tangled confusion.

Sir Jennet looked down at the minor disaster, then back to Becca, a frown on his ruddy face.

"You were scarcely so clumsy on the dance floor," he remarked, and it came to her with a slight shock that he was angrier now than he had been last night.

"Dare I hope to receive an apology for last evening's outrageous and immodest behavior, madam?" Jennet continued, his voice hot and hard.

Becca felt a flicker of temper, and took a breath to still it. *You did wrong,* she reminded herself, *and hurt his pride. For that, he is indeed owed an apology.*

"Indeed, sir," she murmured, dropping into the slight curtsy that was the most her one-handed state allowed. "I am very sorry to have distressed you, especially after you were so kind as to offer to sit with me."

There came from Sir Jennet, not a bow accepting this olive branch, but a glare, and a silence so heavy Becca feared it might crush him.

"Is that," he said finally, "what you consider to be an apology, madam? How differently we judge your crime!"

"Crime, sir?" Becca felt her cheeks heat. "Is it a crime in the Corlands to dance at a dance? For I assure you that it is not here!"

"To mock one's husband in public is certainly a crime; and women have been placed in the stocks in the marketplace for less cause than you gave me last night!" His face was darkening toward purple.

"To characterize dancing with one as mocking another, sir—"

"An entire set!" he roared, overriding and shocking her. "Your father *assured me* that the incident which crippled you had broken you of any further desire for wanton and abandoned behavior! I see that what he characterized as an acceptance of proper female modesty was merely a lack of opportunity. Let one pretty man come into your orbit and you immediately throw over every propriety, with no thought of what hurt you may do to those who are responsible for you—and show no remorse, even after your error has been taught to you!"

"Re—" Her voice failed.

Perhaps Sir Jennet took her silence for a sudden understanding of her so-called crime, for his face softened somewhat, and he inclined his head.

"Just so. Come, madam. Soon you will be my wife, and removed to a strange land. It will profit you to be my friend, and not anger me. Make amends, sweetly, as I know you can, and let us begin again."

She stared, seeing—not him, not the ladies' parlor and the bright spill of embroidery across the sun-drenched floor, but long dank hallways, and a room so cold her bones ached with the thought of it.

If I die, she thought, very clearly and calmly. *If I die up there, of cold and neglect, he will have my portion. It is that which he wants, not me. No one will rescue me, not Dickon, nor even Irene. What woman needs rescue from her husband?*

To place yourself wholly in his hands, Altimere spoke from memory—*it is a bold act. But is it a wise one?*

No, she thought, panic rising. *Not wise at all.* Nor was it wise to anger him again—and already his face was beginning to darken.

Becca dropped into the lowest curtsy she was capable of sustaining, head bowed modestly.

"Sir Jennet, I do apologize most humbly for my folly of last evening," she said, her voice chaste and soft. "Of course I cannot wish to anger you, or to harm you in any way."

Sharp scythe, she thought, staring down at the floor, *let that be sufficient.*

The silence grew, then he moved, his heels hitting the floor hard, and his boots came into her line of vision. He reached out and raised her. When she lifted her eyes to his face, he smiled.

"There, then," he said, jovially, all trace of his former anger vanished. "I knew a firm hand was all you needed. We'll get along famously, you and I. And you will never mock me again, will you, Rebecca?"

She glanced aside, hoping he would take it for maidenly modesty.

"No, sir," she whispered, and swore in her heart that it was true.

"Good—indeed, excellent! Then I know that you will be pleased to know that your father and I have agreed that it will benefit no one to put off our marriage until Midland's harvest. I am here, now. There is no need for me to make a second lengthy journey just as winter is setting in. He has today written to the Governors' Counsel, requesting a special license." Jennet smiled, and Becca felt her blood freeze in her veins.

"We shall be married and on our way home to the Corlands before the week is out!"

They would not tell him how long he had slept—or perhaps the one who attended his awakening simply did not know.

He bore scars, livid against his brown skin, which argued for a slumber of some uncommon while. The wounds he had borne were terrible, and in his lucid moments he had not expected to survive them. That he had done so was well, however, for duty lay before him.

They brought him clothes, the leather leggings and vest of a Wood Wise, and good, sturdy boots, which was also well. They gave him a belt, but neither knife nor bow, from which he deduced that one with more insight into his case than his present attendant would soon wish to speak with him. Those who were newly wakened were sometimes confused in their minds. Naturally, one would not wish to arm such, for fear that they might do themselves a hurt.

He was in no danger of doing himself a hurt—but no matter. They would learn so, soon enough.

He dressed himself deliberately, covering the scars with clothing, stamping into his boots. The belt he considered, frowning, for it were very nearly an insult. Yet, the healers would think of it as honoring his *kest*.

Not wishing to offend those who wished only to convey honor, he threaded the belt 'round his waist, settled the patch over his right eye, and turned as the door opened, admitting the attendant, who bowed low, stammering that the chyarch would see him now.

Chapter Twelve

"SO SOON?" LADY QUINCE STARED AT MOTHER OVER THE RIM OF her teacup. "Obviously, the gentleman is smitten."

"It would seem to be so," Mother murmured. "He sees no reason to subject Becca to a journey at what is, in his own country, the threshold of winter."

"And by marrying now, there is time for a honeytrip before he may be wanted at his own harvest. That is well-thought, I must own." At last, her ladyship sipped her tea, placing the cup back on the saucer with a tiny clink.

"Well, then, Miss!" she said, with a gaiety that seemed entirely horrible to Becca. "Did I not tell you that he would soon overcome his annoyance and realize that he must make a push to secure that was promised?"

Becca swallowed in a dry throat, and made shift to smile. "Indeed, you told me just that, ma'am," she murmured, and raised her own cup so that she need not speak further.

The tea, she knew, was quite good—Lady Quince's tea was always perfectly brewed. It must, therefore, be only what her father was pleased to style an "overwrought imagination" that produced the burning in her throat, as if it were not tea, but vinegar that she sipped.

Her "overwrought imagination" could not, however, be blamed for yesterday's shocking series of events. It was a fact that she had been forbidden to leave the house without her father or mother as escort—"by order of the Earl," so the footman who had barred the front door against her explained apologetically.

She had not been allowed to visit Sonet, nor to tend her garden, nor to repair to her workroom. Which was, Mother said brightly, when Becca laid these same facts before her, just as well.

"For you have a prodigious amount to do, you know, Becca! And a very short time to do it in. Now. What do you think about—"

"I think that I would like to visit Sonet," Becca interrupted. "She expects that I will be here through the summer; this sudden, unexplained departure—"

"Need not be unexplained," Mother interrupted in her turn. "You may write her a note. Any of the servants will be happy to carry it for you."

But Becca did not write to Sonet when she left her mother. Instead, she had walked firmly and briskly down the hall to the door of her father's study—and paused, with her hand on the knob.

Beyond the door, her father was shouting—which was, regrettably, not . . . entirely unknown. It was, however, no luckless lackey whom he disciplined this day, for a second voice, not—quite—shouting, cut across his, and it was that which gave her pause.

For the second voice had been Dickon's.

Prudently, she had removed down the hall to a position of less exposure, and had scarcely ducked into the shelter of the library when a door slammed, and slammed again, and angry footsteps approached.

Becca stepped out into the hall—and stopped, her hand flying involuntarily to her lips.

She had often seen Dickon angry, but this—surely this was fury.

"Becca!" he snapped, sounding more like her father than himself. He caught her arm and snatched her back into the book room, closing the door quietly behind them.

"You will not go to Father," her brother told her, his voice breathless and tight.

"But—" she began, and started back a step when he slashed the air with an impetuous hand.

"Yes, yes, I know! You are not to go visiting on your own, nor are you allowed the solace of your plants, or your work. Protest it and you will find yourself locked in your room until your wedding day!"

Becca swallowed. "Dickon, I cannot marry Sir—"

Again, he slashed the air between them, turned and strode energetically to the window.

"There is no choice," he said flatly, staring out over the formal garden.

Becca gasped. "There must be a choice! I must send a message to Sonet—"

"No. Any notes will be taken directly to Father."

She went to his side, and touched his sleeve. "Would—you—not carry a note for me, Dickon?"

His laughed so bitterly that she winced, and snatched her hand away.

"I might have done, but—not after this. I had no idea that Father—" He shook himself, turned and put his hands on her shoulders. She looked up into his face, seeing sorrow, now, and affection, and something else, for which she had no name...

"There is no choice," he said, his voice so low she could scarcely hear him, as close as they stood. "For either of us."

"... dress?" Lady Quince asked, loudly enough to startle Becca out of these distressing memories.

"The wheat will do splendidly," Mother answered, calmly. "The event is on us so suddenly that it will only be family—and close friends, of course!—in attendance. If it is fine, perhaps an outdoor wedding, in the formal garden."

"That should please the bride," Lady Quince said, with a roguish glance at Becca, who bent her head, pretending to be considering the biscuit-plate.

"Why should we not try to please the bride?" Mother murmured, giving Becca a fond smile. "We are all very proud of Becca for her—"

A tap at the door interrupted her, for which Becca could only be thankful. Lord Quince stepped into and made his bow.

"Madam," he greeted his wife. "Lady Beauvelley—and Miss Beauvelley! Just the lady I was wanting to see!" He turned to Mother. "Might you spare her for a few minutes, ma'am? I've that item I discussed with you here to show the young lady."

Mother sighed and put her tea cup down. "It is a handsome gift," she said slowly, not quite meeting his yes. "I fear the Earl will consider it *too* handsome."

"Is that so? You leave Robert to me. As far as 'handsome'—well, ma'am, so it is! A bride gift is supposed to be handsome! Besides that, this filly was born to be Becca's. I knew it the instant I saw them together. It would be cruelty to keep them apart."

Mother laughed, hand up and palm out. "Pray save your eloquence for the Earl! You will need it!"

Lord Quince grinned and gave a bow. Straightening, he beckoned. "Come along, young lady, and tell me if you think she'll do."

Becca rose, eager to be away, and eager, indeed, to see Rosamunde again.

"Ma'am?" she said to her hostess, but that worthy merely moved an indolent hand.

"Go on with you! And mind you look her over minutely! Your mother and I have many things to speak of!"

Yes, Becca thought, she imagined so. She curtseyed and followed Lord Quince out.

Rosamunde whickered as they approached the fence, and Lord Quince rumbled a laugh.

"She recognizes you," he commented, and pulled a carrot out of his pocket. "You know your duty, I'll warrant."

Becca took the proposed treat and stepped up to the fence, her mood suddenly lifting, as if she had just stepped from deep, winter dark, into the full blare of summer.

"Good day, Rosamunde," she murmured and smiled at the flick of expressive ears. "Would you do me the honor of accepting this?" She offered the carrot across the palm of her hand.

Disconcertingly, the horse did not immediately attend the carrot, but looked into Becca's face, for all the world as if she were judging her.

"Lord Quince," Becca murmured, keeping the carrot on offer, "has kindly thought that you and I might suit. I would . . ." She paused, and the large eyes never left her face, as if there was an intelligence beyond the mere equine listening to her words.

"I would," Becca said, the words coming from her very heart, "very much like it if you would consent to be my mount."

There was a small silence, and a certain . . . warmth, as if someone had lit a candle in the center of her chest. Then Rosamunde bent her beautiful head and lipped the carrot off of Becca's hand.

"I'd take that as an acceptance, myself," Lord Quince said comfortably.

Becca took a breath, her eyes on the elegant curve of the filly's neck.

"Was her grandsire as . . . attentive?" she asked.

"Fey horses are . . . extraordinarily perceptive," a cool, accented voice said from close at hand. "The beautiful lady is quarter-Fey. Surely, she listens, and judges—and determines for herself where her power is best allied."

"Altimere." She turned, her heart suddenly soaring. *Here,* she thought. *There is a choice.*

The tall Fey leaned on the fence beside her, and smiled.

"Good day, Miss Beauvelley," he murmured. "It is a pleasure to see you again. Lord Quince."

"Altimere," said his lordship in his bluff way. "M'wife tells me we're losing your company."

"It is so, I fear," the Fey said. "My business here is complete, and I am wanted in my own land."

"Well, I'll be sorry to see the back of you," Lord Quince said. "You still thinking of that parcel up near Eastkirk?"

"I am. Indeed, I plan to pass by again on my return, and to speak to Mr. Smythe regarding his price."

"He's asking high," Lord Quince said, and it was clear to Becca that both men had forgotten her presence. She leaned closer to the fence and raised her hand to stroke Rosamunde's soft nose. A feeling of satisfaction filled her, and she narrowed her eyes in pleasure.

"Still," his lordship went on, "even if you meet his price, you'll make it back inside a season. I can't think of a man of my acquaintance who wouldn't want one of those horses of yours!"

"I may do well enough for a few seasons," Altimere murmured. "However, I think I may soon be redundant."

"Horses producing more of themselves, as they're wont to do," Lord Quince said. "I see your point, but I'm thinking that what you need to do during those first few years is fix it in folks' heads that the man to go to for the real thing, no imitations, not side breeding, nothing but pure blood Fey—" He stabbed an emphatic forefinger at Altimere's chest—"is yourself."

"You fascinate me. Perhaps we should ally ourselves in this matter."

"I tell you what, that's not a bad notion at all! You write me once you've got everything set the way you want it and I'll—yes, Dobbs, what is it?"

"It's the bay, sir. You asked to be told the next time he loosed that front shoe by stepping on with his back foot in the walk ring."

"Blast!" Lord Quince nodded curtly to his guests. "I'll be just a moment. Sorry, but this has to be tended to immediately!" And with that he strode off, hard on the heels of the stable boy.

Becca sighed, and shivered, suddenly queasy in her stomach. Surely, such a meeting was fated?

If only she believed in fate.

"Altimere," she said softly, stroking Rosamunde's nose the while.

"Miss Beauvelley. How may I serve you?"

She turned, deliberately, to face him, her hand falling from Rosamunde's nose to grip the fence.

"I would like," she said, keeping her voice steady by long practice. "I would like very much to embrace the second possible future you showed to me."

"Ah, indeed?" He looked down at her. "We have said that the customs of your land are not the customs of my own, so I will ask, in order to be certain: You offer to ally with me; to place your *kest*—your power—in my hands?"

Her power, thought Becca, and might have laughed, had Rosamunde not blown lightly against her hair.

"I place my power, my honor, and my future in your hands," she told, and if her voice shook, who could blame her? It was a terrible step she was about to take—and, yet, to find succor, where she had been so certain that all was lost . . .

"The small, angry man?" Altimere said. "He has been informed that he will not profit from an alliance?"

"He has—not." Becca swallowed. "I—if I tell him so, my father will lock me in my room until the day of the wedding, which is—very soon, now. A matter of days. I—if you accept my—my alliance—we will have to go secretly—swiftly and with the possibility of pursuit."

Altimere looked, faintly, amused, but his voice was brisk. "It is well that the moon is just past full, and fortunate that Quince has bestowed upon you this horse." He glanced at the cloudless sky. "If you are able, we may leave tonight at moonrise. Say to Quince that you will come for the horse later; I will bring her to you."

"Yes," breathed Becca, "thank—but her tack, I don't—"

"Leave all to me. For yourself, you need bring only those things which are necessary to your *kest*, but nothing more than will fit in a saddlebag. You will not need jewelry, or coins, or any medium of trade or exchange."

Becca looked up at him. "But, how will I purchase—"

"You have allied yourself with *me*," he said, and there was a note of arrogance on that last word. "I will provide those things which are needful."

"I—see." Her heart quailed, but Rosamunde blew again, a gust of warmth against her ear, and she giggled instead.

"The beautiful lady has heart and courage for two," Altimere said, and looked over Becca's head. "The excellent Quince returns to us. Moonrise, at the servants' door. I will be there for you."

He turned away, calling out a question to Lord Quince. Becca leaned into Rosamunde and closed her eyes, letting the warmth of her mount's regard soothe her spirit and calm her racing heart.

The chyarch was found in a bower of sandelkirk, a book on her knee and a wood's cat curled at her feet. She looked up at his approach, and dismissed the attendant with a nod. He bowed, the performance of which courtesy gave him time to recover from his surprise.

It was most usually the Elder Fey who were called to the healing arts. While it was not impossible to find one of the Wood Wise among the healers, yet it was—unusual.

That one such would rise to chyarch—that was unlikely, for the Wood Wise dislike confinement and are happiest when they rove.

"Chyarch," he murmured respectfully, straightening from his bow.

"Meripen Vanglelauf," she replied, marking her place and setting the book aside. "I would have had you sleep for some while longer. Alas, I have been overruled." She pulled a roll of birch paper from her sleeve and sat holding it in her hand, considering him gravely. Her eyes were pale—grey with a touch of brown, like bark seen through morning mist—her aura a faint shimmer of autumn yellows.

"The Lady of Sea Hold sends for you, by name. Perforce, you must be wakened and set upon the way."

He blinked. "The Lady of Sea Hold?" he repeated the phrase as if the sleep, or what had gone before, had robbed him of sense.

"Indeed," the chyarch said solemnly. "Precisely that most gracious and puissant Lady."

"I—" He paused, trying to think. Unlike some of the Forest Gentry, he had no fear of leaving the land. Indeed, his own mother had ranked as a captain among the Sea Wise, and he had learned the lore of wave and wind at her side. That he had accepted the duties of the Wood Wise was more accident than destiny. He knew and was acknowledged by kin on the seaward side, and had been fostered at Sea Hold in his youth. The last he had known, however, Sea Hold had rejoiced in a lord—one Velpion, whose title had been, properly, Engenium. To find that there was now a *lady* in that dour Elder's place . . .

He wondered again how long he had been inside the healing sleep.

"Forgive me," he said to the chyarch. "Why does the . . . lady . . . send for me?"

She shrugged. "I had hoped perhaps you would know what urgency drives her. But it would seem not." She held out the roll of bark. "You may read for yourself what she writes. And then, if you feel able, you may draw what you need from stores and—"

"No." He said flatly, hands fisting at his sides as he recalled what he must do.

The chyarch raised an eyebrow. "Could you be more explicit?"

"I cannot go to Sea Hold," he said. "There is a matter of duty which must be satisfied before—"

"Yes, yes . . ." She waved the bark at him, impatiently. "It's all in here. I am, in a word, *commanded* to wake you and to send you forth. It may be argued—persuasively, for your reputation precedes you, Ranger—that I cannot be responsible for where you go once you leave here, but leave here you must and shall. And I do think, myself, that you will go to Sea Hold."

Goaded, he snatched the bark, unrolled it, glared—and blinked.

You will, he read, *awaken my cousin Meripen Vanglelauf and put him on his way to Sea Hold as he is needed here. This by the hand of Sian, Engenium.*

He read the brief message in the bold, plain hand again—and a third time. *Sian* had risen to rule Sea Hold? But Sian was—He looked up to find the chyarch watching him, her eyes holding a certain foggy amusement.

"Forgive me," he said again, though his voice was abrupt in his own ears. "How long—"

"Ah." She bowed her head. "Nine thousand nights have passed

since you came here, raving, powerless, and very nearly dead. Your wounds were terrible; we thought at first that we would lose you to them. As it came about, the burns and the abuse were not the worst of it. I would have had you sleep longer, a full ten thousand nights, to equal the sleep of Jonga, Ranger, and then I would not have sent you to Sea Hold, but deep into the Vanglewood. However, as you read—" a flutter of fingers at the message he still held—"my wishes count for naught.

"I do most earnestly counsel you to obey the Engenium's summons of your own will, for she has also provided me with this, in case you should prove . . . recalcitrant." She reached into the pocket of her vest and withdrew a cord of braided seaweed, an ordinary fessel shell suspended from it, the compulsion woven into it so strong that Meripen shivered where he stood.

The chyarch nodded. "It is no gentle invitation the Lady of Sea Hold sends you, Ranger, but a stern order. Be prudent, I beg, for I do not wish to be the one to place this burden upon you."

Standing there among the plants and live things, Meripen acknowledged that he felt not the slightest stirring of *kest*. Should the chyarch apply her will—which she had not done, and which, so he read in her face, she did not desire to do—he would be powerless to resist her.

Stiffly, he bowed.

"It would seem that I have no choice," he murmured. "I will draw what I need and be gone before moonrise."

The chyarch sighed. "Haste is needful," she agreed. "Headlong flight is not. Take time to eat, and to rest again after you have assembled your kit. Sunrise will be soon enough to set out."

Chapter Thirteen

SONET'S HERBAL SHE WOULD NOT LEAVE BEHIND, NOR HER OWN, nor could she travel without easewerth, aleth or fremoni, or the few packets of seeds, including Sonet's gift of duainfey, she had on hand. Which left little enough room for clothes and womanly necessities. In the end, she bundled a single change of clothing together in her heaviest, most serviceable shawl. Happily, her day-clothes had been tailored with her handicap in mind; her riding shirt laced, and while the split skirt did require buttoning, she had a buttonhook for just that purpose. By necessity, she wore her hair loose. It would be well enough, she thought, with the cloak fastened over it—and in any wise, there was nothing else she could do.

Her boots were the worst, and by the time she had them on, she was shaking with effort, her ruined arm aching up into her back teeth.

It was then—just then—as she sat there, aching and weak, that she bethought herself of what she was about to do.

What, in truth, did she know of Altimere? That he was Fey and—how had Harin said it? Not human-folk. Yes, and her grandmother, who had seemed to have a fondness for them, still warned her granddaughter never to trust them.

And yet, Becca thought, what choice had she? She might very well question Altimere's "small power," and put the scene she had been "shown" in the wine cup down to exhaustion, or hypnotism, or

107

hysteria—any of that, or all of it. What she could *not* do, however, was to discount the evidence of her own senses. Jennet had *meant* to hurt her. Nor did his manner of demanding an apology—an abject apology, far out of proportion to her misstep . . .

Having seen Jennet thus, the future in the wine cup, however it had been formed, seemed to her possible, even probable. Whether he knowingly wished her ill, or was merely possessed of a . . . masterful nature . . .

"No," she whispered to the dim room, "it will not do."

Better by far to trust Altimere, who was odd, though no more a stranger than her promised husband, who had furthermore offered her no harm, and indeed seemed to have some concern for her welfare. Traveling in his company would ruin her, of course, but she was accustomed to that.

The clock in the entrance hall struck the hour, its chimes reverberating throughout the house. Becca stood and dragged her cloak on, clumsily one-handed; twisted the brooch shut, and picked up her parcel.

It was time. Whatever doubts and dangers attended this night, she would meet them as they arose.

Soft-foot, she went down the back stairs. Once, she paused, thinking she had heard something—but the soft noise was not repeated and she put it down to nerves, or perhaps the stealthy incursions of a mouse.

She eased the door to the kitchen open and stepped inside. Shadows danced, misshapen under the influence of the banked fire, and it took her a moment to tease the familiar room—with its work tables, and stools, and the cook pots all hung away in their proper places—out of the—

Someone was sitting at the pastry table, leaning against the pillar. Becca gasped, and froze.

The man at the table did not move. Becca held her breath, trying to think. Surely he knew she was here? He would have seen her open the door. Why did he not speak? Why—

The sound of a gentle snore reached her.

The guard was asleep.

Relief made her giddy. She bit her lip so that she did not laugh, took a deep breath, and very slowly, very *quietly* eased past the table, crossed in front of the fireplace, to the door.

The latch worked silently. Becca let herself out into the night.

The moon was a great yellow cheese lumbering above the tree tops, the stars glittering like pins spilled across black velvet. Ahead of her were shadows, and within those a flicker, as if a horse had moved an impatient ear, followed by a soft ladylike snort.

Becca let herself smile as she walked carefully down the flagged path to where Rosamunde—and Altimere—awaited her.

"Miss Beauvelley." He was at her side before she saw him, pale hair covered with a dark hat.

"You placed your power into my keeping. Do you wish to withdraw your word?"

She blinked up at him. Did he not understand? Or did he think that she did not understand? Better him and what he offered—better anything she could imagine!—than that bitter, ill-used future she had seen.

"I stand by my word," she said to Altimere, and he bowed to her, as graceful as always, before stepping to Rosamunde's side and opening the saddlebag.

She handed him her bundle, and he paused, looking down at her, so she thought, quizzically.

"Pots?" he murmured. "Books?"

"I'm an herbalist," she said to the note of query in his voice. "The books are my references and the pots contain medicines we might have need of on the road, and . . ." She bit her lip, but continued strongly, ". . . and a salve, for when my arm pains me."

She felt the weight of his glance against the side of her face.

"I had not understood that the angry man had wounded you so grievously."

Becca opened her mouth—and closed it. This was not, she thought, the time for a protracted conversation regarding the realities of a withered arm.

"But!" Altimere continued, in a lighter tone. "I see that these things are, indeed, necessary to your power. It is well." There came subtle rustlings and the groan of leather being pulled, then Altimere spoke again.

"With your permission, I will lift you to your saddle."

"Thank you, I—"

"No!"

Becca spun, her feet tangling in the uneven ground; she fell heavily against Rosamunde's side as Caroline darted out of the shadow of the house, hair unbound and the moonlight poking bold yellow fingers through her muslin shift. She had not even bothered to snatch a shawl to cover her against the night chill and her feet were naked on the dirt path.

Altimere strode forward and Caroline ran into his arms—or, rather, he caught her above the elbows and held her at arm's length, as if she were an overexuberant puppy that he wished to prevent from leaving mud on his trousers.

"It is *I* who love you!" Caroline cried, her voice ringing with passion. Becca cringed, certain that the noise would rouse the sleeper in the kitchen, and all would be lost.

"Becca is a cripple," Caroline sobbed. "She's ugly and willful—you can't want her! She only uses you for her own gain. When she is done, you will be like poor Kelmit Tarrington. It is I who loves you! I loved you from the first moment I saw you! Have pity, my lord! Take me, take—"

"Silence."

He did not raise his voice, yet Becca felt it crackle over her skin like Sir Farraday's electric current. The effect on Caroline must have been the same, for the outpouring of words stopped at once, and she hung boneless between Altimere's hands, mute and adoring.

"Return to the house," Altimere said in that same even, oddly forceful voice. "Return to your bed. Return to sleep. Forget that you followed your sister to this place. Forget me." He leaned forward, and Becca thought that he was going to kiss—but, no. He merely blew across her eyes, then stepped back, loosing her.

"Go."

And before Becca's unbelieving eyes, Caroline turned, wordless, and passed silently down the path and through the door. She held her breath, waiting for a scream that would rouse the house, but all she heard was the snap of the latch, loud in the still air.

"So." Altimere was at her side once more. "If you will allow me to lift you to your saddle, Miss Beauvelley? The moon is our friend, and it would be ill done of us to shun her bounty."

"I—" She looked up at him. "Caroline will raise the house," she said, the words feeling tentative in her mouth.

He shook his head, clearly amused. "No," he said softly. "She will not."

And with no further ado he put his hands around her waist and threw her into the saddle. Rosamunde stood steady as a rock as she picked up the reins, then turned with no signal from Becca, following Altimere and his mount out of the shadows and into the moonlight night.

Meripen settled the pack on his back, touched the patch over his right eye, and the hilt of the knife at his belt. Despite the pack, he felt curiously unfettered—unfocused—*light,* as if he were one with the pearly dawn even now creeping along the treetops. It was a sensation that he had experienced before, when it had sat less oddly upon him. He paused with one hand on the gate, seeking warily after the memory—

"Are you able?" his companion murmured at his side. "There's no shame in waiting for another sunrise."

"No shame," Meripen murmured. "Yet you carry something for me in your pack, should I choose not to go on."

"I carry it, true enough," his companion, one Ganat Ubelauf, admitted cheerfully. "But we both know it's only because the chyarch will not have it here. Therefore, *someone* must return it to the lady—and I have a long-standing role as the chyarch's *someone.*"

"No," Meri said slowly, and turned to face him. "You carry it because I am not strong enough. I feel—I feel as if I have no substance. As if I were nothing more than a doll cut from fog, and stitched with moonlight. As if—" He had it, the memory of his previous similar state—"As if I were a child again, without experience, purpose, or *kest*—"

"Aye, aye," Ganat said placatingly. "The long sleep'll do that. Your strength will rise quick enough, now you're awake. A few days on your own land and you'll be better than ever—see if not! Why—" He moved forward, pushing the gate open and stepping out onto the path. "You'll hardly credit it, but back when I was scarce more than a sprout myself, a patch of my wood took fire."

Without consciously willing it, Meri's hand flew up, fingers forming the sign for "avert."

Ganat nodded. "Well you might say, brother! Well you might say. Worse to tell, there was a bitter wind egging the flames on, and it was all that half-a-dozen of the Wood Wise and twice that again of the Brethren could do to smother it."

He shook his head, settled his pack and moved down the path. Scarcely attending what he did, Meri followed, the gate swinging shut behind him.

"But you did smother the flame," he said, coming even with Ganat. *Of course he had,* he told himself. *The man stands here, does he not?* Meri sighed quietly, wondering if the long sleep had leeched his wits as well as his power.

"Oh, we smothered it. But there was damage done, and it broke my heart to see it." He slanted a look to Meri. "I knew my lore, and I had the advice of my elders. But it was *my* place that had burnt, mark you, and it wasn't in me to leave it as it stood there, charred and black and not a leaf showing green."

"You never tried to heal it yourself," Meri murmured.

"Oh, you know that I did!" Ganat said cheerfully. "But I wasn't quite a complete young flitterwit, I'll have you know! Nay, I was prudent, and careful. I started with just one tree . . ."

"Oh," said Meri.

"You're a man with a rare way with words," Ganat said. "*Oh,* indeed. I poured everything I had and that which I hadn't known that I did into that tree, and it was my pride and wonder to see a single green leaf unfold from an ash-black branch right before I went to ash myself, or near enough."

Meri considered his companion as they followed the path to the top of the knoll.

"I've seen a Wood Wise sublimate," he said quietly and Ganat turned his head to gaze at him. Whatever he saw in Meri's face, some of the cheeriness left his own, and he bent his head soberly, in respect.

"A terrible thing, I'll own, and one that I'll be glad never to witness myself," he answered, and said nothing more.

They walked a dozen paces in silence before Meri sighed and asked, "But what happened to you? Did the tree return the gift?"

"Eh?" Ganat shot him a startled look. "Well. I daresay it might've tried, and I'm not the man to tell you that it didn't. Next *I* knew was waking up at the Hall there, so weak you could see sunlight through me, and not a flicker of *kest* to my name. My kith bore me back to my place—aye, that same charred and blackened spot that I'd all but killed myself trying to save."

They reached the top of the knoll, and paused by silent agreement, looking out over the dawning meadowlands.

"Turns out, I'd slept so long the land had healed itself, just as my elders had said it would," Ganat finished. "I sat down 'mong my growing things and by the time I'd got up again, I was solid and strong." He nodded, and sent Meri a sidewise look. "Same'll happen for you. All we have to do is get you to your home wood."

"It seems good advice," Meri said slowly, not wishing to startle his companion into silence again. "Unfortunately, Sea Hold is not my home, though Vanglewood lies not too far distant."

"Eh? Why're we taking you to Sea Hold, then?"

Meri shrugged. "Because the Engenium has commanded my presence."

"So she has. So she has. But—you'll forgive me—that begs the question. Which would be . . . *why?*"

Meripen sighed and started slowly down the hill, the long grass rippling ahead of him like waves along the shore.

"I don't know," he said.

"Here?" Becca turned in her saddle to look at Altimere, much good it did her. All she could see was his strong profile, cast in shadow by the moon.

"It is a very comfortable inn," he said. "Does your power show you otherwise?"

"My common sense," Becca said, with an asperity born of panic, "tells me that we're scarcely off Beauvelley land, and on a main road! Searchers must ask here for news almost immediately I'm discovered gone—and so they will find us."

There was a small silence, man and horse almost preternaturally still. Then Altimere's mount shifted, blowing lightly against the breeze.

"It is possible—in fact, probable—that there will be no searchers," Altimere said, quietly. "But if in fact my small skill has proven inadequate and searchers come to this inn and ask—they will find that none of the patrons looks in the least like those they pursue." He moved his arm in a wide sweep, shadow slicing shadow. "They will then move on, and we will not be discommoded in the least."

Becca frowned. "How can you be certain of that?"

"In the same way I am certain that foolish and vain Miss

Caroline did nothing more than return to her bed like a good child, forgetting that she had ever seen me," he answered, sounding amused. "Come. Let us bespeak a room."

He shifted and his horse moved, silent as the moonlight falling upon the land. Becca took a breath, leaned forward and laid her head against Rosamunde's neck.

Bespeak a room.

She closed her eyes. *Rebecca Beauvelley, you are a fool.*

And yet—who but a fool would choose death over life?

She straightened, and flicked the reins gently.

"Follow them, beautiful lady," she murmured. "We've made our choice, for good or ill."

Chapter Fourteen

"EVENING, SIR! MADAM! WHAT MIGHT WE DO FOR THE PAIR OF YOU this fine evening?"

If the innkeeper of the Dash and Tondle found anything amiss, with themselves or with the hour of their arrival, he kept it well away from his wide brown face. Indeed, thought Becca, the man looked uncommonly pleased to see them—or at least, to see Altimere. Upon her, he had bestowed a single benevolent glance so broadly incurious that she was quite sure he would be unable to provide a description even of her cloak, had Altimere asked.

"We require a large room with a private parlor," Altimere told the man, sweeping off his hat and tucking it under one arm. "Also, a cold collation, the house's best wine, and a bath."

A bath? Becca thought. *At this hour of the night?* And a meal? She could scarcely think of food without an unsettling cramping of her stomach. Still, she thought, it was certainly possible that Altimere was hungry; in her experience, gentlemen were often hungry at peculiar times. And if Altimere were kept occupied by his meal, she thought, then perhaps she might slip away while he was at it, and pretend to sleep . . .

"Will there be anything else, sir?" the innkeeper asked.

"I believe that will suffice."

"Very good. I'll just show you to your rooms, and—would you like the bath first, sir, or the meal?"

"The bath, and the meal laid in the parlor for us."

"Very good," the innkeeper said again, grinning. He looked to Becca, his glance sliding off her face as if it were a window he was determined not to look through. "This way, if you please," he said, catching the lamp up.

Altimere turned to her, offering his arm. "Miss Beauvelley," he murmured.

In the act of raising her hand, she froze, as if all her muscles were as useless as her withered arm. She tried to draw a breath—to scream? to speak?—but her cramped chest admitted no air. Her heartbeat was loud, frantic in her ears, and stars danced at the dark edges of her vision.

"Miss Beauvelley?" His voice pierced the panicked thunder of her heart. "You placed your power into my keeping. Do you withdraw your word?"

She looked up into eyes that seemed to glow in the dimness like a cat's. Warmth suffused her, as if his glance heated the very blood in her veins, and she felt her mouth relax into a smile.

"Withdraw my word?" she repeated, tucking her hand around his arm, her fingers delighting in the sturdy weave of his traveling coat. "Certainly not, sir."

He smiled, his eyes narrowing into glowing slits, as if he were a cat in truth, and put his hand over hers, there on his coat sleeve.

"You relieve me," he murmured, and then said nothing else as they followed the patient innkeeper down the hall, past the empty common room, up a wide staircase to a door.

"Here you are, sir and madam!" He pushed the door open and would have gone inside, but Altimere spoke.

"Give me the lamp and leave us," he said, receiving that item into his free hand. "We will be wanting the bath and our food as soon as they may arrive."

"The fire wants—" the landlord began.

"I will see to the fire, and the lady will see to the lamps. You will see to those other needs we have indicated."

The innkeeper bowed. "Yes, sir!" he said smartly, and took himself off, his footsteps firm and certain in the dark.

"Come," Altimere murmured, and drew her into the room.

The lamp threw his shadow, macabre and towering, against the spotlit walls. He set it on a table, raised his hand and snapped his fingers, once.

Becca flinched in the sudden blare of light as every candle in the room took flame.

She gasped, and looked to the tall Fey.

"How—"

He laughed, the first time she had heard him do so, and reached out, capturing her chin in cool, thin fingers.

"So powerful and yet so childlike." He looked down into her face seriously, like a man contemplating the heart of a flower. "You have much to learn, Miss Beauvelley." He bent close, his breath warm against her cheek. Becca felt her blood heat until she felt she must surely melt—and the thin mouth brushed hers, the merest touch of lips against lips. She shuddered, longing for—for what, she scarcely knew, though she leaned toward him—

"Much to learn," he whispered in her ear.

He withdrew, turning from her to toss his coat onto the chair.

Trembling, she gripped the chair back, watching him stride across the room to the fireplace, the poker in one long elegant hand.

Happily, the room was provided with a boot jack, which Becca made use of while Altimere showed the boy where to place the tub.

She shivered, standing there in her stocking feet, and almost wept. Plainly Altimere expected her to bathe and, truth told, she would welcome warm water on tired muscles. But to *bathe* . . . Becca dared a glance at the glass, wincing at the tangled mass of her hair, all too like that cold, doomed future she had glimpsed, and nothing at all like the glittering, immaculate vision of herself among the adoring plants. She was a fool, three times a fool! And lucky she would be if she came out of this night's work with—

The door opened, and Altimere stepped within. He rid himself of his boots, and unbuttoned his shirt, showing a narrow chest as smooth and as pale as alabaster. Becca took a hard breath, feeling her face heat. Altimere paused, head tipped to a side, and a small smile along the side of his mouth.

"You do not look ready to bathe, Miss Beauvelley. Perhaps you require assistance?"

Perhaps, Becca thought, the man had enlisted a housemaid to assist her. She gave him a smile.

"As it happens, yes. I do require some...minor...assistance."

The small smile deepened, and he stepped forward. "It is my pleasure to offer such...minor...assistance as you may require," he murmured, and cupped her cheek in his palm. "So pale, Miss Beauvelley. And you would have had us ride further." He rubbed his thumb lightly along the line of her cheekbone. Becca shivered.

"Nay, you have nothing to fear from me," he said, dropping his hand. Becca felt a pang at that separation, and bit her lip.

"Tell me," Altimere said. "What assistance may it be my pleasure to render unto you?"

"I—" She took a breath and met his eyes firmly. His smile widened in delight.

"Yes," he urged. "Tell me."

"If you will only recall it, sir, I did tell you—at the dance. I am less than perfect."

"But of course I remember this discussion, for it seemed absurd to me."

"Yes, and so it seems to many people. But the truth of the matter is—my left arm is crippled. It has no strength and very little range of motion. I require assistance in the smallest things. Washing and dressing my hair, for instance. Putting on or taking off clothing..." She looked down at herself ruefully. "These I can manage, but anything more...convenable, let us say, and I must have help." She raised her head and met his eyes again.

"If I must bathe tonight, I will have to ask you to summon the innkeeper's wife, or perhaps a chambermaid to assist me."

Altimere considered her out of warm amber eyes. "There is no need to summon a stranger to this task when I, in whose hands you have placed your power, stand ready to assist you and care for you. Come."

He stepped toward the door. Becca hesitated, her hand fisted in the fold of her skirt.

"I don't—"

"Come," he repeated, without heat, and Becca moved forward obediently. He held the door open for her and followed her into the parlor.

"Stand there by the tub," he directed, and she did as she was told.

He came up to her, smiling softly, and began to unlace her

shirt. Becca shook her head, and stepped back, her hand rising.

"Please, I—"

Altimere caught her hand, his touch cool and intoxicating. Becca swayed, feeling as she had when they had danced, only—

"You need fear nothing from me," he repeated. "I will care for you, and comfort you."

"Why?" she whispered, swaying toward him, as if she were the moth to his flame.

"But why not? Would you not have groomed your Rosamunde and fed her and seen her in all ways comfortable before tending to your own needs, had there not been a stable boy present?"

"Why—yes . . ."

"And so it is with us. Come now." This time, he reached for her skirt, unbuttoning in a trice what had taken her hard minutes to secure. She stood docile under his hands, watching his face as he let the skirt, and then the petticoat, down to pool 'round her stockinged feet before he reached again for the laces.

The blouse fell open. He slid it off her shoulders and let it fall to the floor. For himself, he stood very still, his face bearing an expression she had no hope of reading. She did not think it was repugnance; rather it looked like . . . exhilaration.

"This?" he breathed at last. He ran his fingers down her ruined arm,

leaving trails of pleasure in their wake. "*This* is what makes you—how did you say? *Less than perfect*?"

"Yes," Becca whispered. "I—"

"They are fools," Altimere said. Taking her strengthless fingers in his, he raised her hand, bent, and kissed her wrist where the bruises from Jennet's outrage showed.

"This must never be hidden again," he murmured, and his voice made Becca shiver.

"But now," he said, practical again, "we must finish what we have begun." He released her hand, gently, dealt with the rest of her clothes summarily, and held her right hand as she stepped into the tub.

"Oh . . ." she sighed as the warm water enveloped her.

"Yes." Altimere knelt beside, shirt gone entirely now, cloth and soap in his hand. "Allow me."

She should, Becca thought, be terrified, scandalized, given over to remorse—any or all of those emotions which the romances had taught her were the territory of a maiden who was about to have her virtue reft from her. Instead, she felt . . . peaceful, drowsy, cherished. Doubtless, she thought muzzily, her sensibilities were coarsened by reason of having been ruined once, already.

All too soon the bath was done. Altimere brought her out of the tub, wrapped her in warm towels and sat her on the stool in front of the hearth, while he combed out her hair.

"Our dinner has arrived," he murmured. "I will bring you a plate and some wine."

This he did, setting a low table between them, and they ate together, companionably silent, while the fire dried her hair.

"You should have your bath," she said, over her second glass of strong red wine.

"First, I will see you settled and comfortable for the night," he said. "Do you wish for more to eat?"

"Thank you," she said, "but I have eaten enough."

"Very well, then." He slipped her wine glass out of her fingers and stood. "Come," he said, and as before she rose unquestioningly and followed him into the bedroom.

He lifted her into the bed and covered her tenderly, as if, Becca thought muzzily, she were a child, instead of a wanton woman.

"Peace," he murmured and leaned down to stroke her forehead with a mother's gentle touch. "You are safe here with me. Now, sleep."

Rebecca closed her eyes—and did just that.

The air was intoxicating; lush with reds, oranges, and royal blues—the colors of passion, power, and determination. They washed over him in warm, sensuous waves, filling his senses, awakening again the sick, desperate longing.

He lay on the dead wooden floor, the burning in his flesh as nothing beside the burning of his desire for the rich opiate of those colors. His *kest* rose, beyond his will, beyond outrage or shame, blindly seeking to join, power to power, and if it were subsumed, what matter?

For a long exhalation, he hung poised between horror and need. If he were to cede control, allow his base nature rein . . . Depleted as he was, he would most certainly be overcome—subsumed, dead to agony and desire alike.

His essence joined forever to that which he hated.

"No . . ." he whispered, and exerted himself, trembling with the effort. The first lesson of childhood, and almost, it was too much for him. The colors poisoned the air, and he retched weakly—then screamed as the lash stroked his chest—screamed, and screamed—

"Wake!" The voice was loud, and something about it suggested to his disordered senses that it was not the first time that command had been uttered.

He gasped, the memory binding him, every muscle locked in horror—

"Faldana! 'ware, 'ware!"

"Meripen Vanglelauf, I command thee—*wake*!"

The ripple of power was nothing more than a spatter of raindrops against his face, yet it was sufficient. He snapped into wakefulness, and blinked up at Ganat, grim-faced in the starlight.

"Your—pardon," he whispered, aware then of the other's hands gripping his shoulders, holding him hard against the living land, as if the other had sought for him some aid or healing.

"Are you truly beyond the dream?" Ganat asked warily, and Meri sighed.

"You were gentle, and I am powerless. Indeed, I am awake—and I thank you for your care."

Ganat blew his breath out hard, and sat back on his heels, letting his hands fall to his knees.

"They woke you too soon," he said, then lifted a placating hand, as the night wind brought his words back to him. "Bearing in mind that I am not a chyarch."

"Though you are a healer," Meri said with a sigh. "I should have suspected that."

Ganat shook his head, leaf-brown hair brushing his shoulders. "Not so much of a healer, either. Only a Wood Wise who has been given some art and set loose to wander as I will. The chyarch would have it that the Forest Gentry are in want of ministering—or at least of sense. We crawl back to our own small-lands when we're wounded, which is all very well, but not perhaps as wise as might be. Some healing might speed the process, drain less of one's power—and so she trains any of us she can lay hand over and sets us loose again, to heal where we find harm—and perhaps to persuade those who are grievous hurt to seek the Hall." He sighed. "It's the accursed walls," he said, "and the staying in one place. None of us willingly embrace such things."

"I know," Meri said softly, and sat up, wrapping his arms around his legs and resting his chin on his knees. "I apologize for disturbing your rest, Ganat. Please, if you can, sleep."

"Well." Ganat paused, and Meri turned his head to look at the man out of his uncovered eye.

"The thing is, you're weak, and you've been wakened too soon and you need all the things that an invalid needs—*and* I can say that without giving offense because I *am* a healer and I'm here to help you." He glared, unconvincingly.

Meri snorted lightly.

"Even if I were offended—which I assure you I am not!—there's very little I could do about it in my present state."

"Exactly my point. You need sleep, for I'm thinking the Engenium Sian wants you delivered in some reasonable shape."

Meri shuddered and turned his head away, looking out into the quiet night. "Thank you," he said politely, "but I'm wakened now."

"I can give you dreamless," Ganat said quietly, and Meri raised his head, meeting the other's eyes.

"Can you," he said, inflectionless. Ganat raised his hand, fingers curled toward the palm. "I swear it on my small-land."

Meri shuddered. To slide back into the dark, where the horror awaited for him, bound to unconsciousness by whatever art lay at Ganat's hand? Did the other lack sense entirely, to think that he—

No, he told himself, recalling the other man's open, earnest face. *Ganat wishes to assist you. He does not understand.*

"This is not dream," he said slowly, "but memory."

For a long moment, Ganat sat utterly motionless. Then he sighed, and bowed his head.

"Memory . . . heals last," he said slowly, and for third time—"They woke you too soon."

"So it would seem," Meripen agreed, lifting his head to look at the dusty stars. "Better, perhaps, that they had not wakened me at all."

Chapter Fifteen

THE SCENT OF COFFEE WOKE HER, AND A GENTLE HAND ON HER hair. She smiled, and stretched, her newly opened eyes falling immediately upon Altimere's face.

"Good," he murmured, smiling gravely. "Breakfast has just arrived. I've brought you coffee, here." He nodded to the cup steaming gently on the bedside table. "I will also bring you something to eat, if you will tell me what you would like."

Becca pushed herself up against the pillows, the blanket falling away from her breasts and her ruined arm. She grabbed for the covers, then let them go as contentment washed through her, and picked up the coffee cup instead.

"You are not my servant," she said, slowly. "I can rise and come to table."

"Ah, but I wish to serve you in this manner," he said gallantly, and lifted a thin brow. "Also, it is prudent, until we can find you proper lounging clothes."

Becca felt her cheeks heat, and bent her head to her coffee.

"No," he murmured, stroking her ruined arm, his fingers sowing warmth, just as they had last night. "No shame, sweet child. Never any shame, for aught that you may do."

She looked up at him quizzically, searching the cool face. "No shame? Have *you* no shame, Altimere?"

His expression altered; she was aware of a slight chill in the air, and then it was burned away by the pride in his amber eyes.

"I am ashamed for *nothing* that I have done," he said austerely. "I may be the last of my house, but none will say that I am the least. I have continued the house's work, and increased it. I reside within the seventh tier of the Constant, second only to Diathen the Queen, and my workings do not go awry."

Rebecca stared up at him, feeling the strength of his pride. "Indeed, I see that you have no shame," she stammered. "But I *have* shamed my house, and if I have increased my own learning, it is in small things."

Altimere placed his finger against her lips, silencing her. "You are a woman of deed and power. That your deeds were denounced by those with little understanding and your power went unnoticed by those who are blind is nothing to cause you shame. The shame is theirs, sweet child. Only and forever theirs." He took his finger away, smiling.

"Now, tell me what it is you wish to eat, and I will bring it. Then we will dress and call for our horses and ride out into this marvelous, sunny day."

"That sounds delightful," she said truthfully, and looked up at him. "Toast, please, and jam and—if there is ham . . ."

"There is all of that," he said, rising. "I will bring it while you drink your coffee."

Obediently, Becca sipped carefully, delighting in layers of flavor, the sweetness of cream complementing the acrid brown flavor. She felt it flow through her, bringing her nerves to full alert. She finished the cup with regret, and set it aside just as Altimere stepped back into the room, bearing a tray, which he placed over her lap.

"Eat," he said, gently.

Rebecca looked from the tray to his face. "This is rather a lot of food for one person—won't you share?"

He smiled and inclined his head. "You must hold me excused. There is a small matter I must pursue with the host. We will have many meals together, you and I."

He ruffled her hair as if she were a child, indeed, and left her, murmuring, "Eat," once more.

Becca looked down at the laden tray—surely enough to feed Dickon and Ferdy, too!—spooned jam onto a piece of toast, and picked it up.

"I remember when I was a sprout," Ganat's voice came dreamily out of the darkness to Meri's left.

"I remember when I was a sprout, too," he said when the breeze had whispered long enough in the silence.

"D'you remember the tales they used to tell you?" the other murmured. "Of those who had gone before? The names you would be fortunate to be able to stand before, much less equal in deed?"

Meri sighed. "I do. Vamichere Pinlauf, Zuri Skaindire, Janoh Wavewalker..."

"Drakin Fairstar," Ganat took up the litany, "Kainen Denx, Meripen Longeye, Zozan Lochmeare..." He sighed, softly, and Meri heard him shift against the cushioning grasses.

"Names of glory," Ganat murmured. "Names on which to hang an hundred tales or more. And yet you wonder, don't you? Drakin Fairstar burned her hands terribly carrying starfire to the leviathan. Vamichere Pinlauf saw his wood vanish into the *keleigh*. The tales never talk of the time after—when the deed is done, the price met, and all that remains are the wounds."

"Some do," Meri said quietly. "The sea healed Drakin Fairstar's hands."

"Aye, that's so." Ganat sighed. "Is there a tale that tells us how she was healed of the death of her heartmate?"

Meri raised his head and looked at the stars shimmering against the indigo sky.

"Some wounds," he said, softly, "never heal."

The sunlight poured out of the sky like honey, coating the day with sweetness. It was as if she and Rosamunde were one creature, so well did they move together through the flavorful air, surrounded by bird song so piercingly lovely that Becca several times felt tears start to her eyes.

They rode easily, on the main road, which Altimere had pronounced perfectly safe.

"The innkeeper did allow me to know that two men had stopped by while you were still abed, asking after us. He denied us, of course, and the men went on their way, after looking in on the stables."

"So there was pursuit." Becca smiled up at him. "I wasn't foolish, then, was I?"

"Indeed you were not," he responded. "I had underestimated the value placed upon you by certain parties, and I beg your pardon."

She laughed. "Rather you should beg *their* pardon!"

Altimere tipped his head, apparently considering this. "I suppose that I should," he said eventually. "But I do not think that I will."

Becca laughed again, and Rosamunde flicked her ears, and very soon after that, they took the left fork in the road, following the sign for Selkethe.

"I've never been to Selkethe," Becca said. "What shall we find there?"

"Why not wait and see with your own eyes?"

"Because I would like to hear how it seems to you, and then compare my impressions." She glanced at him shyly. "An exercise, you see, to help me know you better."

"I do not see," he said after a small pause, "but I am willing to be taught. This has the promise of being as diverting as your question game."

"So," said Becca, after they had gone some little distance in companionable silence. "What do you like best of Selkethe?"

"Best?" He guided his horse over to the side of the road, and Rosamunde followed. Hoof beats sounded from ahead of them, coming rapidly closer. Becca urged Rosamunde to stand beside Altimere's horse.

"I believe that the thing I like best about Selkethe is that one can occasionally feel the winds of home against one's face there."

Becca laughed. "But you are cheating, sir!"

Altimere turned his head, and Becca felt her heart stutter at the icy look in his eyes. His voice, however, was merely curious. "Cheating? How so?"

In the few, strangled moments required for Becca to catch her breath, the sound of the racing hoof beats were loud.

"Why—why because you have not chosen something of Selkethe at all, but something of your home!" she managed, and leaned forward to put her hand against Rosamunde's neck. That lady blew lightly, in encouragement, Becca thought.

Altimere's thin brows drew together slightly.

"I . . . see," he said slowly. "It is the game that I am to choose something admirable of the *place itself.*"

"Exactly!" Becca said, with considerable relief.

"Well, that will require some thought," Altimere mused. "If I am not allowed the winds of home, then certainly I cannot call upon proximity. I wonder . . ." He lapsed into silence just as two riders came 'round the curve in the road, riding hard.

Rosamunde stamped a foot as the pair hurtled by, but they four might have been invisible, for all the attention the riders spared them. So quickly did they ride that it wasn't until the dust of their passage hung in the air that Becca cried out—"Dickon!"

Rosamunde turned in obedience to the shift of her weight. Becca gathered the reins firmly in her hand. Dickon, she thought, and the second rider—surely that had been Ferdy? And—wait! There had been two searchers at the inn this morning, Altimere had told her so. The innkeeper had denied them, and they had gone on—to the next inn, Becca thought, and finding no sign of them there, were returning—

"Hold." Altimere's voice was soft, and he did not deign to put his hand out to take Rosamunde's bridle, but the quarter-Fey horse stopped just the same.

Becca turned to face him.

"That was Dickon!" she exclaimed. "My brother—and, and Ferdy Quince!"

"Yes," he said calmly. "I recognized them."

"But—"

"They are gone," he said, and Becca felt suddenly lightheaded; her thoughts melted, running like honey, and the day took fire around her, abruptly and painfully beautiful. She looked down, becoming instantly lost in rapt contemplation of the texture of Rosamunde's mane as it fell across her neck . . .

"Now then," Altimere said.

Becca looked up, smiling at him. "You, sir, are unhandsome! Is there no single thing in Selkethe which is admirable? Almost, I begin to believe you find all of us here on the far side of the Boundary despicable."

"No, no," said Altimere soothingly, setting his mount into motion. "You wrong me, Miss Beauvelley. I do not find all of you here on the far side of the Boundary despicable. Not at all.

And as for Selkethe—there is a very pleasant little bridge over a quick-flowing stream at the edge of the village. You and I will walk there, if you like, and you will give me your opinion."

"Done!" she said happily. "Now, sir . . ."

"What, is there more?" He glanced back at her, eyebrows elevated. "How much do you wish to know of me?"

"Everything," she told him, surprised by the fierceness of her voice.

"You do me too much honor," he murmured. "But I think, instead of another game, we should let the horses run." He leaned forward slightly, and the big stallion took his leave immediately.

"Catch them, beautiful lady!" Becca cried, and gave Rosamunde her head.

Of course they did catch Altimere and his mount eventually— at Bordertown Inn. He had already dismounted by the time Rosamunde and Becca galloped into the yard. A boy ran out to grab Rosamunde's bridle, and Altimere stepped in front of the stable boy, holding his arms up with a smile. Becca slid out of the saddle, trusting him to catch her, as if they had done the same numerous times. It warmed her, this trust that had risen so quickly between them.

Altimere treasures me, she thought as they strolled arm-in-arm into the inn. *Dickon would be so pleased.*

And wasn't it odd, Dickon passing them on the road like that? She should have called out sooner, to let him know she was well and with someone who treasured her, just as he had wanted her to—

"A private parlor." Altimere's voice broke her thoughts into an hundred bright pieces. "A cold nuncheon, wine and tea."

Selkethe was larger than she had expected, its high street lined on both sides with shops, and thin off-shoot alleys fragrant with the aromas of baking breads and savory cooking. From the sheer number of bistros and restaurants, it would appear that none of the population of Selkethe ever cooked for themselves, or needed to.

At the end of the high street was the market square, empty this late in the day, except for a few townsfolk clustered 'round a booth beneath a flowing orange canopy.

"Ah," Altimere said, and patted Becca's hand where it rested on his arm. "Shall you like to meet another Fey, Miss Beauvelley? To see, perhaps, if you have made a bad bargain?"

"I'd certainly like to meet another Fey," Rebecca responded. "Is he a friend of yours?"

"A friend?" Altimere appeared to taste the word. "No, I do not think a . . . *friend*. Say rather, an old acquaintance."

"Surely, then, a friend?" Becca said, as they walked toward the tent.

"What makes you insist upon that, I wonder?"

"Well, one would hardly continue an association that was repugnant to one long enough to have achieved an *old* acquaintance?"

They strolled on, close enough now for Becca to see that the goods offered in sale were fabrics.

"How charmingly naïve," Altimere said. "Be a good child, now, and mind your manners."

They paused at the edge of the booth, waiting politely while a portly lady with the red scarf over her hair finished dickering for a shimmering length of fabric so green it looked as if it had been loomed from new grass.

Content to stand there with her hand on Altimere's arm, feeling warm and pleasantly languorous, Becca watched the Fey trader. He was every bit as tall as Altimere, and slightly slimmer, with the same strong nose and thin features. His hair was a riot of pale copper ringlets, and his gestures, as he displayed the bolt to the lady in the red kerchief were made with a familiar casual elegance. He might, Becca thought, be Altimere's younger brother, dressed in gypsy colors and flowing sleeves for market-day.

"Done!" The trader sang out strongly. The lady reached into her pocket and pulled out three coins, which she placed on the plank before reaching for her bolt. The trader, for his part, extended his hand to the coins—and snatched it back.

"Madam," he said reproachfully to the lady. She colored, hurriedly snatched up the center coin and produced another to take its place.

"Excellent!" the Fey trader said, giving her a broad and not quite completely sincere smile.

"This cloth will keep its virtue even if made up into clothing," she said, sounding anxious now.

"Indeed," the Fey assured her, and she gathered the bolt close to her bosom and moved off.

"If she cuts it, the virtue will be lost," Altimere said, so softly that Becca scarcely heard him.

The trader Fey's ears were sharp, however. He turned and gave Altimere a brilliant smile only slightly less false than that which he had bestowed upon his late customer.

"She said nothing of cutting it," he pointed out, and inclined his head. "Altimere."

"Jandain," he replied, and brought Becca forward.

Jandain's eyebrows lifted. "But what delight is shown me here?"

"This is Rebecca Beauvelley," Altimere murmured. "My ally."

"Ah, is it so?" Jandain stepped forward and extended his hand. Becca felt pressure, like the sudden onset of a headache. Her hand twitched where it lay on Altimere's sleeve, and relaxed.

Gravely, keeping her eyes modestly lowered, she curtsied.

"Jandain, I am pleased to meet you," she murmured.

"And I am *very* pleased to meet you, Rebecca Beauvelley," he asserted, smiling into her face as she rose. His eyes still on her face, he said, "Altimere, she is exquisite. Allow me to make her a gift."

"Thank you, no," Altimere said, and Becca felt the pressure behind her eyes fade away into the familiar, pleasant warmth. "We cross the *keleigh* tomorrow, and then ride for Artifex."

"You are taking her with into the Vaitura? Is that wise?"

Becca felt a flicker of irritation, immediately extinguished by Altimere's mellow reply. "Why should I not bring my ally to the Vaitura? She is a woman of power and altogether admirable."

"Indeed," said Jandain. "*Altogether* admirable. And likely to quickly obtain admirers. Of which you may count me, Miss Beauvelley," he said, bringing his attention back to her so suddenly that she felt the tiniest bit of headache return—"your first, and most ardent."

Becca shook her head, giving him a smile. "Your admiration is a gift, sir, but Altimere is first in my regard."

"And are you first in his?" He held up a slim hand before she could answer. "Nay, heed me not! I will happily be your second admirer, cruel beauty! I trow you will find me ardent, indeed."

What, Rebecca thought suddenly, *was she doing, flirting in the marketplace like a—a—* Her cheeks heated, and she dropped her gaze, staring at rough table with its burden of fragile clothes.

"*Wholly* delightful," breathed Jandain. "Altimere, where discovered you this pearl?"

"A pearl beyond price," Altimere murmured, "and rare, as well. Jandain, you must come to call on . . . us . . . when your business here is done."

There was a short, charged pause, during which Becca dared to raise her eyes, accidentally crossing Jandain's golden gaze.

"Yes," he murmured, then more strongly, "yes, Altimere, be assured that I will visit you both ere long." He leaned forward slightly, and Becca felt that unwelcome pressure again above her eyes. "Remember me, cruel beauty."

"Of course I will, sir," she responded, most properly, and with relief allowed Altimere to guide her away from the booth and back toward the high street.

"*Will* he come to visit . . . you?" Becca asked some while later, as they paused in the center of the bridge to observe the rush of the stream beneath their feet. "Jandain."

"Surely, he will come to visit *you*," Altimere said in a light, teasing tone. "You have made a conquest, Miss Beauvelley."

"But, he must be disappointed," she said rubbing her arm absently. "For it is you—"

"It is I to whom you have entrusted your power," he finished for her. "But, you see, Jandain is of . . . a new house. He is fond of sensation and he has never aligned his power with another's."

Becca thought, watching the stream swirl white among the rounded stones. "Then he must be very powerful, mustn't he?"

"How quickly the child learns," Altimere said fondly. "Yes, my sweet, he is very powerful, indeed."

"And do you wish to . . . join power—to align yourself—with him."

Altimere laughed. "Droll child! I do not."

"Why not, sir?"

He glanced at her, his amusement filling her with a giddy sense of wellbeing.

"Well you should ask," he said, after a moment, and more soberly. "I am of an old house. One of ours was present when the *keleigh* was made—indeed, was instrumental in its construction. Jandain's house was a mere cadet branch, which would never have risen to the first rank—had the war not cost us so much."

"*Keleigh*," Rebecca repeated. Altimere took her by the arm and turned her about.

"Look."

To the north, just behind the gables of the town's outlying houses, was a shimmering curtain of lights—purples, greens, and oranges dancing against the dusky sky. Becca shivered, as if in a cold wind.

"That is—the Boundary, is it not?"

"The *keleigh*," Altimere corrected.

"But, the Boundary—your pardon! the *keleigh*—has been in place for an hundred years or more!"

"More," he said. "Considerably more."

His voice woke another shiver.

"Come, what am I thinking!" he said abruptly, and drew her hand through his arm. "You are chilled and wanting your supper. Let us walk back. There is a restaurant on Savory Lane which I think you may find acceptable..."

Chapter Sixteen

THEY HAD TRAVELED THE LAST TWO DAYS UNDER LEAF, AND MERI was the better for it. Though they were not Vanglewood, the trees had been generous to him: the pack he bore grew lighter with every step, the steps themselves firmer and less likely to wander, his wood-sense sharpened—it even seemed to him that he felt a bare flutter of *kest*, far down at the base of his spine, like sap, waiting to rise.

It worried him not a little that he was to meet an Engenium in this powerless state. He had no illusions regarding his ability to resist such a one—Root and branch! A babe in arms could over-come his will! Sian—even the giddy, haphazard Sian he recalled from . . . before—would have no problem binding him.

Why she should want to do so—that remained a puzzle. The ocean had taught the Sea Wise to be cautious with their powers and niggardly in their use, a lesson the High Fey might profit from, as well. And though she had been fostered among the Sea Wise, as he had, himself, Sian was tied by blood to the Queen herself, in Xandurana.

She had demanded that he be waked and sent to her, ensur-ing that her order would be followed by sending the charm that, depleted as he was, he could feel vibrating from the depths of Ganat's pocket.

That these acts boded well for him, he very much doubted. The girl he had known would have been . . . incapable of forcing him to her will, even had she the means to do so.

The woman who had sent that . . . thing . . . to ensure his obedience . . .

"Let us stop here for a meal and a rest," Ganat said from behind him. "We'll raise Sea Hold by sunset."

Sunset?

Meri turned on a heel and considered his escort. "Shall we fly, then?"

"Near enough," Ganat said, shrugging off his pack and dropping it at the foot of a gnarled elitch.

They had traveled together long enough for Meri to know that Ganat treasured a mystery almost as much as he did a joke. Indeed, the two seemed interchangeable in his happy mind. He also knew that silence would elicit the same response as the direct question that Ganat craved.

On the other hand, he thought, shrugging off his pack, what else did they have to talk about?

He sat down on the moss and leaned his back against another elitch, feeling the tree take quiet note of him.

Is it you, Ranger? The voice in his head was slow and warm.

Now, that was a question, wasn't it? Meri thought privately. And trust an elitch to ask it.

I was once a ranger, Elder, he told the tree, striving for exactness. *How may I serve you?*

There was no immediate response, nor had he expected one; trees were unhurried beings. Meri reached into his pack for trailbread. A faint creak of leather warned him and he raised his off-hand casually to catch the culdoon Ganat had thrown.

"You are *much* improved," his companion observed, unwrapping his own rations with a sigh. "It will be a pleasure to stop at Sea Hold and taste something other than waybread."

Meripen sent him a sharp glance, but it appeared that this was a rare moment of seriousness. "I never thought to hear one of the Wood Wise speak ill of trailbread."

"You forget that I have been tainted by my time in training," Ganat said, in a return to lightness.

"True, I had forgot that," Meri said, biting into the fruit.

I think the proper question might be, the tree's voice rustled inside his head, *how I may serve you?*

Meri choked slightly and swallowed, tart juices starting tears to his eyes.

I can think of no service necessary, he answered, which was true; those things that ailed him were far beyond a tree's power to heal. *I thank you for your care,* he told the elitch politely. Vanglewood was home to many elitch, and they had drilled him well in courtesy.

He cleared his throat.

"So," he said to Ganat, "when will you summon the giant birds to bear us to Sea Hold? If you wish to arrive for dinner, it had best be soon."

"Giant birds, indeed," the other mumbled around a mouthful of trailbread. "You think small, Meripen Vanglelauf."

"Teach me to think more widely then, O farwalker."

Ganat snorted. "A few paces on there is a shortcut, created and held by Sea Hold."

Meri blinked. Shortcuts were—expensive of power, and because of that, fleeting.

"That's a great deal of trouble to go to for a poor, empty Wood Wise," he said slowly. What in the name of the Vaitura itself did Sian *want* with him? he thought, panic building in his stomach.

He took a swallow from his water bottle and settled his back more firmly against the tree.

"Well, it would be—but it happens that it's not for you. There was a bit of trouble with the Brethren some while ago and Sea Hold placed the thing for their own ease."

That was understandable, though this news of difficulty with the Brethren was disturbing . . .

"I thought there was a treaty."

"Oh, any number of treaties—as many as you will! And however many you like there will still be some of the Low Fey who feel themselves mistreated by the High, and take exception in ways that are the most trouble for Wood Wise, and disturb the High not at all."

"Except they disturbed the Engenium at Sea Hold enough to create and maintain an extremely expensive bit of artifice—"

"Nay, that's where you're out," Ganat said, dusting crumbs off his fingers and settling back against his tree. "It's not expensive at all."

Meri finished his fruit and wrapped the pit in a fallen elitch leaf before stowing it in his pack. Old habits . . .

"I can see," he said to Ganat, "that there is a great cleverness involved in this that you are bursting to share. Please, don't stint yourself on my account."

Ganat grinned at him. "It draws off the *keleigh*."

Shock struck him, as Ganat must have expected it would, and it must also have shown on his face, for the other laughed aloud, and shook his head.

"Oh, it's nothing but a trick of geometry! Of course the *keleigh* is anchored—if it weren't, it would have long drifted free over the Vaitura—and the other place, too. The heroes who constructed it knew better than that! It happens that one of the anchor points is just a short walk out from here, as some clever Book Scholar at the Engenium's House found one day as she was pursuing her studies. She brought it to my lord, my lord brought it to his artificers, they did the calculations, crafted the appropriate permissions and accesses—and there it's been ever since, convenient in times of trouble—or of sloth—and largely ignored otherwise."

"And are we trouble, or merely lazy?" Meri asked, forcing tight muscles to relax. Warmth eased into him from the tree—which was a welcome service, after all—and he relaxed further.

My thanks, Elder.

Ganat shook his head, his eyes serious for the second time in an hour. "That question has troubled me since the chyarch bade me stand your escort," he said. "Can you think of *no* reason why Sian of Sea Hold requires you *now*?"

Meripen moved his shoulders, hearing leather scuff across bark. "Sian and I are cousins," he said. "When last I saw her, she was scarcely in control of her powers, and the last of the line I would have looked to find in Velpion's chair."

"Well." Ganat sighed. "By all accounts, she is a puissant and prudent lady. For which I suppose we must thank her time at court."

"Sian was at court?" How long, Meri thought, his stomach tightening, had he been asleep?

Many seasons, if you are in truth the Sea Ranger, the elitch said inside his head. *Seedlings have grown into full canopy since last your footfall was heard 'mong the trees in this wood.*

Oh. Meri's thought came on a sharp inhalation. *Dear.*

Elitch matured slowly. If the tree's reckoning was correct—and whose reckoning was more exact?—then there had been time a-plenty for Sian to learn both court-craft and prudence—aye, and to take Sea Hold well in hand.

Unfairly, this realization only made the root question more poignant. If he had indeed slept so long, what possible use was he—to anyone? Even his revenge—the men who had imprisoned and tortured them, defiled Faldana, and slain her—

Ranger, you go unprotected.

Elder, I do. I was . . . sore wounded, and have been . . . long away from the care of trees.

Have you been so long away that you have forgotten the care of trees? You do not walk alone into danger.

There was a sharp *snap*, and the scent of broken greenwood. A branch struck his shoulder, bounced, and came to rest on his pack.

Thank you for your care, Elder, Meri said.

Came back, when you are stronger, and tell me what went forth.

I will.

"Well," Ganat said, his voice a little too brisk and cheerful. "If you've done, we'd better be getting on."

"I suppose we had better," Meri agreed.

He stood, picked up the branch and slid it into his belt on the side opposite his knife, then slung the pack over his back.

"Lead on," he said to Ganat. "It will not do to be late to the feast."

Ganat nodded at the elitch branch. "It's possible that you tree-bound me and walked away. By the time I was released, you were long on your way to Vanglewood."

Meri laughed. "And a message is sent to the chyarch, who gives her oath that I was empty as a babe, and scarce able to hold my head up, much less amaze and overpower a Wood Wise in his prime, and a healer trained, too."

Ganat flushed, his brown cheeks darkening. "A ruse. It would give you time . . ."

"Aye, it would, at the cost of your dismay. And, do you know, my curiosity almost—almost!—overweighs my concern. If I have been asleep so long, why wake me now? If I have been asleep so long, what use am I?" He turned, jerking his head at the other to take the lead. "No, let us go on, by your leave. I would have the riddle's answer, now."

Ganat hesitated a heartbeat longer, then nodded once, sharply, and stepped forward, taking the lead to the shortcut.

"How far beyond the Bou—your pardon! the *keleigh*—does your house lie?"

They were in their private parlor at the inn, eating breakfast tete-a-tete. Altimere had opened the window, so that they might have the benefit of the warming breeze. Becca gazed out at unclouded blue sky, wearing a skirt of smudged purple, which was the weird glow of the Boundary.

"It will seem no distance at all, once we have the *keleigh* behind us," Altimere said, replacing his cup in its saucer with a tiny click of porcelain against porcelain.

"Is it so very wide, then?" Becca asked, pushing her plate aside.

"Sometimes it is very wide. Sometimes, it is scarcely three steps across." He leaned forward slightly, catching her gaze with his, and she shuddered with the weight of his regard.

"Understand me, Miss Beauvelley, the *keleigh* is a dangerous and uncertain place. Strange things happen there—strange even to those of the Fey. Very often things are lost in the *keleigh*. I speak not only of possessions, but of those infinitely more precious—memories, small powers. One's name."

Becca blinked. "One's name?"

Altimere smiled. "I said that even the Fey find the *keleigh* strange, did I not? How much stranger must it seem to you, who have lived all your life among . . . those who are not Fey, to whom the *keleigh* is merely a pretty curtain of lights?" His smile faded. "To return to the topic—treasure is easily lost in the *keleigh*. Most often, it is the inexperienced travelers who lose the most. You," he smiled at her and she felt her whole body warm. "You are fortunate in that you travel in company with an experienced guide. Still, it would pain me to find that you had lost any small thing. I will guard you as best I might, but it would perhaps be best, before we cross, if you were to give me your name."

Rebecca paused with her coffee cup halfway to her lips. "Give you my name?" she repeated. "How might I do such a thing?"

"It is very simple," said Altimere. "You merely say, 'Altimere, I give you my name to hold in safekeeping until I ask for its return.'"

Becca laughed. "Forgive me! It seems very cool and civilized," she explained to his raised eyebrow. "However, I have held my name this long. I think that I may hold it a while longer yet. Though if this crossing is as dangerous as you tell me, I fear for Rosamunde—and for your own mount."

"And yet they are in less danger, for they have so much less to lose."

"Surely, their names and their memories are precious to them," Becca said.

"Do you think so? I consider that memory is a burden upon those creatures of a lower order," Altimere said, glancing down to spread jam on his toast.

"Why so?"

He looked up, his amber gaze holding her riveted. "Why, because they are so often at the command of a will that is not their own, and required to perform actions which they might not, for themselves, perform, and which they may even find to be—distressing."

"In fact, you hold that animals are slaves," Becca said slowly. "I had heard that argument when I was in the city. I think, rather, that animals and men are partners in the husbandry of the land."

There was a small pause while Altimere finished his toast and dusted the crumbs from his fingers.

"That is certainly a viewpoint with some merit," he said politely. "We shall have to discuss the matter again, after we are home and settled. In the meantime, child, allow me to braid your hair. The sooner we begin our ride, the sooner it will be done, however wide the *keleigh* is, this journey."

Altimere's touch on her hair was soothing—too soothing, thought Becca, her eyes drifting shut despite her best efforts.

"Truly, child," Altimere's voice was so low that it seemed to originate inside her skull. "I wish you to sacrifice nothing to the *keleigh*. Would it not be wise to allow me, your most devoted ally, to hold your name safely for you? Think what might happen, if it were stolen away. Not only would you lose your memories, but also those memories Rosamunde must have entrusted to your keeping, for she has placed her power into your hands, just as you have placed your power into mine. Allow me to protect you, and all that you treasure..."

"I . . ." Becca forced her eyes open, and straightened her shoulders. "I think it would be best . . ."

"Yes?"

". . . if I kept watch upon my own name, and Rosamunde's, as well. You are, as you say, our guide and our guard across a strange and dangerous land. It would be churlish of me—and would endanger our entire party—if I were to burden you with that which I can easily bear myself."

"Ah." Altimere finished off the braid and stepped back. "I will fetch our cloaks," he said, and was gone.

Becca blinked, abruptly and entirely awake. Shaking her head, she rose to her feet. Really, what an odd thing, to have been so sleepy when they had just an hour ago arisen! But she was perfectly alert now, and as ready to ride into a strange country as she might ever be.

"Here you are," Altimere draped her cloak tenderly over her shoulders and fastened the brooch, then stood with his hands on her shoulders, looking down into her eyes.

"You are not afraid," he said after a moment. "Excellent."

"Of course I am not afraid," Becca said, smiling up at him. "You will be with me, after all."

Chapter Seventeen

THE WIND WAS COMING OFF THE SEA, SO HEAVY WITH BRINE THAT Meri's eye teared, and the familiar shoreline blurred. He sniffed, shook his head, and there—there were the cliffs, glowing like a sea-rose in the rays of the lowering sun, banners snapping smartly in the wind, and the sound of surf against the land.

Out, past the rosy cliffs, was the sea itself, its restless surface glittering turquoise and gold. Tide was coming in, Meri judged, watching the boats at anchor dance on the rich surface—and hard. The wind tasting so much of salt bespoke a storm bearing down upon the land, though the sky showed only the least swirl of orange and grey cloud.

He took a deep breath, forcing the salty air down into the very bottom of his lungs. From his belt came the whisper of leaf as the sea-wind teased the elitch branch. Meri exhaled and drank in another breath, hoping, only that. His was a mixed heritage; the sea as well as the forest held virtue for him—he exhaled on a sound that might have been a laugh.

Yes, surely, the sea had virtue for him. The sea-breeze? Perhaps not so much.

Beside him, Ganat cleared his throat.

"Not so bad, was it?" he said. "The transfer."

Meri shook his head. The transfer had been effortless: a slight blink of darkness between one step and the next, like stepping from light into shadow and back into light.

"I had expected something more . . . nightmarish," he admitted. "You had said the power came off the *keleigh.*"

"The power comes off an *anchor* for the *keleigh*," Ganat corrected. "It's thought by those whose power resides in such thoughts, that this is an important difference. If you'd like to know why they think so, I suggest you apply to Konice, the Queen's philosopher. He'll be pleased to explain it to you over a period of days, and if you understand more than one word in ten, you're vastly more clever than ever I'll be."

Meri smiled. "I think I'd best capture one square at a time. First, let me survive a meeting with my cousin."

Ganat gave him a worried glance, and settled his pack nervously. "I suppose we'd best go on, then," he said. "Having come this far."

"It would seem the . . . most direct trail to an explanation—and your dinner," Meri agreed, and started down the stone stairway to the courtyard below.

They passed the last homestead at mid-morning; the road thinned to a thread of dusty track through country overgrown with sparse, leggy shrubbery.

Becca recognized redthorn and thessel, punctuated by wild carrot, coinflower, and bluebows. Fire plants, the lot of them, their only virtue that of quick growth and quicker die-off, to enrich the ground so that sturdier, more useful plants might re-grow.

The sound of their passage was unusually loud in the absence of both bird-song and breeze; overhead, the sky faded from azure to grey to purple. Becca felt herself shrink into the saddle, and straightened into proper alignment with an effort. Ill-at-ease she might be, but to communicate her forebodings to Rosamunde was unforgivable.

Not that Rosamunde seemed unaffected by these eerie surroundings. She followed Altimere's mount closely, and set her feet carefully, as if wary of what unwelcome surprise might scurry out of the dust.

Ahead, Altimere guided his horse to the edge of the path, and reined in. Becca brought Rosamunde beside, sent a worried look at his profile, and followed the line of his gaze.

The track ran straight for another few horse-lengths, then

curved sharply. Across the raddled landscape she saw a shimmering curtain of dark light, baleful and bleak, and took a breath that sounded more like a gasp.

Altimere turned to look at her.

"You are very right to be afraid," he said severely. "The *keleigh* is a sore test, even for one of the Elder Fey. I ask you again to allow me to hold your name."

Becca swallowed, staring ahead at the dire, billowing light, and shook her head.

"You to guard your treasures," she whispered. "I to guard mine. I will follow you."

"You will follow me most nearly," he said sternly.

Becca inclined her head. "As you will. If this place is as dangerous as you tell me—what should I do, if we become separated?"

Altimere bent upon her a look so grave she felt her heart chill in her chest.

"If we become separated, it will be because I have failed you. Should that occur, give Rosamunde her head, and trust to your power—and luck."

"Luck," Becca repeated, dully, and looked up, amazed to hear Altimere laugh.

"Luck is often discounted, even among the Fey, yet undeniably it is a power, capricious and uncontrolled as it may be. It bestows its patronage as it will, for no reason that can be discerned. So, yes, if you should become lost in the *keleigh,* trust to luck, Rebecca Beauvelley."

"Very well," she said slowly. "I will do so, if we are separated Before we go on, I wonder if you will tell me—what force created that—the *keleigh*?"

Altimere was amused, she could feel it, but he answered her seriously enough.

"Why, the Fey created it, of course. Who else would have had the power, or the need?"

He leaned over and placed his hand briefly over her left, where it rested on the pommel.

"We will go slowly. Do not fall. Do not for any reason dismount. Do not speak, and in no wise answer, if something should speak to you. Do you understand me?"

Becca took a breath and met his eyes firmly. "I do."

He smiled. "Bold heart," he murmured, awaking an echo of a

voice that—but, there it was gone, dissolved in the warmth of Altimere's regard.

"Now," he said, and gave his horse the office. That gentleman moved forward delicately, as if he knew what awaited him around the bend, as of course, Becca recalled, he did.

"We must," Becca murmured. "Don't fail me, lady."

Her horse sighed, ears straightened, and she moved forward, docile and wary, 'round the curve and into the unknown.

"Names and business." The guard on the door was one of the Sea Wise, grizzled hair braided with fessel shells, boat-hook in her belt. Corded brown arms were crossed over her breast in what one might take for an attitude of careless insolence.

If one were a fool.

Meri met her pale, canny eyes. "Meripen Vanglelauf, at the command of the Engenium."

He had meant to speak mildly, but the twitch at the corner of the guard's firm mouth told him he had missed the mark. She only nodded, though, and looked past him to his companion.

"Ganat Ubelauf, Healer and Wood Wise. I bear a message from the chyarch of Ospreydale to Sian, Engenium of Sea Hold."

Oh, indeed? thought Meri.

"You bear something else, Healer. I can smell it from here."

"A jewel which the lady desired to be returned to her with all speed." Ganat's voice was frankly acidic, which made a startling contrast to his usual light-spoken mode. Before Meri could decide whether he preferred it, the guard spoke a soft word, and the salt-wood door behind her swung open.

"Susel?" the guard asked, without turning her head.

A younger edition of herself strolled out, and paused to survey them out of fog-colored eyes, her thumbs hooked in her belt.

"Captain?"

"Escort these worthy Wood Wise to the receiving hall. They are here for the Engenium."

Susel nodded slightly, then jerked her head in the general direction of Meri and Ganat. "Follow," she said and swung about, never looking to see if they obeyed.

"Best keep close," the door guard added. "It's a tricksy route and we don't have a lot of time to rescue lost Wanderers."

Ganat stepped forward, placing his boot heels with such firm-
ness that the stone floor rang, and echoed off the stone walls.

Meri, who had been fostered at Sea Hold, frowned in protest
of the unnecessary racket; after all, it was easier to walk silent
on stone than it was among the trees. Moving considerably more
quietly, he came up to the other Wood Wise.

"I thought you'd said you'd been here before," he said, hoping
to leach some of the man's palpable nervousness. "And that the
food was good."

Ganat sighed and slanted a sheepish glance at him. "Oh, aye.
I've been here before, though as little as I might. Say that I don't
care to be enclosed by stone, and excuse me for ill-temper."

"There's nothing to excuse," Meri said honestly. "Well I recall,
when first I came here, how difficult it was to reconcile myself
to living *inside* the land, rather than atop it." He tipped his head.
"One does become acclimated." Of course, he added to himself, it
did help one's acceptance of an unnatural order to be able to feel
the staunch regard the stone treasured for all those it guarded.
This chill and echoing emptiness was . . . disquieting.

"I doubt I'll be here long enough to become acclimated," Ganat
said wryly; "therefore, I had best reconcile myself to accept discomfort with good grace."

The hallway branched and their escort bore to the left—toward
the sea. They were not bound for the Engenium's formal audience
room, then. Meri tried to decide if that was good or bad.

He was still undecided when the guard struck the bell outside of
a door that, in Velpion's day, had opened into a small parlor where
messengers had been put to await the Engenium's summons.

The guard paused, head tipped to one side, then bent forward
and opened the door, waving the two of them through.

"The Engenium will see you now," she said, with the perfectly
blank face the Sea Wise showed to those who were considered
outsiders, or enemies.

Meri felt a cold draft run his backbone, and touched the elitch
branch thrust through his belt. Then, as Ganat had not yet moved,
he stepped across the threshold.

The room was still small, but it was no longer merely a bare
rock cave with the simple table and chair that only a messenger
exhausted from his ride might find comfort in. Now, there was
a window in the far wall, opening over the sea, allowing the last

rays of the setting sun in to fill the space with rich light, waking glints of silver and gold from the depths of the stone.

A woman stood before the window, turning as they entered. She moved toward them, 'round the desk set by the window, threading her way through a clutter of chairs made out of canvas in the way of the Sea Wise.

She wore the sharkskin leggings and wide-sleeved shirt of a captain of the Sea Wise, her skin was the color of alabaster that had been left to soak in strong tea, her features angular and thin.

A leather cord caught her tawny hair at her nape, and another bound her brow. Her eyes were blue-green, and extremely clear. They widened slightly as they met his, and she pressed her thin lips together.

His little cousin Sian, all grown up.

Meri folded his arms, boots braced against the stone floor, noting a spot of warmth where the elitch wand nestled against his side, and a spot of coldness where the fear lay in the bottom of his belly.

Abruptly, Sian turned her head, and strode forward, her attention now fixed on poor Ganat.

"Wood Wise, you have a message for me from the chyarch?" She held out an imperious hand.

Ganat considered that hand for a moment, sighed and raised his eyes to her face.

"Most gracious Engenium, the chyarch asks merely that the next time you have urgent need of one of those under her care, you send more reason, and less force."

He reached into the pocket of his vest, withdrew the fessel shell on its cord, and placed it, gently, on the outstretched palm.

"The chyarch also sends, Lady Sian, that this charm would have slain its intended recipient, had he been forced to carry it so far."

If Sian was angry, or abashed, or bored, one did not, Meri thought critically, learn it from her face. Her fingers were another matter, as they closed hard around the charm, the fist dropping to her side.

"I am grateful to the chyarch for her care of my cousin," she said, her voice cool and pleasant. "Will you be returning to Ospreydale, Ranger Ganat?"

"Lady, my path now lies toward my own wood, from which I have been absent too long."

"I understand," she said calmly. "Before you go, allow me to thank you personally for your escort, and to offer you a meal, and a bed for the evening."

Ganat hesitated, threw Meri a glance overfull of some meaning he could not read, and bowed, deeply.

"You are kind, lady, but I hunger for the voices of my own trees. The moon is bright enough to light me along a path I know so well. By your leave, I will continue onward."

Sian inclined her head. "Certainly. Walk safely across our land, Ranger."

Behind Ganat the door opened and the guard Susel stepped within. Sian moved her hand.

"Escort the Wood Wise to the gate, first stopping at the kitchen so that he may replenish his supplies."

"Yes, Engenium." The guard gave the casual nod which is a high mark of respect among the Sea Folk.

Ganat bowed once more. "Lady," he murmured. Straightening, he gave Meri a smile that was not the best he had from the man during their journey, though it was perhaps the most earnest.

"Rest safe, brother, and heal among kin," he said softly. "Send word through the trees, when you're able."

Meri's eye stung. He reached out and gripped the other's arm above the elbow.

"Walk canny, Ranger," he said.

"And you." Ganat turned and followed Susel out of the room.

The door closed, leaving Meri alone with his cousin.

For the moment, however, she seemed to have forgotten his existence. She raised her fisted hand, opening the fingers one-by-one, and stood staring at the charm nestled in her palm as if she had never seen such a thing before.

Abruptly she spun on her heel, casting the charm down on the desk, and swung back, her eyes on his face, her own showing a tinge of pink along high cheeks.

"You cannot think I sent that thing to you!"

Oh, thought Meri, could he not?

"As of this moment," he observed, "I am free to think what I might." He raised an eyebrow, unable to resist. "Though that, of course, may speedily change."

"Oh!" She spun away from him and stamped over to the window, staring out over the sea with her arms folded tightly across her chest.

Meri sighed, walked over to one of the canvas chairs and sat himself down to wait while the Engenium of Sea Hold grappled with her temper.

There had been a time when Sian could not have risen to rule. Connected by blood to the Queen as she was, yet that blood was mixed, as was Meri's own. His, however, was a simple admixture of Wood and Sea Wise. Sian was Sea Wise, well enough—but her mother had been High Fey, of one of the lesser houses. The Queen's mother proceeded from that same lesser house, which was, to hear any of the full remaining of the Elder Houses tell the tale, an abomination.

Meri had been born after the war, and had never known a domain under the proper rule of the Elder Fey, nor had he much patience for those arguments which were firmly based upon purity of blood. In his experience, ability counted—and the present Queen, upstart house or no, had no equal in state craft. She could lead, she did lead, and so she ought to lead.

His cousin Sian, however . . .

She whirled away from the window and came to where he sat, falling to her knees beside his chair. The face she raised for his scrutiny was damp with tears.

"Cousin, let us call truce until you are rested at least. Hostilities may commence tomorrow after breakfast. But for the moment, allow me to see you! It has been so long . . ."

She raised a hand to his face, her fingers tracing the thin scar across his left cheek, then the long one that slanted up from the patch, across his forehead, and into his hair.

"They said you were . . . terribly wounded," she whispered.

"Those are the least of what they did," he answered, his voice rough.

"I would not have had it happen," Sian murmured. "And to see you thus, after you have been asleep so long! Your *kest* . . ." She looked down, extended a hand and touched the elitch branch at his belt, setting the leaves to whispering.

"The chyarch," he said, striving for a mild tone—"and Healer Ganat, also—suggest that I may wish to retire to Vanglewood."

Sian shook her head. "I think it is perhaps best that you stay here."

"What—" he began, but she put her fingers over his lips.

"Tomorrow," she said. "Now that you are home, tomorrow is

soon enough. For tonight, let us feed you and settle you into your rooms." She moved her fingers and rose, holding her hand down as if to help him rise.

Or as a gesture of peace.

Sighing, Meri put his hand in hers and came, slowly, to his feet.

Chapter Eighteen

OVER THE YEARS BECCA HAD LEARNED NOT TO PERMIT HERSELF to startle suddenly. Not only would such movement set her sister to nattering about fidgety invalids but it would also, depending on circumstance, serve to spill the tea, or tear the roots or leaf of a growing thing, or distort the pattern of thread-count or lead to any number of unhandy outcomes. Treasures to guard . . . well! Of late, her isolation and social invisibility had oft been her greatest treasure.

And so she rode with that will-not-to-startle foremost in her thoughts, then, feeling a slight reprieve from the oppression about her, she mindfully wrapped that will about her like an over-large shawl, covering herself, and her saddlebags with the precious journals, seeds, and herb kit, over Rosamunde's back and croup, and mentally sealed it with the strongest brooch she could imagine, with a pin almost as long as a dagger.

Sensible or not, the sealing of that imaginary shawl settled her and drew a backward, arched-eyebrow glance from the not-quite imperturbable gentleman who led them into ruin. His expression was that of surprise, perhaps, or merely distraction.

The bend in the road was much further than she had supposed. The air grew heavy; breathless. Rosamunde's paces felt mis-paced until Becca realized that the steps were solid—but the sounds were odd.

Altimere's lead took them to the right of a sudden branch in the trail. She looked down from her perch, past Rosamunde's shoulder, hearing the step, *then* seeing the hoof strike.

Well, she thought with relief, *it's only that the sound precedes the footfall.*

Looking ahead, and listening intently in the dead air, she learned that the same was true for Altimere's mount: first the sound of hoof against gravel, then the placement of the hoof. How odd.

For a time, she simply rode, watching the hoof strike belatedly, unaware of anything else, her head heavy and her limbs languorous.

Just before she slipped into sleep, she did start, for Altimere now led them into the distinct bowl of a valley, surrounded by sere, mounded hills. Surely, they had not come far enough for such a change in the terrain! Unless . . . had she fallen asleep, in truth?

Directly before them, terrible above the humpbacked hills, the flickering balefire filled the sky with an iridescent fog belying the depth of the darkness growing at the edge of the trail.

Her good hand as light as possible on the reins, Becca reached with her weak left hand for Rosamunde's withers at the saddle-edge. Hah! Altimere rode courtly, did he? No blanket here, between saddle and withers, but all dependence placed on the leather panels. True, she was used to country ways, where oft a horse might be expected to sweat.

Motion in front of her . . .

A man's figure limned in darkling light, astride a flickering shadow of a horse, waved at her, his long fingers drifting like snowflakes in the turgid air. Heart in her mouth, Becca caught, looked about her, and gasped. In her inattention, she had nearly allowed Rosamunde to veer onto a thin track to the left, which spiraled away, ghostly, toward the terrible hills with their crown of black light. Carefully, she eased her mount back to the proper trail, and sighed.

The left-ward track beckoned with flickering fingers, teasing her side vision. Surely, Becca thought, that way was shorter? Perhaps she might—

But no, she reminded herself sternly; she *would not* take her own path. She had agreed to this trip, and to the terms. This was a dangerous and tricksy land, as she now knew for herself. She would not allow it to lead her astray. She would follow . . . she would follow . . . Yes. She would follow.

Do not lose sight of them, my brave! she thought to her filly.

She moved the reins, a gentle motion being sufficient, the lightest tap of heel ...

Rosamunde was willing to close ranks with the lead horse, though it seemed that horse was ignoring her existence. The sounds of hooves on gravel echoed all about them, as if there were a dozen or more horses to be caught, and if Altimere approved or even noticed her new attention he gave no sign.

Even at this distance, following was not easy. Not only was Rosamunde's sudden tendency to bear left and go off the track a concern, but Becca found the lack of color in the world disheartening. Worse, there was an annoyance she couldn't lay her thoughts on around a plague of aches and pains, as if all the wounds and injuries of her life were complaining at once. . . .

Rosamunde shied from a rock, and then another, both large enough to cast them down if misstepped, rocks Becca should have seen as she looked between her mount's ears, over her star, at the slow moving gravel they transited.

Becca could scarcely see the tail of the horse they followed, the colorlessness absorbing light as if they rode in the midst of a hundred rainstorms.

She felt, in truth, as if she were beaten down by those rainstorms, and the minor aches came upon her at once and in full force: her crippled arm screamed from shoulder to pinkie, each muscle declaring itself afire, and she nearly swooned as the memories of bug bites, stubbed toes, and sisterly pinches took ...

There! Ahead was the darkling stallion! She mustn't lose sight! She *would not* die here, alone and in pain. She *would not* be lost!

And yet it seemed that she was lost. Fog enveloped her, rain beat her, and she could scarcely see the ears of the ... of the ... horse ...

There was no light, no color, no sound. She tried to speak, but the fog forced its way down her throat, muffling her voice.

There! An image in the fog: A man, his hair golden and his eyes steady; a quiet smile on his pale lips ...

Altimere!

His name! She grasped, hurled it out into the fog on the wings of her thought. Altimere! Altimere was why she was here! Altimere was the connection she had with this place! Altimere was ahead leading her through this terrible land!

Sound was all around her like a thunder and wind rolled into one, like the sound of a splintering thill combined with her own screams, or the angry buzz of . . .

She must flee! There was no safety, up here so high, so exposed. She wanted to leap down from this absurd perch and rush to safety, to—

No! If she fled now all was lost. . . .

Her hand, tucked hard between leather and . . . hair. Horsehair, warm and living. Horse . . . her horse was with her . . . brave horse had a name, must have a name, as she must. Altimere was not her name, the horse was not Altimere . . .

The hand—her hand!—between soft coat and hard edge of the saddle—and the name Rosamunde bloomed in her mind, reflecting back to her *Lady Becca I know you,* colored with determination—a determination to push through, to arrive at the other side, each with a would-be master behind them, neither with any other place that would accept them, except what might be *forward, away from—*

Hold your seat came into her mind, and she knew not if she thought it or the horse, but she tucked her hand hard, touching saddle and horse, concentrating her thought on a place where there was clean water, flowers, grass, *light,* someplace where they could rest, and she might draw on the slim store of balm and herb that rode, suddenly recalled, in her saddlebag, to leach the agony out of her arm, and soothe away the clamorous small pains.

Ahead of them only a small eldritch glow outlined a horse's hooves; a greyer patch in the gloom showed where Altimere moved, bent against rain that did not fall and wind that did not blow. The cold swirled with the heat; she was sodden with sweat, as her hands and feet froze.

It was dark. Even the hateful flickering of unlight ceased.

Becca leaned forward, one hand gripping the reins, the other gripping the edge of the saddle, her eyes straining until she saw blue flashes, and crimson. Until she saw—

The star.

Yes.

The star on Rosamunde's forehead, beneath the darker fore-lock, that star was more visible now. The wretched arm ached with the strain of holding on with the hand she still had tucked 'neath the saddle—when had she managed that?—that throbbing in her good arm where her sister always pinched her was no longer a piercing reminder, and the tears—had she been crying the while?—were slowing.

Sounds. Hooves against earth, the creak of leather. And ahead there was a definite horse and a definite rider and even enough of a track to be called a trail.

Rosamunde puffed and snorted, wishing to run now, not from fear but toward the places promised ahead. There was scent on the air, and it was clean scent, no matter that the plants suddenly visible here mirrored those she had seen at the start—they were plants, growing things, and there, just ahead, a blade of sunlight crossed the track!

Becca dared look behind her, at a sheet of fog rising from the ground into the heavens, stitched with flares and shimmers of hideous light.

There came the sound of hooves on gravel, the unexpected flit of some tiny, urgent bird . . .

Before them, the dark horse slowed. The rider turned, his face filled with honest dread.

The dread gave way to some other expression Becca could not name . . .

He nodded, did Altimere, as Rosamunde drew aside.

"That meadow ahead," he said without preamble, "is entirely outside the reach of the *keleigh*. We will rest there; water the horses, and partake of a small meal to recruit our strength."

Exhausted, shivering with the remnants of pain and fright, Becca hardly knew what to say to these curt commonplaces.

Rosamunde snorted though, and Becca looked into Altimere's face.

"You sir," she said, striving to sound as matter-of-fact as he, "will wish to dust your coat."

He looked down at himself, his chest, his waist, his legs—all wrapped in the slenderest ropes of their poisonous metal. If he craned to the right or left, he could also view the destruction of his arms, likewise bound in chain and secured to staples set in the cold stone wall.

His flesh was corroded, the wounds seeping, but if they had hoped to undo him with agony, they had miscalculated. The pain had long since exceeded his capacity to feel it.

He did long for death, yes—as an end to confinement, and the continual assault of their terrible auras. When the one called Michael stepped into the room bearing a poison-metal knife, his first impulse was one of relief.

Fool.

Michael's aura was a strong sky-blue, with lightning flashes of orange. Passionate, purposeful and seductive. He held the knife like it was an old friend, and smiled at Meri gently.

"Give us the secret of creating gold from leaves."

"I cannot," Meri said, as he had many times before.

Michael sighed, and moved, the knife flashing at the edge of Meri's eye. It was only when the blood fogged his vision that he realized—

"Hack me to bits, and still I cannot tell you," he said tiredly.

Michael nodded sympathetically.

"I told Lord Wing that you'd say the same as you'd done. He said to give you another chance, and this was it, but, hey—you're a regular fella. A hunter, like me. So I'm going to ask once more, nice, see? Tell the man what he wants to know, or worse than you've had done will happen. You don't think that's possible, maybe. Take it on trust that there's worse, and think about it."

The knife flashed again, slashing his cheek. Meri said nothing.

Michael sighed, shaking his head, and walked over to yank open the door.

They had been kinder to Faldana than they had to him. That was what he thought at first. They had taken her Ranger leathers, as they had taken his, and given her a plain white robe. Her wrists were bound with common rope and her flesh was whole. She walked as one in pain, however, and the subtle mauves of her aura showed flarings of a sickly yellowish green.

"Meri!" Her broad face lightened with joy—then horror, as she took in his situation.

"Oh, my love—"

"Silence!" Lord Wing strode through the door, swinging his arm out in casual cruelty, striking her across the face.

The auras filling the room flared into one lightning bolt of crimson, abruptly dissipated as Michael's elbow went into his gut.

"It ain't the worst he can do," the man snarled.

"Correct." Lord Wing stood before Meri, his hands fisted on his hips.

"Michael?"

"He won't talk, your lordship. I didn't figure he would."

Lord Wing nodded. "The time has come for strong measures, then."

"I cannot tell you what you want to know," Meri said, struggling with the mangled notes of the man's tongue. "If you are not as we are, you cannot do what we are able to do."

"Yes, yes. You've said so, over and over. You're a brave man, and your ability to withstand pain is both prodigious and admirable. However, I must have the information, and time has become short. Therefore, I am forced to resort to . . . less savory means. Michael."

Michael stepped forward, grabbed the robe at the shoulders and tore it from Faldana's body. He put her on the stone floor, not ungently, fastened her bound wrists over her head and each leg wide. After making certain that the bonds were secure, he rose and stepped back against the wall.

"Very well." Lord Wing pulled an object out of the pocket of his coat. Meri stared. In form, it was not unlike a male member.

Except that it was cast from poison-metal.

"Remember," he said, holding the thing so close that Meri felt the dire essence burn his cheek, "that you can stop this at any time."

Chapter Nineteen

EVEN THE KITCHEN GARDEN AT ARTIFEX WAS KEPT FORMAL, WITH not a creeper nor a blossom out of place. Becca had yet to discover the stern policeman-gardener who kept all in order, for she had met no one during her extensive rambles around the grounds.

Possibly, she thought, opening the gate and stepping out onto the flagged path, the Gossamers kept the gardens as part of their duties, or perhaps it was simply fear of Altimere's displeasure that kept his plants so orderly. At least, that was what Elyd would have her believe. On the other hand, Elyd would have her believe trees spoke, sprites danced in the water garden, and dangerous monsters lurked hidden in the wild wood beyond Artifex's perimeter—or, rather, beyond the point where Altimere's *kest* extended.

Elyd was kindness itself, and Becca was quite fond of him, not the least because of his care for Rosamunde. But she suspected that from time to time he told her bouncers, to amuse himself and relieve the tedium of answering her endless questions.

Not that his answers were always helpful.

When she had asked him how it was that fosenglove, teyepia, and tea rose were all at bloom together, all she had gained was a sideways look and a muttered, "Who will tell them otherwise?" In answer to her inquiry as to why it was that she never saw him in the garden or the kitchen, he had shaken his head and answered very slowly, as if he thought her wits had gone wandering, "Because my place is in the stables, unless the master wishes otherwise."

And when she asked if he had served Altimere long, his only answer was a blank stare, as if he had forgotten how to speak.

It was, she supposed now, as she walked along the pathway away from the water gardens, perfectly possible that Elyd did not know how long he had been in Altimere's service. The days were so pleasant and unruffled that it was difficult to keep them separated, or, indeed, to experience any sense of time's passage. As if, thought Becca, events marked time, and, lacking anything save peace, its passage was suspended.

Certainly, the inconstancy of the growing season did not help one keep a sense of time. Since she had come here with Altimere—eighteen dinners ago, she told herself scrupulously—she had observed two serath bushes, side by side, in what appeared to her gardener's trained eye to be in identically robust health: one dormant, and the other blooming madly. Closer inspection showed her that this was not unusual. Here, a stand of fosenglove waved its belled stalks in the breeze, while three steps further on, there were only the broad leaves and the shy head of a new stalk barely peeping beyond them.

If the plants themselves could not keep the seasons . . . Becca shook her head, pushed open the second gate and stepped into a small, chaste garden very nearly under the branches of the wild wood. This point, as near as she could tell, was the furthest from the house, and, to hear Elyd tell it, Altimere's influence. To be honest, these factors—and Elyd's insistence upon the monsters inhabiting the wild wood—had made her spurn it as a likely spot for her own garden. Unfortunately, a thorough inspection of the rest of the grounds surrounding Artifex produced no other place so promising, and Becca had returned today to study it once more and be certain that her memory had not played her false.

It had not.

Broad-leaved climbers bearing glossy blue fruits that Elyd had told her were *winberige* clambered over the stone wall, daring even to shoot tendrils into the shadows cast by the untamed trees beyond. From the right, the path was lined with penijanset, wagging their copper beards in the breeze. To the left an escort of lord's purse tossed their golden heads.

Directly before her was an elitch tree, the gold and copper flowers pooling 'round its sturdy trunk, and a stone bench beneath.

Becca walked over to the bench and sat down with her back

against the firm trunk. There had been an elitch and a bench in her garden at home—perhaps it was that circumstance that had convinced her that this was the only place for her herb garden?

But no. It was the fact that here, unlike any of the numerous other gardens at Altimere's house, there existed land that was not already being used for plantings. Beyond the brilliant swirl of flowers a silky expanse of meadow grass rippled like water under the gentle breath of the wind. Despite the nearness of the wood, and the presence of the elitch, there was sun enough for those plants that loved it, and shade a-plenty for those shyer and more delicate. She dared to believe that her few seeds would find this land as nourishing as the other plentiful growth. If she planted thoughtfully, she might make a more restful transition between the flowers in their ordered imitation of carelessness and the untamed trees beyond.

It was settled, then, she thought. This was the spot. She would ask Altimere's permission this evening, and request the services of an under-gardener, or a pair of Gossamers to turn the soil. The way things grew here, she would have a proper medicinal garden started by the time she and Altimere had shared eighteen more dinners.

Meri leaned his elbows on the balustrade. The rock was warm and slick against his skin, the salt breeze sharp as a slap on the cheek. Below, the sea assaulted the shore, its black surface picked out in the pale reflections of stars.

He could, he thought carefully, jump.

Of course, there was no guarantee that Sea Hold would allow him to do so, nor that Sian had not seen fit to place a tiny geas upon him, after all—for his own good. He might test either proposition merely by mounting the rail. If he was wrong—about Sea Hold, about Sian—then the agony might stop now.

If he was right, there would be alarms, and guards, and a room deeper inside the hold, without windows.

His stomach clenched, threatening the return of the meal Sian had insisted he eat.

"'What a strange sort of coward you are," he murmured, salt puckering his mouth. The storm he had tasted earlier would make landfall at the turn of the tide, he thought absently, or he was a lubber and the despair of his mother's kin.

Not that he wasn't necessarily so, in any case.

The wind freshened, scraping along the rock face, whining in crevasses, the various pitches conspiring to sound like conversation. Indeed, the Sea Wise said that the dead rode the storm wind and would speak with any brave—or foolish—enough to say their name.

Meri closed his eye, listening to the wind gabble in the night.

"Faldana?" His voice was hoarse; his inner eye seeing her as he had seen her last—broken, drained, and defiled on the dead stone floor in a windowless room on the very wrong side of the *keleigh*.

The wind gusted, throwing grit into his face, twisting his hair in wet, spiteful fingers, but Faldana did not answer him.

Or, thought Meri, as the first driven raindrops bruised his face—perhaps she had.

"Thank you, Nancy." Becca smiled at her maid in the mirror. "That's lovely."

The tiny creature gave one more, and quite unnecessary, pat to the glossy dark curl trailing in counterfeit abandon from the orderly cluster at the top of Becca's head. The curl drew the eye from imposed perfection, past Becca's left ear, following the curve of her cheek before plunging to her shoulder, and spilling wantonly over the swell of her breast, bringing the admirer to a doubled delight.

Altimere had explained these things to her, and she learned them, despite secretly finding it more than a bit silly to be referred to as a "treasure of art." That this mode pleased Altimere must be her only concern, and that she learn to dress herself to please him her only care.

Not that she needed to keep such close care as all that while Nancy tended her, her maid being, in Becca's opinion, even more of an artist than the master of the house.

The glass reflected a sharp flutter of jeweled wings; Nancy was never patient with wool-gathering.

"The amethyst drops, do you think?" she asked, and watched in the mirror as the tiny creature tipped her head consideringly. She hung in the air just behind Becca's shoulder, her wings moving in a blur of garnet, green, and gold—then suddenly darted off across the room.

Becca shook her head, noting the sensation of the renegade tendril feathering across her tender flesh. Altimere had been teaching her other things, as well . . .

A flash in the mirror warned her of her maid's return, bearing, not the expected ear-drops but a deep purple flower from the bowl on the bedside table. Hovering so close to Becca's right ear that she could hear the hum of the busy wings, Nancy delicately seated the flower among the careful curls, then zipped away so that Becca might study the result in the glass.

Study it she did.

"Yes," she said eventually; "I see. The ear-drops would have distracted the eye from the fall of the curl."

Behind her, Nancy turned a handspring on the air. Becca bit her lip, careful not to laugh. One did *not* laugh at the infirmities of others, and it was no fault of hers that Nancy could not speak, and must thus make her feelings known in—other ways.

Why Altimere had chosen not to give the maid a voice, Becca did not know. He had turned her questions on the point, asking if she wished to always be gabbled at by a mere servant. It would, Becca thought privately, have been nice to have someone else to talk to—though of course she did have Altimere and Elyd.

The Gossamers likewise being voiceless had led Becca to suspect that the lack was far less what Altimere termed "deliberate design," and much more because he hadn't known how to go about it. He was a proud man, and proud of his skill as an artificer, so naturally he would not wish to admit to such a thing—and Becca had stopped asking him to give Nancy a voice.

And, truly, aside from that one small thing, she could not wish for a better attendant, though it be a mute mechanism that drew its ability to move from the sun's rays or no. It had been Becca's whim to name the tiny creature "Nancy," for it was not overtly female, its naked silver body slim and sexless as a dragonfly. Still, a lady's maid *ought* to be female. . . .

Nancy zipped between Becca and the mirror, and darted toward the door, which as hints went was quite broad enough.

Becca laughed and rose, her skirt rustling like leaves. She smiled once more at her reflection, approving the deep purple bodice with its lacing of silver ribbon, the single sheer sleeve covering her right arm, while the left remained uncovered and unadorned. The bodice hugged her upper body, the skirt merely clung, reproducing every line of her limbs in shimmering, silver-shot amethyst. She recalled the first time Altimere had dressed her for dinner—that had been before he had given her Nancy—and her insistence that she must wear at least *one* petticoat. He hadn't laughed at her silliness, but had taken her onto his knee and petted her, explaining that custom was different in the Vaitura. So patient and kind . . .

She laughed again, softly, and nodded cordially to the woman in the glass, with her fine eyes and her glowing brown skin. And here was Nancy, darting back from the door in an agony lest she be late, flitting around Becca's head, the agitated flash of her wings almost seeming to crown her with flames.

"I'm going!" she said, and did, relishing the cool slide of fabric along her naked limbs as she walked. Her feet in amethyst and silver slippers made scarcely a sound as she moved down the hall. She paused at the top of the ramp leading to the receiving hall, and there he was at its foot, wearing plain black shirt and trousers, his hair flowing loose upon his shoulders.

He looked up as she hesitated and smiled, opening his arms. Laughing, she ran as fast as she could down the slippery wood, until he caught her up and swung her about, his lips brushing the tops of her breasts before he set her on her feet.

"Yes," he said, stepping back, the better to observe her. "You are extraordinary, Rebecca Beauvelley."

She laughed up at him. "If I am, it is because you have given me the means to be so."

"Now, can that be true?" He tipped his head, his amber eyes teasing her. "No," he said, after a long moment of consideration. "No, I cannot allow that to stand, *zinchessa*. You were extraordinary when first I was privileged to look upon you, astride a quarter-Fey horse, full of *kest*, and with an aura to challenge the sun's pallid rays. If I have done anything, it is only to give you the scope that is your birthright, and to guide you toward performing great deeds."

He offered her his arm and she stepped forward to put her hand on his sleeve.

"Shall I do great deeds, then, sir?"

"Oh, undoubtedly you shall," he murmured, leading her toward the dining room. "Together, we shall accomplish marvels."

✻   ✻   ✻

It was just the two of them at dinner, lounging on pillows with the meal laid out on the low board between, and music wafting from the golden harp in the corner. There was a specific order in which to address the meal: first, a cup of sorbet, which dried the mouth and prepared it for the tart cold soup; after the soup, one savored a plain cracker before moving on to the next course of skewered vegetables—every possible vegetable, from every season, presented at one time, flavored with butter and hot-salt—removed by another cup of sorbet, and then on to cheese and fruit and wine.

Conversation was as delicate as the foodstuffs. Altimere had chosen this hour to tutor her in his language, and her part was scarcely a complement to the meal. However, he never complained, nor lost patience, but smiled and encouraged her, and leaned over to feed her choice bits from his own hands when he considered that she had been especially clever.

After the meal, they repaired, as always, to the terrace overlooking the night garden. There, Altimere sat in his chair, and she curled onto the cushion at his feet, leaning her head on his knee.

"Altimere?" she murmured, as he stroked her hair.

"Yes, my child?"

"May I plant in the elitch garden?"

"Now, which is the elitch garden, I wonder?"

"It is—" He traced her ear with a light fingertip, and she shivered deliciously—"Mmm."

"Mmm, indeed," he agreed, his rich voice languorous. "But the elitch garden . . . ?"

"It is in the shade of the wild wood," she said, while his fingers followed the errant curl. "An elitch, and a bench beneath it, guarded 'round by penijanset and lord's purse—surely you remember it, sir!"

"I believe I do have some vague recollection," he murmured, cool fingers against her cheek. "But it appears that it is planted already. Unless you do not care for penijanset?"

"There is . . . some space merely given over to grass," she explained. "I would like to plant an herb garden there, if you will allow me the service of an under-gardener—or perhaps some Gossamers—to dig the beds." His fingers stilled. "I will be *most* careful, Altimere," she added, wondering if she had at last overstepped.

"I wonder," he said after a moment. "This herb garden—I apprehend this would be for the raising of medicinal plants?"

"Yes," she agreed. "Aleth and easewerth . . . fremoni." She hesitated. "I am an herbalist," she continued, when he said nothing more. "I do not wish to lose my lore."

"Of course not," he answered, his voice easy once more. "Let me consider this, *zinchessa*. It may be that there is a . . . more apt . . . location for such a garden. The elitch—as you say, it stands close upon the wild wood. I would not risk you needlessly."

Becca smiled and rubbed her cheek against his knee. "Thank you, Altimere," she murmured.

Chapter Twenty

THE SUMMONS CAME AT DAWN, AS THOUGH SIAN WERE AWARE OF his wakefulness. Or, Meri thought, recalling his youthful residence within these walls, as if the rock had informed her.

He closed the book he had been reading—a history of the settlement of Sea Hold, and dry stuff it was, but he would by no means have the volume of poetry that completed the room's slender library—and stood, inclining his head to the page sent to guide him.

"I am ready," he said, and followed the child along corridors lit with a pale pink glow from the walls itself to the Engenium's audience chamber.

He was in for it now, he thought, touching the elitch wand in his belt. For a moment the walls receded, and he smelled—not salt air, but a pure, leaf-washed forest breeze. A breath only, but it put heart in him.

Then the page opened the door and he stepped into the room, reminding himself to bow nicely to the Engenium's honor.

He might have saved the effort.

Sian was sitting, knees drawn up under her chin, on the wide stone windowsill overlooking the sea. Breakfast was laid on a table directly before that same window, and two chairs drawn up, facing each other across the board.

"Meripen Vanglelauf," the page stated in a high, sweet voice, and departed, the door closing softly behind him.

Sian turned her head and gave him a smile.

"Cousin," she said, softly. "Will you break bread with me?"

Traditionally, an offer to share a meal was a guarantee of accord—at least so long as the meal was in process. What happened when one rose from the table was uncertain, but, Meri reminded himself with a sigh, so was life.

"I will be very pleased," he said, "Engenium."

She laughed and slipped out of the window.

"I really would rather a rousing scold, you know," she said, pulling out a chair and waving him to the other.

"I know," he said, lips twitching despite himself. After a moment, he moved forward and took the indicated seat.

"Of course you do. But, Meri, I think I have been punished enough." She pointed at the tureen in the center of the table. "Chowder?"

If he had awakened without knowing his location, the offer of fish chowder for breakfast would have immediately given him his bearings.

"That would be delightful," he said, trying—and, to judge from Sian's quirked eyebrow, not entirely achieving—a less formal tone.

She ladled stew into a sea-green pottery bowl and passed it to him, the aroma waking an unexpected hunger. He broke the loaf before him, and passed half of it to her, winning a grin and a nod.

"Eat," she instructed, and he found that he needed no such urging. Sian apparently shared his hunger, for there was very little conversation until both had sopped their bowls dry with ends of crisp bread and Sian had refilled their cups with ale.

"You slept badly," she said then, throwing one slender leg over the arm of the chair, and cradling her cup between her hands. "In our house."

Meri sat back in his own chair, feet flat on the floor, the elitch wand digging into his ribs, a little, and gave her a direct look. "I slept badly under leaf, too."

Her brows drew together in a frown, and she looked down into her cup.

"That is . . . unhappy news," she said eventually, and said nothing more, her attention apparently focused on the contents of her cup.

Meri waited with what patience he might muster, nursing his own ale. Finally, though, he could bear it no longer.

"Sian."

She looked up, blinking as one newly awakened.

"Cousin?"

"Why did you have me wakened?"

She shook her head, sea-colored eyes wide and guileless. "I did not."

He raised a hand, frowning. "Your letter to the chyarch, and the—"

"I did *not*," Sian interrupted forcefully, "send that *thing* to you!" She shook her head and added, quieter, "Nor the letter. I swear it, on the tides."

The elitch wand warmed against his side, but even he could feel the prickle of a true-oath along his skin.

Meri let his hand fall to his knee. "Who, then?" he asked simply.

"The philosophers are at work; they have orders to find me, wherever I am, whoever I am with, when they have the answer to that question," she said, and he heard anger running beneath the true-telling. "Someone wished you ill, Cousin."

Ill. Almost, he laughed.

"Well." He finished his ale and sat with the cup in his palm, taking comfort from the weight of it. "If you did not send for me, and never thought to do so, then there is nothing here for me. I will, with your permission, withdraw to Vanglewood, and take up the life of a simple Ranger."

Across from him Sian laughed aloud.

He waited, head tipped to one side, an eyebrow up, until she had subsided into chuckles and raised a hand to brush the tears from her cheeks.

"I am pleased to have amused the Engenium," he murmured, which tipped her over into hiccuping giggles.

"You . . . were," she gasped, "*never* a simple Ranger, Meripen Longeye!"

His fingers tightened on the cup, but he thought he managed not to flinch.

"Clearly I was once a very simple Ranger, indeed, and have lately reverted to type. Let it lie, Sian, and grant me leave to go home."

She sobered then, and shook her head. "I cannot."

"You did not send for me—" he began, and stopped when she raised a long hand.

"I did not send for you," she agreed. "But *some*one did, using my name and my influence to do so."

Meri thought about that, the cup cold against his palm. "What reason could there be? I—"

"Come now, Cousin," she interrupted, softly this time. "A hero is always of use to someone."

He closed his eye. "There were those who were pleased to name me a hero," he said, keeping his voice steady. "Once. Since that time, I have done only my duties, as Ranger and as Longeye, until I chose a course that endangered me, and brought doom and destruction upon the blameless."

Sian tipped her head. "You speak of Faldana Camlauf."

Tears pricked. "I do," he whispered, and cleared his throat. "I must go to her kin . . ."

"Her kin," Sian said coolly, "are aware of her fate. You need not put yourself at their disposal."

It struck him to the core, that chill note, and he opened his eye to stare at her. "Sian—yes, I have been long asleep! But surely custom has not changed so much as that! Faldana gave up her *kest* to me. Wounded as I was, I would never have won through the *keleigh* without—"

Her hand rose again, stopping him in mid-sentence.

"*Dear* Cousin Meri, I ask your indulgence. Stay at least until the philosophers have done their work, and we have both heard what they have to say." She smiled at him. "Is that a bargain?"

He thought of Vanglewood, the sunlight filtered green and sumptuous through the leaves, and the wind tasting of growing things. And yet—he was weak, wounded. If he was also hunted, it were only prudence to know it—and the names of those pursuing, if they might be learned.

So thinking, he returned Sian's smile, and inclined his head.

"It is a bargain," he agreed. "Cousin."

The bath water was like heavy silk, rippling intimately over her skin, kissing her breasts, stroking her private parts. Becca drifted, drowsy with pleasure. Of all the things Altimere had taught her, this *savoring* of pleasure was the strangest. Indeed, it seemed to her that, before she had come away with Altimere, that she had never truly experienced pleasure. Oh, she had known satisfaction—in a successful planting, in seeing a patient regain health through her offices, or—more rarely—in duty done. Pleasure in the simple sensations of daily life—the scent of growing things, the firm stroke of a brush through one's hair, the taste of sorbet, or the feel of Rosamunde's coat beneath her palm—no one had spoken of such awareness at all, as if everyone she had known had moved through their days with eyes closed and hands fisted in pockets, refusing to see, to touch.

To be.

To be in the moment, Altimere had taught her, thinking neither of the past's mistakes nor the future's uncertainties—*that* was the greatest pleasure of all. Becca rarely achieved such an exalted state of sensation, and she suspected that Altimere, with his correspondence, and the projects that kept him all day in his laboratory, approached it even more rarely.

In the bath, Becca sighed.

"Altimere?"

"Yes, my water sprite?"

"Does your work give you pleasure?"

"Certainly it does, or I should not pursue it. Though I will own it to be a different sort of pleasure than that which will have you at one with the bath water, if you do not rouse, just a little."

She laughed dreamily, and opened her eyes to show she was awake. Altimere reclined upon a cushion at the edge of the bath, his head upon his hand. His hair glittered like a king's ransom in the soft illumination from the fog-bowls.

"You will also find," he said, giving her a slow smile that edged her languor with . . . anticipation, "when you are as old as I, that your pleasures will change. Those which beguiled you in your youth will interest you no longer, while sensations you had scarcely noticed will exert a . . . fascination that cannot be broken. Some pleasures will cool and be taken sparingly between warmer delights."

"Like sorbet," Becca murmured, moving her fingers to feel the water swirl between them. "How old are you, Altimere?"

He raised an eyebrow, by which she knew she had surprised him.

"I am of the Elder Fey, child. Did you think it just a pretty claim?"

"I don't know what it means," Becca said, smiling. "Certainly it is pretty-sounding. But tell me, sir—were you in . . . the war?"

There had been a war, so she had learned, though it had been unimaginably long ago. There were surely books dealing with the topic in Altimere's extensive library, and she doubted not but that one day she should read them. For the moment, however, her work was to learn to decode the strange, swirling pictographs that made up the written Fey language. No easy task, when Altimere could spare her only a few moments in the mornings before his own work called him to the laboratory, and Elyd with only the patience to bear with her for a page or two.

"I was in the war, yes," Altimere said, and put a languid hand down to stroke the water.

"The bath grows cold," he said, sitting up with his boneless, effortless grace. "Come out now, *zinchessa*."

Obediently, she rose, the water clinging to her for a moment like a garment, then falling away, leaving her to tremble deliciously in the scented air.

"Stand still," Altimere murmured, and began to towel her dry. The cloth was light but very absorbent, the texture as rough as a kitten's tongue, rasping every inch of flesh into tingling attention.

Altimere knelt, the towel never ceasing its rough ministrations. Becca looked down as he bent closer to his task, his hair trailing golden threads along her brown skin. She moved her left arm and stroked his head; his hair was light and soft—like feathers—and warmed her weak fingers where the tendrils 'round wound them.

He dried her legs, and her feet, one by one, then looked up, his smile squeezing her heart.

"So," he murmured, trailing long, white fingers across her belly. "Do you like this, pretty child?"

Like was not the word she would have used, though certainly the sensation was . . . compelling, even riveting. Breath caught, she watched as he played his fingers along her flesh, and felt the fire flicker in her belly, heating her blood until she shook with it, and now his lips were following the burning path his fingers had left upon her, and she clung to him, wrists bound with golden tresses.

"Please . . ." she whispered, and shuddered when he laughed against her breast.

"Please what, I wonder?" he murmured, his breath cool against her flesh. "Please stop?"

"Please . . ." she gasped. "Please let me touch you . . ."

"Ah, how the child grows . . ."

He rose suddenly, sweeping her up into strong arms, her heat pressed against his coolness. He kissed her throat, her temples, her eyes. Becca moaned, and moved her head, capturing his mouth on hers, all the heat in her body pouring into the kiss . . .

Sensation erupted into color, into light—into the wide world. She was every plant in Altimere's formal gardens, the water in the pool, the elitch in the far garden; she was the stars, signing in the great, curving wheel of the—

She was, some timeless while later, a gently glowing and langorous body lying between cool sheets, her left hand cradled between Altimere's long fingers. He was smiling down at her with such pride and wonder that tears started to her eyes.

"No, *zinchessa*. There is no need to cry. You have exceeded yourself. I am very pleased."

His words comforted her; the tears evaporated and she smiled.

"I believe," Altimere murmured, leaning over to stroke her hair, "that you are ready."

"Ready?" she asked, sleepily.

"Indeed. What do you think keeps me for such long hours in my workshop?" He smiled at her, sweetly, and put his smooth cheek against hers. "I have been making a gift for you."

"But everything you give me is a gift!" She lifted her good hand and touched his face. "Please," she murmured. "Is there nothing I can do for you?"

He paused, then turned his face into her caress. His lips grazed her palm.

"Perhaps there may be something you might do for me," he murmured. "Very soon, now." He leaned closer, still smiling, and blew across her eyes.

"Sleep," he whispered.

Becca slept.

Chapter Twenty-One

"WERE YOU IN THE WAR, ELYD?"

The stable boy turned, Rosamunde's saddle in his arms, and gave her a hard stare out of stone grey eyes.

"Do I *look* like I was in the war?" he snapped.

For all his peevishness, he walked light around the horses. Becca followed him and stood to one side, watching as he put the saddle gently on Rosamunde's back.

"How would I know?" she asked reasonably. "Altimere was in the war—"

Elyd snorted. "Oh, aye, *he* was in thick of it, no mistake there."

"Well, then," Becca persisted, "why can't you have been, also?"

He brought the belly strap under and tightened it with a steady, unaggressive pressure, shaking his head the while. "Because I'm not an Elder Fey." He gave her a sideways glance. "Very few of the Elders left—nor should there be, for what they'd done."

Becca blinked. "What they'd done?" she repeated. "But—what did they do?"

Elyd sighed heavily. "There's books about nothing else, you know."

"Doubtless there are," she retorted. "And I would read them, if some people were a little less jealous of their time."

"It's not my job to teach you to read," he said, snappish again. He turned away to pick up Drisco's saddle. "I'm a stable hand."

"I know that," Becca said, "and I'm sorry. I wouldn't trouble you at all except there are only you and Altimere to teach me, on this whole vast estate. If I'm to learn how to read, it must be one or the other of you who helps me, and Altimere—"

"Is continuously busy with his work," Elyd interrupted and pulled the cinch tight across Drisco's belly. "I know."

"Well, then," Becca said, as he went to get the rest of the tack, "you can see why I have to ask all these idiotish questions. I'm very fortunate that you and Altimere both speak my language, at least!"

Elyd turned, giving her a look that was perilously close to pity. He shook his head and returned to his task.

"I don't speak your language."

Becca laughed. "But of course you do! We're talking even—"

"We're talking, right enough," he said. "But I'm no more speaking your language than you're speaking mine, no matter what either of us hears."

Becca studied his craggy brown face, and after a moment decided that he was serious. "How do we understand each other, then?" she asked quietly.

He shrugged. "The trees whisper your meaning to me. Perhaps they do the same for you."

"The trees?" Becca frowned. "No, I hear your voice, directly."

Another shrug. "Likely some artifice involved, in that wise—don't ask *me* what it is! I'm Wood Wise."

Wood Wise, as Becca had come to learn, were the foresters of this world beyond the Boundary. And if Elyd was ignorant of Altimere's work, he was absolutely eloquent in regard to anything that set roots in the ground and put forth leaves to soak in the benediction of the sun. It was from him that she had learned the names and habits of the unfamiliar plants in Altimere's extensive gardens. She doubted not that the trees whispered to him, so comfortably did he move among them.

"Are you riding today, or not?" His voice was sharp, bringing her out of reverie.

"Yes." She gave him a smile, and extended her hand. "Elyd, forgive me for badgering you! It must be maddening to be required to explain what the least child knows! You must think me utterly mad—and unschooled, besides!"

She had meant to make him smile, and ease the strain between them. But Elyd—Elyd stood as one transfixed, staring down at her extended hand.

"Come," she prompted softly, "cry friends, Elyd, do."

He took a breath, and cast a furtive look into her eyes, seeming in that moment a wild thing and utterly alien to her. Then—

"Friends," he whispered harshly. His hand darted forward, callused fingertips barely brushing her palm, then he turned away, dropping lightly to one knee, his hands ready to receive her foot.

Becca smiled and stepped forward. He tossed her neatly and was astride Drisco by the time she had gathered the reins into her hand and leaned over to whisper proper greetings into Rosamunde's waiting ear.

"Where?" Elyd asked shortly, and she cocked a whimsical eye at him.

"The Wild Wood?" she returned, mischievously.

His eyes flew to hers, such longing in them that Becca felt the heart squeeze in her chest. Tears pricked her eyes—and then he was leaning over to pat Drisco's withers.

"The Wild Wood being out of the question," he said, his voice excruciatingly even, "is there another ride that would please you?"

Rosamunde shifted, stamping her foot with energy, and Becca laughed. *That* was decided, then.

"The southern field," she told Elyd. "Rosamunde wants to run."

They rode in silence for a while, the horses walking mannerly side by side. A breeze came up, damp against Becca's face, and she looked up at the sky.

"It won't rain until evening," Elyd said, in answer to her unspoken concern.

She shook her head at him. "And how do you know that?"

"The trees," he answered, and gave her a brief, sideways smile. "They are sometimes wrong, but not often. We'll have time for that run the lady commanded."

Becca laughed. "Rosamunde rules us all, does she not?"

He blinked, then inclined his head. "She does, at that," he agreed.

"I wonder," Becca said, as they passed along the border of the water garden, "how you came to serve Altimere?"

The silence stretched so long that she thought he didn't mean to answer her, then he spoke, so low that he might have been murmuring encouragement into Drisco's ear.

"He is one of the last Elders. His House is old and he is awash in *kest*. Of course I serve him."

Which, Becca thought crossly, was scarcely more informative than his continued silence would have been.

The path widened somewhat, and there was the meadow, ahead and to the right, down a short slope, the fence that kept the Wild Wood at bay a full furlong distant. Rosamunde quivered, her yearning translating into Becca's yearning.

She leaned slightly forward in the saddle, tucking her heels and stirrups up gently, and whispered, "Good girl," before she looked to Elyd and let Rosamunde have her head with the word they all waited for.

"Go!"

Rosamunde ran, outstripping Drisco in the first moment, and the very wind in the next. Meadow grass flowed beneath them like water, and still they ran faster. Where Elyd and Drisco were—Becca neither knew nor cared. The whirlwind of their passage, the exhilaration of speed—that was all, everything. Enough.

Ahead, the fence! Becca leaned, and Rosamunde turned right, running along the barrier, slowing of her own will, until, quite suddenly, she stopped, ears pricked, and nostrils wide, staring across the fence.

Into the Wild Wood.

Biting her lip, Becca scanned the wood, shadows deep beneath the branches even now, at midday. Rosamunde was alert, not alarmed, but—concerned. Yes, definitely concerned.

Beneath the trees, at the near edge of shadow—was that—

What was that?

Rosamunde snorted, lightly, and the thing in the shadows jumped like a squirrel for the nearest tree. Except it wasn't a squirrel. It was—

Perhaps it was a man. A bandy-legged man scarcely higher than her stirrup, with a tufted tail and—

"Are you mad?" Drisco stormed up, driving between Rosamunde and the fence, Elyd blocking Becca's sight of the—thing—as he grasped her bridle.

"We stopped," she said mildly, and pointed over his shoulder toward the edge of the wood. "Elyd, what is that?"

He turned his head briefly, then looked at her again, anger—no. *Fear* in his face.

"I don't see anything," he said harshly.

"You did!" she snapped. "There was no other reason for you to set Drisco between it and us!"

"You are *not* to go under the trees!" Elyd snapped back.

"And why not?" Becca took a hard breath, to cool her temper. Elyd was her friend, and truly, he would know the dangers of the Wood far, far better than she.

He shook his head. "You are *not* to go under the trees," he repeated, stubbornly.

"Very well," she said, trying to keep her voice calm. "We did not go under the trees—and did not intend to go under the trees. I am sorry to have alarmed you, Elyd." She leaned forward and put her hand over his, where he still gripped Rosamunde's bridle.

He froze, and Drisco under him, the two of them seeming to have been carved of the same vast block of mahogany.

"Elyd?" Even as Becca frowned, her fingers moved, delighting in the taut knuckles and firm flesh. His hand was warmer than Altimere's, his pale eyes fixed in a glazed fascination on her face, like a mouse, frozen under the scrutiny of a cat.

Becca laughed, and leaned back, removing her hand. "Well, you needn't look as if I were going to eat you!" she cried. "You are unhandsome, sir! I only want my reins back."

Elyd licked his lips, and closed his eyes—and dropped the bridle.

"It's time to return," he said, tonelessly. "I have duties."

The breeze was off the land this morning, bearing the scent and the vigor of green growing things. Meri paused on the seaward path and turned his face uphill, filling his lungs; feeling the tug toward home.

The faint, and perhaps wholly imaginary, tug toward home. Still, he needed no beacon to guide him to Vanglewood. He had walked the path so many times his feet surely knew the way....

He winced slightly as the elitch switch in his belt developed a sudden sharp edge and dug into his side.

"I gave my word," he muttered, and resolutely turned his face away.

The path he had chosen to the ocean's edge was the quickest. It was also the steepest, and, unless one had spent considerable time at Sea Hold, was indistinguishable from a goat track.

When he was a youth, it had been Meri's favorite way down, the hungry crashing of the waves upon the toothy rocks below adding a thrill to the descent. He had taken it as a mark of his mixed heritage, for it was said that the Sea Folk thrived on danger. His mother was pleased to express the opinion that dancing on daggers was a folly of youth. Especially those youth with wooden heads.

It came to him, halfway down, and sweating his balance among the treacherous stones, that his mother had perhaps been correct.

Still, he had chosen the path, and he was damned if he would turn about and climb an almost perpendicular hill strewn with shattered rock to find a safer route. Even his foggy-headed younger self had known better than *that* ascent.

The flat stone walk which led to the pier was only a half-dozen *careful* steps distant. Meri, poised on shifting stone, distinctly remembered *leaping* this last distance, which, given the almost complete lack of footing, was perhaps not as mad as it now seemed.

Except for the probability of landing badly, falling and dashing what might be supposed to be one's brains out, or skidding on the damp walk and plummeting into the sea or—

The rocks with which he had achieved his uneasy truce turned abruptly beneath his boots, destroying his balance. Instinct sent him into a leap, knees high, arms extended like wings, and he hit the walk solid, boot heels hammering the rock, breath leaving his lungs in a shout.

For a moment, he stood there, knees bent, arms half-furled, then slowly straightened and looked about him.

It seemed that his mode of descent had gone unwitnessed, which was, upon reflection, too bad. Perhaps a song celebrating Meripen Longeye's graceless descent of Sea Hold would instruct those who hallowed heroes.

Or perhaps not.

Meri shook his head and looked out over the bay. Only a few ships in; and the tide on the turn. He had come down here to the sea's edge for a purpose, and, as he seemed to have survived the descent, he had best get on with it.

One more deep breath, the air thick and tasting more of sand than salt, and he was moving, down the walk until it met the pier, then another jump—a hop, really—to a soft landing in wet sand.

The sea lapped the shore tamely here at this hour, lulling those who did not know it into the belief that all was protected and safe. He supposed he would be safe enough—and in any case, he did not see that he had a choice. Sian held his word, thereby binding him to this place, among these folk. And while the Sea Folk were in no wise as . . . fierce in their acquisition of *kest* and of precedence as were the Elders, yet there remained a distinct danger in standing amongst them protected only by Sian's will.

Not, he thought wryly, unlacing his shirt and pulling it over his head, that Sian's will was to be discounted; even as a child she had been noted for her willfulness. It was rather that she could not be everywhere, and even Sea Hold might not consider itself bound to protect one who was empty of *kest* as a—

Light burst before his eyes, shockingly real. A blaze of hot blues and molten yellows. For a moment, he hung, his will suspended, *kest* rising, his whole being yearning to merge with—

The vision faded. Meri was on his knees in the wet sand, retching.

He shuddered, and pushed himself to his feet. Deliberately, he shook the sand out of his shirt and folded it onto a dry rock, yanked off his boots and put them up, as well, his belt following. For a moment he stood with the elitch wand in his hand, while he looked out over the turgid ocean.

"It were better," he murmured, "if I might seek the trees. I thank you, Elder, for your care."

He pressed the branch to his lips, then put it atop his shirt, stripped off his pants, folded them, walked to the place where the wavelets lapped the hard sand and the ledge fell away, through layers of shifting blue and green—and dove into the ocean.

The water was like acid along his skin, the salt entering each scar as if it were a fresh wound. Meri's muscles convulsed, his breath locked in his chest, and he was sinking, bound for the bottom of the bay like a boulder. He had a moment to appreciate the irony of the sea's healing before the pain vanished, his muscles warmed and he kicked for the surface.

His head broke water, and he drank air in noisy gasps, raising his hands to skin sopping tendrils of hair off his face.

Eventually, his gasping stopped, his breathing deepened and he lay back upon the water. The sea held him as firm as any comrade's arms. For a long time, he stared up at the sky curving like an egg blue bowl above him, dotted here and there with frivolous, curly white clouds. He thought to lift the patch over his right eye, but in the end he closed the left, and let the sea have its way with him.

Chapter Twenty-Two

NANCY DRESSED HER SIMPLY THIS EVENING: A WHITE BLOUSE CUT low on her shoulders, and a soft skirt the color of cranberries. Her hair was caught up off her neck with a plain silver comb, which was her only jewelry.

"I do not," Becca said to her maid, "appear to be very well dressed for dinner. Am I to expect a picnic on the grounds?"

Nancy of course did not answer, unless the sharp movement of one dainty shoulder could be interpreted as a shrug. But, thought Becca, even if it were so, was it a shrug of ignorance—dismissal?—general insolence?

It occurred to Becca that Nancy did not care much for her—which was . . . unsettling. The servants in her father's house—Cook, Mrs. Janies, Lucy—had been fond of her in various degrees. Those in the city had perhaps not been quite so fond of a strong-willed, countrified miss who had brought scandal on the house of Beauvelley, but that had hardly mattered, so long as they did their duties—which they did, punctiliously.

Nancy, though . . . Nancy was a *device*.

Altimere had said that she had no more feelings than a buttonhook, or a quill, or a fork; that she had been created to mime all the motions of a living creature, yet experienced neither thought nor emotion. And *that* was even more distressing than the notion that her maid might dislike her. As unsettling, in its

183

way, as the shadow of the bandy-legged, tuft-tailed man shape she had glimpsed beneath the shadow of the trees.

She wondered if she would tell Altimere about that sighting, and decided that she would not. Elyd had been horrified enough of the possibility of her escaping over the fence and into the wood, as if Altimere's estate were some prison that she wished to flee! She was shrewd enough to suppose that the stable boy was under strict orders to keep her upon tame land, and she had no wish to expose her friend to Altimere's displeasure.

In the mirror, she saw Nancy flitting back and forth. It seemed to her that the tiny creature was . . . annoyed, which would seem to put the lie to Altimere's claims. Though why he should wish to prevaricate over such a matter was more than Becca could fathom.

"Yes, I see," she said, standing up and shaking out her skirt. "Thank you, Nancy. That will be all."

"And how did you spend your day, child?" Altimere's dress this evening was a simple as her own: a dull gold waistcoat over a creamy shirt, and long pants in smoke gray.

"Elyd and I went for a ride," she told him, taking care with her pronunciation of the Fey words. She paused, and sipped her wine with trepidation. While most of Altimere's wines delighted the nose and tongue, there were two in particular that she found unpleasant—a red that bore a strong aftertaste of pepper and a white that tasted so much of cinnamon that she could not drink it without her eyes tearing up.

"It seemed a pleasant day for a ride," Altimere murmured. "Did you go far?"

"Only to the south field," she said, finding that the wine this evening was one of her favorites, lightly chilled and tasting of peaches. "Rosamunde wanted to run."

"Rosamunde would run from here to Xandurana," Altimere said fondly, placing the cheese platter near her hand. "She is very much her of her grandsire's line. Try the blue, *zinchessa,* and tell me what you think."

Obediently, Becca took a slice of the purple-veined cheese and nibbled.

"I think it excellent, sir!" she said, surprised. She reached for another slice.

"Do you? I had been concerned that it were too . . . wild a flavor."

"Not at all!" she assured him. "The flavor is just what it ought to be and the texture is delightful."

"Well, it does me good to hear you say so, child, for your *kest* never leads your wrongly in such things. Did you see anything untoward, in the south meadow?"

There had been something . . . Becca frowned and sipped her wine. Oh! She had decided not to discuss the day's ride in detail with Altimere! What a strange idea. As if she could not tell Altimere everything and anything! He held her *kest* and her future, how could she make him free with so much, and not trust him with the simple events of her day?

"We saw something at the edge of the Wild Wood, Rosamunde and I," she said, setting her glass aside. "Elyd swore he saw nothing, but I think that was because he was angry with me."

"Angry with you? How very odd. I had been certain that he was . . . fascinated by you."

"No, I annoy him," Becca said seriously. "Badgering him with silly questions, and nagging at him to take time from his duties to teach me to read."

"Can Elyd read? You surprise me."

"Well, I own that I found it odd, too. But he can read quite well, sir, and he is very good at explaining—"

"But . . ." Altimere coached gently.

"But, he has his duties in the stables and for the horses. It is not his job to teach me to read. As he rightly points out to me." She paused, suddenly struck by a thought. "Altimere?"

"Yes, my child?"

"Could—*we*—not hire a tutor to come and teach me reading?"

"Why, I suppose we might," he said, sounding much struck. "Let me think upon it."

"Thank you," she said.

"There is no need to thank me," he said, nudging the platter nearer. "The pinchmelon is quite good, I think. Do try some."

After the meal they rose, as always leaving what remained of the meal to be cleaned up by invisible and efficient Gossamers, but when Becca stepped toward the door that led to the inner garden, she was restrained by a gentle hand upon her arm.

"Let us come into the small parlor for a moment," Altimere murmured, sliding his hand slowly up her withered arm.

Becca felt her skin heat under the light fabric, and allowed herself to be guided down the hall.

She had been in the small parlor only once. It was an oddly shaped space that ought not really have been a room at all. Situated behind the dining room, it was a weirdly shaped cave of a place, with neither prospect nor art to recommend it.

This evening it was . . . less ill than it had seemed on that previous occasion, for someone had laid a small fire, and lit real candles. The dance of live flame against the darkness served to conceal the room's odd proportions, and made it seem a safe and cozy haven.

"Here," Altimere murmured, guiding her over to a small table where two candles burned merrily, casting their light onto polished wood and a pouch of some material so dark and dense that it seemed to absorb any flicker that touched it.

"Now," Altimere said. "Do you recall that I said it pleased me to make you a gift?"

"I do, indeed, sir. And I recall that you have given so many gifts already—"

"Peace." He raised his hand, his smile flickering in the candlelight. "I have said that it pleases me to do this. That does not mean, however, that you should feel in any way compelled to receive what I offer. Take it only if you desire to possess it."

Impossible to read his face in this light. Still, he sounded serious, his voice resonate with meaning, as it had been when he had taken her life and her future into his hand.

"Of course anything that you give to me is precious in my sight," she said slowly. "And it must please me to receive any token of your regard."

"All very pretty and proper." He sounded—amused, now. "I say again, child: Receive it only if you desire to possess it."

He extended a long hand, his fingers washed in golden light, and plucked the fabric away.

Starlight burst across Becca's vision, impossibly bright; a thousand scintillant points burning against the dark.

Diamonds, she understood slowly. A diamond collar, the stones so pure they burned blue at the heart.

Another vision rose, partially obscuring the glory spread before her—the vision in the wine cup, of herself gowned like a queen, strolling at ease among her attentive trees, and around her throat, a diamond collar, glittering like all the stars of summer.

The memory faded, leaving the reality of the collar, sparkling in the candlelight, colder and more brilliant than the moon.

She wanted it. Of course she wanted it! More, she was meant to have it! Had she not seen it? Did the vision not mean that she had *already* accepted and treasured this gift? Why else, indeed, was she here, except to make that vision true and real and her own.

Becca extended her right hand, felt the reflected glory sparkle across her skin.

"I will require assistance . . ." she murmured, hardly hearing her own voice.

"Perhaps not," Altimere answered, his voice so low it seemed she was hearing it inside her head. "Remember, *zinchessa*: Receive it only if you must possess it."

She shook her head. There was no question that she must possess it! Possession of the collar would make her future perfectly . . . real.

Shaking, she slipped her right hand beneath the stones, not at all surprised to find them pleasantly warm. A moment later, concentrating, she was able to slip her left hand also beneath the collar. It clung to her fingers as she raised it, shaking harder now as pain shot the length of her ruined arm, but she persevered.

The collar was hers. She *would be* worthy of this gift.

Her whole future depended upon it.

Sweat ran her face, and tears, and still she pushed, demanding that the strengthless limb do as she desired, ignoring the agony that threatened to burn her bones into ash.

The darkness edged tighter, the candlelight glaring cruelly, and still she demanded, and still her ruined arm rose, inch by torturous, agonizing inch . . .

The collar was against her throat now, warm against sweat-soaked skin. Becca gathered herself, and *pushed*, driving dead muscles to do her bidding. Her arm jerked, the necklace slipped in feeble fingers, she *pushed* once more, and the two ends met, meshing with a snap that was loud even over her scream.

"My brave, beautiful child!"

Altimere's arms were around her, cuddling her against his chest. He stroked long, clever fingers down her back, down her arms, and the pain died, cooled by his touch. A kiss and her tears dried. She lay against him, content, fulfilled, the collar an unaccustomed weight around her throat.

"Well done, well done! Your strength is of legend. There were heroes who had not done so much!" Altimere crooned, and kissed her cheek once more before setting her away from him and smiling down into her face.

"Now, if you will, we shall have a small demonstration."

"Demonstration?" Becca looked up at him in amusement. "What sort of demonstration can we need?"

"A definitive demonstration," he answered, quite seriously. "We have come far, and gone boldly, but it will not do to become overconfident. So." He moved away, one step only, and smiled at her.

Becca smiled back, dreamy and content, not much surprised when she felt the silken tumble of her hair against her neck. She threw the silver comb lightly to the table, where it landed on the cloth that had hidden the collar, glinted once in the candlelight—and was extinguished.

Smiling still, she felt a tug at her breast, and looked down to see her busy fingers languidly unlacing her blouse. As the laces loosened, she stroked the curve of her breast, sighing pleasurably. The ribbon slipped through its last eyelet and dropped to the floor from negligent fingers. Becca was busy looking down, watching her hand move across her own body, shuddering with pleasure, though with a yearning, a yearning for . . . *something.* She scarcely knew . . .

No, she realized. She *did* know what she desired. And she knew where it was to be found.

Without a word, she left Altimere, walking down darkened halls with no misstep and let herself out into the night. The breeze was cool and sportive against her exposed breasts. Her feet were sure on the path. The door swung open at her touch.

Elyd leapt from his bed of straw, shirtless, his hair unbraided, and a look of horror on his rugged brown face.

"No," he whispered. "Becca—leave me."

"Leave you?" she asked and her voice was thick with anticipation, for this, yes, this was what she wanted. *This* was what she *would have.* "But we are friends, are we not?" She stepped closer, fingers at her breast, pinching the upright nipple.

Elyd stood like a man transfixed, his eyes wide, his face sick with longing. Becca closed the distance between them, pushing her body against his, flesh to flesh, his maleness hard against her belly.

"No . . ." he whispered, as a shudder ran through him.

Becca laughed, twisting her fingers through his hair, and pulled his mouth down to hers.

He shuddered again, and his arms went around her, bruising, exciting. She felt the warmth pooling in her belly, rising from the base of her spine, exalting her, making every touch an agony of pleasure.

Elyd clawed her shirt down and bent, licking her breasts, her belly . . . She put her hands on his head and stepped back, undid the single button and stepped out of her skirt.

He moaned, his face suffused with an expression she had no trouble recognizing as desire—and yet he shook his head.

"Go," he said harshly. "Root and branch—" He reached out, arms trembling. "Stay. You are so beautiful. I must . . ."

"Must you?" she murmured, stepped close, rubbing her nakedness against him. "Must you?" she asked again, and licked his cheek, feeling his panic, his yearning.

One hand on his chest, she pushed him back; back and down until he was flat on his bed. His eyes looked into hers, as he unbuttoned his breeches, freeing himself. Becca smiled and bent to place her lips on his hardness.

Elyd sobbed, his hands twisting in her hair, whispering over and over, "I must . . . I must . . ."

He grabbed her shoulders, urging her up, and she kissed him tenderly on the lips as she lowered herself onto him, his hips rising to her—and she rode him until they both screamed with pleasure, his body arcing under hers—

And going utterly limp, as light, desire, and life left his eyes.

Chapter Twenty-Three

THE SEA SENT HIM BACK TO THE SAND SPIT ON THE BACK OF A rising wave, which delivered him with a fine boom and a brave showing of foam, withdrawing even as Meri rolled to his feet.

Laughing lightly, he gave a nod to the swelling waters, marking the boats and fishing rigs sweeping toward safe harbor on the incoming tide.

Still smiling, he turned away, fairly skipping across the sand to the rock where he had left his clothes. However long he had slept under the care of the healers, it had not done him as much good as this morning's drowse in the arms of the sea. He felt . . . stronger, less weary—and considerably less sullen. Whether these improvements were indicative of a deeper sea-change, he thought, drying himself with his shirt, remained to be discovered.

It was plain that immersion in the sea had not eradicated the pale scars stitched across his skin. Eye closed, he ran his fingers down his chest, feeling only smooth flesh, beginning to pebble slightly in the breeze. His shiver had nothing to do with the freshening breeze off the water.

"I must have slept an age," he whispered. The breeze snatched the words from his lips and bore them off, up the hill, inland. To the trees. Perhaps, to the trees.

He sighed slightly, and shook out his wet, bedraggled shirt as best he could before dragging it over his head, and pulling on his leather pants. He would have to draw another set of clothes from stores and put these in for a thorough cleaning.

"No more sense than to wear wood's clothes down to the sea," he grumbled to himself, hearing his mother's voice behind his own. "Small wonder they let you sleep so long, Meripen Tree-son. They were hoping you would sprout some sense."

He cinched his belt, made sure of the elitch wand, and picked up his boots. He'd take the common path up to the Hold, and—

Behind him, a wave struck the sand with a crash and a roar. Meri spun, the leading edge washing over his feet, and the whole wave receding as suddenly as it had come, leaving wet-combed sand, and an—object, perfectly round, perfectly white—and perfectly dry.

He did not hesitate—one did not refuse a sea-gift, no matter how chancy such gifts were known to be. Darting forward, he snatched the object from the wet sand, its dry-as-bone surface rough against his palm, and danced back from the next wave, all the way to dry sand before opening his fingers and looking at what the sea had brought him.

The wand flared to white heat against his side, proving yet again that the elitch was the wisest intelligence in the Vaitura. Meri—Meri merely stared, breath-caught, and wondered what the sea might ask of him, for placing such a treasure into his hand.

Sunshields were never found; they were always given—by the Sea Wise, rarely; by the sea, more rarely still. For all they appeared to be merely dry, untenanted shell, each housed a living intelligence, acute, reclusive, and occasionally whimsical. Meri had heard it said that the spirit of the sea itself worked through the shells. He supposed that this was possible in much the same way that any single elitch tree seemed to possess the knowledge and wisdom of all elitch trees.

And, as elitch trees demanded courtesy, so did this strange token. Meri drew a careful breath.

"Welcome," he said, trying not to sound as ambivalent as he felt.

The elitch wand warmed approvingly against his side.

The sun shield made no sign at all.

"Elyd!"

Becca was on her knees, sobbing as she groped for his wrist, his flesh still warm, stone-gray eyes staring sightless, and there was nothing beneath her questing fingers, nothing—

"No! Elyd!"

Her voice locked, and quite abruptly she stood, tears running her face, turned and walked out of the snug little room, leaving him where he lay and her clothes scattered on the straw-covered floor. Into the color-soaked night she walked, naked, sure-footed, and silent. Inside the house, she moved down hallways, through shimmering curtains of light, and up the ramp to her rooms.

Altimere awaited her by the bath, his hair streaming like sun-light across the dark shoulders of his dressing gown, his whole form haloed in silver.

Smiling, he opened his arms. Becca went to him, raising her face. He kissed her, deeply; the liquid fire coursed up her back-bone and along her veins, leaving her chill and shaking.

She was swooning against his arm when he broke the kiss, and stroked her face with his long, cold fingers.

"Why do you weep, *zinchessa*?"

The question unlocked her voice, and she began to sob anew. "Elyd! Oh, Altimere, he is dead! I—I killed him!"

"Indeed, indeed," he murmured, leading her toward the bath. "And most gloriously. I stand in awe of you, Rebecca Beauvelley. You are more than ever I had hoped to discover."

"Altimere—Elyd is dead. He was my friend and—"

"He expired at the peak of his joy, insofar as one of his sort might be said to experience joy. Into your bath now, there's a good child. As deaths go, it was a kind one, and worthy of a friend."

"I—" The water enveloped Becca, blood warm and smelling strongly of roses, driving away the lingering odors of straw, and of lust.

"I don't understand you," she whispered, as Altimere picked up the sponge and began to bathe her.

"No, I see that you do not." The sponge moved in hypnotic circles on her back. "All that you need to understand is that you have exceeded my expectations and that I am very pleased." Altimere's voice was slow and liquid, filling her head, drowning her horror in contentment.

"Did you enjoy yourself, my child?"

"Yes," she murmured. "Yes, I—enjoyed myself very much."

"Good." The sponge moved over her shoulder, circled her

breast, and moved down her belly. Becca lay back in the water, drowsing.

"You must let go of this shame," Altimere said, his voice smooth and honeyed. "You have put yourself and your *kest* into my keeping, and I use both to further my goals. Oh, you will be the darling of the High Fey. Who can resist you?"

Becca struggled. "I—will they all die?"

"Hush. Hush. They will not die. They will scarcely know what it is that they have given away."

"But, Elyd—"

"Elyd Chonlauf died because he was weak. He could not resist the meld, and once he had melded, he lacked the strength to withdraw."

"Why?" Becca whispered, looking up into Altimere's amber eyes. "Why did he die?"

"Because you absorbed his *kest,* and left him powerless to survive. Be still now and let me finish bathing you."

Becca drifted, awake only enough to come out of the water when she was told to do so, to stand while he dried her and wrapped her in her dressing gown, to sit before her mirror.

She watched him in the glass as he braided her hair, his dark gown disappearing into the dark room, his hair lifting and spreading as if he floated in a pool of black water.

"What happened to it?" she mumbled as he laid her down in the bed.

"Happened to what, my treasure?" He pulled the sheets up around her shoulders and looked tenderly into her eyes.

"Elyd's *kest.* You said I . . . absorbed . . . it?"

"Indeed you did." He stroked her cheek, smiling softly. "As to what you did with it—why, child, you gave it to me." He leaned closer and blew across her eyes.

"Sleep now," he whispered.

And she did.

Chapter Twenty-Four

"AND WHO," MERI SAID CAREFULLY, "WOULD ZALDORE BE?"

Sea Hold's master philosopher looked down at his hands, and studiously said nothing. Sian, seated at Meri's left hand, sighed sharply.

"Is there anything else you can tell us of the work?" she asked the philosopher. "Any innovation, or . . . peculiarity?"

"Engenium, no." The man looked up, seeming glad of a chance to face away from Meri. "A simple compulsion, albeit stronger than we are accustomed to finding."

"And you are certain of your identification?"

The philosopher looked slightly less eager.

"As certain as we can be, Engenium. These matters are not as precise as we would hope. And, while we did not discover a third level, it remains . . . remotely possible that someone else had forged her signature." He hesitated, glanced down at his hand, and—unwillingly, so it seemed to him—looked at Meri. "Zaldore is quite accomplished in the Higher Arts."

"She springs from a philosopher's house," Sian added. "Though she is not herself a philosopher."

She pushed her chair back and stood; the philosopher scrambled to his feet as Meri rose more casually.

"Thank you, Master," she said formally. "You have given us much to think upon."

"Engenium." The philosopher bowed to her honor, straightened—

195

considered for a heartbeat, and bowed also to Meri. "Master Longeye."

Meri inclined his head politely, and waited until the door had closed before turning to face Sian.

"Zaldore?" he said again. She sighed sharply and strode across the room to the table.

"Wine?"

Meri considered her. "If it's going to be that sort of answer, I'm not certain I want to hear it."

"It's a dry tale," Sian said.

"Then by all means, wine." He moved over to the table and received the cup from her hand.

"Tell me what you think of it," she said, swirling her wine lightly. "It's something new."

He failed to point out that far too many things were "new" to him since he had wakened, and glanced down into his cup. The wine was the color of heart's blood, its surface glossy and smooth. The scent was full of fruit, and the taste, when finally he sipped it, exploded into half-a-dozen distinct notes.

Meri raised and eyebrow and sipped again, appreciatively.

"You like it," Sian surmised, with a deal more satisfaction than he could account for.

"I do like it," he acknowledged. "I hope it isn't your last barrel."

"Not quite. And if we are clever in our trading, more barrels will come."

Meri raised his cup in a mock salute. "To clever trading!"

Sian smiled and sipped.

"Very good," Meri said. "Must I ask it a third time, Cousin?"

She gave him a long, direct look, turned and strode to the window. In times of stress, Meri noted, his cousin tended to favor the sea view.

"The Queen," she began. And stopped. And sipped her wine.

Meri wandered over to the window, hitched a hip onto the broad sill and looked up into her face.

"The Queen," he said, encouragingly. Sian glared at him.

"It's difficult to make a precis," she said tartly, "for someone who has less information than a new sprout."

"I can understand that it might be. Certainly, it is difficult to give good game, as worthy quarry ought."

Sian's cheeks colored.

"You are safe here, Cousin."

"So you say, and so I am certain you believe." He gave her a smile, feeling it sit lopsided on his mouth. "The chyarch assuredly believed the same."

Her lips parted; she raised the cup and turned her head, to stare out over the sea while she drank . . . perhaps more deeply than the wine deserved. Lowering the cup, she took a breath that lifted her shoulders and turned back to him.

"Zaldore sits on the Queen's Constant," she said, her voice flat, emotionless. "She has risen quickly, and gathered many allies to her cause. Very nearly, she has sufficient pledges to allow her to mount—let us say a *credible opposition* to Diathen."

Meri considered that, tasting his wine to give himself time to think. He had no patience with subterfuge, but he had ties—blood ties—to Sea Hold and to the Queen's house, and so he had been taught—and unwillingly learnt—statecraft.

He had never, alas, learned to like it.

"Credible opposition," he said now. "To what?"

Sian's mouth pursed, as if her wine had suddenly turned on her. Abruptly, she swung 'round and sat on the sill beside him.

"I'm sure you'll recall that the . . . New Folk . . . beyond the *keleigh* was the subject of much curiosity and discussion." She paused, head tipped as if awaiting an answer.

"I do recall that, yes," he said, keeping his voice absolutely even.

"I thought you might," she murmured. "Well, to say it as short as possible—the discussion has become more acrimonious, to the point where it divides the Constant and the Houses. The Queen had wished merely to maintain the balance: We, they, and the *keleigh* to keep us apart . . ."

"Except," Meri said, from bitter experience, "the *keleigh* can be breached."

"It can, has been, and will be again," Sian agreed. "Still, it is we more than they who cross it, and even we may be forestalled by the dangers. I do not see intimacy growing, under such conditions."

But if we cross the keleigh, Faldana whispered from memory, *then we would know what sort of folk they are!*

Meri's stomach clenched, his chest tightening. He closed his eye and concentrated on breathing, deep and slow . . .

"Cousin?" Sian's voice was concerned.

"It's naught—a moment . . ." The nausea faded. He took a sip of wine to dampen his dry mouth.

"What opposition does this Zaldore—does she offer?" he asked at last. "Does she wish to bring the *keleigh* down?"

Sian looked at him soberly. "Indeed she does not. She invokes the memory of the war—too vivid in those of long memory—and argues that the Newmen are best shaken from the land, and that speedily, before they learn how to threaten us."

Meri was on his feet without quite knowing how he had gotten there. He couldn't breathe, couldn't *see*, his flesh burned—

"Meri!"

A hand on his arm. He focused on it. Drew a breath in. Let it, unsteadily, out. And again.

"Meri?"

He opened his eye and gazed into Sian's eyes, reading only concern there.

"They know," he gasped. "They know how to threaten us, cousin. That metal—"

Her eyes widened. She moved her hand from his arm to his scarred cheek.

"Meri. Cousin. I am so very sorry . . ."

"No more so than I," he whispered, pulling away from her and seating himself again on the sill. "Forgive me, Cousin; I'm a fool."

"Not a fool," she said softly, sitting beside him. "Never a fool, Cousin Meri."

He drank his wine, draining the cup, and looked back to her face.

"So you say the Queen's former path of imperfect isolation loses favor before this . . . proactive Councilor Zaldore?"

"It does. And the Queen being the canny woman that we both know her to be has shifted her ground."

"Ah."

"Yes. She has put forth the notion of strengthening the *keleigh*."

Meri blinked.

"I am no philosopher, but—would that not have the effect of increasing the damage we have already incurred, and thrusting what we are pleased to call our land even further out of true with the whole?"

"It would," Sian said serenely, "require much study by the philosophers."

"She means to stall them, then. But Zaldore does not wish to be stalled, does she? And she very nearly has what she needs to carry her point."

"There are some," Sian murmured, "who are done washing their hands in blood. And others who see the damage we have wrought. The Queen has made some gains. It is possible that she will carry the day—or at least win a delaying action."

Meri nodded, looking down into his empty cup.

"And all of this has something to do with Zaldore's attempt to . . . assassinate me?"

Sian finished off her own wine. She rose, took his cup and walked back to the table.

"I do not believe," she said over her shoulder, "that Zaldore wished to assassinate you, Meri. I think she created the letter and the necklace as a ruse."

"A ruse?" He stared at her narrow back, and shivered at the memory of the fessel shell necklace, the compulsion roiling off it like poison. "I could not have borne that geas to Sea Hold and survived it!"

"Precisely! And it is my belief that you were never intended to carry it so far. The note was meant to force the chyarch to wake you. The necklace was to put you on the road. Once you were traveling, and in a known direction, it would have been simplicity itself to pick you up, relieve you of the necklace, and enlist you in their cause."

She walked over to him and handed him a refilled cup.

"Enlist *me*? I have no standing in the Constant."

Sian laughed. "You do yourself too little honor, Cousin Meri. Indeed, what better way to further her ends than to display a hero, bearing the so very visible marks of his treatment at the hands of the Newmen? Even better if the hero, wakened too soon and feeling his losses too keenly, would speak against the Newmen and call for their annihilation." She raised her cup in an ironic salute.

"And it would be fitting, as well, to carry on that which Faldana Camlauf had begun, at the urging of her dear cousin Zaldore."

She drank, her eyes holding his.

There was a high, hurtful buzzing inside Meri's ears. He tried to ignore it, to focus on Sian.

"You accuse Faldana of . . . conspiring to bring me over to her cousin's politics?" His voice sounded thin in his own ears.

Sian moved her shoulders. "The possibility exists," she murmured. "She was of the House, by blood."

"Faldana sacrificed herself, that I might have a chance to win free of our imprisonment."

"That is not," Sian said softly, "inconsistent, given the situation in which she found herself." She sipped wine, her face taking on a ruminative cast. "I own it is merely speculation. Zaldore had not yet risen so high, though she was under Nanterik's wing by then." She sighed. "No. I have steeped too long in the stew of politics. . . . Forgive me, Cousin."

Meri shook his head, and came deliberately to his feet. Politics, statecraft, lies and deception. And the fact that she spoke at all was nothing more than a ploy, designed to shake the roots of his assumptions and make him rethink all of his certainties.

The joke being, of course, that he could see very well what she had done—and still his certainties shook, like a sapling in a strong wind.

"Your pardon, Cousin," he said to Sian's waiting eyes. "I am—I require time to . . . consider these things."

"Of course," she said politely, stepping back to let him by. He was at the door when she spoke his name. He paused, his hand on the latch, and looked at her over his shoulder.

"I think it would be best for you to remain at Sea Hold for the foreseeable future," she said calmly.

Meri felt anger flicker through his bewilderment. "And do what, noble Engenium?"

Sian smiled. "I'll think of something," she said, and waggled her fingers at him. "Go. Think."

Chapter Twenty-Five

THEY CAUGHT UP TO THE WOUNDED BOAR AT TWILIGHT, DEEP INTO the rocky badlands at the edge of the *keleigh*'s influence. Conditions favored animal over hunter, except that the animal was ill and exhausted and a danger to herself and everything in the Vaitura. She had already savaged a Low Fey hamlet, leaving several badly mangled; and had gone on to gore Indella Lachenlauf, the Wood Wise summoned by the Brethren to deal with the problem. From Indella, the charge had gone to Faldana Camlauf, roused from the arms of Meripen Longeye to take the message.

"Heading toward the rocklands," she said, looking worried, which was only sensible. Boars were chancy at the best of times, and a threat even to Rangers. A wounded boar could do incalculable harm. A wounded boar in the badlands, on its choice of terrain? Not something a single Ranger wished to face alone, no matter how seasoned or skilled.

Two Rangers would scarcely be sufficient to bring such a creature down, Meri thought, arms crossed behind his head as he lay in their mossy nest, looking up into Faldana's face as she considered the situation once more.

He did not offer to go with her—Faldana was a canny and competent Ranger, and the charge had come to her. It was not his place to offer advice or assistance. She would ask for what she needed, and of whom.

"It's in bad shape," she said, holding up the bit of tusk that constituted the physical part of the charge. "Blackened fur along its left side, and something ... unfortunate going on with the rear legs."

"Sounds as if the poor beastie was caught in the lightning and hail a few days ago," Meri offered. Faldana nodded.

"If a tree came down on those hindquarters ..."

Meri understood. It took a lot to hurt a boar; even if it had taken its death-wound, it would linger overlong. Had already lingered overlong.

"I'll go at once," Faldana said, raising her head to give him a rueful, tender smile. "It's hardly the sort of sharing we had envisioned, love, but—I would like it, if you would hunt with me."

"Of course I'll come," he said, sitting up and reaching for his shirt. He felt a pang for the lovingly constructed nest, and the thorough sharing they had promised each other. The Wood Wise, especially those who followed the Ranger's calling, tended to be solitary, meeting seldom and in small groups to drink and tell tales, make love and share *kest*. He had met Faldana Camlauf at one such seldom gathering, and had taken note of her, as she of him. They had shared then, and several times after; then their paths had diverged.

Four seasons passed before their wandering feet brought them along the same path again, and each had immediately felt the old bond rekindle. Thus, they had agreed to meet, and renew their relationship.

They pledged each other that *this* sharing would be deep, complete; and had taken the time to construct the moss nest.

Meri shook his head, giving Faldana a wry grin, which she returned.

"The Wood waits for no one," she quoted.

"A boar," he answered with a quote from his Sea Wise mother, "is the most inconvenient creature alive."

"*Inconvenient* is not the word I would have chosen," Faldana remarked. She pulled on her shirt and reached for her vest.

Meri grinned and extended a single finger to trace the line of her cheek. "Nor I."

Faldana leaned forward and kissed him, lingering somewhat longer than a Ranger on charge ought, then stepped back.

"Come. We should find it before it does more damage."

They had at least managed that much, sending those Brethren

who were willing ahead of the beast with warn-aways and cautions. Still, and among plentiful signs that the animal was weakening, they had not been able to close with it. It almost seemed, Meri thought, as if the boar knew it was being followed and was hurrying to advantageous ground before its strength wholly failed.

And so it had been.

"I don't like this at all," he muttered. He went down on one knee and ran his fingers over the stony ground, feeling the boar's hitching walk, and the depth of her rage, fright, and hatred. They were close, for him to pick up so much.

Faldana stood a little ahead of him, nearly invisible in the dusk and among the scant growth. "Meri, what is that?"

He was at her side in a heartbeat, sighting along her pointing finger. There was a . . . shimmer at the very edge of his left eye.

"Surely, it's an aurora," Faldana said, but there was a thread of doubt in her voice.

And she was wise to doubt it. An aurora was transparent to the eye; it did not thicken the air upon which it danced, nor belch sickly green flame toward the milky sky.

"The *keleigh*," he murmured.

"I . . . hadn't realized that we were so . . . very . . . close . . ." Faldana shook herself. "The boar—could it have been bred—*here*?" She sounded profoundly troubled, nor did Meri blame her.

Boars tended to range wide, and to return to their home ground in times of stress. And every Wood Wise knew that animals which had been born inside the *keleigh*'s influence were . . . strange. Odd.

Wrong.

"As if a wounded boar weren't bad enough . . ." he muttered.

"We have to go in after it," Faldana said firmly. Meri thought she might be saying it for herself as much as for him. And she was of course correct.

A wounded boar was dangerous, and this one had already killed. If it . . . shared something of the nature of the *keleigh* . . .

"Under other circumstances," Meri said, trying for a light tone, "I would have counseled waiting until the morning gave us better light."

Faldana nodded. "We dare not wait," she said, and threw a tight smile at him over her shoulder before ghosting forward into the dusk.

Following the boar to ground.

*   *   *

The rocks grew larger, and more numerous. There were no trees. Ahead, the *keleigh* belched and danced, soaking the landscape with its unhealthful glare. Meri squinted, trying to make sense out of their surroundings, piecing the jagged outline of a rock fall out of the weird light.

He held up a hand. Faldana paused, looking at him worriedly.

"We cannot go back."

"We cannot go forward much longer. Happily, I think I see where it has gone to ground. Take your bow to the top of yon boulder, and I will take mine to that. You are the better archer, so I will shoot first, to flush it. You, I depend upon to bring it down."

She tipped her head, considering—then nodded and turned without a word to the boulder he had indicated.

Meri vaulted to the top of his chosen rock, drew an arrow and set it. He lifted his hand and moved the patch from his right eye to his left.

The blasted, unnatural landscape leapt into focus so sharp he winced, and closed both eyes. Two breaths to steady himself, and to recall that they sought a boar.

He opened his eye. The landscape blurred dizzyingly, bile rose in his throat, and there—there was the quarry, belly down on the stones. Its burned flank was peeled and raw, the ugly wounds weeping, and he could *feel* the effort it made, simply to breathe. It was dying—and yet it could not finish.

His focus still on the suffering animal, Meri carefully raised his bow.

More often than not, longsight created more problems than it solved. On the one hand, it was possible to see what was desired, many furlongs distant. However, it was damnably difficult to *know* how far the desired thing lay from the seeker's physical presence. It was also all but impossible to know *where* it was, for the longeye focused tight, and any attempt to gain context or a sense of near surroundings usually resulted in a loss of focus and a debilitating headache for the seeker.

Meri had learned through hard lessons to use his longeye sparingly. Indeed, this particular situation—where they were near enough to the creature they sought that they needed no context—was one of the few where his gift was exactly as useful as it ought to be.

The animal in his sight shuddered where it lay, and Meri paused, wondering if he witnessed its death, after all.

But, no—it abided. In misery. But it abided.

Meri pulled the arrow back. He had told Faldana that he intended to startle the beast into running toward her position. In truth he would do his best to kill it where it rested; he hardly had the heart to force it to rise again.

Back came the arrow. The boar lifted her heavy head.

Meri released.

The arrow sped true—and buried itself to the fletching in one enormous eye.

The animal roared, hurtling to its feet. Meri brought another arrow across the bowstring . . .

And the boar crashed to the stony ground, shaking the boulder Meri crouched upon.

Faldana slit its throat, to be certain, and straightened with a tired smile.

"We should have thought of that sooner," she said.

Meri shook his head, and gazed around him with his left eye. "It had to be here. We were near enough, and she had put her back against a wall. Startled, she could *only* bolt toward us."

Faldana nodded, absently, her eyes lifting to the ghastly display of the *keleigh* against the obscured, starless sky.

"Have you ever wondered?" she said softly. "What they're like—the Newmen?"

Meri shrugged. "So long as they remain on their side of the *keleigh* and we on ours, there's no need to wonder."

She looked back to him, her body taut against the unnatural sky. "What if the *keleigh* falls? What if time and place reassert themselves and thrust them into the Vaitura *with* us? Should we at least not scout them out and learn what sort of folk they are?"

"Since we're so close?" Meri frowned. "What brings this to you now?"

"We *are* so close," Faldana pointed out. "And it is our charge, to scout ahead, to be certain that the land is safe for travel, that no boars lie in wait to savage the innocent, that the trees are cared for, and the covenant upheld."

Faldana stepped closer and put her hand on his arm. He felt her *kest* rising, and his stirred in answer. Indeed, it was their charge, but even more than that, to cross the *keleigh*, to spy out the Newmen in their natural habitat—what an adventure it would be, at the side of a companion his equal in craft and spirit. . . .

"I would like it," Faldana whispered, "if you would hunt with me, Meri."

The morning was pleasant—as were all mornings in this place—giving the lie to the horror of her dreams. What could happen here, that was less than fair or beautiful? And yet, such a dream . . . Becca shuddered under sun's caress and hurried to the stables.

Rosamunde whickered from her stall, and Drisco snorted. Altimere's black stallion gave no sign that he had even noticed her presence.

"Elyd?" Becca called. "Elyd, are you here?"

The only reply was the sound of Rosamunde's hoof striking the floor of her stall—firmly.

Becca bit her lip. "Elyd!" she called again, voice shrill, chest squeezed with the memory of the dark dream.

Not even Rosamunde answered this time.

"No," Becca whispered, hearing her breath rasping. "It can't have been *true*. . . ." She tried to slow her breathing; tried to *think*. Elyd could simply be—somewhere else. Surely, duty called him to other segments of the estate from time to time. Perhaps— Perhaps Altimere had given him the day off. Perhaps—

Becca moved to Rosamunde's stall, which looked as if it had just been cleaned and reprovisioned, and the other stalls, as well.

"Well, then," she said briskly, though the pressure in her chest was no less. "He can't have gone far."

She turned, ignoring Rosamunde's offended snort, and moved to a door set in the right wall. That Elyd's room lay beyond it, she knew. She had seen it once—if one did not count the dream—a modest bed with a straw mattress, and clothes hung carefully on hooks. There was another door that opened out into the courtyard.

The door she had entered. In the dream.

Biting her lip, Becca pushed the interior door open—and stood staring at the tidy storeroom: buckets, sacks, rakes, and spare tack all neat and orderly. There was no bed, no clean, tattered clothing hung up off the floor.

No sign that Elyd had ever been here.

Becca felt a stab of pain, tasted blood, turned and bolted, the door banging shut behind her and Rosamunde's whinny shaking in her head long after she had run past the water garden, shoved the gates open and pelted into the elitch garden.

Panting, she collapsed onto the bench, pulling her feet up and leaning into the tree's firm, warm trunk.

"Oh, Scythe! Oh, Scythe . . ." she moaned, and dropped her head to her knees.

It was true. She had—she had taken cruel advantage of her friend, had gloried in his terror, and reft him—reft him of life.

"How . . ." she cried, shivering in self-loathing.

The necklace. She raised her hand and touched it, hard and hot around her throat. Altimere had given her the necklace, and she had suddenly felt—different. Abandoned. Powerful. And she had gone to Elyd—but the dream, or the memory, did not provide her with a reason for his seduction. She had simply—acted, with no more thought or choosing than if she had been a gleeman's doll, responding to twitches along her wires . . .

And then! He had died—died under her, in the midst of their debauch, and she had tried to help him—she had!—only then to rise, thoughtless again, walking naked out into the night, returning . . .

. . . to Altimere, who kissed her and petted her and told that her she had done well!

"I'm mad," she whispered, rubbing her wet face against her skirt. "How could such a thing happen? How could he think it *right*? How could I—"

She stood suddenly, and turned toward the gate. A low branch caught at her sleeve, as if the elitch sought to detain her, but she shrugged it off without a glance, walking briskly down the path, letting the gate fall closed behind her.

Chapter Twenty-Six

IT WAS, BECCA THOUGHT, AS NANCY RETURNED WITH THE COMB and began to dress her hair, an altogether confusing dress.

The color was old gold, which set off her brown skin beautifully, with a demure square neckline that barely revealed the swell of her breasts. The sleeves were wide, banded tightly at the wrist; the silver-bound slashes in the left sleeve alternately revealing and concealing her ruined arm.

The bodice that Nancy had laced so tightly was a fantasy webwork of silver, drawing the eye to her waist, and from there, following the sparkle of dangling cords, down to her belly and to her legs, faithfully outlined by the clinging fabric.

In short, it was a puzzling mixture of the demure and the hoydenish and she wondered what was meant by it.

Perhaps, she thought, wincing as Nancy pulled a knot, it was a comment on her—her base treatment of Elyd? But, no—*he* had been pleased. Therefore, the dress was not a punishment.

Was it—could it conceivably be—a *reward*?

Nancy pulled another knot, so hard that tears flooded Becca's eyes.

"Oh!" she cried. "Nancy that—"

"That is quite enough," a quiet voice overrode hers smoothly. Altimere's reflection appeared behind her shoulder, dressed for dinner in cream and sable. He took the comb from Nancy. "Go to the workroom," he said coolly.

The little creature hung in the air for a moment, wings vibrating, her hands lifted in what might have been supplication.

"To the workroom," Altimere repeated, pulling the comb softly through Becca's hair. "Shall I say it a third time?"

An explosion of silver, a *poof* of displaced air and Nancy was gone. Altimere smiled at Becca in the mirror.

"There, this is better, is it not?"

"Yes . . ." Becca said hesitantly. It *was* better; she adored it when Altimere brushed her hair, but—

"You won't . . . discipline Nancy too harshly, will you, dear sir? It's true that she's—peevish—sometimes, but she's a magician with my clothes and hair." She smiled at him in the mirror. "You can't dress me every day, after all."

"As much as I might wish to . . ." he murmured, amber eyes downcast, as he watched the comb glide through her hair. After a moment, he looked up and met her gaze in the mirror.

"I will not deprive you of your dresser, *zinchessa*. Merely, I will perform an adjustment, so that you are not subjected to these petty tyrannies. You are a treasure of my house and you will be honored as such. Nothing shall harm you—certainly not your own servant. Stand a moment and let me finish this."

In a trice he had her hair coiled atop her head. Diamond pins came to his fingers and he set them with casual artistry; they sparkled slyly when Becca moved her head.

"It feels—a little loose, sir," she said tentatively.

His hands cupping her shoulders, Altimere bent and brushed a kiss along her earlobe. "I think it will hold as long as it must," he murmured, and looked at her in the mirror, his cheek against hers.

"Excellent," Altimere murmured. "You are exquisite."

"It is a . . . very fine dress," Becca said slowly.

"It becomes you perfectly," he said. "Yes, you *will* captivate. I doubt it not."

Becca rubbed her cheek against his softly. "Captivate whom, sir? Yourself?"

"But I am already in your thrall," he said, straightening and turning her to face him. He slid a cool finger under her chin and looked down into her eyes, his hooded and amused.

"Tonight we will have a guest with us at dinner. By the end of the meal, I am confident that you will have added another slave to your retinue, cruel child."

"A guest? Who?"

"Do you recall in Selkethe, we met a Fey at the market? He was much taken with you."

"Jandain," she said, remembering masses of copper ringlets and gypsy silks beneath a brilliant orange canopy.

"Precisely Jandain! He has taken up my invitation to visit. I imagine that we will have him for . . . some days. His entertainment will fall largely to you, I fear, for my work has reached a point where vigilance is imperative. Indeed, now I think on't, this visit is timed well! You need not grow pale and listless for lack of company while I tend my tedious experiments."

"But I will miss you, sir!" Becca cried, panic suddenly roiling in her stomach. "I do not know this Jandain—and you said he was no friend of yours! What if he—"

"He will not harm you," Altimere said with a cool assurance that was at once terrifying and infinitely comforting. However, that answered but half of the question.

Becca looked down, biting her lip. "But how if *I* harm *him*, sir?"

"What is this?" Altimere sounded frankly surprised. He raised her head again, the touch of his fingers sending a thrill along her nerves. "How do you imagine that *you* might harm Jandain?"

She wanted to fall to the floor and hide her face. Instead, she licked her lips and forced herself to meet his eyes firmly.

"In the same way in which I . . . harmed Elyd," she said steadily.

Altimere's face clouded, and Becca felt her courage fail.

"Did I not tell you that Elyd Chonlauf died because he was weak?" he asked sternly.

"Yes, but—"

"Jandain is High Fey. He is an upstart and a heathen, as is the Queen he supports in Xandurana, but he is not a weakling. It is not possible for you to harm him, nor do I expect that you will attempt to do so." Altimere smiled. "After all, he is a guest in our house, and blessed."

"Yes . . ." Becca whispered.

"Poor child!" He bent and brushed her lips with his. "Come! Allow yourself to be pleased with him. If you recall, he named himself your most ardent admirer."

"He did," Becca her spirits rallying, "but I would not have it."

"Indeed you did not." Altimere laughed softly. "Perhaps you

will be kinder this time." He took her left hand and placed it on his sleeve, pressing gently with cool fingers.

"Shall we go down and greet our guest? I am certain that he is eager to renew your acquaintance."

The flowing sleeves, tousled ringlets, and bright colors were gone. In their stead was a sober man in a sapphire velvet coat, and silver lace at throat and wrists. The copper colored hair was confined in a tail that flowed to the small of his back. There were rings on his fine, pale hands, stones flashing azure and orange. He smiled when Becca came in on Altimere's arm, and met her eyes boldly. His were the precise sapphire blue of his coat.

Becca lowered her eyes modestly and curtsied.

"Jandain. How good it is to see you again."

He bowed, with a fanciful flourish that seemed to make mock of the courtesy.

"Rebecca Beauvelley, I am entirely enchanted to see you again."

He straightened, and gave his host what seemed an almost insultingly casual nod.

However, Altimere did not react as if he had been insulted, merely nodding in return. "I am pleased that you grasped the opportunity extended to you," he murmured, stepping forward and bringing Becca with him.

"Will you accept Miss Beauvelley's escort to dinner?"

Jandain bent slightly, and smiled down into Becca's face as he offered his arm. "I will be in all ways delighted to accept Miss Beauvelley's escort," he said, his tone uncomfortably warm.

She thought to frown at him, but instead found that she had cast her eyes down, as if in maidenly confusion.

Altimere raised his arm, and Jandain received her hand as if it were a treasure, and placed it gently on his sleeve.

"Lead on, Miss Beauvelley," he said lightly. She glanced at him out of the side of her eye and saw him smiling widely.

"Of course," she murmured, her fingers pressing into his sleeve as if drawing courage from the contact. Eyes still averted, she stepped forward, leading the guest in to dinner.

Through the sorbet, soup and cracker Jandain regaled them with tales of his late travels. He was droll enough to draw laughter from Altimere, which made Becca happy. For herself, she smiled politely, though she did not always understand the jest, and watched the guest from beneath her lashes. The wine which accompanied the cheese course was the peppery red; she sipped, tears starting to her eyes, and sipped again before replacing the glass.

"How do matters stand at Xandurana?" Altimere asked into the pause. He chose a sliver of cheese from the platter and held it out, as if he would pass a tit-bit to a favorite hound. Becca leaned forward, lips parted to accept the offering, her gaze held by Altimere's amber eyes.

She swallowed the cheese and leaned back on her pillow, reaching again for her wine glass. A glance beneath her lashes showed Jandain watching, lips parted, as if entranced. He reached for his own glass and forcibly moved his attention to Altimere.

"The Queen is beset, which will perhaps amuse you," he answered, leaning back on one elbow and twirling the glass between his fingers. "Indeed, it seemed that Zaldore was very close indeed to calling the question. Certainly, she has pledges enough."

"But how many of those pledges will stand with her to see the thing through, should she prevail?" Altimere murmured, half of his attention seemingly on choosing another bit of cheese. He found one and once more held it out. Once more, Becca leaned forward, head tipped back, to receive the treat from his fingers. He brushed her cheek, and looked over to their guest, who appeared to be studying the contents of his wineglass.

Becca reached for her own wine. She drank deeply, the peppery taste burning her throat, and lay back, raising the glass, and watching in dismay as the Gossamers refilled it.

"Your pardon," Altimere said to Jandain. "You had said Zaldore had been close to calling the question. As I have received no word that the Constant is called to attend the Queen, I must suppose that she was forestalled." He sipped his wine and chose yet another piece of cheese—this one, happily, for his own consumption, as he relaxed in boneless elegance into the pillows.

"I trust that Zaldore enjoys her accustomed good health?" he murmured.

Jandain laughed, short and sharp.

"Oh, she's healthy enough! As to what stayed her hand—" He glanced at Becca and inclined his head politely—"it is, I feel, the sudden interest of some parties in trade and intercourse—with those on the far side."

Altimere raised a languid brow. "Ah. Are we grown bold enough as a race to try the *keleigh*? You encourage me."

The guest laughed lightly. "Nay, nay. There's a move afoot to cast the *keleigh* down, and unite the races."

Altimere tipped his head to one side, elegant brows pulled slightly together. Becca raised her glass, realized what she was about and tried to set the thing aside. Despite her will to the contrary, her hand continued to rise, the glass came to her lips, and she drank deeply, head thrown back as she drained the glass. She leaned forward with a toss of her head to replace it upon the table.

Her hair, too loosely confined by the pins, shifted as she did so, and tumbled willy-nilly around her shoulders.

"Oh!" she cried, snatching at the fall too late. She felt a blush flame into her cheeks, and struggled upright, the dress suddenly clinging in all the wrong places, tying her to the couch more surely than—

"Peace." Altimere leaned over and touched her lightly on the forehead. A feeling more like languor than peace filled her, drowning her dismay in honeyed waves. "Gently, child. How many times have I said to you that the customs of your homeland are not the same as we observe here in the Vaitura?"

Becca looked down, swallowing hard in her abraded throat. "Many times, sir," she said humbly, her voice husky and subdued.

"Indeed. Why should we not admire your lovely hair—unless—" He looked to Jandain.

"But perhaps this display disgusts the guest?"

Jandain leaned forward, extending a hand across the table. "Miss Beauvelley," he said softly. Becca drew in herself, wishing she might dissolve into the pillows, as her head rose and she met his eyes shyly.

"It is inconceivable that you could offend any of my sensibilities," Jandain said. "It is as Altimere has taught you—our customs are different—perhaps very different than those you have known. Your hair is lovely, and I am pleased to see it thus."

Becca felt her lips shape a tentative smile. Her left hand rose laboriously, pain shooting like flame through the damaged muscles. Tears started to her eyes, but she did not—could not—cry out, and still her hand rose, until she placed it in his.

He smiled, and ran his thumb lightly over her knuckles. Becca felt a shudder of longing pass over her skin—and then it was gone, leaving only warmth.

"If we are all finished here," Altimere murmured, reaching over to take Becca's hand from Jandain. He kissed it, lingeringly, and placed it on her lap before looking up to the guest. "Let us repair to the terrace for another glass of wine. I would be grateful, Jandain, if you would honor me with your opinion of my evening garden."

As always, she curled next to Altimere's chair and leaned her head on his knee. His fingers stroked her hair lazily. They sat quiet for a time, overlooking the garden as dusk fell and the flowers began to shine, giving back, so Altimere had told her, the light they had taken in from the sun all day. Everything was precisely as it always was, with the exception of the man sitting on the chair at Altimere's right hand.

It was wrong, she thought rebelliously, that they should have a stranger sharing their special time and place. It was intrusive and distressing. She wished that Jandain would simply go—

The thought faded, and she nestled more closely against Altimere, eyes half-closed as she watched the moonbees flit between the flowers.

"So you tell me," Altimere murmured, "that Zaldore has challenged the Queen outright?"

Jandain laughed. "Indeed not! I tell you that Zaldore failed of asking the question that we were all poised to hear. Instead, she implored we of the Constant to create a new seat among ourselves, as per the Mediation, and that seat to be given to a hero. This was, as you might imagine, diverting, and we all strained to hear the name of the one she would propose. Instead, what should she do but call for an adjournment, to consider this weighty matter, and so we were twice disappointed. "

Altimere's attention was wholly on the merchant; Becca's more distant attention wavered between the two Fey, each with certain admirable qualities of person . . .

"Such disarray scarcely seems like her," Altimere commented. "I wonder if she had some deep plan which went awry?"

"That would be most like the Zaldore who has been a gadfly amongst us since she took her chair," Jandain answered. "And I believe you may have the right of it. For a moment it seemed as if she expected this hero to appear from smoke and air to be seated at once. When there was no such manifestation, then came the appeal for an adjournment." There was a slight pause, as if Jandain savored his wine. "She has since been calling on everyone, regardless of their known affiliations. I had not yet had the pleasure of a visit before I felt it necessary to take up your invitation, but it scarcely seems likely that all this politicking is aimed at the creation of a single new chair."

"It seems strange in the extreme," Altimere conceded after a time. "But surely all will soon be revealed? The adjournment must swiftly be drawing to a close."

"So it is. There was rumor that Zaldore has another string to her bow, but what that may be, no one I speak to has been able to discover."

Silence, in which Becca floated, the night garden blurred to an agreeable smear of light before her drowsing eyes.

"Well," Altimere murmured, twining his fingers through Becca's hair. "But what are we about, to sit talking of politics! Do tell me what you think of the garden! I know you have an artist's eye, whereas I am merely a technician—"

Becca drowsed, their voices a pleasant rise and fall, like the sound of the wind in the trees. How long she might have dozed, she did not know; but she was roused by Altimere's voice.

". . . poor child is exhausted! Come, there will be an end to our cruelty. Rise, rise and make your goodnights . . ."

She lifted her head as he rose from his chair. He lifted her to her feet and turned her toward Jandain, who had risen to his own tall height. She made an unsteady curtsy.

"Good night, Jandain Sleep well in our house."

He bowed. "Good night, Miss Beauvelley. Please forgive me for having kept you so long from your rest!"

For some reason, she smiled, then turned to Altimere. "Good night, sir," she murmured, and stretched high on her toes, her face turned up to his, lips parted, her right hand on his shoulder.

He laughed lightly, slipping his fingers through her hair and holding her head between his hands. "Greedy child," he whispered, and kissed her, his lips bruising hers; his tongue forcing her mouth wide.

Liquid flame shot up her backbone; she leaned into the kiss, demanding—and then he withdrew, setting her gently on her feet, and slipping his fingers free of her hair.

"Good night, *zinchessa*," he said. Becca turned and walked in to the house, along the dim hallways, and up to her room.

It was dark in her bedroom. Altimere was busy with his guest and Nancy had been banished. She would never be able to remove the dress herself, and she did not wish to ruin it by sleeping in it.

She was so tired! Becca yawned and stopped by the bed. Hands, or gloves without hands, appeared, casting pale shadows against the darkness. Becca smiled. Of course! Altimere would have thought of her needs, and left orders.

The Gossamers had the dress off in a trice; two took her hands and led her to the bed, tenderly drawing the covers up to her chin.

One stroked her forehead, and it seemed that Becca heard Altimere's voice, murmuring, "Sleep."

Chapter Twenty-Seven

SHE WOKE ALL AT ONCE, WITH THE FEELING THAT SOMEONE HAD spoken her name. The room was awash in sunlight, but as far as she could tell she was alone—no, even as she thought so, the door to her bathing room swung open, and the coverlet was drawn gently back. It could, Becca thought, hardly be any clearer what was expected of her.

So thinking, she slipped out of bed and went to have her bath.

Jandain rose from behind the table and bowed as she entered the dining room, bathed, her hair in a demure knot at the back of her head, dressed in a green split skirt and a white shirt laced with green cord.

"And now," he said dramatically, "it can truly be said that the sun has risen!"

That was quite ridiculous, of course, and it was on the edge of her tongue to tell him so, but instead she looked down, as if confused by his compliment, and slipped into her place.

"I hope that everything is as you like it," she said, watching her cup fill with coffee.

"I am pleased by everything," he said lightly. "Altimere is a generous host." He leaned forward suddenly, and felt herself compelled to raise her head and meet his blue, blue eyes. "Ah." He smiled and leaned back. "Indeed, I hear that he has outdone himself in generosity, and that you are to be my hostess today."

"Yes," she said, as the precise amount of cream she preferred was added to her coffee. "I am at your disposal today, sir. Is there something in particular you would care to do or to see? The gardens are quite . . . amazing. We might go for a walk, if you desire it. Or we could ride."

"I think that I should like to ride this morning," he said, watching her even as he broke a muffin and spread jam on it.

Becca felt a thrill of pleasure at the prospect of riding Rosamunde—and then dread. For Elyd was dead and there was no one to saddle—

"Miss Beauvelley," Jandain murmured, and once again she felt compelled to raise her head and look into his eyes. "May I call you Rebecca?"

"Certainly," she heard her voice say, before she had time to consider the matter, and Jandain smiled.

"Excellent," he murmured, and picked up his cup. "Please, do not feel that you need to make small talk with me. I am content to lie here and bask in your beauty while you break your fast."

Becca felt her cheeks heat again, and looked down into her coffee cup.

"You, sir, are quite ridiculous," she heard herself say.

Jandain laughed. "So it has been said—many times!"

Becca cast him a sideways look from beneath her lashes. He smiled at her, and sipped his coffee.

"Now, *there's* a filly in want of a ride," Jandain commented as they entered the stables, and Becca smiled for the praise of Rosamunde.

"Indeed, she is a very fine horse!" she said, seeing with relief that the horses—Rosamunde and a big-chested white stallion—were both saddled and waiting. The Gossamers, of course. She hoped that Altimere would give them a gift, to compensate them for the extra work that had fallen upon them.

"Rosamunde is the granddaughter of one of Altimere's horses," she continued, laying her hand on the filly's nose. Immediately, she felt the warmth of Rosamunde's regard, tempered by—something. She hesitated, but here was Jandain, setting his hands around her waist; Becca gasped, shrank back—and caught up against Rosamunde's shoulder.

"Gently," Jandain murmured. "I only wish to lift you to your saddle."

His hands were firm, and Becca looked up at him shyly.

"Of course," she whispered, and he smiled.

Once she was up and gathering the reins into her good hand, he swung onto the back of his own beast, which danced under him in a show of impatience that seemed utterly lost on Jandain.

"Pasha wants to run," he commented. "Shall we have a race?"

"Certainly, if you like it. But what shall we have for a prize?"

"Why not a kiss?"

Becca frowned. "Are you so certain of victory, sir?"

He laughed and held up a hand. "No, you mistake me! If I win, *I* shall kiss *you*. If you win, *you* shall kiss *me*! Surely, that's a fair division of wealth."

Becca clicked to Rosamunde and that lady moved out of the stable.

"Very well," she heard herself say as they passed Jandain and Pasha. "The stakes are acceptable."

The white stallion gained an early lead across their impromptu course. Becca threw herself along Rosamunde's neck, and dropped the reins, letting her run.

Run she did, passionate, fleet, and determined, the ground a blur beneath her hooves and her mane lashing Becca's cheek. Together, they ran, they flew—

They gained. Inch by inch Rosamunde closed the distance between them, until she was at Jandain's stirrup. And there she stayed, unable to gain more, unwilling—determined—to lose an inch.

Hooves pounding, they rounded the third corner, heading for the finish.

The white horse stretched, and Rosamunde did, keeping her place, but unable to gain. Becca clung to her neck, exhilarated—and there! There was the finish! Certainly, they were going to lose, but the white stallion knew that he had been in a race, by good seed, and Jandain the Fey as—

Ten lengths from the finish, the stallion checked, slowed—and Rosamunde tore past, passing the fourth corner, and coming around—guided now by Becca's hand—to where Pasha stood, Jandain smiling at her from the saddle.

"You, sir, are unhandsome!" Becca cried angrily.

He laughed, and moved his hand, showing her the post they had agreed on as the finish.

"You and your lady won, did you not?"

"We did not!" Becca said hotly.

Jandain blinked, his smile vanishing.

"You pulled back and let us pass! Did you think I would not see? Do you think that *she* would not know? That was no win, but a cheat!"

Jandain's pale cheeks flushed bright red.

"Do you say I cheated?" he asked in a tone so quietly dangerous it pierced Becca's fury.

She drew a hard breath, and leaned over to stroke Rosamunde's neck. "Swift, my lady," she murmured, "and beautiful. You have spirit, grace and heart, and you ran with all—an admirable race, my lady . . ."

"*Do you say,*" Jandain asked again, as Pasha walked toward them, "that *I* cheated, Rebecca?"

She raised her head and met his eyes. "I do," she said, slightly more temperately "—and it is nothing nor the truth, sir. You pulled up. 'Twas not a fair race." She took a deep breath, meeting his eyes firmly. "You mock my horse, sir, and her lineage."

Jandain's lips parted—but he closed them again without giving voice to whatever he had thought to say. The color receded, leaving his cheeks properly pale, his eyes a glittering deep blue. He considered her for a long moment, then bowed low from his saddle.

"Lady Rosamunde, your pardon. It was never my intention to mock you—or to anger your fair rider."

Rosamunde flicked her ears, and he smiled slightly.

"I see my poor manners are forgiven." He tipped his head. "And you, cruel beauty?"

Becca looked down at Rosamunde's mane, suddenly overcome with shyness. "If Rosamunde accepts your apology, it would be churlish in me to refuse it," she murmured.

"Reprieved," he said, lightly, flashing his wide, brilliant smile that was so different from Altimere's.

"Where shall we ride now, Rebecca? The horses must walk." He jerked his head toward the Wild Wood, looming dark and moist just over the wall. "Perhaps a short ride beneath the trees might amuse you."

Becca shook her head quickly. "I cannot," she said, her voice sounding breathless in her own ears.

"Are you timid of the wood? There's no need, you know. I doubt the Brethren come within a league of Altimere's land. If by chance there is some danger, I will protect you."

"No." There was a high ringing in Becca's ears; her chest was tight, and it was hard to get enough air—"I cannot!" she burst out, tears springing from her eyes. "I cannot cross the wall!"

"Cannot—ah. I understand." Pasha was suddenly very close. Rosamunde began to sidle away—and went still. Jandain leaned over and gently wiped the tears from Becca's cheeks with his fingertips.

"Hush, pretty child. Hush, hush. There's no need for distress. I had not understood. He keeps you very close, indeed. Of course he does; I would do the same, did I hold such a treasure. There, don't cry. There's no blame to you."

Becca sniffed, swallowed, and blinked up into his face. "I'm sorry, sir—"

Jandain lifted a hand. "No need. Come, let us walk the horses back to the stable."

❧❧❧

Meri slept, finally, stretched along the broad branch of a ralif tree, rousing only when a grey whistler sang a shrill inquiry into his near ear. It was mid-morning by then, and his mind was clearer. Sian might well think that she had sound reason to believe that Faldana was but a cat's paw for her ambitious kin. In fact, Faldana *could have been* just that. Even so, she could not have dreamed that she would endure what horrors came to her on the far side of the *keleigh,* nor did anything she had—or might have—done before negate the fact that she had died a hero, granting him the means to cross the border in one burst of power.

That sacrifice, Meri thought, as he climbed down from his arboreal couch, *yet requires an answer. Whatever Sian might think.*

He put his hand against the ralif's smooth ebon trunk. "Thank you, friend," he murmured, and felt a brief warming against his skin, which meant that the tree had heard him.

Well. Meri looked about him, caught his direction and strode off into the trees. He had walked a goodly distance last evening while he struggled with his memories, but he was still on the

Engenium's lands, which meant that—technically, at least—he had not violated his parole.

Perhaps Sian would even see it that way.

He plucked berries as he walked, and broke his fast; followed a silvery giggle to a spring where he drank, and washed his face.

Thus fortified and refreshed, he came back at last to Sea Hold, and sauntered up to the main gate.

The Sea Wise standing guard there looked to be the same who had passed him and Ganat, a small age ago. Certainly, her frown was familiar, and also the ironic cant of her brow as she surveyed him. He braced himself for a sarcastic greeting, but she had better in her arsenal than mere sarcasm.

"The Engenium desires to see you," she said, her voice studiously bland. "Immediately you return."

"Wine and a light luncheon," Jandain said as they came into the house. "On the evening terrace."

Becca wondered if the Gossamers would serve him—and then decided that of course, they would. Altimere had doubtless left word with them, as well as with her, regarding the guest and his comfort.

She considered mentioning that the evening garden did not have its best face on so early in the day—and did not. If it pleased the guest to overlook night-blooming plants in the full light of day, well, then, his pleasure was hers.

Or, to state the case as exactly as possible—Altimere would be pleased that she had cared for the guest so well. And to have Altimere pleased with her was everything she desired.

Jandain stepped out into the garden, Becca at his heels. She noted that the Gossamers had wasted not a moment in carrying out his instructions. Wine, two glasses, and the requested light luncheon sat on a small table between the two chairs.

She was, Becca realized suddenly, quite hungry. Exercise—and the aftermath of anger—were the likely culprits. She moved toward Altimere's chair, but Jandain was there before her, settling into it as if it were his by right.

"Sir!" Becca said—or thought to say. Despite her intention to speak sharply to this man who usurped Altimere's place, she said nothing, but meekly went to her place at the side of the chair and curled up, leaning her head against Jandain's knee.

"Ahhh . . ." He exhaled, and it seemed to Becca that he shivered. His hand dropped to her hair, very lightly, smoothing it where it had come loose during the race.

"Yes," he murmured, perhaps to himself. "He keeps you very close, indeed."

He said nothing else for a time, merely stroking her hair as he overlooked the garden. Becca tried to ask him what he thought of it, in daylight, but her lips would not form the words.

"Are you hungry, little child?" Jandain asked eventually, sounding as if he were thinking about something else entirely.

"Yes, sir," Becca said truthfully, and nestled her cheek closer against his knee, as if he were Altimere!

She tried to lift her head away, to put distance between herself and this stranger—but it might have belonged to someone else, for all the success she had.

"If you are hungry, then it will be my pleasure to feed you," he said, lifting his hand from her hair. "Come and sit on my lap."

As if his words had released her, she raised her head, and waited a heartbeat, but—unlike Altimere—it seemed that Jandain was not going to lift her to her feet. Gritting her teeth, she rolled clumsily to her knees, unbalanced by her crippled arm, and staggered upright, nearly missing a headlong tumble off the terrace and into a silver-thorn bush, showing black and toothy in the mid-day sun.

Disaster averted, she turned to find Jandain watching her intently, as if he had never seen someone almost fall and break their heads open before. He met her eyes, forcefully, and patted his knee, as if, Becca thought hotly, she were a lapdog.

And, precisely as if she were a lapdog, she went to him and sat, stiffly, upon his knee.

Jandain laughed softly. "Such an obedient little one," he murmured caressingly. He lifted a wine glass and sipped, with every evidence of enjoyment, then held the glass to her lips.

"Drink," he murmured, and Becca, who wished to do nothing other than rise, dash the glass from his hand and retreat to her room, meekly did as she was bid.

He sighed, as if deeply affected. Becca felt her face heat, and tried to concentrate on the flavor of the wine—her favorite, tasting of peaches.

The glass was removed. Jandain reached to the tray and selected a piece of cheese, which he held out to her.

She lifted her head without wishing or desiring to do so, lips parted to receive the morsel from his hand. He caught his breath, watching, rapt, as she swallowed, and extended his hand once more, fingers tracing the line of her throat, down to the lacing, leaving trails of fire down her flesh.

No! Becca thought. *I don't—he's not—*

"Fear not, little Rebecca," Jandain crooned, his voice slurring slightly, as if he had drunk too much wine, but—a sip? How could he be drunk on so little?

"I will do nothing that you do not like," he murmured. His fingers ran along the margin of her shirt, and Becca gasped, shaken to her core.

"Do you like that?"

"Yes . . ." she breathed, truthfully, her voice wavering.

"Good. And this?" He touched her breast, covered as it was with shirt and undergarment. Her nipples hardened, and Jandain laughed, low in his throat. "I feel that you do."

He took his hand away, reached negligently for the wineglass, and sipped slowly. Becca, watching him, licked her lips, craving the taste of peaches. Jandain watched her from hooded blue eyes, glass cradled close.

"You said," Becca heard her voice say, small and timid, "that you would care for me, sir."

"And I do care for you." Abruptly, he brought the glass to her lips. She drank thirstily, and when he took it away, it was empty.

"Greedy little one," he whispered, slipping his hand along her waist. Becca's stomach clenched; all at once she felt the urge to laugh uproariously, coupled with a yearning so poignant she felt that she must weep.

"Come closer," Jandain murmured. "Let us find what else you may like."

He tucked her against his chest, her head on his shoulder, and his right arm like an iron bar around her waist.

"Do you like that?" he asked.

"Very much, sir," she said shyly.

"Excellent. And this?" He stroked her cheek with a light fore-finger.

"Yes . . ."

"Ah. And we have already found that you like this . . ." He

cradled her breast, kneading gently, then his clever fingers were between her legs.

It was as if there were no barrier between her womanly parts and his fingers. Becca moaned, bit her lip and tried to hide her face against his shoulder.

"What a rare, lovely and astonishing prize she is." Jandain crooned. "Look how her *kest* burns . . ." He withdrew his hand, and Becca moaned again, as he took her chin between forefinger and thumb and forced her face up to him.

He covered her mouth with his; his tongue twining with hers as his fingers teased the lacing wide and pulled her shirt off her shoulder and down her left arm, the slide of his fingers along her ruined flesh exciting, tormenting— She moved her head, and suddenly it was not she who was being kissed, but who was kissing him, demanding.

Jandain pulled back with a gasping laugh, looking away from her face to stare at her arm, something like awe in his face.

"Land and weather, look upon you, Rebecca Beauvelley," he whispered. "Your *kest* burns like the sun, and you wear the evidence of your power proudly." He ran his hand down her arm, Becca moaned in pleasure so fierce it was nearly pain.

"Ah, and you like that very much, do you not?" Jandain murmured. He moved his gaze from her arm with an effort Becca felt in her own gut, and looked into her eyes.

"We will share *kest*," he announced, his voice a weight against Becca's will; "now and completely."

"Yes," she agreed, and lifted her head, mouth questing for his . . .

"Greedy bird. Let us find a more seemly nest." He gathered her against his chest and stood, striding into the house, and down halls she had never explored, until a door opened before him and he strode in, to lay her on the wide, deep bed.

Chapter Twenty-Eight

IT WENT WITHOUT SAYING THAT THE ENGENIUM WAS IN HER formal hall at this hour. One might almost think that she had known he had spent the night sleeping in a tree.

And what if she did, Meri thought, sauntering down the hallway. He was Wood Wise and a Ranger—and the Sea Folk expected far stranger behavior from such a one than a mere nap among the branches.

Ahead of him, the living stone floor flashed briefly pink, as if Sea Hold urged him to a brisker pace.

"Ah, if only I had the patience of stone," Meri murmured, and chuckled when the walls went dark.

"Well," he commented, coming to a leisurely halt, and crossing his arms over his chest, "this will certainly speed things along."

Pink light flooded the hallway, and Meri squinted his eye in protest.

"Don't you think it might be best if I simply continued at my own pace? At least then I'll be certain to arrive."

The blare of light faded until the walls were suffused with their usual gentle glow.

"Thank you," Meri said, and moved on at a slightly less lazy pace, amused to see that there was no recurrence of the encouraging flickers in the floor.

It was said that Sea Hold never forgot its Folk, and that the rocks truly mourned those who had returned their *kest* to the sea, even as they delighted in births, and teased fosterlings newcome to their care. It was . . . profoundly comforting to find that Sea Hold at least had not forgotten *him,* or the silly game they had devised between them.

. He reached the formal hall too quickly. The Sea Wise on the door didn't even ask his business, but merely stepped aside to let him through. Well, Meri told himself, Sian had left orders that he was to come to her immediately. Certainly she would have told the door—

Two steps into the hall, he stopped, blood gone to ice and stomach heaving, the room blurring out of sense as he fell to his knees, retching, every scar burning as if the chains still wrapped him. He heard voices and braced himself for some new torture all the while the beauty and power of their auras seduced his will and—

"Meri!" Cool hands on his face, quick words spoken over his head, the sound of boot heels on stone, and of the door, closing.

Meri gasped, struggling for breath, but the seductive, unnatural colors were gone, leaving only the cool misty turquoise that was Sian's aura, and the glow from the heart of the stone.

"Meri?"

Slowly, he raised himself, though he would far rather have sunk into the heart of Sea Hold and never be seen again. To have made a display of his weakness, here before Sian and whomev—

"Newmen!" he spat the words, straightening to stare into her face.

Sian sat back on her heels, eyebrows raised.

"Am I to take it that you are recovered?"

"Why does the Engenium harbor one of them?" he snapped, ignoring both her question and her station in the sudden boil of anger.

"The Engenium may do whatever she pleases in her own place and among her own folk," she snapped back. "Meripen Vanglelauf."

"Send it away!" He heard the bleeding edge of his own voice, and took a hard breath, and another, as he touched the elitch branch in his belt.

"Your pardon," he managed. "I—"

"You are distraught and ill," she interrupted him. Her words at least were gentle, and if her tone was still snappish, who, Meri thought, could blame her? Certainly not Meripen Vanglelauf, ruined and useless as he had become.

"Tell me, Cousin, what illness is this that afflicts you? It seems to have passed now—is that so? Shall I call for a healer?"

"I was with the healers, an' you recall it," he answered, and raised a weary hand. "I know you had no part in drawing me away; I merely say that . . . I think I see why I was still bound to the sleep." He shuddered, and took another breath to center himself. "I sometimes . . . experience the . . . memories of my time . . . beyond . . . the *keleigh* as if they were in fact happening, here and now. I—apparently suffered such an attack when I entered the room. It seemed to me that I was seeing the aura of one of the New Folk—"

"You were," Sian said crisply, and came to her feet in one fluid move. She held her hand down to him. "I am pleased to see your *kest* so much restored, Cousin."

Meri did not take her hand. "Tell me," he said. "Sian. Why do you have Newmen at your court? They are dangerous, devious and cruel. I—"

"Do not, I pray you, be absurd," Sian cut him off coldly. "Sam Moore was born on Sea Hold land. He and his owe allegiance to the Engenium. As to why he was here—he came to apply for assistance with his landhold." She looked down at him haughtily. "Would you like to hear his petition?"

"No," Meri said tiredly. He took her hand and was grateful for her assistance as he climbed to his feet. "But doubtless you believe I should."

"I do," she said, "because it concerns you closely." She turned away and walked over to the sideboard, Meri following more slowly.

"Here." She handed him a glass half-filled with amber liquid. He sniffed it. Double-wine.

"You do look as if it might do you some good," she said softly, pouring herself a simple glass of water from the carafe.

Well, and it could hardly hurt. Meri sipped, welcoming the potent burn of the liquid.

"It happens," Sian said, leaning against the sideboard, glass in one hand, and the other thrust through her belt. "It happens that Sam and his folk are settled in a section of our land on which there are many older trees, some, perhaps, not in the most robust health. The Newmen are clever farmers, and they know plants. They have respected the trees, and the land. For all of their excellencies, however, they have not the tree-wisdom.

"And so Sam has come to ask me to send them a Ranger." She sipped her water. Meri, dread gone to sand in his gut, threw the rest of the double-wine down his throat.

Sian nodded. "Just so. You had expressed to me that you wished to return to your fictitious former existence as a simple Ranger, and—I tell you honestly, Cousin—I have no one else to send. Once you have yourself in hand, you will—"

"No," Meri said firmly. "I will not."

Sian raised her eyebrows, and tipped her head, inviting him to go on.

"I will not place myself in the hands of those—of Newmen. I have scars and wounds enough, Sian."

"Agreed. And yet—you *are* a Ranger, and the charge has come to you. Will you deny the trees, Meripen Vanglelauf?"

"It is not possible. You have seen—"

"You were taken unaware," she interrupted, "and given no time to shield yourself. It need not happen again. Indeed, I trust that it will not."

He looked into her face, and read resolution there; her misty aura was threaded with gold threads of determination. He wondered, briefly, if she would compel him—and then knew that she would have no need.

He *was* a Ranger, and the charge had come to him. He could no more deny the trees than refuse to breathe. And yet—

"I will need time to . . . prepare," he said slowly. "Truly, Sian. I do not know if it can be done."

She put her glass on the sideboard with a firm click, and came forward to place her hands on his shoulders. "Meripen Longeye was a strong and canny Ranger. I do not say a philosopher, or an artist, but skilled and practical. Deny him a hero, if it amuses you, but do not deny his strength." She leaned close and kissed him on the cheek.

"Go. Make your arrangements, as I trust you can and will. Come back here tomorrow after you have broken your fast. Sam will be here, waiting."

Jandain's white skin was touched with a rosy glow, as if an hundred wax candles burned at his core; around him pulsed a nimbus of palest lavender. For all of which, his fingers were cool, and clever, and his lips and tongue even more so.

Becca lay in the wide bed, trembling, her limbs heavy, so that she could not even lift her right hand to stroke his hair. Each knowing touch of his cool, clever fingers inflamed her more; she moaned, and cried out, beyond speech, half-mad with sensation, her eyes and senses dazzled, the lavender nimbus deepening, and she reached—*reached* . . .

"Ah, no . . ." His fingers stopped, and Becca screamed in frustration, though she made no sound.

Jandain bent over to look into her eyes, his hair brushing her face.

"You are a greedy, greedy child," he murmured, breathless and unsteady. "But you will—I *insist* that you will—obey the proprieties. Why, pretty Rebecca, you are still dressed! We will remedy that."

Still dressed? Rebecca thought, as his fingers slid over her shoulders, upward, toward—

"No!" she cried, suddenly terrified. "You may not remove Altimere's gift!"

He paused, and looked at her curiously. "Are you so fond of him, then?" he murmured, his voice so low it seemed she heard her own thoughts. "He collars you and keeps you hidden here, whereas I . . ." He bent even closer, his breath hot on her cheek. "I would take you to Xandurana, and show you all the delights of our land, and protect you. Ah . . . protect you . . ." He licked her cheek; she closed her eyes, shivering, and he kissed her eyelids. "Say you will come with me, Rebecca Beauvelley," he whispered, his hands at her throat . . .

Words rose to her lips. "I forbid you," she whispered, and opened her eyes to stare into his. "I forbid you to remove Altimere's gift."

He laughed.

"Stop me, then, mighty philosopher." His fingers slid 'round her throat, tightening, as he sought the clasp—

Jandain cried out, jerking back, hands before him as if he had been bit, or burned. He blinked, and looked down at her, his long fingers curling into fists. The lavender nimbus showed flickers of red.

Fear washed through her, icing her belly and her heart. She struggled against the invisible bonds that bound her to the bed—

Jandain laughed again, low in his throat. He reached down to stroke her crippled arm, she shivered—and gasped as his fingers closed painfully.

"I see the game," he whispered, his eyes like sapphire flames. "You like to be helpless, do you? You toy with me, and think me your lesser . . ."

"No," she whispered, her voice shaking. He was going to break her arm!

He smiled. "Perfect," he murmured. "See her eyes, so wide and frightened. Hear her voice tremble." His eyes moved, as if he gazed upon something just beyond her face. "And her *kest*—see it blaze, and beckon. Seductress." He smiled, Becca thought to scream for Altimere, but her throat closed. She lay there looking up at him, her breath coming in short, shallow gasps.

Jandain's smile widened. "We will share *kest,* fully," he said. "And you will come with me, Rebecca. You will want nothing else."

The kiss was brutal, horrifying—wrong. Yet the familiar molten gold rose from the base of her spine, and her breath came short now with passion. He thrust his member into her mouth and she spent at once, cresting again when he did, and the golden fire coursed her veins and overflowed her.

He brought her up onto her knees and rode her as a stallion rides a mare, his fingers knotted in her hair, pulling her head painfully back; and the room filled with flame. He threw her down and impaled her, again, again—and at last her voice was her own. She screamed, and *reached,* snatching at the boiling violet, while above them the ceiling went to ash, the stars burned gold against the night.

How wise the Engenium, Meri thought sourly, as he watched the moon rise over the sea. For soothly she had said, he was not a philosopher.

"If all the healers could think to do was put me to sleep until I forgot . . ." he muttered.

That it might, indeed, be possible to create a charm that would shield him from the—from Sam Moore's damnable, sickening aura, he had no doubt. There were marvelous things created by the artificers—witness the *keleigh* itself. Alas, he was not an artificer, nor had he any wish to be one. And if he had once possessed a certain small, clever talent, he doubted he possessed it any longer.

Fire and flood! He wasn't even certain that he could best the—Sam Moore—if the Newman turned violent.

Shaking his head, he stepped off the balcony, back into his room, robe rustling about his ankles as he paced.

His leathers had been cleaned and were draped over the chest, ready for wear. How if he simply left now, faded into the woods . . .

. . . forswore himself . . .

. . . and ignored the fact that there were *Newmen in the Vaitura.*

They held land under Sian's aye; they had not been unseemly—and yet they were dangerous, savagely beautiful, senselessly violent . . .

He paused, looking down at the table where he had put out his few possessions—knife, elitch wand, sunshield—and sighed. Surely it was a virtue to travel light, but even a Wood Wise might find this kit scant. And while the kitchen would provision him, even, perhaps so far as a carven cup and small pack of dried teas—he wanted a bow. Badly. Also a rope.

More than bow, or rope, or tea, he wanted some assurance that he might bear the company of Sam Moore and however many of his kin-group he was destined to encounter without succumbing to a fit, wherein he was entirely vulnerable . . .

He frowned suddenly. The elitch branch had not yet lost its leaves; indeed, they were as new green as they had been when stick had first dropped into his hand.

And they were waving—though there was no breeze.

Meri picked the branch up and closed his eye. The scent of elitch tree was strong, and he heard the voice of the elder tree whispering between his ears. *You need not walk alone, Ranger.*

"Help me," he whispered. "Please."

She woke, crushed beneath heavy limbs, tangled painfully in the twisted sheets. Though there was no candle burning, nor fog light in the room, but Becca could see quite clearly by the golden light spilling from her hands—indeed, from her entire body. She did not spend much time in wonder of this, however, but wriggled carefully out from beneath Jandain, pausing for an anxious moment until she was certain that he slept on. Satisfied, she slid out of the tall, wide bed, and padded across the room, casting golden shadows before her.

She went purposefully, but slowly; she was bruised, stretched and sticky, which made walking difficult.

But, after all, she had not so very far to walk.

Only out to the terrace, where he waited for her, overlooking the silver-washed garden. He turned, opening his arms, and she walked into them, her brilliance dulling the garden's glory.

"Yes . . ." Altimere murmured, and bent his head somewhat. She stretched high, her torn mouth questing for his. He kissed her, long and thoroughly, and it hurt, but she could not pull away. When he finally set her upon her feet, there was only the garden for illumination. She staggered, giddy and chill, and he put his arm around her waist to steady her.

"So, *zinchessa,* did you enjoy yourself?"

She shook her head. "I was afraid," she whispered, her voice strained and rough. "He hurt me." She blinked up at him through sudden tears. "He . . . seduced me . . . and he says—he says he will take me away with him."

"Really? Would you like to go with him? It might be diverting."

"No!"

"Then you shall not," he murmured, stroking her knotted hair back from her face, and touching her brow lightly. Immediately, she felt soothed and at peace, her tears drying before they fell.

"And as for our honored guest seducing you—I beg you to understand that you have seduced him—and to good effect, as well!" His arm tightened about her in an affectionate squeeze. "I am pleased, my child. Very pleased."

"I—seduced him?" Becca shook her head. "Sir, he—it was so strange! I felt his will move me, he forced me to speak words that I had no wish to say, and, and—do things that—"

"Nay, nay, you were never so entirely in his power! You sat safe in the hollow of my hand, speaking and acting as was necessary to fulfill our goal." Another slight hug. "I say again that you are a marvel and a wonder, darling child."

"You?" She stared at him in the silver light of the garden, feeling the sluggish surge of horror in her belly. "*You* made me say and do those things? Why?" She swallowed. "How?"

He looked down at her, elegant eyebrows arched. "To further our goal. As to how—did you not give your life and your *kest* into my keeping? Did you not accept the collar? You are my willing vessel, Rebecca Beauvelley, and you do as I will." He smiled at her tenderly.

"With great passion."

Her stomach cramped. She was going to vomit. She was going to scream. She was—

Walking into her rooms, where candles were burning, striking golden notes from the dark wood. The Gossamers ushered her into the bath, cleaned her, dried her, and wrapped her in a spotless white nightgown.

It all seemed to happen from a considerable distance, and to someone who was not precisely herself. She thought, when she finally slipped between the sheets, that she might not be able to sleep, then wondered why.

And then wondered nothing.

Chapter Twenty-Nine

DAWN FOUND MERI IN THE KITCHENS, CAJOLING PROVISIONS FROM the staff. He was either unusually persuasive, or they unusually sleepy; in either case his pack was filled in very short order and he was on his way to the Engenium's formal hall.

He went slowly, each step an argument between self-preservation and duty. The elitch wand warmed his side, and he did not doubt that it would do for him what it might. Indeed, he was aware of the subtle aroma of growing things as he walked on, as if he moved inside a sphere of greenwood. Perhaps he would not fall into distemper merely upon observing the Newman's aura. He very much wished for that outcome.

Even if he managed to keep his wits about him, he was vulnerable. All honor to the sea and to the trees, his *kest* was rising, but was yet dangerously low. If the Newman exerted influence, Meri was not at all certain of his ability to preserve his own integrity.

He stopped there in the center of the hall, hands clenched, stomach roiling so that he was glad he had refused any of the breakfast meats offered him in the kitchens. If the Newman exerted his influence, Meri thought, what recourse had he? A dagger rode in his belt, but—granting the Newman any amount of skill—he would have no opportunity to use it before he was bound to the creature.

Perhaps, he thought, his heart hammering in his ears; perhaps if he sought out his cousin Sian and begged the boon, she would kill him now.

The elitch wand dug into his ribs, and the aroma of green growing things faded. Beneath his boots, the floor flickered, thrice, and subsided.

"Rabbit-hearted, am I?" He put out a hand and pressed his palm against the living stone wall.

Strength flowed from the stone, gritty, chill, and deliberate. Meri closed his eye, feeling his panic cool, and his heartbeat slow. Certainly, there was risk in this undertaking, but he had taken risks before. He knew how to keep watch; and how to defend himself, and if the worst came about—well, then the Newman was land-bound to the Engenium of Sea Hold, who would perhaps not wish to see a kinsman enslaved.

Perhaps.

Meri sighed and took his hand from the wall. His skin gave off a faint pink luminescence, fading as he watched. He took a breath, soothed by the aroma of new leaves, and took a step down the hall toward the Engenium's audience hall. And another, after that.

At the door, he paused for only a heartbeat, to touch the elitch wand, and his dagger.

The door opened; he crossed the threshold—and stopped, senses reeling under the assault of colors so varied and sharp that they might have been cut and pieced into a window. The room swam out of focus, its textures suborned by the blare of color, its reality challenged—

He took a hard breath, the scent of elitch leaf steadying him. The colors faded; the room solidified. At the windows, framed in the dawn light, stood a thin young man in scruffed and serviceable traveling clothes. He wore a beard, as seemed to be the habit among the Newmen; an auburn fringe outlining a square face as brown as Meri's own, from which a pair of soft blue eyes considered him with no small amount of wariness.

Meri took another deep breath and made shift to bow.

"I take it that you are Sam Moore?" His voice sounded odd in his own ears, as if he had been breathing thin mountain air.

The Newman produced an answering bow. "I am. And you are Meripen Lo— Vanglelauf."

"Indeed," he answered, and his voice sounded . . . more substantial now; "I am Meripen Vanglelauf." Another careful breath. The assault of colors was—not fading, no—but he was able in some measure to ignore it. If he concentrated on the broad, brown face, the wary blue eyes, on the scent and the sense of the safety of trees—he could contrive. Already, he told himself rallyingly, he was much improved. Had he not only failed to fall into a swoon, but held rational conversation with the—with Sam Moore?

The Newman licked his lips. "The Engenium is everything that is kind," he said—carefully, to Meri's ear—"and certainly our need of a Ranger is, um. Is acute. But, I would not put the journey on you, sir, if you are ill. She tells me that there is no one else to send—"

Meri cleared his throat and Sam Moore stopped, his face stricken. "She tells me the same," he said moderately, breathing in the calming scent of the trees. He spread his hands. "If the trees need me, then my duty is plain."

The Newman nodded, lips compressed. "I understand. But your illness, sir. I—"

"I am not ill," Meri said curtly.

There was a pause, followed by another plain bow, and Sam Moore bent to pick up his pack.

"Are you provisioned?" he asked as he settled it on his shoulders.

Irritation flared. Did the boy think he was just sprouted—and idiot besides? He thought—and bit his lip to keep from gasping aloud as the room slid sideways, the furnishings pierced by brilliance—no. He touched the elitch wand on his belt, focused his eye on the sturdy brown boots upon the Newman's feet, and the colors faded into the background.

He sighed. Lifting his head, he stared into Sam Moore's face, daring him to say anything. The Newman looked grim, but his lips were pressed together into a straight, pale line.

And, Meri thought, *as it happens, I am not entirely provisioned.*

"I need to stop at the armory," he said, and turned. It was harrowing, turning his back on the Newman, whose belt knife had looked as serviceable as his leathers, his boots and his pack. But there, the blade was nothing more than honest lektrim, such as any Wood Wise might wear, and while the outcome of a knife fight was never certain, Meri need not fear such an engagement, if it came.

No, what frightened him more than the Newman at his back was the prospect of proximity to that disorienting aura. He strode down the hall with an alacrity that another might uncharitably classify as a trot, and heard the sound of Sam Moore's boots striking the stone floor behind him.

Leaf and root, but he could scarcely abide being in the same room with the creature! How were they to travel together?

Perhaps, he thought, it will be different, under the trees.

"Dickon! Dickon!"

She screamed herself out of sleep, and lay coiled in a knot under the covers, sobbing, her throat raw, her body torn and painful.

"Dickon, take me home," she whispered, as kind hands pulled the sheets back, straightened her limbs, and brushed the tears from her face. They held her head and gave her a sup of water, freshened her pillow and tucked the covers 'round her.

"No . . ." she protested, struggling feebly. "I must go home!"

There was no answer, save the soft pressure of a hand against her forehead—and sleep swept her away.

It *was* different under the trees.

Sam Moore had taken the lead, Meri following at a compromise distance; neither so close as the Newman seemed to feel necessary— did he think a Ranger could become lost in a wood?—nor so far removed that Meri need see neither man nor aura.

He had half feared that the strength of the Newman's aura would blind him to the trees. Instead, the sharp-edged colors were blunted under the greenleaf, and Meri sighed in relief. Not only did the bow he had wheedled from Sian's armorer buoy his spirits, but the terrain now favored him. Too, the necessity of focusing to keep the Newman's aura from overwhelming him was less of a burden under leaf, where there was so much else for him to heed.

As he walked, he listened to the stroke of wind along leaf, while the birds sang him riddle-bits of news. There was an art to piecing together sense from bird-song, and he was inordinately pleased to find that he had not entirely lost the way of it. Chief among the news items was his sojourn among the high branches,

two nights ago. A Ranger in the Wood was cause, it seemed, for
some excitement, which made him wonder if it were actually *true*
that Sian had no Rangers save himself to send with Sam Moore.
He had merely thought it an excuse, but if there were no Rangers
at Sea Hold, which enclosed a not-inconsiderable forest within
its honor, then—where were they?

Possibly the trees knew, though the older ones were likely to
become confused regarding time. Meri snorted lightly. The whole
of the Vaitura had become somewhat confused regarding time,
since the artificers had exercised their skill, for the safety of all
and everyone.

Sam Moore ducked beneath a low branch, scarcely disturbing
a leaf. Meri ducked in his turn—and paused, caught by the hum
of the tree's contentment.

Greetings, he sent, politely.

The humming became not quite so loud. *Greetings, Ranger.*

I wonder, Meri sent, *if the one who preceded me is known to you?*

He and his folk are known to the trees.

And he and his folk have your . . . approval?

*They are a joy upon the land, Ranger. And what is a joy for the
land is a joy for the land's children.*

Of which he, Meripen Vanglelauf, called Longeye, was argu-
ably one.

I see, he said to the tree. *My thanks. Good growth to you.*

And to you, Ranger.

He continued, only to find Sam Moore awaiting him at a curve
in the path, a frown on his square, brown face. Meri hesitated,
hand dropping to the elitch wand, but the Newman made no
threat, nor said a word, merely turned and walked on.

Very soon after, he called a rest.

It was early for it, or so Meri felt—and then reminded himself
that the Newman held the route for this hike, and would have
planned his rest stops and night-overs. The spot was likely enough,
next to a swift-running streamlet, and near a culdoon tree. Meri
helped himself to a fruit and sat down on one of the rocks near
the stream, his shoulder to the Newman.

He should, he thought, ask where they were bound, but it was
far more restful to listen to the discussion of the squirrels in
the aspen tree growing on the far side of the stream. Something
about the Brethren and—

Sam Moore cleared his throat and Meri started, the comfortable woodsy scene momentarily lost behind a mosaic of glassy color.

Meri bit into his culdoon, concentrating his entire attention on the sharp flavor. The colors retreated somewhat; the woods returned; and Sam Moore spoke, hesitantly.

"The Engenium said that you had taken harm from—from men, on the far side of the hellroad. I—it is doubly good of you, to consent to help us."

Anger flickered and Meri fought it down, putting his attention on the complexity of smells born on the wood-breeze, the sound of water racing over stones, the feel of the culdoon in his hand. When the world felt stable, and his anger had retreated to mere annoyance, he looked up and met the Newman's eyes.

"I go with you because the charge came to me," he said slowly, "to aid the trees." And if, he added silently, what aided the trees discommoded the Newmen, none would see Meripen Longeye weep for it.

Sam Moore bit his lip, but his gaze did not wander from Meri's face. "I would try to persuade you that—even as the Fey—we are not all the same. There are good folk among us, and ill; strong and weak. Foolish and wise." He paused, his expression earnest, apparently expecting an answer, and prepared to wait for it.

Meri took an irritable bite of his culdoon. Thorn and stone! Was it not enough that he came with the creature? Did he have to converse with it, too?

"There is a saying, among my folk," Sam Moore said quietly. "*A dark heart will tarnish the noblest deed.*"

"And the remedy 'mong your folk for lightening a heart that bears the burden of a death?"

The Newman blinked, and looked aside. "The Fey healers are—" Meri raised a hand, and he stopped, pressing his lips tight.

"Leave it," he said shortly, and frowned as the squirrel's discussion erupted into argument. Silently, he rose from the rock and silently moved downstream, toward a clump of redthorn bushes, their fruits trembling in the breeze.

Or perhaps not.

Meri threw the half-eaten culdoon into the heart of the bush, which burst into agitated movement, accompanied by squeals and complaint. A short, cobby body sprang up and out of the thorns, hit the ground, took a running step—

"Hold." Meri did not raise his voice, nor did he move.

The Brethren stopped and stood as if frozen, growling softly, its horned head lowered, and the tip of its tail twitching. From the side of his eye, Meri saw Sam Moore rise from his rock, and raised his hand, freezing the Newman, as well.

Such power.

"Good day to you, Brethren," he addressed the horned one, mildly.

"Release me," the other snarled.

A non sequitur, or a pleasantry, since Meri had not—indeed, could not—extend a compulsion. Still, it was best to observe the forms.

"Of course, you are free to go according to your needs and will," he said, and paused. The tufted tail twitched, stilled—but the Brethren did not otherwise move.

"I only wonder," Meri said, tucking his hands into his belt, "if you have news."

"News?" The Brethren shook its horns lightly. "What news would you? A High Fey fell off his horse and lay in the road, smiling up at the sky while those of the Brotherhood made free with his pockets and saddlebag. The horse would not be frightened off, more's the shame, and eventually the Fey returned to the saddle and rode on." It shook its head, and stood on one foot, staring up at Meri over its shoulder.

"The Barrens are widening. We lost one of our own down a crack in the earth."

Meri bowed his head. "I grieve for your loss," he said politely, and the Brethren growled deep in its throat.

"The land trembled to the west and south last night. It could be that some trees fell." It pivoted at the waist to stare the silent Newman. "It could be that some trees fell on huts, or gardens, or Newmans."

The Brotherhood were indeed a wealth of information, Meri reminded himself, but they also, some of them, valued making mischief above all other pursuits. He glanced aside, expecting to see the Newman striding forth, but Sam Moore stood where he had stopped, his eyes on the stocky, horned form.

"Anything else?" Meri inquired patiently.

"Meripen Longeye, who quenched the madfire, is back underleaf. The trees natter of nothing else."

"Thank you," Meri said. "I appreciate it, that you took the time to share your news. Is there any service I might perform for you in return?"

"Might be," said the Brethren. "I'll think on't."

It put its foot down, hopped across the stream—and vanished from sight.

Across the clearing, the Newman sighed noisily, spreading his hands when Meri turned to face him.

"What chances," Sam Moore asked, and Meri could see the effort he made to speak calmly. "That it was . . . telling a tale . . . regarding the damage at the steading?"

Meri shrugged, walked over to the rock and picked up his pack.

"Best we go see for ourselves," he said, pulling the straps up over his shoulders. "How far distant?"

Sam Moore shook his head, and settled his own pack. "Two days, walking at a—walking gently."

Meri froze, while the realization that the leisurely pace and early rest had been for *him*.

In respect of his *illness*.

A sparkle of too-vivid color warned him; he snatched at his temper, caught it, and managed to say, evenly, if not with the best of grace, "There is no need to travel gently on my behalf, Newman."

Sam Moore licked his lips. "I would not see you come to harm through me." His voice was faint, but steady.

Meri flicked an impatient hand in the direction the Brethren had taken. "Lead. And do not stint."

The Newman took a hard breath, his various worries plainly at war across his square face. All at once, he nodded, squared his shoulders, turned and led on, moving at a trot.

Meri smiled and settled his bow before following, taking the stream in a low leap.

This, he thought, was more like it.

Chapter Thirty

NANCY DRESSED HER IN A BROWN SPLIT SKIRT AND A PALE GREEN
shirt, combed her hair out so gently that tears came to Becca's
eyes, and put it into a single loose braid down her back.

"Thank you, Nancy," Becca murmured. She rose and shook
out the skirt, eyes averted so that she need not see the woman
in the glass. Outside her window, the day was fine and blue; the
breeze that danced past the curtains bearing the sweet tumbled
scents of the garden below. She yearned to be outside in the day,
to walk among the flowers and take her ease beneath the elitch
tree at the far garden.

And yet—how could she leave her room? What if she met
Jandain and he—and he—

She covered her face, feeling cheeks hot with shame against her
palms. What had she done? She had degraded herself, accepted—
reveled in!—acts that no woman of gentle birth—

There was a tug on her sleeve. She raised her head to see Nancy
hovering on busy jeweled wings, plucking at the cloth with tiny,
anxious fingers.

"No," she said, her voice wavering and full of tears. "I cannot
go down to eat. I cannot go down for anything. Nancy, I am—"
Ruined. In a far different, and far more damning way than—

Nancy plucked her sleeve again, tugging her toward the door,
agitation plain in her small, scrunched face. Becca bit her lip,
ashamed once again.

She had been sunk so deeply in her own misery that she had failed to think about what might happen to Nancy, who Altimere might hold responsible for Becca's failure to attend breakfast.

Nancy, who had been "adjusted" once, and whom Becca had not even had the grace to welcome back into her service.

She smiled, or tried to. "Yes, I will go down. You are quite correct; I'm only being foolish." She took a deep breath. "Thank you, Nancy. It is good to have you back."

The little creature dropped her sleeve and rose, until she was staring into Becca's face. Suddenly, she extended her tiny hand and patted her cheek, then zipped off to some far corner of the room, where Becca, turning to follow her flight, could not spy her.

"Thank you," she called softly, putting her hand over the cheek Nancy and patted. "Thank you."

She had trembled and cringed for nothing; the dining room was empty when she went down and remained so while the Gossamers served her coffee and cheese scones, which she ate, to her own surprise, with a great deal of enjoyment.

While she was drinking her second cup of coffee, a note appeared on the table at her elbow. She blinked at it, wondering why she hadn't noticed, but there—one of the Gossamers must have brought it when her cup was refilled. Carefully, she broke the wafer and unfolded the stiff paper.

The note was written in the flowing script of the Fey, which Becca had yet to master. She frowned—blinked, and the symbols shifted before her eyes, making what had been unreadable very readable, indeed.

My very dear child, I hope this morning finds you well and radiant as always. You will perhaps be relieved to know that Jandain our guest departed while you slept, citing pressing business in Xandurana.

Do as you please today, but pray do not tire yourself. We shall be entertaining another guest this evening; an old and dear friend of my youth. Her name is Sanalda, and I think you will like her extremely.

Once again allow me to express my delight in you and in our association. Truly, you are a marvel, Rebecca Beauvelley. I kiss your hands.

Altimere

*   *   *

It was cool beneath the elitch tree. Becca sat on the bench with her feet drawn up, and her back against the warm tree trunk. The lord's purse and penijanset lining the walk had gone to seed, and there was the faint, musty smell of old leaf in the breeze. The elitch itself showed no sign of incipient autumn, and Becca shook her head, astonished all over again at a land where all seasons coexisted, and the rain seemed never to fall.

Dropping her head back against the tree, she tried to order her thoughts.

While it was a relief that she would not have to face Jandain after—after what they had done together, yet she could not but own that her own actions remained a mystery to her.

She tried to examine what she had done—what she had been thinking, but it was as if the actions of the night before had taken place years ago. The details seemed to slide about, misty and half-recalled. Why, even having met Altimere, afterward, in the moon garden . . .

Wait.

She screwed her eyes shut, battering at the memory, and again heard that soft voice, *Wait. Allow it to rise.*

Becca took a breath, and another, letting her eyes droop closed, and little by little the memory arose: Herself stepping out onto the terrace, golden light spilling from beneath her skin that put the night-plants to shame. Altimere's arms around her, and her stretching up, eager for his kiss. The fading of the light, of her awareness of the night. The creeping chill and pain. His praise.

His assurance that she was safe in his hand, as he suborned her will and forced her to act as she would rather not—and how? Becca wondered wildly. How did he have this terrible power over her? She—

The collar.

She had accepted the collar. Her hand rose, touching the cool stones at her throat, recalled with sudden vividness Jandain reaching to remove it, and the sparks with which it defended its position.

That meant . . . *Did* it mean that Altimere could read her mind? Yes! she decided, cold to the bone; it must! That by itself was enough to make one swoon.

There was, however, no time for swooning, even if she had been prone to such things. She must act to insure her liberty and her safety.

Which meant that she must remove the collar.

She bit her lip. Well she recalled what an ordeal it had been to affix the thing; she *had* almost swooned them, from the pain.

And yet, she thought, while a catch might want two hands to fasten, it was entirely possible that it might be *un*fastened with only one.

She raised her right hand, groping 'round to the back of her neck—

Gasping, she snatched her hand back, staring at the blood welling from her sliced fingertips.

The stones were not that sharp! She had touched them many times, taking pleasure from the liquid feel of the surface.

Becca fumbled a handkerchief from her skirt pocket with her left hand, and wrapped her wounded fingers.

Obviously, she thought, gulping against the rising bubble of wild laughter. Obviously, she would need both hands—and gloves, too—in order to undo the catch. Doubtless Nancy could provide her with gloves, though that meant returning to the house.

She did not wish to meet Altimere before she had—

...before she had...

With no direction from her conscious mind, she came to her feet, her thoughts sliding away like water. She took a step—and paused, an elitch branch tangled in her braid. Patiently, she freed the branch, being careful of the tender leaves, then turned and walked out of the garden, leaving the bloodstained handkerchief fluttering on the bench.

Sam Moore could cover a bit of ground, when he wasn't cosseting the halt and the infirm, Meri thought. Indeed, he had so far forgotten himself as to range beyond Meri's sight, which was not particularly worrisome, as his trail was plain to see.

This was not to say that Sam Moore blundered in the wood, or was bewildered under leaf; indeed, as the leagues fell under their boots, Meri began to form the opinion that the trail was clear because the Newman wished it so, and that matters might have been different had he not wished to be followed.

He was startled to find the Newman so accomplished in wood-craft. Had not Sian said that her band of Newman land-held were farmers, lacking in tree lore? Though Sam Moore must know this ground well, if he was spokesman for his kin-group and traveled often to the Engenium in Sea Hold.

There was a danger, with the aura out of range, in thinking of the Newman as a fellow Wood Wise. He must guard against that, and recall what he had learned beyond the *keleigh*. The Newmen who had tortured them for secrets they did not hold had lived separate from the land, unlike Sam Moore, on whom the trees doted. Still, the thoughts and reasons of trees were sometimes strange, even to a Ranger. He must hold his—

A hard edge of color obtruded on his vision. Meri paused, testing the air, listening . . .

Ahead, was the sound of labored breathing, and whispers of what might have been curses.

Meri frowned and crept forward, his passage displacing not so much as a blade of grass. The cursing thinned out and stopped, the breathing seemed to ease somewhat, though the sound was still hoarse and strained.

Pausing in the shelter of a spinictus bush, Meri surveyed the scene before him.

Sam Moore, on his knees in the dirt, one hand clutching a simple pine, for support, Meri thought, rather than for strength or sustenance. His head was bowed, his shoulders tense.

Had the Newman taken harm? Meri wondered, then sighed silently, and moved away from the sheltering bush.

There was only one way to find out.

"Sam Moore?" His voice was as neutral as years of state craft lessons could make it. "Are you hurt?"

"I'm not hurt," the Newman said shortly, a faithful echo of Meri's bad behavior of the early morning.

"What's amiss, then?" he asked mildly.

No answer. Well, and it wasn't as if he really needed one. It would seem that Sam Moore had driven himself too hard, and now suffered his body's rebellion. The cause for that, now . . . Meri settled down on his heels at some small distance from the Newman kneeling next to the pine.

"The Sea Folk say that a wandering mind steers a wandering ship," he commented. "If you drive yourself to exhaustion, you will come later to your people, rather than sooner."

Sam Moore shook his head. "I know that," he rasped. "I can keep the pace. I just—wish I knew . . ."

. . . if the Brethren had only been about the work the Brethren did best—sowing mischief and discord—or if indeed his home and his folk had taken damage when he was gone away and unable to protect them.

Meri pressed his lips together, and looked about him. The land had changed since the last time he had walked these paths, but it would have taken more years than he had slept to wear away the spystone.

"Near here there is a naked hill of rock—the same sort that forms Sea Hold. Do you know it?"

Sam Moore turned his head to stare. His breathing, Meri noted, was no longer so harsh.

"I know the place," he said. "We bear north of it."

"Let us instead go to it," Meri suggested, and raised his hand as the Newman drew breath to speak. "Agreed, it is out of our way. But we may discover something of your home there."

Sam Moore frowned. "What?"

Meri shook his head. "I cannot say until I have seen," he said curtly and came to his feet. "But I am willing to look."

"No," Becca said, staring at herself in the mirror. "Nancy—I cannot wear this to greet a guest!"

Her maid darted off, hopefully to return with a dress more becoming to the occasion.

This dress—this *robe*—she wore now was modest in design: round-necked, long-sleeved, with the hem sweeping the floor.

The fabric was utterly transparent. It was rather like wearing a small gold-tinged fog.

"I might as well," she said to the room at large, "go down naked."

Actually, she thought, it would be better to merely be naked. The robe somehow . . . put her on display in a way that transcended mere nakedness. Becca shivered, and looked up hopefully as she caught a flash of wings in the glass. Alas, Nancy bore only her brush, which she began to apply in long, gentle sweeps from the top of the head to below her waist.

Becca's eyes drifted shut, and she opened them by main force, staring at her reflection in the mirror to keep alert.

"Altimere *can't* want me to wear this!" she said finally. "I *will* have another dress, Nancy! No more of your pranks."

Nancy fluttered up and down, which Becca took to mean that Nancy was innocent of pranks.

"Fine," she said. "I will chose my own dress." She turned and stalked off across her room to the wardrobe on the wall next the bath, and put her hand on the latch.

She half-expected that it would be locked, and staggered a little when the door came open readily in her hand.

And after all, there was no need to lock the door, she saw.

The wardrobe was empty.

Becca stood for some minutes, staring into the vacant depths. Nancy rushed over, and fussed about, pulling the collar straight, tucking the ends of the belt up, tweaking the sleeves.

"Leave it!" Becca snapped. "I will not wear such a—"

Still speaking, she turned, and walked on bare feet toward the door of her room. Her unbound hair belled behind her like a cloak. The door opened as she approached, and she passed down the hall, to the ramp. At the foot, Altimere and a gilt-haired lady slightly taller than he awaited her.

Becca paused at the top and lifted her chin haughtily. Altimere, dressed in russet and black, his hair caught over one shoulder with a jeweled clasp, smiled at her and bowed, hand over his heart.

The lady—was this, after all, Sanalda, his old and abiding friend? The lady tipped her head, frowning slightly, for all the world like a housewife considering the merits of a particular piglet.

"Come," Altimere said, holding his hand out.

Becca glided down to him, and set her palm against his. He smiled again, and inclined his head, turning her to face the lady.

"Sanalda, I make you known to Rebecca Beauvelley. Is she not exquisite?"

Chapter Thirty-One

"SO, ALTIMERE, WHAT MAD START IS THIS?" SANALDA'S VOICE WAS
light and dry, sounding much, Becca thought as she reclined at
Altimere's side and accepted tid-bits from his plate, like a garden
snake's skin felt. She could only be grateful that the lady's regard
of herself fell into the lines of distant curiosity.

Altimere favored his friend with one of his slight smiles. "Am
I mad, then?"

"I've had occasion to think so, from time to time," his friend
answered. She sipped her wine and set the glass aside. "You would
hardly be a son of your house, if you did not excite some speculation in that direction. But." She raised her head and favored him
with a grave look from silver eyes. "You will note that I accused
not you, but your—project, shall we say?—of madness."

"My project." He sipped from his glass and extended it to
Becca, who leaned forward to drink, though she did not wish
to do so.

He took the glass away, placed it on the table and looked at it
for a moment before raising his eyes again to his friend.

"My project seems to be delightfully simple, with a low probability of discovery. I would be interested in hearing in what way
you find it to be . . . may we agree on 'unsuitable'?"

Sanalda appeared to be giving her entire attention to the cheese
plate. She made a leisurely selection before she answered.

"Simple," she said eventually, "I allow. However, I am inclined to view the risk with nothing short of alarm, and wonder how you can commit yourself to such a scheme. When last we spoke, you had been a man of reason."

"And my reason tells me that this plan, now underway, possesses the twin virtues of simplicity and surprise. It will succeed because it is not possible to harvest *kest* one bright pebble at a time, adding each to the same pile."

"Oh, nonsense, of course it is possible to annex *kest*! It's done all the time. The bedraggled Wood Wise you keep caged in your stables demonstrates my case. Where is he, by the way? The Gossamers were most unsettling to my poor horse. Did the trees come for him at last?"

"In a manner of speaking. But you have imperfectly understood what I am about, Sanalda! What I propose—what I have done!—is no brutish act of dominion." He raised an elegant white hand, as if he placated her. "The stronger dominates the weaker—that is natural law. And as so many natural laws, it lacks finesse." He leaned forward, speaking intently.

"What I will do, with the willing assistance of my pretty child, here, is to detach the merest morsel of *kest*—a single, golden nugget caught in the net of her aura, then transferred—"

"Forgive my interruption of these poetical flights," the lady said dryly. "Her *willing* assistance?"

Altimere raised elegant eyebrows. "Indeed. Would you like a demonstration of her willingness?"

Sanalda settled back upon her cushions, wine glass in hand. "I would like such a demonstration," she said. "Yes."

She raised her glass, and Becca rose, also, uncoiling from her cushion. Facing the reclining lady, she placed her right hand over her heart and bowed deeply from the waist, then turned and glided in a manner entirely unlike her usual form of locomotion to the center of the floor. There, she bowed again to the lady and straightened into an attitude of attention, her right hand clasping her left.

The harp, which had been providing its usual pleasant background music, went silent.

In the absence of sound, and staring directly into Sanalda's ice-colored eyes, Becca began to dance.

She moved gently at first, merely swaying, shaking her head so that her hair rippled and shimmered in the light from the fog bowls. As she swayed, her right hand rose, pinched each of her nipples in turn, and glided in a long, sensuous stroke down her crippled arm to her shoulder, then back, her palm skimming the silky-smooth diamonds of the collar, and descending to her right breast, which she fondled for a time, her hips lazily thrusting, while her left arm . . . her left arm began to rise away from her side. Pain flashed along the ruined muscles, while she pinched her nipple hard, harder, her hips moved more urgently now, and her left arm was at right angles to the floor, fully extended, pain and pleasure woven together, indistinguishable each from the other, and suddenly her ruined arm thrust straight up, fingers pointing at the ceiling. She screamed, falling to the warm wood and rubbing herself against the floorboards until she released, screamed again . . .

. . . and lay there, her face against the wood, strands of hair stuck to her sweaty cheek, and wished to die, then and there.

Even as the thought formed, she began to move again, worming her way across the floor on her belly, until she reached the cushion where Altimere's friend reclined, coolly sipping her wine.

Becca nuzzled the inside of the lady's knee, feeling the liquid gold stir.

"Enough," Sanalda stated, and Becca was withdrawn to rise and sit back on her heels, her breasts thrust wantonly forward against the transparent fabric.

Sanalda turned her head to address Altimere.

"You had said, I believe, her *willing* assistance."

"I did."

The lady shook her head. "You have fashioned yourself a slave. I confess to . . . disappointment. One has come to expect a certain . . . elegance and flair from you, even at your most . . . unsuitable. This—" She flicked a negligent hand in Becca's direction. "—is only sordid."

"You fascinate me," Altimere said lazily. "Tell me what you see."

"I *see* a changeling, unschooled in the use of *kest,* and with an aura bright enough to burn, wearing an artifact with what would appear to be her signature upon it—which I allow to be clever. For the rest of it—" She shrugged. "The artifact compels the girl, and she dances as you will it." A sigh and a flicker of white fingers. "So tedious, Altimere."

"You miss two points of interest," he murmured. "Shall I elucidate?"

The lady inclined her head. "Please do."

"The first point is that this girl—this so rare and beautiful girl—has given her *kest* and her life into my keeping, willingly and without coercion."

Sanalda's eyebrows twitched, and she turned her head to study Becca from cold eyes for a long moment before she turned again to Altimere.

"And the second point of interest?"

"She has by her own choice retained her name."

The lady was so still upon her cushions that she scarcely seemed to breathe, and Becca feared—but then she leaned forward and placed her glass on the table.

"She retains all memory of what transpires?"

"That is correct."

"Do you mean to leave her here when the Constant is recalled to Xandurana?"

"What would be the purpose of that? I intend to introduce Rebecca Beauvelley to everyone, and she will know no lack of company."

"And what will you do, should one of her future legions of lovers compel her to answer questions?"

"She cannot be compelled by another; the collar guarantees it."

"And if the collar is removed?"

"It can be removed only by she who accepted it."

Sanalda nodded. "And if she who accepted it wishes to remove it?"

"Wishes," Altimere murmured, "are not horses."

"I see." She turned again, and Becca lifted her chin to meet those cool eyes.

"I believe you delude yourself, Altimere," she said at last. "This plan is neither simple nor is it likely to succeed. I advise you to give over."

Altimere stirred, and Becca wondered if he were angry, or hurt, but his voice was mild when he spoke. "Do you not wish to see Diathen the Bookkeeper Queen deposed? You had used to want it beyond anything."

The lady shook her head without looking at him. "Indeed, I wish the upstart deposed, the Elder Houses restored to their previous position, the *keleigh* dissolved, and the war that has brought us to this pass unfought." She did look at him then, long and serious.

"However, as we have just agreed: Wishes are not horses."

Altimere said nothing.

Sanalda sighed. "I believe there is a flaw in your work, my friend. May I demonstrate it to you?"

"Of course."

She nodded and looked into Becca's face. "Remove your compulsion, old friend. If you please."

Shame suddenly burned Becca; she dropped her eyes, unable to meet that chilly gaze, and flinched at the sight of her naked thigh, seen through fabric no thicker than a spider's web.

"Look at me," Sanalda said.

This was not a lady who tolerated disobedience, Becca thought, and forced herself to raise her head once more.

Sanalda nodded. "What is your name and condition?"

"Rebecca Beauvelley, eldest daughter of the Earl of Barimuir, of the Midlands, beyond the *keleigh*."

"Attend me carefully, Rebecca—did you give your *kest* and your life into Altimere's keeping?"

Becca nodded. "Yes," she whispered.

"Ah. Why did you do such a mad, desperate thing?"

"He—he showed me two futures, and I—I asked him to save me from the, the one where my husband abused me and I was dying of the cold. He asked if I put my power in his hands and I said I gave him my life and my future, because, after all," Becca finished plaintively, "all I had was my life and my future; it was ridiculous to speak of my possessing the least bit of power!"

"There is power and power," Sanalda commented, and leaned forward slightly. "Nor can a future be given away." She tipped her head, consideringly. "Why did you keep your name? You had offered Altimere everything else. If he held your name, you would at least be free of these things you do as an agent of his will."

"I—" Becca swallowed, trying to remember. "My name is my own possession. Who will fight for it more strongly—I, who have born it my entire life; or Altimere, who has a name of his own which must be protected before mine."

"So," the lady murmured. "Pride."

"Of a sort," Becca agreed, looking down and plucking at the thin cloth. "It seemed necessary at the time."

"I am certain that it did, though it cannot add to your comfort at present. Look at me."

Becca raised her head.

"Now, Rebecca Beauvelley. Do you wish to remove this artifact which makes you only an extension of Altimere's madness?"

The garden, her decision to remove the collar, the sharpness of the stones—had it only been today?

"Yes," she said, not allowing her gaze to wander to Altimere's face. "I want to remove it."

"Then do so," Sanalda said. "I give you the opportunity."

Becca smiled, her right hand rose, snatched the knife from the cheese plate—

And plunged it into Sanalda's throat.

They reached the summit of the spystone by late afternoon, and stood for a moment, shivering in the cool breeze. The zig-zag path up the side of the stone had not improved over time. In fact, it was worrisomely overgrown, as if the Sea Wise had given over minding the stone, and the signal fire he had expected to find stacked and ready to light at need was merely a few sticks pushed into a pile, and a firestarter tucked inside a waterproof bag. There was no sign that the place had been visited by a fire guard in some time.

"Well," he murmured, more to himself than to his companion, who was not listening to him anyway, but looking out over the domain of the trees.

This might not have been, he said to himself, as he slipped his pack off and had a drink from his water bottle, *one of your better ideas, Meripen.*

Still, there was no harm in trying.

"Which direction?" he asked Sam Moore.

The man came to his side, aura blaring and blowing in the breeze. Meri forced himself to stand firm, and not retreat.

The Newman pointed—north and east, where the trees were tall and old.

Meri sighed, nodded, and braced his legs. He moved his patch from his right eye to his left and looked out to the northeast.

An elverhawk toyed with the wind, caught an updraft and was lost as Meri adjusted his sight past the trees, down—down to the ground, where he saw a fallfox trotting along a path, and two Brethren tucked companionably together beneath an overhanging weepertree, beyond—and there was a house.

Or what had been a house. A branch had fallen from the enormous elder under whose friendly canopy the Newmen had constructed their home. There were people about this late in the day, and Meri counted them out, for Sam Moore's sake.

"I see a down branch which has damaged a house," he said. "Two tow-headed boys are playing a game with a stick and a ball. A red-haired woman has a basketful of eggs on her arm. There are sawhorses set up near the damaged house, but I see no workmen."

He winced at the sudden stab of pain through his head, and recalled that using the longeye for extended periods was likely of producing a headache.

He reached up and moved the patch, cutting off the woman, the boys, the house under repair, and finding a carpet of treetops at his feet, and Sam Moore staring at him.

"That," said Altimere sadly, "was unfortunate."

Becca stared at him, screams locked in her throat, her fingers tight 'round the sticky hilt.

"Doubly unfortunate," Altimere corrected himself, and leaned across the table, fingertips brushing Becca's forehead.

"Poor child, you know I would never use you so, unless the need was dire."

Warmth coursed through her, dissolving the screams, relaxing her throat and her muscles. Her fingers fell from the knife to her thigh, leaving wet red smears across the transparent fabric.

"Why?" she whispered, looking into his eyes, that were so wise and so kind . . .

"Why?" he repeated, one eyebrow up.

"Why—did I kill her? Was it like Elyd?"

Altimere shook his head. "Elyd died because he was too weak. Sanalda had to die because—she was too strong. She would have exposed us, and we cannot allow that." He rose, and stood looking down at what was left of the other Fey, sprawled gracelessly against cushions bloated with her blood.

"My best and oldest friend," he murmured. "Who taught me

everything. She would have done the same, were our roles reversed. Well." He sighed and Becca saw a tear slide down his alabaster cheek.

Of a sudden she stood, turned sharply, lifted a foot—

She fought it, hysteria bubbling in her stomach. "No!" she cried. "Altimere, for the love of life!"

"Rebecca, do not try me." His voice was stern, but still she fought—and fighting, watched her foot sink slowly toward the floor.

"Take it!" she shouted, her chest so tight she thought her heart might burst. "I give it to you!"

Her foot completed its descent, but she did not take another step.

"Take what, child?" Altimere came to stand before her, his face sad and stern.

"My name," she gasped, forcing herself to look into his eyes. She snatched at his hand with her bloodstained fingers, but he easily eluded her grasp. "My name—take it."

The sadness in his face deepened. He shook his head. "The time for that has passed. You have chosen, and I admire you for your choice. It confirms that you are worthy of the part you have accepted." He moved an elegant hand, indicating the tragedy behind her. "This was . . . unfortunate. Unlooked-for. And it grieves me beyond the telling of it. Yet, we are committed. We must do that which is necessary to achieve the goal, you and I, and recall our deeds proudly."

He placed his hands gently on her shoulders, leaned over and kissed her forehead.

"Go now," he said, "and sleep. I will wake you, when there's need."

She thought to tell him that she would never sleep again. She thought to tell him it was beyond her to take pride in murder. She thought to tell him—

But her feet were on the ramp, and her thoughts flowed away like water.

"What ails you?" Meri snapped as Sam Moore stood there, face gone pale, and mouth gaping like a landed fish.

"I—it—" the Newman took a breath and forcibly brought himself to hand.

"Forgive me," he said firmly. "I—I had thought you blind in that eye, at the hands of those who had—who had used you ill."

Meri stared at him out of his uncovered left eye. "Yet you knew I was called Longeye."

"Oh, aye. But it is—humor among us to sometimes name a thing for its opposite. For instance, my brother's dog, which would far rather sleep than hunt, and even when roused is the laughingstock of anything that climbs or burrow. The name of this sterling hound being 'Lightning.'"

It did, Meri allowed privately, tickle a certain sense. He judged it something that the Newman did not need to know, so he frowned and shook his head.

"It is not a . . . humor . . . shared by Fey," he said flatly. "Did you attend nothing that I said about the homestead?"

"Indeed," Sam Moore stammered again. "I attended most closely, and I thank you for your trouble on my behalf. The house damaged by the tree is worrisome, but I am encouraged to learn that the hob—the Brethren exaggerated the damage."

"So it would seem," Meri muttered, and rubbed the back of his neck, where the spark of pain was trying to become a full-fledged headache. Three times a fool! He knew better than to look so long.

"Best we move on," he said to Sam Moore. "Unless you need to rest?"

The Newman frowned slightly, obviously put on his mettle. "I have no need to rest," he said shortly.

Meri grinned despite the headache, and swept his hand out.

"Lead on, then," he said loftily. "Lead on."

Chapter Thirty-Two

SHE WOKE ALL AT ONCE, WITH THE FEELING THAT SOMEONE HAD spoken her name. The room was awash in sunlight, but as far as she could tell she was alone—no, even as she thought so, the door to her bathing room swung open, and the coverlet was drawn gently back. It could, Becca thought, hardly be any clearer what was expected of her.

On the edge of the bed, her feet swinging above the floor, she glanced 'round again, beguiled by the play of light along the deep green tiles set along the line between ceiling and wall. The curtains, drawn back to admit the buttery rays of the sun, were cleverly woven into the seeming of flowering vines, rustling now as the breeze slipped by them, bearing the scent of flowers and green growing things.

Her combs and brush were laid out on a vanity to the left of the bed, neat and glowing against the carved blond wood.

Becca took a breath.

This was not her room.

Someone patted her lightly on the shoulder; ahead, the door to the bath moved encouragingly. Wherever she was, the Gossamers at least were familiar, and also the insistence that she rise *now* and have her bath.

Slowly, she did just that, pausing short of the door to spin on a heel and consider the room.

"Where am I?" she asked aloud. The Gossamers could not answer, of course, no more than—"Where is Nancy?"

Silence. Before her, the door waggled impatiently on its hinges. Sighing, Becca went in to take her bath.

It wasn't as if she had a choice in the matter.

Nancy was waiting for her when she emerged from the bath and quickly got Becca into a dress of silver cloth over the sheerest of petticoats before setting to work on her hair. Becca, sitting docile beneath her maid's tiny, fierce hands, looked at herself in the glass.

The dress, she decided, was a ball gown; the bodice cut low and the sleeves nothing more than a few short fluttering silver ribbons. Despite the lack of a stiff petticoat, the skirt was not binding; she would be able to dance. Altimere living retired in the country as he did, the puzzle was who she might dance with.

And that was, she admitted to herself, a puzzle to which she did not wish to know the answer.

Nancy had rolled her hair and secured it with a silver net; diamonds—or, more likely, cleverly cut pieces of glass—made it glitter and bounce when she moved her head. Between it, and the dress and the diamond collar, Becca thought, she looked a veritable snow queen.

"Thank you," she said, but Nancy was not yet done with her. She zipped off, returning a moment later bearing a pair of square-cut diamond earrings.

Becca shook her head, harder than she had intended—and might as well not have moved at all, for the attention that Nancy paid to her.

The diamond earrings completed the image of ice, and snow— rather a stark contrast to the warmly sunny day outside her window.

Becca sighed. "Where am I?" she asked again.

"Why, you are in the Queen's own city, fair Xandurana." Altimere slipped in from the edge of the glass and stood behind her, smiling at her reflection.

He was dressed in black, with masses of snow-white lace at throat and wrists.

"I don't remember riding here," she said, watching his face in the mirror.

He lifted an eyebrow. "You were sleeping; there was no need to wake you simply to exhaust you with a tedious journey."

"Did we come by coach, then?" she asked.

He laughed softly. "Child, the coach is an abomination of your people, not mine."

"So, I rode," she persisted, even as she wondered why this was so important to her.

"So, you rode," he agreed blandly. "Attend me now, my treasure. Tonight, I host a party, and you shall be my hostess."

She felt ill. "Hostess," she repeated.

"In fact and in action." Altimere smiled at her gently in the glass. "The so-ambitious Zaldore comes to *me*, to persuade me to align myself with her agenda and lend my countenance and my *kest* to her bid to unseat Diathen, the upstart Queen."

Altimere, she recalled suddenly, wished to depose the Queen, and so had— She flinched from the memory and met his eyes firmly in the glass.

"So you will join forces with her," she said, keeping her voice even. "And make common cause?"

"For a time, I believe I shall," Altimere said, bending down to nuzzle her ear. Becca shivered with longing, even as she cringed from his touch.

"What is this?" he murmured. "Does my pretty child no longer find pleasure in my attentions?" He kissed her behind the ear, and Becca bit her lip, wanting and not wanting . . .

"I—you give me so easily to others, sir," she said, and her voice was no longer even.

"Nay, nay—those are but necessary sacrifices, to further the goal. I adore you as I have done from the first, and count you the chiefest treasure of my house. It pleases me exceedingly to pleasure you, and I very much hope that you will not deny me."

Deny him? Becca thought. When he directed her every movement, even to causing her hand to—*no*. She took a hard breath, watching her reflection's bosom strain against the gown as she did. *I will not think of that. I will not.*

"Certainly," she said unevenly, "your touch does fire me, sir. I am torn, however, between pleasure and fear . . ."

Altimere laughed into her ear, his hands moving slowly, enticingly, down her arms, until his fingers encircled her wrists. She tensed as his grip tightened, aware that he could snap her bones so very easily . . .

"That is the cruelest pleasure of all, is it not?" he whispered. "How the child has grown . . ."

Abruptly, he released her and stepped back. His eyes met hers in the mirror.

"You grow lovelier, Rebecca Beauvelley. I predict that you will make many conquests here in Xandurana."

Again, she shivered, half in anticipation and half in horror as she rose to face him. "To further the goal, sir?" she asked boldly, and tossed her head.

Altimere chuckled and extended his arm.

"But of course," he murmured. "Everything we do must further the goal."

He stood on the flanks of Mount Morran, elverhawks sporting below him, his breath icing on the thin, cold air. Far out, a league down and many to the east, rose a thick column of blacker-than-pitch smoke, its oily coils half-obscuring the rising sun.

"Xandurana," he breathed, the horror in his belly colder than the arid mountain air. "They're burning the Queen out."

There had been rumors—there were always rumors, and he had not paid any more attention to these than those that had been whispered before. Despite the Mediation and the Queen's Constant, which gave representation to every House and tribe, there were some of the Elders who wished only to have all as it had been.

As if that were possible.

But to burn Xandurana! His heart ached—for the Queen, yes, but moreso for the old trees of the city, soaked in wisdom, who had protected and nourished the Fey since the beginning of the world.

A gout of flame shot high, dazzling Meri on his far-away vantage, and he felt his *kest* rise, burning with the will to aid the trees.

As if he could do anything from here.

And yet—

Looking toward the sun was always uncomfortable, and sometimes actively dangerous. If he wasn't careful he would bring on a debilitating headache and sickness. Still, he thought he might—he must!—risk it.

He placed pack and bow to hand and settled as carefully as he could with his back against a firmly-rooted ralif tree, then moved the patch from right eye to left, to see what he could see.

He was surprised by the gentle disorientation, which was not nearly as bad as it would have been from the walls of Sea Hold or the mast of a ship at sea, for both of those placed him close to the horizon and distracting waves, birds, and sails. No, this was—

Ranger, there is a fog upon the trees of the city of the Queen, said the ralif tree he was lodged against; *and from there are only whispers of dangers, for they mostly drowse who live there. Others seek to wake the world, for this is no storm fire nor careless woodswork you see.*

The voice in his mind was a deep presence. At the same time his eye adjusted, hurling him past birds and clouds of fluff, down, down—and there! There was movement around the base of the smoke column.

Ranger, you have trod my roots since nearly you rose this day. I was a seed before the strangeness that ended your war enveloped our seasons.

The minute movement of his jaw as he was trying to frame a reply in his mind was enough to smear the scene before him.

"After," he said aloud, and pressed his head harder into the receptive bark.

It was not, he realized, Xandurana that burned.

No, not Xandurana.

Rishelden Forest was burning.

The oldest forest in the Vaitura, comprised of oak and elitch, absent the City of Trees itself, the wisest entity known to the Fey.

Meri was sobbing as he looked down, down further, to the very base of the trees, to the confusion of Brethren and Fey and horses hitched to—

Drags! Cut of local tree limbs and branches, and . . .

With horror he saw a horse whipped as the drag behind it was set afire. Screaming, the horse plunged into the forest, and there were Brethren, whipped like beasts, unwillingly loading another drag with brush.

Ranger! The charge comes to you, the tree pushed into his mind. *End this.*

Meri moved his head, the scene so far away jittering in his long sight. He? From here? Impossible.

And yet—the charge had come to him.

Longeye yet uncovered, he groped his way to his feet, found his bow, and set his back against the ralif. His *kest* rose; he exerted his will, and saw the clouds forming overhead, spinning with

270   *Sharon Lee & Steve Miller*

unnatural force. He shuddered, knowing that he would pay for such work, later, and yet—the charge had come to him.

The clouds whirled faster, sucking moisture from Morran's snow-peak. Meri left it to do what it would and looked again, down among the burning trees.

Three Fey standing there in the shade of an elitch, unconcerned as trees blazed and died around them.

Even as he watched, a heavy branch split from the tree, crashing down upon the Fey, leaving one writhing, one still, and one hastily retreating, to snatch up a tool—an instrument of some sort, and turning again, released a stream of liquid fire, engulfing elitch and scurrying Brethren alike, destroying . . .

Someone screamed.

Meri raised his bow, reached to his quiver and pulled out the arrow that he never thought to use. The arrow of Gerild Vanglelauf, inherited from his father and his father before him, said to have been first fletched during the war itself.

His father's word was that this arrow would find any target its archer could see.

He drew.

It was the seeing that was hardest now; as he struggled to pull bow and pour into it all the strength of his *kest* and all the strength of his body—and all of the sight he could.

The cloud he had made boiled down the mountainside, heavy with rain, obscuring—no! There was the target!

Meri released.

The bow flexed, shattering in the aftermath; thunder boomed, wind whipped and rain slapped his face.

Meri screamed, his fingers bleeding, his head afire, but still he watched—watched the arrow find its target, and the rain pour down upon the burning land . . .

He woke, hand fisted in his mouth, face wet with sweat, or tears, and sat up, looking about him at the dark wood, full of the thoughts of trees.

Across from him Sam Moore the Newman slept rolled in his blanket. He shook his head and sat up, putting his back against the tree he had chosen to sleep under.

The trees remember, Meripen Longeye, a voice so deep and resonant that it must, indeed, be the voice of the entire wood.

We remember. And we honor you.

Chapter Thirty-Three

"STRENGTHEN THE *KELEIGH*, THEN!" THE FEY WITH THE TRUCULENT chin shouted. "There's no need to go hunting the grubbin' things!"

"Indeed," Altimere said, so smoothly that Becca thought only she in all the very full room understood that he was irritated. "There are many who agree with you, Venpor. Isolation is strength! We've all heard that cry often enough. Yet what thing, of all possible things, will occur if the *keleigh* is strengthened so that neither Fey nor Newman may pass?"

Venpor frowned, chin quivering. "Why, what *will* happen is that we shall be inviolate."

"*Safe*," Altimere said, with an edge to his voice that made the word seem an insult. "And yet would we be—safe?"

He looked around at the dozen Fey faces, seemingly transfixed by his words. Zaldore alone did not have her eyes on Altimere. She, rather, watched those who watched him, a calculating cast to her cat-green eyes.

"You suggest," another said, "that we would *not* be safe."

"I suggest," Altimere corrected her with a smile, "that *we would not know* if we were safe."

There was a stir at that, then silence as Altimere raised his hand. "Think. If we were to strengthen the *keleigh* so that none could pass, how would we know what the Newmen might be about? They are a clever race, and their devices are cunning. I would not put it beyond them to find a way through the *keleigh*, if they conceived a need."

"Oh, come now, Altimere," Venpor said. "You speak as if they are something above brute animals, which we know they are not."

"Do we? How many times have you crossed the *keleigh*, Venpor, and walked among the Newmen?"

There was a short silence, before Altimere bent his head.

"I see. In fact, you know nothing of them from first-hand observation, and base your decisions on rumor and fear."

Venpor drew himself up, but before he could say something that was bound, so Becca thought, to be regrettable, Altimere put his hand into his pocket and withdrew a watch.

He flipped open the silver case and placed it on the table before him. The gathered Fey bent low to study it. Becca, from her shorter vantage, could see that it was a very fine watch, indeed, with a painted porcelain face, and a hammered silver case.

"Observe this sample of their skill," Altimere murmured. "See how finely it is made."

"May I?" Zaldore murmured, and at Altimere's nod bent forward to pick the watch up. She held it in her hand for a time, gazing down into the face, then blinked and looked up.

"There is no *kest* tied to this."

Altimere smiled. "No," he agreed, "there is not. It is a machine— an artifact. Properly constructed, it operates itself, with no need for continued input of *kest* from the artificer." He extended a hand and reclaimed his watch, turned it over and opened the back.

"Look at this!" he commanded, and his guests bent forward as much in response to the power of his voice as in genuine curiosity.

"Observe the intricacy of the work; the *sophistication* of concept. A beast did not fashion this. Nor is this the least of their works. Do not suppose that they rest with the counting of time. I have seen great metal machines as long as this room, stoked with wood, achieve speeds beyond a horse—even a proper Fey horse!"

"Are they kin to the Wood Wise, then?" Someone—Becca could not see who—asked from the far side of the table. "Do the trees serve them?"

"The machine I saw was powered by the reaction of fire and water," Altimere answered. "Steam drove it. And it was a marvel, indeed, to see how the energy was captured and contained to be released at need—all, *all*, without a candle-flash of *kest* expended." He sighed. "Indeed, I was sorry not to have an opportunity to study it at length."

"What prevented you?" Zaldore asked.

Altimere closed the watch and slipped it back into his pocket. "The device unfortunately exploded," he said. "A matter, so I understand it, of faulty calibration, which might happen to any artificer in the throes of experiment. Lost with the device was its maker, and the plans were taken by the law-givers of that place—for such devices go against the word of the Newmen rulers—and burned."

"A sad outcome," Venpor said, his tone suggesting otherwise.

Altimere bowed his head. "So I thought and still believe," he said gravely. "You speak of *kest* as if its acquisition and manipulation is the mark of a higher being," he continued in that grave voice. "Having seen the Newmen, walked among them . . ." He turned his head to smile tenderly at Becca, ". . . associated closely with them—I would say that it is not so simple a line to draw, between man and beast. And as for power—I have seen a Newman take one wire, bring it toward another—and watched power visibly arc between the two!" He shook his head slightly. "No, *I* would wish to keep the Newmen under my eye, rather than have my reason in rags through not knowing—and being unable to guess!—what new artifact they might be a-building."

He paused while the Gossamers circulated among the guests, refreshing depleted wine glasses.

"There is another . . . difficulty," Altimere said slowly, "with this notion that we might simply strengthen the *keleigh*."

"And that is?" inquired the soft-voiced Fey leaning against Zaldore's chair.

Altimere smiled at her. "Why, that the *keleigh* itself is no simple thing! Would you care for a demonstration?"

"Very much," Zaldore said before anyone else could speak, and Altimere gave her a bow before raising one languid hand.

At once the Gossamers appeared, carrying a thin sheet of highly polished stone. This they placed on the table before Altimere. He, in the meantime, had reached into his other pocket and withdrawn—

A child's top.

No, Becca thought; not precisely a *child's* top. This was painstakingly painted with flowers and birds—more art-piece than toy. Altimere held it up for all to see, smiling.

"A simple device," he murmured. "It does one thing well,

much the same as the *keleigh*. It spins. When the *keleigh* spins, it reweaves and strengthens itself, but spin it does and must, precisely—*so!*"

The top struck the polished stone and spun, the Fey watching breathlessly. It was marvelously well-balanced, thought Becca, for it neither wavered nor bounced and kept on spinning long after she had thought it must fall and stop.

"Ah." Altimere shifted slightly in his chair and several of the groups started. "How pleasant to watch the pretty thing spin, is it not? And yet I fear it is beginning to waver. It will stop soon, unless it has some assistance. You, ma'am—" He nodded at the soft-voiced Fey. "Would you indulge me by insuring that the top continues to spin?"

Pretty brows drew together, but the Fey inclined her head. "Certainly," she murmured and the toy immediately recovered itself and recommenced spinning, tall and true.

"How much *kest* do you expend on this task?"

The soft-voiced Fey looked up, obviously surprised. "Very little."

"Of course," Altimere said politely. "Now, if you would do me the honor, slow it so that its revolution matches the span of a day."

"Matches the—" The Fey frowned. "I cannot," she said slowly. "If I slow it so much, it will fall."

"Yes. Excellent. The top must spin at a certain speed to maintain its position. And in order to spin without faltering, it requires a steady input of *kest*." He opened his hands. "So, with the *keleigh*. It uses energy, and, as we all of us know, it is so constructed that it draws what energy it uses directly from the land."

"Which in turn," the soft-voiced Fey said, "requires energy—or it will die."

"You have been studying!" Altimere exclaimed, obviously pleased. "Precisely that is our conundrum." He looked around at the watchful faces. "The *keleigh* was created as a solution to a problem—a most dire problem. It has served us well, but now, I submit to you, it serves us no longer. And it was our error, that we never considered that the *keleigh* itself would one day require a solution in its turn."

There was a small silence, then Venpor spoke again.

"So, what would you, Altimere? Throw down the *keleigh* and mix blood with the Newmen?"

"Throwing the *keleigh* down is—also not as simply done as

said," Altimere murmured. "And as for the Newmen—they are, as I have said, clever. They might serve the Fey well, if they are put under strict governance. Indeed, they may well flourish under such governance. I see that as a beneficial course for all, and one that does not repeat past error."

There were mutters at that, and it seemed that there would be more questions—but just then Zaldore rose from her chair with a lazy smile, and reached her hand down to Altimere.

"I am sure you have given us much to think upon with regard to the *keleigh* and the Newmen," she said. "But, come, Altimere! You and I must speak in private, if your guests will forgive you."

"Of course." He took her hand and rose gracefully to bow to those gathered. "Pray excuse me. I don't despair that you will find a topic or two of conversation in my absence."

There was laughter at that, and the group began to dissolve into small clumps, while Zaldore led Altimere away. Becca took a deep breath and, recalling her duties as hostess, set herself to moving among the guests.

The Gossamers, of course, were much more efficient than she was at keeping glasses filled and circulating trays filled with savories. As she moved among the guests, Becca began to understand that she was present not so much as hostess, but as a reminder—or a provocation—to those who held her own people in such low regard.

She found that she did not mind playing the part of the provocateur, either. *What right have they,* she thought, as she strolled from the main room to the small parlor, *to declare us beasts? If we possess this precious* kest *of theirs and choose not to use it as they do, does that make us any less admirable? Surely, the genius for mechanics—for art, and for healing, too—surely that is* kest, *only expended in a manner unlike—*

"I tell you," an unfortunately familiar voice said, too near at hand. "She's nothing more than a beast, no matter what the artificer's son may say! *He's* besotted, obviously."

"Altimere, besotted!" scoffed his friend. "The wine has the best of you, Venpor. Certainly, he may take some pleasure in the company of a comely woman strong in *kest*. Who would not? But—"

"Strong in *kest*!" Venpor interrupted. He threw what was left in his glass down his throat. No sooner was the glass empty than the

Gossamers were there, offering a full one in trade. Venpor scarcely seemed to notice that he had received a new glass, his attention on his friend, who was, Becca saw with surprise, the soft-voiced Fey who had grasped the lesson of the top so adroitly.

"That cow possesses no more *kest* than this glass!" Venpor announced, raising it exuberantly, and it was a credit to his nerves—or to the other Fey's deft application of *kest*—that not a drop was spilt. He held his pose for a moment, then lowered the glass, turning slightly so that his gaze fell upon Becca.

He frowned.

She lifted her chin and met his eyes, striving for that look of iced haughtiness perfected by Celia Marks.

"Arrogant beast," Venpor muttered, and jerked his head, calling his friend's attention to her. "If I prove that she's no more than a lower form, will you come speak with Harow?"

"How will you prove it?" the other Fey asked, and Becca admired how adroitly she failed of giving her word.

"By dominating her, of course. Here."

Becca felt an unpleasant pressure behind her eyes, as if someone had pushed at her thoughts. The feeling was eerily familiar, and she was still for a moment, trying to recall—

The second push was harder; hard blue light flashed, dazzling her, spiking a headache. Irritably, Becca *pushed* back. The blue light snapped out; the headache vanished.

The soft-voiced Fey laughed.

"Apparently," she murmured, giving Becca a tip of the head. "She does not wish to be dominated this evening."

Venpor's pale face flushed hot pink, and Becca had no trouble at all in reading hatred in the stare he brought upon her.

"It's the collar," he snapped. "She draws power from it."

"Come now!" the other chided. "If she does, surely that disproves your theory!"

"How so?" Venpor snarled, his gaze never leaving Becca's face.

She met his eyes, defiant, and felt a thrill of fear. His hate was hot, she could feel it. Venpor *wanted* to hurt her—possibly to kill her. She should, Becca thought coolly, scream for Altimere, or run, or—or curtsy and beg his pardon.

Notably, she did none of those things, merely held his eyes with hers, while the soft-voiced Fey said—

"The collar bears her signature, therefore, she created it. And if it was fashioned, as you believe, to protect her, then it is hers, it functions as it should, and she is thereby no dumb beast, but a woman of *kest* and cunning." She shook her head, smiling, but Becca thought she looked more worried than amused. "Give over, Venpor!" she said, urgently. "If nothing else, recall that you are a guest in this house."

"I forget nothing," Venpor grated. "And I say again, without the collar she is a worm, an insect, a *thing* to be dominated by a higher order and used as seems best."

"If you believe that my jewelry in some way impedes you," a voice that Becca belatedly recognized as her own said frostily. "Then remove it."

He will kill you! a small voice screamed inside her head.

Good, she answered herself, and smiled at Venpor.

Wineglass in one hand, the other outstretched, he lunged. She stood her ground, whether by courage or idiocy, she scarcely knew.

There was flash, a sense of heat, a thump of displaced air—and a crash, as Venpor struck the wall across the room, and collapsed bonelessly to the floor.

The soft-voiced Fey had not reached his side when Altimere arrived, Zaldore with him, and a great many people in train.

"Rebecca," he said sternly. "Venpor is a guest in my house."

"Yes, sir," she said, meeting his eyes no less boldly, and felt another, more potent, thrill of fear. "A guest in your house tried to *dominate* me, as is his natural right."

"The lady speaks sooth," the soft-voiced Fey said, kneeling next to the fallen, who was beginning to moan and shake his head. Becca tried to feel relieved, that he had survived—and failed. "He insisted that the necklace gave her . . . unearned . . . protection, wherefore she most courteously invited him to remove it."

She raised her head and smiled at Becca. "With what result you see here."

Altimere, however, was still stern. "It was a great deal of force," he said, as if Becca had indeed been in control, rather than simply allowing the necklace to do what it had been made to do.

Becca did not hesitate in her answer, for surely it was to her advantage to seem to be the woman of *kest* that Altimere claimed she was, rather than a captive to another's will.

"Indeed," she said, her voice cool. "I was concerned for my safety, sir. It is possible that I overreacted."

"She wants schooling," Zaldore commented. "If she cannot control her *kest*, she will do someone a hurt, Altimere."

"So she might," he agreed. "Now that we are here in Xandurana, I shall engage a tutor." He raised his voice. "Venpor, are you hale?"

A moan answered him.

"I'll tend him, Altimere," the soft-voiced Fey said. "He's in his cups, and ought to make his bows."

"You are too kind," Altimere told her. "I thank you."

"No need." She rose from Venpor's side and bowed. "Altimere," she murmured. "Zaldore." She straightened and smiled directly in Becca's eyes. "Rebecca, allow me to express my admiration."

She curtsied. "Thank you, ma'am," she murmured.

"Now that we have put this disturbance behind us," Altimere said, turning toward the crowd that had followed him and Zaldore into the room. "Perhaps it is time to sing rounds."

There was a general murmuring of pleasure at that, and Becca stepped forward, to do what a good hostess ought, and direct the guests to their places.

Chapter Thirty-Four

THE DRESS WAS SILVER WHITE LACED WITH DEEP GREEN, ITS NECK square and modest, the sleeves full and fluttering. Nancy took special care with her hair, brushing it until it shone in the rich yellow light spilling in from the windows, and braided it with a ribbon-thin vine bearing flowers no larger than snowflakes.

Becca stood, shook out her skirt and looked at herself in the mirror. Suddenly, she was cast back to the over-bright ballroom, stifled by the sound of human voices, talking, instruments playing, a cup of wine in her hand and her own voice, low and intense beneath the racket of gaiety, "Show me another choice."

"Another choice!" she cried and began to laugh. A choice where she was not a puppet, entirely subject to the will of another, upon whose whim she thrived or died, with no one to succor her, friendless in a country of savage strangers.

The laughter grew wild in her own ears, while Nancy fluttered about her shoulders, wings agitated, and finally darted off. Becca leaned against the vanity table, laughter shrill now, and her stomach roiling with nausea—

A hand whipped against her cheek, knocking her head back. She gasped, the laughter dissolving into tears, and the Gossamer struck her again, on the other cheek.

Shuddering, she gasped for breath, squeezing her eyes shut to stop the tears. The Gossamer did not strike her again, but she had no doubt that it would, if she did not bring herself under control.

And slowly, she did regain—not calmness, but at least an outward seeming of composure. She pushed away from the table and looked at her reflection. There were no marks where the Gossamer had struck, though when she raised her hand, she found her cheeks tender to the touch.

"Invisible bruises," she murmured, and swallowed the spasm of laughter that threatened again to overwhelm her sense.

She shook her skirt out in order to buy herself another moment, then moved away from the vanity, walking toward the door. None impeded her, and the door itself misted out of existence as she approached.

Last night, she had traversed this hallway on Altimere's arm, her senses disheveled, and she had scarcely taken note of anything but the feel of his arm beneath her hand.

This morning—if, indeed, it was morning, and not a flawless sunlit afternoon—she noted her surroundings carefully, in an attempt to focus her intellect and push that horrified and horrifying laughter further away.

Altimere's country house had been elegant, and appointed with every luxury that an Earl's daughter might expect. The hallway that led to her room had been hung with expensive tapestries, and rich carpet had covered the floor. By contrast, the city house was plain, the floor seemingly cut from a single, vast board, the walls mottled silver-grey; rough, as if—she ran her fingers down the surface—yes. As if the walls were covered in bark.

Further along the hall, one entered a ramp, which executed a lazy spiral along the outer wall. Becca paused on the landing, then turned to the left, meaning to follow the ramp upward, to see what lay above her own room, but a light, invisible touch to her shoulder steered her to the right, and down.

The ramp was covered in the same barklike material. It gripped the sole of the shoe, which was, Becca thought, a good thing, there being no banister to catch at, should one trip. It was a dizzying descent without Altimere's arm to steady her, and she hugged the wall, trailing her fingers along the rough surface.

The ramp ended in the flagged entry hall she recalled from the night before. Here, she had stood beside Altimere and welcomed his guests as they were made known to her. Some names left her memory as soon as she spoke them—the soft-voiced Fey who had later in the evening escorted the drunken Venpor away being one—and others remained with her even now. Venpor, alas, was all too clear in her memory, nor had Zaldore faded.

Becca crossed the hall toward the dining alcove. Zaldore, she thought, was a dangerous woman. Certainly, Altimere was not without his dangers, and he, too, wished to depose his Queen, though for what cause Becca could not have said.

Zaldore, however, wished to *be* Queen, and for a specific purpose. Becca shivered and paused on the threshold of the dining room, glancing sharply to the right and left—but the room was empty, save for some covered dishes steaming gently on the table.

She forced herself to enter, to approach the table, and sit on the bench that seemed to grow out of the wall. No low table, dining cushions, and thickly carpeted floor here. There was a harp in the far corner of the room, but it was silent this morning, as it had been last night.

Her coffee was poured, the precise amount of cream that she preferred was added. Becca leaned back, sipping the hot beverage gingerly; savoring the bitter warmth.

She rested her head against the rough wall and closed her eyes. Once again, she saw the vision that Altimere had shown her—her *other choice*. How stupid had she been, she wondered now, to ask him to show her only one more? Surely, where there were two choices, there were three? And if there were three, then certainly there were four, five, six—until one achieved an infinite number of Beccas, each making her own unique choice, each leading to—a unique and special torment.

She shook her head against the wall. No, she told herself carefully. Surely—*certainly*—some of those infinite Beccas had made happy choices. Why! Perhaps, somewhere, there was a Becca who had chosen not to accept Kelmit Tarrington's offer of a ride, and who was now whole in spirit, heart, and body, married and—

Her face was wet. Hastily, she leaned forward, placed the cup carefully in its saucer, and caught up a napkin to dry her tears, wincing when she patted bruised cheeks. When she had done and opened her eyes again, she saw that her plate had been filled for her with the pastries she had so loved at the country house, and thin crisp strips of bacon. The Gossamers meant for her to eat, no matter how troubled her heart. Nor should she, Becca reminded herself as she picked up a pastry, think hardly of them for this. After all, they received their orders from Altimere, as Nancy did, and Elyd had . . .

As she did.

The pastry was too sweet; she swallowed coffee too hastily, to clear her mouth, and burned her tongue. Gasping, she shook the tears of pain away, and reached again to her plate.

The bacon, at least, was just as always, waking a hunger she would have sworn she did not feel. In the end, she ate four strips of bacon and a piece of toast brought by the Gossamers, and drank another cup of coffee.

She was not prevented from leaving the table afterward, though she was guided away from the library, and down a hall she had not previously traversed, to a strong wooden door at the end of it.

As upstairs, the door misted into nothing when she approached and she stepped out into a garden.

The garden.

The glimpse in the wine cup had not been the half of it. She had never seen such a multitude of flowers, all in full rioting bloom. There was a narrow pathway, but it had been ceded reluctantly; there were portions only a few steps beyond the door that were covered in flowers. Among the flowers grew trees, noble branches arcing against the flawless pale sky, casting shade and shadow amidst the crowds of color. The air was rich with the perfume of growing things and there was a constant murmur of sound—bees and birds, surely, gilding another, deeper sound, which might have been the voices of the trees themselves.

Her spirit rose. She stepped onto the path, moving carefully lest she crush a blossom. The gradials, sunbursts, and other tall sun-lovers for which she had no names, bowed their heavy heads as she passed, chickadees came to her shoulder and exuberantly declared themselves, their sharp toes pricking through the thin fabric to her skin, and flew off again, calling out to their less bold kin. Low-hanging branches stroked her sleeves as she walked, and she heard a murmured low welcome . . .

Her senses reeled, but she pressed on, deeper into the riot of growing things, and eventually she came to a bench. She sank onto it with gratitude and never a thought for her fine dress or fragile sleeves, closed her eyes and listened to the voice of the garden.

The birds, the bees, the wind, filtered through green leaf . . .

Welcome, Ranger.

"I thank you," Becca murmured, "for your welcome. But I am no Ranger."

Indeed she is not, a different voice said.

Or not precisely, a third put in, while the first asked, *How shall we call you?*

"I'm a gardener," she whispered, feeling her throat close with longing for her own dear wild garden, never—not a tenth!—as wild or as glorious as this!—"An herbalist."

Gardener, she's a gardener, the trees told each other, the words moving on the breeze.

Becca smiled and took a breath, drawing the scents and the strength of growing things deep into her lungs.

Possibly, she dozed. Certainly, the chickadee that landed on her shoulder and shouted into her ear thought so.

One comes, the deep voice that had first spoken to her said, *seeking you, Gardener.*

Altimere? Her heart pounded and she rose, turning—and froze, her body no longer her own.

The garden had gone silent; she heard the quick, light step clearly. The flowers parted and she came forth, long, white hands outstretched.

The soft-voiced Fey from the evening before; she who had not wished her name to be recalled.

Her eyes were so blue that they seemed purple, there in that place awash with color, and they crinkled at the corners when she smiled.

"In the heart of the garden, I find the bloom that puts the rest to shame," she said, with the air of one quoting poetry.

Becca lifted her chin. "Pretty words," she—she, herself!—said. "From one who did not trust me with her name."

The Fey's smiled deepened as she stepped forward. "What can my excuse be, but that at the beginning of the evening I did not know who you were? By the end of the evening, precious flower, I regretted my lack of courtesy very much indeed."

"And so you have come to make amends?" Again, her own words, spoken by her own will. A wild flicker of hope sprang up in Becca's breast as she gazed into the pale and lovely face. Surely, so noble a woman, gifted with so quick an intellect, surely, were she appealed to directly...

"I have come," she murmured, her blue, blue eyes intent on her face, "to propose that we two share *kest*."

Becca opened her lips, "Help me," she said—rather, she willed to say.

"You have Altimere's permission, of course," her voice said haughtily, and the nameless Fey laughed.

"Altimere is thought to be the deepest and most powerful of all the Queen's Constant," she said, bending down to take Becca's left hand. "It is a reputation not undeserved. But if he will leave a treasure so lightly guarded, then he must pay the consequence. Do you not agree?"

She pushed the sleeve up off Becca's ruined arm, her breath quickening as the damage was fully revealed.

"Enchantress, tell me that we may share, now, here, and fully. We will both be the stronger for it, and I swear to pleasure you as no other."

"There is," Becca murmured, her knees trembling as cool fingers continued to caress her arm, "a toll."

The Fey moved her eyes with an effort, and focused on Becca's face. "A toll?" There was stern pride in her voice, and a certain cool amusement. "Name your toll, fair tormentor, and I will decide if it is too dear."

Becca stepped back, pulling her arm away, and the Fey allowed her to escape.

"I still lack your name," she said sternly. "Is this how the High Fey in Xandurana share?"

The Fey women threw back her head and laughed, then dropped to one knee on the pathway, recapturing Becca's hand, and raising it to her forehead.

"I am Benidik, woman of power. Remember me."

"Certainly," she said coolly, "I will remember your name." But her right hand moved and stroked her pale hair, belying the coolness of her voice.

Benidik laughed again, softly, and raised her head, looking up into Becca's face. "Is that a challenge?"

"If you wish to hear it so," her voice said.

Benidik pressed her lips against Becca's left hand.

Still on her knees, her hand pushing the sleeve back slowly, her lips traveled up Becca's ruined arm, paused a moment to use her tongue on the sensitive skin inside the elbow and continued. Becca shivered where she stood, her head tipped back in pleasure. The garden was gilded in light, as if an aurora danced among the leaves.

Benidik's lips reached her shoulder; she nuzzled Becca's flesh, and looked up, blue eyes dazzled.

"Already, we take fire from each other," she said, her soft voice husky. "I begin to see why Altimere keeps you hard by him." She smiled. "You tremble, woman of power."

"I tremble," Becca answered, and her voice trembled, too, "with desire."

"We are well matched, then," Benidik murmured, and slid her hand slowly down Becca's arm, letting the sleeve fall. "And yet we must be certain that we do not stint each other..." Her hands slipped beneath the white skirt, cool palms skimming Becca's limbs, her thighs, lifting the fabric until she suddenly leaned forward, head and shoulders beneath the skirt, hands gripping Becca's buttocks tightly, and her mouth, her tongue—

Becca cried out, and the garden melted away in waves of desire.

They lay tangled among the flowers, Benidik's alabaster skin slick with sweat, her form outlined in a blue as deep and flawless as the sky. Becca kissed her breasts, feeling the other woman's desire as if it were her own. The cool hands were warm now, urgent, but Becca resisted her urgency, teasing, drawing out the moment to the final sharing, feeling their pooled *kest* build, interweaving into a fabric made wholly of light and spirit.

The garden crackled, green power interweaving into what they made between them, sharing, strengthening . . . strengthening, and it seemed that they would melt together in the conflagration of their need, and from the ashes rise a new and marvelous creature neither Fey, nor human, nor plant, but partaking of the excellencies of all.

In the heart of the conflagration, Becca found her voice.

"You must swear," she said, and there was no pride, but only naked need in Benidik's voice when she answered,

"I swear!"

"When we have shared, you will take me away," she gasped, fighting her desire—her *need*—for culmination, for union, fighting the will that drove her, and that locked her voice, too late, into her throat.

"I will," Benidik gasped. "On my name, which you know!"

There was no more waiting then. Around them, *kest* burned the air, and the very ground reverberated with their passion, as they shared, and melded, and shouted aloud with one voice, fulfilled.

Chapter Thirty-Five

ONE COMES, GARDENER.

The deep voice roused Becca from her drowse against Benidik's shoulder. She stirred, and was abruptly yanked to her feet, muscles protesting.

"Benidik!" her voice cried. "Altimere is come! You must away!"

The Fey was awake and on her feet between one moment and the next, full clad in the third, her smile in place, and an arm around Becca's naked waist, turning her away from the house, down toward the unexplored bottom of the garden.

"Come," she said. "We shall go through the Queen's Day Garden."

"Rebecca!" Even muffled by leaf and flower, Altimere sounded angry, and it was in Becca's heart to run.

Instead, she shrank from her escort, and pushed her away.

"Go!" she hissed. "I would not have him harm you!"

Benidik laughed and shook her head, silvered hair flying.

"Foolish child," she said fondly. "But go I shall, remembering my promise. I will return, precious flower, and bear you away. You have my oath and my name on it!"

She bowed, kissed her fingers to Becca and was gone, vanished into the garden like one more blossom.

"Well," Altimere said from quite near at hand, "that went . . . differently than I had planned."

Because she must, Becca turned. Fear thrilled through her, and the garden went grey around her.

Courage, Gardener, the tree's raspy voice said. *We will keep safe what is yours.*

Altimere strolled into sight down the reluctant path. He paused to gaze down upon the flowers that had been their bed, and Becca felt her heart quail in her breast.

"That was . . . rather surprising," Altimere said to the crushed and fragrant flowers. He raised his head and looked into Becca's eyes, and if not for the grip of his will she might have swooned at the anger she saw there.

"Would you abandon me, Rebecca? You find the noble Benidik more to your taste? Now that she has what she desires from you, do you imagine she would treat you as well as I do? That she would treasure you and hold you as closely?"

She stared at him, shaking, her skin pebbling in the breeze.

"You make a fine picture," he commented coldly, "smeared with leaves, crushed flowers, and berry juice. If my patronage wearies you, perhaps I will give you to my good friend Venpor." He cocked an eyebrow. "Well? I give you leave to speak."

It was true; her voice was her own.

"Altimere," Becca gasped. "For the love of breath, what is this if not domination? You make me a stranger to myself; my actions are not my own! I bear the burden of deaths I never desired! I am nothing more than a knife to your hand, a—"

"Silence."

The collar tightened around her throat; her voice choked out.

"I see my error," Altimere continued. "I have assumed that you might hold the goal as high as I did, myself. You gave your power into my hands, you retained your own name. By these actions, I chose to see that you had the ability to understand what must be accomplished, and the courage to sacrifice yourself to necessity."

Becca struggled. The collar was uncomfortably tight, but not so much that she could not breathe. And if she could breathe, then surely—

"Altimere—" she said, her voice a thin croak.

His eyebrows rose. "This is extraordinary. Last night, you challenged my dear friend Venpor, provoking an incident. This afternoon, you plead with the so-noble Benidik to bear you away. Even now, you defy me. I am impressed, Rebecca Beauvelley."

Hope stirred. Perhaps, Becca thought, he would forgive her. Perhaps—

Altimere stepped forward; at the same instant, Rebecca crashed to her knees, her head wrenched back on her neck until the muscles screamed. He looked down on her, his face devoid of expression.

"You will surrender what was harvested in my name," he said. "It need not be as pleasant as a kiss."

Trapped on her knees, unable to move, she stared up into his face, seeing a mist of pale gold rise, and take shape—a scythe, or a hook or—

The hook plunged, set into the core of her, and began to pull. Pain threw the world into blackness. She bled joy, love, memory as the burnished fire at the base of her spine was dragged out, thread by fiery thread.

Becca screamed and *pushed,* fighting the loss as she had fought Jandain's domination. She screamed again—and could not. The collar was tight, tightening; she gasped for breath, and still it tightened, her body's anguish overriding the horror. Names swirled away in a blood-red mist, faces, once dear, faded and were lost. She *pushed* again, with everything she had left—

The pain ceased. She lay in the dirt, twisted, naked, and sobbing for breath. Altimere was gone.

Be at ease, Gardener, the tree murmured. Slowly Becca caught her breath, though the collar remained too tight around her bruised throat, while around her the garden took up its interrupted rhapsody. She lay where she had fallen, and could think of no reason to rise. Surely, she thought, she was bleeding; impossible that the rape she had just suffered had left no mark upon her.

The lightless ones approach, Gardener. The tree's voice roused her from a dream or hallucination in which she wandered the night-time streets of the city, ragged and miserable, only to spy Irene being handed down from her carriage before a brightly lit house. Strains of music came from the windows, and the sounds of animated conversation. She rushed up to her friend, knowing that she had found the one person in the world who would not shun her, who would love her and care for her, no matter what she had done.

"Irene!" She thrust past the coachman, leaving the rag she called her cloak in his hand, but she had no care for that because Irene would take care of her. Sobbing with joy, she placed her hand on her friend's shoulder. "Irene!"

The woman turned, there was her dear face, shocked, as of course she would be, but any moment she would realize—

Becca trembled, smiling. "It's Becca," she whispered, and saw horror in her friend's face before she was snatched away among a babble of men's voices and pushed out into the street, while hands groped her nakedness, and patted her head.

She cringed, sobbing, but the Gossamers were stronger than she. They lifted her, gently, despite her struggles and cries, and bore her down the path, into the house and up the ramp to what she groggily realized was her room.

A bath had been drawn. She was slipped into the water, and here came Nancy to undo the braid, while the Gossamers bathed her, their touch as soft and as sweet as any woman's.

Sometime during their ministrations, she lost consciousness, and awoke to her full senses in bed, wrapped in a crisp, white nightgown, reclining in the embrace of a multitude of pillows. The bed was softly illuminated; the room beyond was dark.

At the bottom of the bed, half in shadow, was Altimere.

Becca shrank back against the pillows. He smiled, sadly, and shook his head.

"There, child," he said softly. "I allowed my anger to have its rein, and I have lost your trust. How could it not be so? Truly, you deserve better of me. Now that I am no longer blinded by anger, I see how well you have served the goal. Venpor's set-down, the plea to Benidik—both can be used to advantage. Yes, child, you serve me well, and I am pleased with you."

"You *did* send Benidik to me," she murmured, and felt some fragile flower she had nurtured in her breast wither.

"I allowed it to be possible for her to think she had stolen access to you." Altimere laughed gently. "There is nothing the noble Benidik loves so much as thinking she has gotten away with a theft." He was silent, then continued thoughtfully.

"She is a Fey of great power, and also of some cunning, to have left so little of her *kest* to be harvested. She must guard herself more closely than I had thought. Still, the matter is well-ended. I shall put that promise to good use, I think. How clever of you, *zinchessa*, to obtain it."

As always, his voice soothed her, and his words were fair—but the memory of the garden, the violation of her spirit . . .

"I also see that I have not served you as well as I might." He moved forward and sat on the edge of the bed. Smiling softly, he took her left hand and held it between both of his.

"The plan—the goal—it is complex. Even Fey have difficulty understanding the scope of what I would accomplish. Small wonder that you find yourself adrift, making wild throws that—though they have thus far proved to our fortune—might well endanger everything."

She searched his face, but all she saw there was tenderness, and a lingering sadness. "You have already punished me," she said, and was ashamed to hear how her voice shook.

He bowed his head. "I wish you will forgive me that display. It was ill-done." He looked back to her face. "There is nothing here of punishment, *zinchessa*. Merely, I wish to take from you that burden which, in my thoughtlessness, I required you to bear. You have been eloquent in your willingness to do your part, and for that I have and continue to honor you. The error lies—again!—with me. Relative to those others I have known across the *keleigh,* you are strong; your spirit adamantine. But you are not Fey. It is my shame and my sorrow that I forgot that, Rebecca, and so caused you to suffer."

"But," she said, honestly bewildered. "What will you do?"

"I will no longer burden you with these periods of solitary thought during which you weave your own clever variations upon our theme. I had thought that the sleep—but no matter. I am determined to rectify all of my errors and make myself worthy once again of your trust."

Becca licked her lips. Surely he could not mean—but, yes, it was possible. If he could lock her to his will at whim, what prevented him from extending that power?

Nothing, she answered herself. The diamond collar made all possible. And she had willingly accepted it, vain fool that she was.

"Altimere," she said, leaning forward and daring to touch his sleeve. "I—I am flattered by your care and protection, but this—you ask too much of yourself," she improvised wildly, wondering why she had not understood until this instant that he was mad. "To be forever in—in my thoughts. Would it not be better to remove the collar, and allow me to go home? You have made great gains. Councilor Zaldore courts you, little guessing that you are her master. She does not guess that your plan, so carefully made, is the plan that will see success. You are beyond what poor assistance I can give you."

He smiled and shook his head. "That is where you are wrong, *zinchessa*. I need you now more than ever before." His smile grew wistful, and he leaned forward, voice dropping to a whisper that, aleth help her, thrilled along her nerves.

"I will tell you a great secret. The inclusion of yourself into the plan is itself a variation, for how could I plan on—how could I dare hope that there existed on the face of this sickening earth—the precious treasure who is Rebecca Beauvelley? Now that you have been woven into the pattern, you cannot be unwoven without doing violence to the whole."

Becca drew a deep breath.

"The necklace," she said, as steadily as she was able. "Altimere. You must remove the necklace."

He bowed his head. "If you wish to remove it, *zinchessa*, then do so. I impede you in no way." Gently, he placed her left hand on her lap and folded his hands upon his knee.

She stared at him, the blood gone to ice in her veins. "You know I cannot."

He raised his head; his face was calm, his eyes reflecting only sadness. "And yet, you placed it and sealed it, of your own will and power."

Well she recalled putting the necklace about her neck, the pain, the wild sense of exhilaration.

"Very well," she said. She sat up against the pillows, concentrated, and began to raise her left hand.

It was agonizing work; though she used her good hand to force it up, the ruined muscles could not suffer the strain. At last she rested her left hand on her left shoulder, fingers gripping the fabric of her nightgown. She screwed her eyes shut, feeling the sweat running her face, raised her right hand and took hold of the edge of the clasp. The left hand inched its way toward the collar, pulling itself along by tiny pinches of fabric.

An eternity passed, the arm on fire, and Becca weeping, but at last, the weak fingers touched the clasp. She rested then, the silver warm against her skin, her heart beating joyously against the burning pain. She would do it! Only a moment and a push, like so—

Her fingers fumbled, slid, she grabbed wildly for the nightgown— and every muscle in her ruined arm spasmed.

Becca screamed, her body jackknifed, curling 'round the agony in her arm. She felt a hand on her hair, stroking softly. The fire in her arm slowly cooled, the aftermath of pain leaving her drowsy and wistful.

"There, do you see?" Altimere murmured. "You do not truly desire to leave me, to abandon the plan. This is merely a passing distemper, brought on by being alone too often with your thoughts, in a strange country, where the customs are not known to you. My error lay in failing to take your full nature into account. I had simply assumed that you would—but there. I was wrong. I will make restitution. My eye is upon you, my hand ever raised to protect you."

"Altimere, I beg you—"

"Hush," he said gently, and leaned over to kiss her brow. "Sleep now."

Becca slept.

Chapter Thirty-Six

THEY CAME INTO THE NEWMAN VILLAGE AT DUSK, WHEN THE STAR moths were just beginning to flutter beneath the thicker leaves, stitching the shadows with silver.

Meri walked a prudent distance behind Sam Moore, so that his lesser aura was not obscured, and began to feel the local trees take notice. They would, of course, have known of him and his mission; the thought would have begun moving from tree to tree the instant he came under leaf, until the whole of the forest was aware. But travel and arrivals were concepts that trees—even elder trees—accommodated uneasily, so that his actual presence came as a surprise.

They knew him now, though, and their voices clamored for his attention, like so many children plucking at the sleeve of a favorite uncle, who has come late to a gathering. He ought, of course, to answer the welcome in fullness—and would, soon.

As soon as he found whether he would succeed in the trial that was about to overtake him. While it was true that he had come to tolerate proximity to Sam Moore with scarcely any discomfort at all, so long as he kept himself centered upon the trees, or the earth, or the air. He did, however, very much doubt his ability to maintain that concentration in the presence of—*a number*—of auras, each exciting his newly rising *kest*.

Welcome, Ranger, a strong voice intruded into these thoughts.

Meri sighed, and stopped in the shadow of the ancient elitch tree, letting his guide go on ahead.

Elder, I thank you for your welcome. Indeed, the welcome of this grove lifts my heart.

We lift your heart, the elitch commented, *but we do not free you of fear.*

I have heard it said that each man must master his own fears, Elder.

The elitch did not answer immediately, which was perhaps just as well.

"Sam!"

The glad cry came from up ahead, followed by others, accompanied by such a rush and chaos of color that the dusky sky took fire from it. The land lurched under his boots, and it seemed to Meri that the tide had rushed far inland, bearing him up upon its shoulders, drowning out the voices of the lesser tress, obliterating leaf and land.

"Tremor . . . tree . . . Gran . . ."

The wave crashed, thrusting him against the broad, rough trunk of an elitch. Meri twisted, got his back to it and braced himself.

The air around him burned with power, drawing his *kest,* filling him with a desire to embrace that which was not himself; to share, to achieve completeness.

No. He concentrated: The weight of the pack on his back; the breeze that stroked damp cheeks; the scent of sea and salt marsh; the voice of the elitch tree inside his head . . .

Be at ease, Ranger; there is no danger here. These folk have lived beneath our branches. We know them. We honor them.

Faldana screamed, her voice raw with agony; the glorious, seductive auras bathed the walls, piercing him with longing even as horror froze his heart.

Not here, Ranger. Not these.

The noise of Newman voices faded; the colors became less immediate, and easier to ignore.

Meri felt his knees give and allowed himself to slide down the broad trunk, his pack catching on the rough bark, until he was sitting on the cool ground beneath the tree, alone except for the whisper of breeze, the small murmur of the night wood . . .

. . . and an aura of a faint, delicate green, cool, misty, and soothing.

Another Wood Wise. Meri sighed in exquisite relief. Sian had not utterly abandoned him, after all.

He opened his eye, the greeting rising to his lips.

Crouched before him was the merest sprout—hair a riot of leaf-brown ringlets in which a twig was caught there and here, his clothing scuffed and grubby. His eyes were agate blue, startling in the brown face. Surely, thought Meri, a youth of the Wood Wise.

Surely, the elitch spoke dryly inside his head, *a son of the land.*

Meri considered that, and extended his poor store of *kest*, only a little, wisping a tendril toward that delicate aura—and yanking back with a barely suppressed hiss as the contact sparked.

"You're the tree-man Sam went to fetch, aren't you?" the sprout inquired, seemingly oblivious to what had just occurred. "I heard the Old Ones welcome you."

"That's right," Meri answered, slowly, and extended a cautious hand. The sprout surrendered his grubby paw with a grin.

"I am Meripen Vanglelauf, of the Wood Wise."

The boy tipped his head, but did his part courteously enough. "Jamie Moore, of New Hope Village." He lifted his hand away. "The trees call you Meripen Longeye."

"That's another of my names," Meri agreed, as the trees volunteered something of the sprout. "This concept is not unknown to you, as I learn that you are properly called James."

Jamie Moore sniffed. "*That* depends on who you ask," he commented, a small edge to his burry boy-voice. Meri inclined his head.

"That is how it is with names, after all. And, as you had asked me, I gave the name I wish to be known by."

"Oh." The sprout's fine brows pulled together in thought. While he considered, Meri learned, by way of the trees, that the child's mother was Elizabeth, Sam Moore's sister; his father the Wood Wise Palin Nicklauf.

"What should I call you, then?" the boy asked—and his pale eyes grew round. He ducked his head.

"The trees say I'm to call you Master Vanglelauf," he said, subdued.

"And so we achieve a third name," Meri said solemnly, while he put forth the question of Palin Nicklauf's whereabouts.

Jamie nodded and looked about him. "You came a long way to help us," he said slowly. "We—that is, as the headman's nephew and his nearest heir—I welcome you. The rest would do so, but—there was an earthdance two nights ago, and one of the trees came down on Gran's house. They took Sam off to see, because, um—because the village is first in their minds." He slanted an agate blue glance beneath his lashes. "Being villagers."

"Of course," Meri said politely. "As it happened, I saw the downed tree and the damage. I hope that all who were inside escaped safely?"

Jamie looked grave. "Gran, she chased everybody outside, but— they didn't think she was hurt at first. My sister and mother put her to bed and kept her warm, but next day, she was sickening. She's only gotten worse, and it's thought she's dying."

"Thought?" Meri lifted an eyebrow. "Is no one certain?"

"Well—Gran's our healer, see? Violet's her 'prentice, but not so far along as—as she needs to be."

Meri hesitated . . .

"You're not a healer, are you, Master Vanglelauf?"

"I am not—and it is not certain that a Fey healer would be of use. However—"

"If I ask the trees, will they send?" The boy's voice was at once tentative and fierce, from which Meri deduced an elder Wood Wise who had impressed a sprout with his own insignificance, when measured against the trees.

"It is possible," he said now. "If you are respectful, and *ask*—do not demand."

The boy nodded, and closed his eyes. Through the kindness of a larch, Meri heard the boy's request, and most gentle it was. In a trice, it had been taken up by the elders and entered the thought of the forest.

"Well done," he said. "The matter is now with the trees, and you may rest easy."

Jamie nodded solemnly, and rose. "Would you like something to eat?" he asked, slowly. "Or—we weren't sure. My mother made up a room in our house, if you'd rather, but—I made a nest out near the barn, if . . ."

A room—he shuddered, rejecting confinement inside one of their dead structures. And yet—did the boy think he was unable to make his own nest?

They meant it as a kindness, Ranger.
A kindness.
He did not laugh. Or weep.
Merely, he inclined his head to the eager sprout before him.
"I thank you for your . . . care. My preference would be, indeed, to sleep under leaf."
Jamie Moore grinned and leapt to his feet.
"I knew it!" he exclaimed, and held out an eager hand. "Here, I'll show you . . ."

Becca was in the garden before the dew was dry. The seeds she had set the day—or had it been two days?—before were sprouting already. Her task today was to set the seeds into the second quarter of the wheel, before continuing her program of thinning and spreading the plants that overran the rest of the garden.

Though she preferred to set the seeds herself, she had, at Altimere's insistence, a pair of Gossamers with her. And truthfully, they were useful for turning the soil and for grasping those plants that she meant to move while she dug gently 'round their roots. *That* task, she trusted to no one but herself. She was under no illusion that the Gossamers understood, or cared about, growing things. They assisted her because Altimere willed it, not from any interest of their own.

Carefully, Becca laid out her seed packets. Yes. The first quarter-wheel had been planted with fosenglove, penijanset, aleth and sunspear. The second quarter, then, would be . . .

She paused, frowning in thought, her hand hovering over the careful packets. It had been her conceit to create a seasonal garden, the plants in each quarter coming to fruition in proper sequence. If she did it correctly, it would appear that the wheel itself was turning as the plants matured.

But it was so difficult to recall! Did lord's purse bloom at the end of spring or in high summer? Did she deceive herself that teyepia blushed into blossom for a sweet, single day in late summer? And fremoni—no, surely fremoni bloomed all summer long!

And duainfey . . .

"Oh, bah!" she muttered, reaching for her book. It was kind of Altimere to have fetched her herbals and her seed packets back from Artifex—and of course when she had tried to thank him, he had pretended it was the merest nothing. To be able once again to garden and tend to the needs of plants. *That* was a benediction and a kindness that surpassed all the others he had bestowed upon—

Becca sat back on her heels, frowning at the last page of the herbal. Surely, she had sketched in what she had planned, and labeled each plant and the order of planting, just as, as . . . just as she had been taught? She recalled it! No—she recalled . . . she recalled sending the Gossamers for a pen, and then she recalled the evening's entertainment . . . Altimere had become quite a hectic host, now that the whole of the government had been recalled to the city. Why, scarce an evening went by when there were not visitors, and many of course wished to, to—but there! She must have forgotten, in the rush of getting ready to receive their guests . . .

What is this wheel that you construct, Gardener? the voice of the garden asked her. *Since the severing, each plant is always in season.*

Becca shook her head and smiled, fingering through the book until she found the entry for lord's purse. There! *This bloom marks the end of spring and the true beginning of summer . . .*

"Here, there are so many of you," she said, pushing the packet containing the lord's purse ahead of the others. "There are so many of you that no single voice can be heard above the riot and clamor. It is as if we two were trying to hold a comfortable conversation in the midst of a storm, having to shout our gentlest wishes over the blare of the thunder and the roar of the wind!"

Here—it was duainfey that bridged the seasons from summer to early autumn. Becca leaned forward and pushed it to the right. Teyepia, then . . .

But we easily converse amidst this clatter you object to, the deep voice said, pursuing its point. *And each plant obeys its natural cycle.*

"Why, yes it does!" Becca agreed. "Over near the door the daisies have wilted and gone dormant, while by the bench, they bloom as if it it were high summer! It makes my head quite spin to see it. Even if there are no seasons here, still all of one kind ought to bloom with their kin."

Seasons . . . the tree mused, and said no more. Smiling, Becca put the herbal aside and leaned forward. Using the fork, she scored the turned earth and sprinkled the tiny, fur-covered seeds into the tiny furrows, then covered them gently.

Teyepia liked to be planted deep. She poked holes in the soil with a stick, taking care to start inside the row of lord's purse. Dropping a big striped seed into each hole, she asked the Gossamers to cover them, which they did with a delicacy that made her smile again. Perhaps, after all, she could teach them to care for something other than Altimere's word.

Fremoni seeds went shallow, interleaved with the teyepia, so it would seem that the new flowers sprang immediately from those which had passed their time.

Becca reached for the sack marked "duainfey."

These, as she recalled, were something different. Little knots of plant stuff, that required shallow planting, the hairy roots well-covered and the nub of dried stem exposed to the weather. The illustration showed it a leggy plant with a profusion of dark cone-shaped flowers. According to the text, the flowers were deep purple, the leaves a lucent, light green. She hoped it would take to the soil—she had not seen its like among either of Altimere's gardens, and wondered if she had in fact found the one plant that would *not* grow in this changeless springtime.

"It could be," she said, after she had tried to set the first root three times with no success, "that it does not grow here because it cannot be planted." She sat back on her heels, and looked down at her reddened fingers. The dried root gave off a protective irritant, she thought absently. That was interesting. Duainfey thought much of itself.

Well, it would not have the better of her.

"Gossamers," she said, leaning forward again. "Please hold this nub upright while I make certain that the roots are well-covered."

Cool fingers brushed hers as the nub was taken from her control. Becca bent to cover the roots—and sighed in exasperation as the bit fell over.

"Come back here," she said sternly. "I'm not done."

The Gossamers, however, did not forth to continue their task. "Oh, really!" Becca muttered, frowning.

At last, she made a pile of soil, pushed in a pocket, set the nub precariously in the little depression and gingerly covered the roots. They went into the earth not as straight as she would have liked, but perhaps straight enough. And if they were touchy, tender plants, Becca thought, frowning down at the tiny white blisters covering her reddened fingertips, it was best to know so immediately.

That is a strange plant, Gardener.

"I agree, but its properties are said to be beneficial, so we will all profit, if it will grow here."

She pushed herself awkwardly to her feet and walked across to the overcrowded flowerbed she had been trying to thin. To her chagrin, new leaves were already pushing into the small spaces she had created in order to let the settled plants breathe and thrive.

"That is far too quick!" she cried. "They'll be smothering each other again in—"

The words died on her lips; she turned and walked away from the garden, through the misty door and up the curving ramp to her room.

Chapter Thirty-Seven

"A GLOVE, DEAR CHILD? ARE YOU CHILLED?" MONDAIR TIGHTENED her arm, and drew Becca closer to her side. It being one of Altimere's special subscription parties, Becca wore only a long, diaphanous skirt, the diamond collar, and the single, long glove on her right arm, which had been added to her costume at the last moment, and if she were not cold it was because Altimere willed it so.

"What have you done to your fingers, foolish girl?" Altimere had demanded, frowning at the blisters.

"One of the plants I handled today secreted an irritant," she answered, and smiled at him. "It's nothing, really."

She'd placed the vase of new-cut flowers on the stand the Gossamers had provided, arranged them one more time, and turned to smile again, and to accept his thanks for the pretty display.

Altimere, however, had not returned her smile, nor given thanks. "I dislike it very much when you put yourself at risk," he said sternly. "And our guests will not like to see these mars. Glove!" This last was snapped to the air, to be obeyed by whichever Gossamer happened to hear.

Becca shook her head. "I don't understand, sir. Surely, your guests have—have displayed only admiration for my crippled arm. A few blisters is scarcely anything at—"

"Your crippled arm, as you care to style it," Altimere interrupted, "is a potent sign. It displays to the world how much you are willing to endure in the service of your power, and therefore excites the senses. These *few blisters* are merely tawdry. Ah."

He received a single black leather glove from the Gossamer, rolled it and eased it over her fingers and up her arm. The leather was cut in strips, so that it criss-crossed her skin, clinging like skin itself from her fingertips to her shoulder.

Altimere stepped back to survey his handiwork. Amber eyes thoughtful, he extended a hand and plucked a single curl loose from the careless pile atop her head, and guided it down to lay upon her breast. The cool back of his hand brushed her nipple and Becca gasped, ready all at once.

Altimere laughed. "I am pleased to see you so eager. There will be several among this evening's guests who will desire your companionship most particularly. We may also look for some new faces from 'mong the Queen's supporters."

He walked around her, eyes intent, and Becca stood very still. Tonight's entertainment must be critical indeed, for him to care so much about her appearance.

"In the meanwhile, I will allow you to know that your especial friend Aflen will be present, and has requested a private audience."

Becca shrank in on herself. "I hope you refused him, sir," she said, her voice small.

"A joke, *zinchessa*? Of course I did no such thing. Aflen supports the Queen too well. To see him weaker is to find ourselves stronger, and therefore it behooves us to accommodate him in any small thing that he might ask."

She did not answer. Aflen had become—very particular in his attentions, and had begun to bring others to her, which pleased Altimere very much, but—

"It is time," Altimere said, interrupting her thought. Her body drew taut, breasts thrusting, as he came to her and placed her left hand reverently upon his sleeve.

"Now, *zinchessa*, a piece of news," he murmured as they walked through the misty doorway and down the short hall to the ramp. "I will be gone for a number of days, on the business of Zaldore. As she considers you too much of a danger to be let loose among her own supporters, you will remain here."

"Without you, sir?" Becca stopped, staring down at the floor, face hot, her emotions in such turmoil she could scarcely say what she felt. Fear, surprise, desolation . . .

"Peace. It will not be for so many days. My servants will of course be here for you, and you may work as you have been among the growing things." He put a finger under her chin, and tipped her face up to him. "Poor child. If the separation will be too painful for you, you may sleep through it."

"No!" she said immediately, so there, at least was one thing upon which she stood certain. "I—it is only that I will scarcely know how to go on . . ."

"You will be well-protected and receive every comfort. Of course, there will be no visitors for you while I am gone." He smiled, and bent to kiss her sweetly upon the lips, before breathing into her ear. "But we will make up for that lack of society when I am returned."

She shivered, suddenly cold. Altimere laughed softly and began to move on. "Your devotion touches me," he murmured. Becca shivered again; all at once Sanalda was before her mind's eye, knife in her throat, surprise cooling into death, and the stink of blood over everything. She stumbled, and had it not been for the support of Altimere's arm she surely would have fallen. A high whine distressed her ears, her stomach heaved—

"Silence!"

The ghastly sound ceased. Becca moved her head, as if to shake the terrible memory from her mind, but there was blood—the reek of it everywhere and—

"Be still!"

She froze where she stood, muscles locked, and still the horrific memory before her mind's eye.

"What nonsense is this?" Altimere asked. "A little bit of willfulness, to demonstrate your dismay at my absence?" He sounded less angry than amused, Becca thought, the odor of blood still in her nose. "I have, as I said, noted your devotion, and your display. I am gratified, but I cannot have you work yourself into such a pitch, *zinchessa*. Not now. You will calm yourself—"

Honey filled her head, sticky and beguiling, dissolving the terrible memory, overlaying the charnel stink with sweetness; sluggish, it ran her veins, leaving her languorous and eager.

Sighing, she leaned her head against Altimere's shoulder.

"Yes, that is more the mode," he said. "Come now. Let us greet your guests."

*　　　*　　　*

Mondair had finished with her and gone in search of the rest of her party. Becca, her hair long since tumbled into disorder, moved slowly out into the wider library. A breath of breeze stroked her nipples into hard nubs, and she very nearly melted at the sensation of her skirt along her limbs. Already, she had entertained three of Altimere's guests, though she had yet to see Aflen and his friends, a circumstance that both relieved and distressed her.

A tray wafted by, borne by Gossamers. Her right hand rose to receive the glass of red wine, and she drank deeply, feeling the pepper score her throat, near half the over-full glass in one gulp. That was almost enough to clean her mouth of those other tastes. She drank again—a sip only—and lowered the glass, suddenly aware of another scent almost as intoxicating as the wine, and a flutter of yellow light at the edge of her vision.

She turned her head, seeking the source of this unexpected brightness, of the scintillant scent, and sense of willing sharing of the energy of stored daylight. The memory of her exertions over the last while faded under the carress of a quiet thought: *Gardener.*

Ah, there! The vase of fresh flowers, with the greens tucked behind and between the sunbursts, and the coy purple bells of fremoni. She had arranged them this morning, thinking they would freshen the room, and how odd it was that Altimere, who was so meticulous regarding his grounds in the country, never brought flowers inside. She had forgotten, and none of the guests had noticed as they pursued their plotting and their lusts. And Altimere had ignored them entirely.

Something else, then, she'd done not quite right, or only right enough for a moment's fleeting urgency. The glass of wine weighed suddenly heavy in her hand, drawing her eyes momentarily from the flowers. The glint and promise of respite moved her hand and though she meant to sip it became a gulp.

When the glass was empty, she lowered it, to find a lady she had never seen before standing before her.

For a moment, she thought that here was another such as herself, her skin being more brown than white. She felt a touch of concern, even of jealousy. If Altimere grew tired of her failures and meant to replace her, surely such a one as this would do.

Then she saw the hair, and the jutting cheekbones, and the cool green eyes that could only be Fey.

A Gossamer snatched the empty glass out of her fingers. She

curtsied, and came up with a toss of her head, revealing breasts hard with need. Lust warmed her belly and she felt her mouth move in a smile and knew that Altimere considered this one worth pursuing.

"Engenium," her voice said, politely, full of sudden knowledge. "Be welcome."

"Thank you," the lady replied, and it seemed to Becca that there was an ironic note in her clear voice. "What is your name?"

"Rebecca Beauvelley, lady." Becca took a step forward, raising her head with a smile. "How may I serve you?"

"Nothing comes to mind at the moment," the Engenium said in her dry, ironical voice. "If something occurs, I will certainly inform you. In the meanwhile, what do you here, you who speak with flowers?"

"I entertain Altimere's especial friends," Becca heard herself say.

"How fortunate for them. And this is a task you undertake of your own will?"

"Certainly, Engenium."

The lady tipped her head, sea-green eyes speculative. "My name is Sian," she said. "Will you be able to recall it?"

"I have a very good memory, Sian," Becca's voice said, and she swayed forward, face upturned, offering her lips to the lady. "Will you not give me something else to remember?"

The Fey shook her head. "Perhaps—upon another occasion," she said, and moved her hand, showing Becca the library, the clusters of guests—and Korvayte, approaching with hunger naked on his face. "This is rather . . . public."

"Rebecca, sweet child!" Korvayte stepped close and put his hand on her left shoulder. "Surely you haven't thrown me over for the Queen's salty cousin?" He ran his hand possessively down her arm, making Becca to shiver, but his eyes were only for Sian.

"The lady and I were merely passing the time until her next duty arrived," Sian said lightly. She bowed. "Miss Beauvelley, your servant." A flicker of sea-green eyes. "Korvayte."

She was gone.

"Half-breed!" Korvayte snarled under his breath. His fingers tightened around Becca's wrist and pulled her with him across the room to the private alcove.

Korvayte was never gentle; this evening, he was harsh, and spent quickly. He sealed his clothes and left her without a word.

The Gossamers found her there some time later, kneeling where he had thrust her, head throbbing, her face and breasts sticky with his seed, with no will to try to raise herself. They cleaned her with the scented towels they had brought, lifted her to her feet and guided her out to the larger room, thin of guests now, and over to the place where the pleasant arrangement of flowers reposed in its own play of sunlight.

She closed her eyes, standing in the wash of scent; fremoni, giving soft comfort. *Gardener,* the voice whispered inside her head. *Healer.* Was she awake, she wondered, or caught in some dream of Altimere's willing? Who did she heal here? Comfort fell away, leaving her needful.

A wine glass was pressed in to her hand. She drank of her own accord, wishing that the burning pepper were poison, indeed. How had she come to this? she thought wildly—and knew a bolt of fear, that she was able to form the thought, here and now, at the very center of Altimere's party. Had he abandoned her? Left her alone? Was she become so wanton that the will to do these things was no longer his, but hers?

Panting, she thrust the empty glass at the air. "Another," she snapped, and it appeared in a trice.

"Thank you . . ."

Becca drank again, and looked about her. The library was empty, saving her and the little arrangement of flowers; the candles replaced with fog pots. Was the party over, then? Her heart stirred, but—surely not. She had not yet entertained Aflen. But—perhaps. She looked at the glass in her hand, half-full with wine, raised it and dashed it to the floor, where it broke, red droplets scattering like blood. She staggered, retching, pushed her fist against her mouth and ran, naked feet soundless against the living wood floor.

She was free of Altimere's will. What could have precipitated such a thing, she could not imagine. She could scarcely grasp the meaning of such an event, saving only the thought that she would not be forced to endure Aflen. She would run, she thought, and hide herself in the garden.

The dining room was deserted; the kitchen door misted away from her approach and she was in the garden, feet sure on the twisty, overgrown pathway.

Gardener, 'ware!

The tree's shout disoriented her, she staggered, off-balance, threw her hand out to grasp a branch, missed—and her wrist was caught in a crushing grip. She spun and squealed as her naked back struck the rough bark of the elitch tree.

"There! Did I not say she would come here!" Aflen's voice echoed triumphantly. He twisted his fingers in her hair and pulled her head back. Abused neck muscles screamed, and Aflen smiled hatefully down into her face.

"See how *frightened* she is," he crooned. "Deeply, *genuinely* frightened. This, my friends, will be a feast to recall."

"Unhand me!" Rebecca snapped, her voice shaking. Aflen laughed, grabbed her breast with his free hand and twisted it. She screamed; he bent and covered her mouth with his, grinding her lips against her teeth until she tasted blood.

"Come!" He called out, raising his head. "Who will partake with me?"

There were voices, hands. The flimsy skirt was torn away, a knee was thrust hard between her legs, while someone panted, hot and damp, in her ear.

"Altimere!" she screamed, and there was more laughter.

"I am here, *zinchessa*," his voice came out of the dark, calm and soothing as always.

"For the love of life, stop them!"

"Indeed I shall not," he said. "Did I not say that Aflen had requested a special serving of your charms?"

"And so I did!" Aflen cried, his fingers digging cruelly into her breast. "A serving without the interference of your protector—raw passion, pain, anger! *There* lies the power in a true melding. Three of us, Rebecca Beauvelley. And we will all have our fill."

She kicked, her bare feet doing no damage, and tried to twist away from them. They laughed, and Aflen—she thought it was Aflen—struck her across the face and threw her to her knees, one hand still twisted in her hair while he unfastened his clothing with the other.

Someone pulled at her glove, the last of her coverings, and Aflen laughed again, forcing her to look into his face.

He thrust his member into her mouth, choking her, and even as she recoiled, hands caught her hips, pulling her up, impaling her. Pain flared, shaming the stars, sheets of flame danced among the flowers, and the pure liquid fire exploded from the base of her spine, pouring out of her in wave after wave of ravenous color, melding, overpowering, *consuming* their pale, vapid colors, taking them into herself, making them hers.

Making them her.

Aflen spent, and the man in her rectum. They cast her away into the bleeding colors. Fingers closed around her left arm, jerking her to her feet, and hurled her against the tree once more. Ribbon went 'round her right wrist, shocking in its softness; and again, around her left. There was a moment—a lull—and then agony as both arms were yanked above her head, pulled hard and high, so that her toes barely brushed the grass.

Becca screamed, or tried to. Her assailant laughed, low, and brought his hand up under her chin. Light flared, showing her Venpor's face, then he was in her, each thrust an agony, fire bleeding off of him in thick orange sheets. Becca clawed her way back into the heart of the conflagration, reaching, absorbing, making everything that was his, hers, weakening him, draining, taking. Taking everything.

Help me! she screamed inside her head, and suddenly there was help, cool and green, lifting her away from the heat and the horror and the pain, to the top, the very top branch of the elitch tree, where she reclined, coolly at her ease, watching with distant interest as below hateful things were done to a ragged, soiled doll, who was finally abandoned, coiled into a knot among the trampled flowers, light pulsing out of her in rich streams of red, blue, and gold.

Three of the men righted their clothing, nodded to the fourth, seated upon a bench at some small distance from the abandoned doll, and were guided away by the firefly flickers of the invisible servants.

The fourth sighed, and stood, and suddenly she was swept from her aerie, and thrust into the trembling, torn body of the doll.

Whimpering, she lurched to her feet, and limped to him. He took her battered face between his cool hands and looked deeply into her eyes.

"This experiment has been a success," he murmured. "We shall have to entertain in this manner more often."

She swayed, her heart crushed in her breast, and he kissed her, long, deep, and hard.

Pain swirled, interlaced with flares of crimson. The night slid sideways—and disappeared.

Chapter Thirty-Eight

BECCA WOKE INTO SUNLIGHT, SNUG AND COMFORTABLE IN HER yellow-covered bed, with the feeling that someone had spoken her name. She stretched, carefully, expecting twinges and complaints from bruises and outraged muscles. Astonishingly, there was no pain, only a sleepy feeling of well-being, already beginning to dissipate as memory grew sharper.

She raised fingers to her lips, which had been torn and bleeding, and encountered only smooth, soft flesh. The fingers themselves showed a network of spidery white scars where there had been raw blisters only the night before. Her hair was clean—but the Gossamers would have bathed her, after all, rather than sully the bed with blood, and fluids, and mud.

Flinging the covers aside, she slid out of bed and went to stand before the mirror, staring at the brown-skinned woman with her down-tilted eyes and slanting brows, her hair neatly braided for sleeping, swathed in a pure white nightdress, sleeves deep with lace, and the ribbons tied in demure bows. Around her throat, the diamond collar sparkled coldly. Becca raised her hand, then allowed it to drop before her fingers made contact. What was the use? The thing would only protect itself—exactly as Altimere had built it to do.

Color flashed, quick as butterfly wings, behind her left shoulder, and then Nancy was before her, hovering with her little head cocked inquisitively to one side.

"How long," Becca asked her, "have I been asleep?"

Nancy hesitated, then spun full around—once, twice . . . thrice.

Three days? Becca took a deep breath. Very well. She knew that Altimere had sometimes caused her to sleep . . . longer than simply one night through. But even three days would not have been enough to heal the harm she had taken at the hands of Aflen and his—

Bile rose in her throat, and the room seemed to slide sideways, sunlight shattering into glimmering motes. Becca doubled over, retching, snatched at the vanity table, missed, and was caught in a strong, gentle grip.

The Gossamer eased her onto the bench, and kept her shoulder in a light grip until the fit passed and she was able to straighten. A glass appeared, water sparkling in its depths. She received it gratefully and drank.

"Nancy," she said, her voice not at all steady. "Is Altimere home?" Her maid fluttered before her, shaking her head, *no.*

No. She was alone and in her own will. Or, if not entirely in her own will, near enough.

Near enough.

She held the glass out; a Gossamer swept it out of her hand as she rose.

"Please dress me, Nancy," she said, her voice calm and low. "I am going down to the garden."

How quickly things grew here! Becca leaned over the half-wheel, fondling the lush lemon-colored leaves of the duainfey. Her fingers tingled, the pain so minor as to be a caress.

Duainfey, which bestowed clarity of thought—and surely clarity of thought was a virtue, though she sought other of its virtues.

For here, right here—these sweet, bright leaves were the answer to everything. An end to grief and guilt. An end to being a stranger to her own thoughts. An end to dishonor.

An end.

Carefully, not wishing to harm them, she took a leaf from each plant, and carried them with her to the stone seat by the elitch tree.

Gardener, what seek you?

"I seek an end to pain," she said dreamily, turning the leaves over on her lap. So pretty, like filigreed gold.

"And yet an end to pain is too often an end to joy," another voice spoke from beyond the elitch. "Both must be embraced, to achieve a balanced and fruitful life."

Becca laughed, raised the first leaf and took it into her mouth just as Sian the Engenium stepped out of the flowers.

"Good day," she said solemnly. "I hope you will forgive my intrusion. My garden shares a gate with this one. I saw you were out and thought to share news that perhaps might interest you."

"I will soon be beyond news," Becca told her. "If you wish to tell me, however, I will listen for as long as I may."

There was a small pause. The first leaf lay on Becca's tongue; she sucked it like a mint leaf, and almost smiled. She had feared that she would not be able to tolerate the taste, but in truth it was quite pleasant.

"That's fairly said," Sian said at last. She stepped forward until her shadow fell across Becca's face. Today, she was dressed in sharkskin leggings and wide-sleeved shirt, a leather cord binding her forehead. She frowned down at the two remaining leaves on Becca's lap.

"What manner of plant is that?" she asked. "It burns the air between us."

There was a sort of . . . shimmer about the Engenium's slim form, a misty, pleasing blue-green. Doubtless an effect of the leaf, but pretty, nonetheless. How odd that Sonet had not written of this—but, then, perhaps Sonet had not known. Those in need were unlikely to describe the hallucinations of release, after all.

"The herb is called duainfey," Becca said. "It is from—from beyond the *keleigh*. In one of its preparations, it is said to bestow clarity of thought."

Her mouth was damp and sweet; she felt relaxed. She curled the leaf with her tongue and swallowed it, allowing that the touch of it was more satisfying than much she had swallowed of late.

"Certainly, clarity of thought is to be desired," Sian said seriously, and Becca smiled politely.

"You had news of interest, you said?"

"Indeed. Aflen, the Queen's first counselor, is gravely ill. The healers have remanded the case to the philosophers. The philosophers pronounce it a crisis of *kest* and say they can do nothing."

"A crisis of *kest*," Becca murmured. "I have heard that one might die, if one is . . . too weak . . . or too open . . . to guard one's *kest*."

"Have you?" Sian looked at her with interest, but Becca only raised the second leaf, nibbling it daintily.

Sian cleared her throat. "My news continues—Flonyth is likewise ill, which is perhaps not surprising. He and Aflen are never apart, so it is not wonderful that whatever afflicted one should also strike low the other. They share not healers, however, and Flynyth's healer claims his to be an affliction evermuch like those of the war, where great magics oft were loosed with little thought."

Amusement tinged the taste of the leaf; Becca wondered briefly if she appeared harelike as she nibbled the leaf down to stem. No matter; Flonyth and his thoughts were being solved even now. She licked her stinging fingertips, and glanced up into the Engenium's serious face.

"The third piece of news, however—that I own to be odd."

"And that is?" Becca asked composedly.

"Venpor has returned to the elements from which he sprang."

"Good," Becca said, calmly. "There was no joy in him."

There was something . . . very strange . . . happening with her vision, and there could no longer be any doubt that it was attributable to the leaves she had eaten. She knew a momentary sadness, that she had not thought to bring out ink and paper, and so note down these effects, for the education of future herbalists.

Sian was most definitely overlaid with turquoise mist. Indeed, the whole of the garden seemed to be blooming on two levels— the simple, familiar level of earth and leaf; and another, which seemed to exist as interwoven beams of light, the weaving of one strengthening the pattern of all.

Becca blinked, and looked down at the third leaf, pierced now with strands of silver light. Perhaps she would be able to taste the light. She rubbed the leaf between her fingertips, felt the green ribs bruise and break, as the wax coated her fingers. Almost, she was at an end, and it would seem duainfey was kind. An unexpected blessing, that, after so much pain and betrayal.

"Forgive me," Sian said slowly, "if I overstep. But I wonder that you care to wear that collar."

"I do not care to wear it," Becca said serenely, still studying the third, the last, leaf. "However, it is only I who may remove it, and I have already failed twice."

A small pause. "Do you intend to risk a third attempt?"

"I intend to risk nothing, any longer," Becca said. "This kind leaf—" she raised the last of the three "—will insure that."

"In fact," said Sian, "you *mean* to die."

"I do."

"And would you die with such a thing binding you?" Sian's voice was distant, gentle—concerned.

Becca laughed, the leaf burning in her fingers. "Can he call me back from the dead to do his will?"

"It may be that he can," Sian said slowly. "Altimere has worked marvels aplenty in his time. There are those of us who would not say there is anything he cannot accomplish."

Becca stared up at Sian through the misty air, the pleasant taste of the leaves she had eaten going to ash in her mouth "No," she whispered.

"The only way to be certain is to have it off," Sian said. "You dance on the points of daggers, Rebecca Beauvelley: Bound forever if you fail thrice; bound beyond forever, if you embrace doom before you win free."

Becca swayed where she sat. Could it be possible? And yet—Sian surely told the truth; she could taste it in the hot air.

"What shall I do?" she cried.

"Deny it. Reject it. Remove it."

"I have tried, I tell you, and failed. I have not the strength to deny it, much less remove it."

"Then you must find it," Sian said coolly.

"Find it?" Becca demanded, with no little heat. "Where will I find such strength?"

Fie, Gardener, you need no one else to tell you the answer to that riddle. And, now that you have clear sight, it is time for us to return that which is yours. You will find that we have kept it safe, and husbanded it well.

There was a bolt, as if of vivid green lightning. Becca cried out where she sat, pierced to the heart, the garden gone to motes of light, Sian a standing stone among them—

She took a breath, and lifted her hands, the left rising more slowly than the right, but rising. Pain flickered; her muscles shook, as if she pushed against mud. She turned her head, and clearly saw the inky flow of some—anti-light—staining her fingers. She bit her lip and shoved her hands upward those last few inches, until she touched it.

The collar. It felt thick and heavy on her neck now, and as she touched the bottom it seemed to tighten in warning. But there, before, the threat of death had meant something. Now she was merely a kind leaf away from release.

Unexpectedly, she chuckled with the irony of Altimere's failure to measure her resolve.

And there! Altimere's strength had always been her ignorance and need, and her failure to heed the careful traps he had allowed her to build to imprison herself.

Deny it.

Her fingers against the collar, Becca took a hard breath.

"I, Rebecca Beauvelley, in my own voice and by my own name, deny Altimere of the Elder Fey use of my body, my mind, and my intention."

Three seasons, suggested the voice in her head.

Another breath, and the words, again, her voice shaking, her resolve firm. The collar warmed, melting the leaf-wax from her fingertips. She pushed her hands upward until all ten of her fingers were pressed to the bottom of her thrall.

A voice, firm, insistent: "That is but two, Rebecca Beauvelley."

Her hands rose higher; the clasp adamant beneath pressing fingers—

The collar grew uncomfortably tight. It would fight to keep her for Altimere. It was, after all, what he had made it to do.

Becca hooked the fingers of her left hand between the collar and her throat, her breath coming ragged now, as it tightened again.

A third time she spoke the phrase to deny it, and if the collar did not loosen, neither did it tighten.

Reject it.

"I, Rebecca Beauvelley," she said, her voice thin, "have no need of this necklace. There is no beauty in it, nor power. It is not mine to hold, nor is it my greatest desire. I wish it gone."

Words. Mere words. What did she think she might accomplish with such puny statements? She felt despair, and swayed where she sat.

Three seasons, insisted the trees.

She spoke again, the words coming in gasps, her head reeling from lack of air or the effect of the leaves. They came slowly, but she said them, and with each word her fingers clawed into her own flesh.

The words said, she relaxed—and the collar crushed her hands into her throat, drawing on the will to pain . . .

She laughed, wheezing.

"Foolish construct! I . . . mean to . . . die."

"Again!" Sian shouted.

The words. The ideas. Altimere, who loved her and who had given her this collar as a symbol of his devotion and care.

"Lies . . ." Becca whispered

Reject!

Her tongue was not so mobile now; her mouth was dry, and her eyes. Altimere was not here. The necklace was a trap to bind her—she saw it clearly. It was woven with deceit and the will to fail, so that once she had it on, she would never be able to remove it.

The breeze shifted, bringing the scent of the garden to her. She struggled for breath, moved her thick tongue, shaping the words, the words, the—

"I wish it gone!"

Caught! Her fingers were numb and trapped, her crippled arm screamed for surcease from its agony, and her throat was full of dust and panic!

Remove it!

Painfully, she dragged down on the collar with her left hand, freeing her good right hand. Burning fingers sough the catch, touched it, pressed—

The click was audible, and the release so sudden she fell back and would have toppled from the bench if Sian had not reached out and grabbed her shoulder.

Becca looked down.

The collar lay in her lap, touching the bruised and broken leaf. Even as she watched, the duainfey withered and crumpled into ash. The necklace . . . the necklace *melted*, bold diamonds expanding into rugged lumps of coal, the fine golden links twisting into common rawhide cord.

Revulsion filled her soul, the stink of blood so thick she could scarcely breathe; Elyd dying beneath her; Sanalda with a knife in her throat; Altimere petting her, warming her with sweet words of praise.

She was free. Altimere no longer controlled her.

And the hand on her shoulder belonged to a Fey, who lived by dominating those weaker than themselves.

"Now!" Sian said, and Becca heard the frenzy for possession in her voice. "Now, I can help you!"

There was a dagger on Sian's belt. She must act, before she was enslaved again.

Becca lunged, got her hand 'round the hilt—

And sleep fell upon her like a wave.

The nest was well-made; snug for a Ranger grown, but, Meri thought, sliding his pack from his shoulders, t'would do.

"Dinner will be in the common," Jamie told him. "I'll come fetch you." He had then gone off to do whatever duties a child of his village might have, leaving Meri to settle in to his new camp.

He should, he thought, easing down into the woven grasses, go at once to the trees—and he would, after he had taken a moment to savor the simple fact that he was alone, unassaulted by the unnatural brilliance of those terrible auras. The boy—had been almost restful, his aura nothing more than the delicate, washed hues of a Wood Wise born—and wasn't that a tangle! A child of a Wood Wise and a Newman? One could scarcely decide whether to be horrified on one's own account, or laugh aloud and wonder what the High who had deplored breeding with Wood Wise and the Sea Folk would say to *this* misalliance.

Meri smiled and settled back, closing his eye for just a moment . . .

Diathen the Queen looked from the draggled, sleeping Newman to her cousin Sian.

"I had thought the tale was that he had brought her from beyond the *keleigh*."

"It is the tale," Sian said slowly, "and I believe it. The aura—is much like those others I have seen among the Newmen."

"And what shall I do with her, now that she is mine?"

Sian shifted her shoulders. "That depends on what she might tell you, does it not, O Queen?"

Diathen laughed. "How have I landed in your black books, Sian?" She waved a hand. "No, do not speak. Let the poor child sleep for now."